Dear Bronwyn x

From Brandy to Mrs. Van Aarde,
thank you for sticking around long
enough to be one of my oldest, dearest
friends, and for being the first
to help me celebrate this book
with pink bubbly!

I do hope you enjoy the read ☺

Pam x

Something

Pink

ALMOST A TRUE STORY

· · · · · · · · · ·

Pami Simpson

Almost a true story

· · · · · · · · · ·

Something Pink has been an eye-opening adventure to write, wonderfully exciting and the experience of a lifetime. I can't thank the people who have helped me along the way enough! A big thank you to my mom, Alison Shortridge, who not only is my biggest cheerleader and was the first to encourage me to write, but put her heart and soul into believing in me by doing a first read and edit even when she had no time to spare. Laura Shortridge, my little sister and partner in crime, thank you for the endless late night sessions poring over this book with wit, wine and pen – without you this project would never have seen the light of day. Claire Strombeck, the professional editor I hired who became a friend through it all, thank you for being such an amazing inspiration and always lifting me up. Laurey Buckland, my cross-continent bff – thank you for your engaging commentary, helpful suggestions and pretty pink notes in the margins – you continue to fill me with hope and happiness to have made it this far in my literary journey. Natashia Muna, my oldest (though by no means old) bestie – you know without your tiresome dedication to both me and my word-vomit I would have drowned? Thank you for hemming me in…after all, who knows me better than you to offer the best hemline for each season? And last but not least, my husband and favourite human on the planet, Bruce Simpson. It's my book and I'll gush if I want to. Thank you for literally making my dreams come true. I love you most of all, and this book is dedicated to you.

· · · · · · · ·

Chapter 1

This is it. Gearing down in my fourth-hand, seaweed-coloured Opel Monza, I decide this is the moment where my life is about to change forever. I take the right hand turn into Hollywood Drive. It's not really called Hollywood Drive, but as far as neighbourhoods in Johannesburg go, this is pretty darn close. Most of the embassies and consulates and whatnot are here . . . Well, a lot of houses have flags on them so I'm just assuming. I've heard some of the most expensive houses in South Africa are on this street, as well as some owned by high-profile politicians, so naming it Hollywood Drive just seems appropriate to me.

My cell begins to vibrate with a purr.

"Hi Mom," I'm a little annoyed that she has phoned me again. "Actually I'm driving right now . . ."

Mom doesn't seem to understand the cell-phone-to-car-driving illegality ratio and most certainly doesn't believe in the fine I would get if caught.

"Yes, I am on my way to the new job . . . No Mom, it's not that politician's house. I just said they live in the same street!"

Now she's going on about some guy she read an article on in the Sunday Times. I should never have told her he lived in this area. Her voice is suddenly earnest and reminds me of my grandmother who would cling to her seat like a kidnapped victim whenever my dad picked her up and drove her anywhere. Mom's been getting worse ever since I moved here.

"I am just concerned, you know, that you are not thinking this through properly." She pleads. "You're not in Cape Town anymore. You might think it's very glamorous, but Joburg is different – you really have to be careful! I was watching Carte Blanche and that character apparently had sushi served off naked women at one of his parties . . ." Seriously? That sushi incident was years ago. Does she have backdated recordings she sits and watches over and over again? I wouldn't put it past her. Her voice, accelerating to a high-speed quiver, interrupts my thoughts. "Oh, Jemma, I really hope you aren't thinking of becoming that sort of girl. First you take up with that… that girly-boy, and now you are selling your body. I knew this day would come. Ever since you and your brother stopped going to church!"

"Mom! Please calm down. I told you this is an au pair job. Just like the ones I had before. Fully clothed! Nothing to worry about. Just ask Jason. And actually, I really am driving so have to go . . ."

Now is so not the time to get into another argument. I am on an important mission right now. Mission Hollywood Drive.

I have driven past the house, or rather, The Estate, where I will be working, a few times over the last couple of days to familiarise myself with the ins-and-outs of my new work-hood; good thing too, because there seems to be a lock-down feature in this part of suburbia that turns the entire block into a giant security village between certain hours of the day. Giant gates have been erected across all access streets but one, and are barricaded off.

I've done the drive a few times - you have to circle an entire area like a vulture before making your way in, which feels like a bit of a waste of time. But as a criminal deterrent, I bet it works, based solely on the fact that would-be attackers and thieves just couldn't be bothered to put in the time and petrol emissions. Even if they did make it in, that over-enthusiastic private security bunch that followed me while I was rehearsing my first-day-at-work drive would put them off. I mean, they really followed me. Me! With a face like this? I have freckles!

"Babysitting is not a real job, Jemma. I thought we discussed this . . ." Mom is still speaking. I've been able to block her out until now. Sigh.

"No Mom," I resign myself to the fact that we will, in fact, be having yet another one of these conversations. "We didn't discuss anything. And it's not babysitting. They advertised for a 'governess'. I'm an au pair."

"Some people make a career out of it. Who do you think looked after Prince William and Harry when they were small? Not just a babysitter. An au pair! Anyway, Mom, I really do need to go now. I promise to call tonight. Love to Dad!" I hit end call quickly before she can protest.

I drive past the swanky suburban perimeter gates, flash the guards at the entrance boom my most winning "This Time I Actually Do Work Here" smile and take the next right to my destination. Watching the street in my rearview mirror for any potential security inquisitions, I stop the car for a minute. Yes, this all feels right. Well, almost everything. The air is melting hot in my idling car, as usual, and she lets out a loud backfire, inciting further interest from the security post. As much as I love the old girl, as soon as I save up enough for a deposit, I am totally getting a new car. And with this job, that won't take long at all.

My phone purrs again.

"Mom, I told you, I'm driving! Please–"

"Good Gaga, child!" The male voice on the other end of the line is comically surprised, with just a hint of indignation. "If I'm your mother, there are some dark drugs at play here!"

"Oh, I'm so sorry Frederick." Woops. "I thought you were my mother. Was just getting another lecture from her about the job."

Frederick is my bff, the one Mom calls a 'girly-boy'. The concept of genital based gender classification seems to be entirely lost on her.

"Oh good." Frederick breathes out in relief on the other end of the phone. "So I'm not your mother after all. Phew! I was about to start worrying about stretch marks. Having a baby will do that to you, you know. Unless you are Victoria Beckham…"

"Oh, no. Stretch marks? We wouldn't want that!"

"Jemma darling, I just wanted to wish you luck with the meet-and-greet. Knock 'em dead, sweet-bottom."

"Thanks Frederick. You're such a honey. I'll see you later though, right? You're coming over this eve so I can tell you all about it?"

"Definitely. See you then!"

I hang up, look at myself in the rearview mirror once more, dab at my damp face with the handy tissues I always keep in my oven-on-wheels, and add a dust of fresh face powder to hide my pink-cheeked, thirty-five-degree Celsius excitement. So not a good look.

"OK, Peaches," I say out loud to my car, "here we go!"

Happy and hot-flushed-faced, I arrive at my new place of work: 8 Bishop Drive, Sandhurst, Johannesburg. Home of the rich, the royal, and the totally awesome.

I sign the registry (the registry! For a private home!) with a dark man in a crisp white pajama-come-butler suit at the entrance to the driveway, start Peaches up again with the usual splutter, and navigate her along the winding path towards my sparkling future.

The cobbled stone bricklets clink under my car tyres all the way up the shaded drive and I see the beautiful, clear blue Highveld sky peeking through the leaves above me. On the left of the path I keep catching small glimpses of the grounds. Firstly tennis courts. A bit retro – old money for sure - then smooth sheer lawns. Some heavily manicured bushes and shrubs, and I could have sworn I saw a big grey animal galloping up the garden. As I'm about to speed up – this is taking ages – I see it. Rising up above me like a glowing beacon of all things wonderful to come: the main house.

Woooooowwwww. A fresh wave of excitement bubbles up in my tummy and I can't help but grin like the Cheshire cat. This is my new 'office'? No wonder they are paying me so much.

I see Kobus, personal assistant to Mrs. Totally Awesome and the one who hired me, standing close to the side of the house-come-Palace chatting to another dark man dressed in white. There is a parking area to the left, so I pull Peaches up to a stop and switch off the ignition. I make sure my hand brake is as high and tight as it can go – there is no way I'm chancing a freak accident with Peaches rolling into one of those Greek-ish white marble statutes on the other side of the neatly bricked drive. They're surprisingly ugly, but very expensive-looking. All Rands and no sense, as Mom would say.

Kobus is now heading over the lawn towards me. I do one last lip-gloss check in my cracked rearview mirror and climb out of the car. A light January breeze catches my skin as I turn to face Kobus, whipping up the ends of my hair, and it makes me feel all fresh and giddy. In the glorious presence of this house, I am suddenly a bit light headed.

"Miss Richardson!" Kobus stumbles over a few bushes, and then quickly backtracks to make sure he didn't do any damage. He straightens up again and gives me a discoloured toothy smile. "I'm so glad you're here!"

"Please, call me Jemma. Wow, what a place!"

He bustles up to me, slightly out of breath, and sticks out a damp hand to shake mine. "Welcome aboard, Jemma."

I had a full hour-long interview with him two weeks ago at offices belonging to one of the companies my new employers own. I was just about to give up all hope when he called back. I did think it was a bit odd that I got the job before I met the parents or their children, or even found out their real names, but I suppose with this kind of client, you can't be too careful. They're famous, after all. "Practically royalty," were Kobus's exact words in the interview and I am guessing he acts as a buffer against the paparazzi and would-be chancers who might try to pose for the position just to get close to the family. An international flag (Japan? India?) flutters in my peripheral view and I suddenly feel very special. Trusted. Discreetness in this neighbourhood is clearly a necessity, but he chose me.

I wonder, for the umpteenth time, who these people could be? Mr. and Mrs. Totally Awesome, yes, but who are they really? Frederick and I spent hours over pink cocktails discussing the possibilities. He suggested the Dalai Lama, but even I know that's not probable. Is it? How old is he anyhow and is he allowed to, you know, mate? Or is it just the Pope who's not allowed a Mrs. Pope?

My mind starts wandering again: Maybe it's a local T.V. celebrity. Like that guy Mom loves on Carte Blanche – maybe he has small kids. Or it could be a high-profile parliamentarian . . . After all, doesn't that other guy live on this block . . . Oh no! What if it is that other guy? I'm not sure I'm ready for naked sushi parties . . .

Kobus sees the worried look on my face. "Are you nervous?" he asks kindly.

"Oh no," I quickly recover, widening my eyes at him in a show of enthusiasm. "I just can't wait to meet the family. Will both parents be here today?"

"Actually . . ." Kobus lingers on the word apologetically. "Neither. The lady of the house is – er – out, and the father of the children doesn't live here any more. They're divorced."

"Oh," I'm fairly taken aback. This isn't exactly what I was expecting, but I guess he never did specify whether it was a single parent home or not and I never asked. And if the father doesn't live here any more, the chances of naked-sushi parties seem very low. Which makes me feel a bit better.

But neither of them being here on my first day of work?

Too busy to meet the stranger you have just hired to care for your children?

"No matter," Kobus chirps. "Let's go see the girls, shall we?"

He's a funny round sort of man, all jolly like Father Christmas but with the distinct creases of corporate stress lines on his brow. Come to think of it, his eyes also seem somewhat shifty – sort of like his exterior is programmed in saying "Welcome to this happy healthy working and living environment" but his interior is a scrawny, panicked white rabbit man, desperate to scurry away. A stain on his middle and index fingers match the stains on his teeth, confirming a cigarette addiction. He's probably just hyped up on nicotine.

I follow his smoky aroma round the drive-about and up towards the monstrous sky-high glass doors at the main entrance. There is an elaborate fountain positioned with enough space for cars to, I imagine, be valeted to and fro. A deluge of rich watery shrub and glistening rock features coat the walls on either side of the walkway between the drop-off-zone and the front entrance. And is that Koi I see? I love Koi fish! I cannot wait to tell Jason about this place. My twin brother would get such a kick out of it.

"Those koi are so karmatic! I love the colours," I say matter-of-factly to Kobus. I like to use words out loud as soon as I invent them – that way they seem more real and I get to pretend they exist, which is fun. When people don't call me on it, of course. I would never do it on Twitter.

Kobus gives me a strange look, puts his hand on the elaborately carved stone handle, and after a second glance at me (perhaps I should have gone with 'karmic'), pauses and turns his whole body to face me. "You will obviously be using the staff entrance round back normally, but just for today let's go through here." He sort of twinkles at me, as if to convey what a privilege it is for us to be using the 'regular folk' entrance. I nod and pretend to be honoured.

As he pushes the thick patterned glass doors open, I catch my breath. Straight ahead, with a skylight directly above, streaming light down on to its shiny perfectness is a gorgeous white spiral marble staircase. It's as if I've died and been brought to the ethereal stairway to heaven!

Kobus bends down and unlaces his matt-black snakeskin shoes. "No one is permitted to wear shoes in the house," he explains. "Dust from the outside world brings in bad omens."

"Bad omens?" I ask, a small laugh escaping before I can stop it.

"You know, bad luck, nasty demons, the tokoloshe – that sort of thing." He rolls his eyes ever so slightly, but gestures for me to take my shoes off too.

He's funny. I knew I'd like him.

Obediently I start to un-do the buckle on one of my fuchsia pink, wedge-heeled gladiator sandals.

After placing my shoes carefully by the doorway, I step onto the white marble floor. Suddenly I feel disjointed. Those shoes were the final touch to my meet-and-greet outfit. I had started trying different ensembles the moment I got the job, and must have changed my mind about a hundred times since then. 'They're not going to notice your shoes,' Jason had practically yelled at me when I asked if we could go for one last mall search, as I had 'nothing to wear'.

He was right after all – they aren't even going to see my shoes now.

I smooth down my black stretch pencil-skirt, feeling suddenly short. I had chosen to wear the ever-faithful interview top again, even though Kobus had seen it at our first meeting. It's a sapphire blue polar-neck sleeveless top that looks just formal enough for someone to take me seriously, and yet bright enough to make me look fun and interesting – the way I imagine you would want your child-minder to be. The stretch skirt was chosen to reflect flexibility and competence when it comes to running around after toddlers. Corporate-black, of course, to show I am a professional governess, not just a babysitter.

But the shoes were special. They were what made me feel good about myself, giving me the final essential to every outfit: Confidence. I take a deep breath. It will all be OK. No matter how short or incomplete I feel.

"These are all genuine Samurai swords," Kobus gestures in a hushed voice, sweeping his arms round the room. The enormous staircase is in the centre of a wide entranceway with high walls and three separate archways leading off to other sections of the house. The surrounding walls are set off with ancient paintings and magnificently worked swords hanging in glass floating frames. Miniature down-lights highlight the shiny metal.

"Ah, Suda. Jemma, Suda is the head housekeeper here, and the best person to ask any questions you may have about the rules. Suda, this is the new au pair." Kobus steps aside so I can see a small sturdy barefoot woman dressed all in black coming through one of the arched entrances. The black tunic makes her look as though she belongs in an exotic Indonesian health spa, leading me off to have my hot stone massage.

"You no use staff entrance?" she says to Kobus in a blunt monotone. She turns to me and sticks out her hand. "Nice we meet, Jemma." As I shake it, all visions of Indonesian back massages disappear. She must have more callouses on her hands than a hard-boiled lumberjack.

"You have an interesting accent, Suda," I try a friendly smile. "Are you from here?" She stares at me. "Er, from South Africa?" I add, just to be sure.

"No," she says, and turns to walk away.

Sheesh. Tough crowd! No karmatic-ness going on there.

"Erm," Kobus looks at me uncertainly, and then quickly hurries after Suda. "Come on, Jemma," he adds. "Let's go meet the girls."

Kobus explained in the interview that I would be taking care of two girls; one aged five and one aged seven. I would be a live-in au pair from Mondays to Fridays, and be expected to stay on weekends when asked to. Holidays were negotiable, but I would most likely travel with the family over that time. Extra pay would of course apply. My duties would include waking the children, getting them dressed and packed for school, driving them to and from school and any other extra-curricular activities. I would help them with their homework, monitor their progress, liaise with their schoolteachers and report back on everything to their mother. I would indulge them with playtime, but it was also my responsibility to be sure they were spending a few hours a day on non-school-related educational activities. I wasn't sure how the evenings would work, but I supposed there would be family time and I would only be needed if their parents worked late or had engagements to attend to. I was planning on discussing this hidden aspect of the job description with my new employers when I met them, but I guess, considering their absence, that will have to wait.

Kobus and Suda are way ahead of me now so I hurry up to follow them and try not to get any more distracted by the ornate-looking vases and statues along the walls, ignoring the distinct feeling of Alice in Wonderland, falling down that rabbit hole. I walk down a long open passageway, past the entrance to what looks like a sunroom (in the same way Marie Antoinette would describe her "summer cottage") and out some stack doors on to a brightly lit terrace.

I shield my eyes, momentarily blinded by the sun, and hear splashing, giggling . . . shouting . . . screaming . . . galloping . . .? And then thud! Everything goes dark.

Opening my eyes I realise I am lying flat on my back on smooth, buttery tiles, and a giant sea lion is slobbering all over my face.

"Bruno! No! Down, Bruno! Down!"

I scramble to my feet, thanking my lucky fairy-star-dust this skirt goes to my knees with enough give to avoid embarrassing panty-flashing moments, even though they are pink and part of a matching set. In the event of head-on collisions, I hear my mother's voice echoing in my head as I rub at the bump on the back. She never warned me of animal encounters.

Suddenly remembering where I am, I push wildly at the hair stuck in my mouth and turn to see four bewildered faces staring at me. Five, if you count the dog – though he doesn't look concerned at all. He looks more excited than anything, as if he is just itching to have another go at me. Kobus is holding onto the bouncy six-foot Weimaraner who obviously thinks this is all a big game.

"I'm so sorry, Jemma. Bruno! Down! Jislaaik, I'm gonna klap you." His Alberton accent is suddenly much stronger as he wrestles the dog. "Jemma, are you OK? Did you hit your head?"

"I tell he bad dog," Suda looks mildly indifferent. "You want cold cloth?"

"Er, no thanks. I'm fine." My voice has gone up a few pitches, and I am burning red with humiliation. I rub the back of my head again, checking to see if the bump is growing, and wince slightly as my fingertips find the tender patch.

Suda shrugs, and ushers two children towards me. She reminds me of a mother hen with them, all dusty and flustered. "This girls. Girls, this new babysitter."

Great. Even they call me the babysitter.

I look past Suda as two of the most angelic-looking, raven-haired girls step forward. Both still dripping and in matching swimsuits, the little one with arm bands on, they shake off some of the excess water, their eyes fixed on me.

"We are so sorry. He loves to jump at people." The taller one speaks first in an assertively husky, yet childish voice. "I'm Tasanee, and this is my little sister Lola. It's so nice to meet you."

She pronounces her words carefully, formally. She holds out one of her hands to shake mine. Like a grown-up. I can't help hesitating in surprise for a moment. These girls must be used to all kinds of important people being around, I guess – what's one new babysit . . . au pair to them?

"Lovely to meet you too, Tasanee."

She has wide oval eyes and a round face like the sun. Her grin is big and full of oversized teeth, planted with just the perfect level of politeness. She's very sure of herself, evident as I take her hand and feel her firm grip.

The little one hasn't said anything yet and is standing slightly behind her big sister. Head tilted down, she peeks up at me through a silky sheen of black hair falling over one side of her baby face. Her eyes are beautifully oval like Tasanee's, but more slanted in the corners, and her lips are much fuller. She holds no resemblance to her sister's confident exterior, but rather looks like a scared, delicate princess in a Disney storybook. As soon as she catches my eye, she pops two fingers into her mouth and starts sucking furiously. I sink down to my haunches and tilt my head to one side.

"And it is very nice to meet you too, Lola," I soften my voice encouragingly. She is holding a plush toy rabbit to her chest and is swinging her body slightly from side to side. "Is that your rabbit? What's its name?"

Lola takes her fingers out of her mouth just long enough to say "Mu" and goes straight back to sucking the finger-dummy, and cuddling her bunny. She holds out the toy for me to see. She has the cutest shy voice – much sweeter than Tasanee's loud annunciation.

"Those fingers must be very tasty," I lower my voice to a secretive whisper and give her a wink. She giggles sheepishly, revealing tiny front teeth set skew in a jaw of milk-duds.

"Oh, Lola," sighs Tasanee loudly. "You can be such a baby sometimes!"

"Well, I'll let you girls get acquainted," interrupts Kobus, still struggling with the dog-monster. "I'll just put Bruno back in his kennel and have a chat to Suda, then we can all give Jemma a tour of the house."

I straighten up again and watch as Tasanee elbows Lola playfully. She drops her shy surveillance of me and starts chasing Tasanee along the stone patio and down some steps to a pool area. I follow them to see the whole garden open up in front of me like the grand grounds of Versailles. The terraced pool is on a deck overlooking a lush green lawn and has a glass front that overflows to another pool a few meters below. Further down the hill are intricate pathways, trimmed hedges and ponds stretching all the way to the tennis courts at the bottom. No wonder it took me so long to get up the driveway. This place is huge!

"Watch this, Jemma." Tasanee dive bombs into the pool causing Lola to squeal in delight and jump back as water splashes all over her.

"Do you like to swim a lot?" I ask, finding a dry deck chair to sit on.

"Oh, yes!" answers Tasanee, emerging from the luxury pool. She stalks over to where two towels are laid out and lies down on one of them. "I also like to tan," she says with an overly mature air. Lola has trotted across to where her big sister is sunning herself and copies her, lying stomach down on the free towel.

"Dry you self, girls!" Suda's authoritative voice croons from the patio door. "We show Jemma house now."

"Where is Suda from?" I can't help but ask Tasanee as we walk back up to the house. I know she's only seven, but something about her makes me automatically want to relate to her like she's older.

"Oh, she's Thai. The last one left," Her matter-of-fact statement baffles me slightly, but I decide not to push it just yet, remembering she is, in fact, only seven and I should not be gossiping with her like high school teens.

Suda takes Lola's towel from her and starts to rub the little girl up and down roughly, making her look as though she's about to fall over. She squishes up her face as Suda ruffles the towel over her head. "Suuudaaa," comes her muffled complaint from behind the aggressive drying.

"You must dry before walk in house," Suda scolds. "Mummy get very cross."

The tour of the house leaves me breathless. I have never in my life even dreamed of a place like this – a home so decadent and embellished. There are four main living areas downstairs, a spacious, fully equipped gourmet kitchen, and two wings on the top level.

The East Wing – seriously, that's what they all call it – belongs to the mother and I don't get taken beyond the entrance to her passageway. The West Wing contains three bedrooms and a playroom. Each girl has her own double bedroom with a four-poster princess bed, a TV cabinet, walk-in closet, and a sofa lounging area at the bay-style window, littered with enough stuffed toy animals to populate their own plush zoo. Tasanee's room looks like a shrine to Hello Kitty. Her bed linen, throw cushions, wall clock, bedside lamp – all Hello Kitty. Her toys seem to be ninety per cent Hello Kitty related, and even her laptop, strategically placed on a mini pink Hello Kitty homework desk in the corner has a bedazzled Hello Kitty cover and screensaver. Both rooms have en-suites with heated floors, Tasanee's with a Hello Kitty bathmat, of course. They both have rainforest showers, jet stream Jacuzzi baths and stage-lit make-up mirrors. I walk around, taking in every detail in amazement. Everything is pink and purple and silver glitter and white fluffy cushions and Swarovski crystal and fairy lights. It's the princess room every little girl dreams of.

But the best part, the very best part, is my room is exactly the same!

Chapter 2

. . . .

"And there are like fifty hundred different passageways and these massive entrance areas all over the place and the kitchen has a pantry and walk-in freezer like a restaurant, which makes perfect sense, seeing that they have a live-in chef too and there are shelves and shelves of whatever you can think of, bulk boxes, like shopping at Macro, and the maids' quarters are a whole other house on the property and bigger and nicer than our place, Jason, and the garage is this long building but I never went inside but I can't wait to see what's in there tomorrow morning when I start and there are these crazy rugs in the piano room that look like they were hand-woven from like silk or something and the piano! Oh my word, Jason, the piano!"

I stop to take a huge breath. Jason is watching me with genial amusement. I am on such a high from my introduction to the new house, or "The Palace" as I have now nicknamed it to my twin, it's as though my heart is pumping at four times its usual speed and I can feel blood rushing through my head as I gush on.

"It's a grand piano. And it was a gift from the Queen of England. The freaking Queen of England, Jason!"

I'm standing in our dinky kitchen at the flat Jason and I rent, my hands on top of my head as if I'm trying to contain myself. Every time I close my eyes all I can see is the sleek black grand piano on its silken rug, just sitting there on the lower level of the West Wing, unassuming and quiet in the afternoon light, like the sighting of an exotic wild animal.

OK, now I really am out of breath. Jason has clearly given up trying to keep a straight face and is laughing at me.

"Why are you laughing?" I demand, exasperated.

"Come on, Jemma. I've never seen you get so flustered over a house before. Shoes, yes, but not bricks and mortar. And a big garden."

"Oh no, Jason, this could never be called a garden. It's grounds is what it is!"

Jason pauses as if finally to understand something he couldn't before. "Oh, grounds. Why didn't you say so?" His grin tells me I am being mocked. "But seriously, it sounds great. And the girls? Not spoiled little monsters like in the movies?"

"Oh Jase, they are amazing. They speak like mini grown-ups, well, the seven-year-old does. The younger one is very quiet and shy, but such a cutie-pie. And I can tell she likes me too. I may have to work on Tasanee, but she's seven, right? I mean, how hard could it be? After I give them the SpongeBob SquarePants sweet boxes she's gonna love me."

This is something I've always done, sort of like my trademark. I usually buy a small token for the kids in my first week of work. So far I've been spot on with the gifts, never getting one wrong. It's not really bribery like Jason says it is; it's just a small gesture to break the ice – and children are all the same . . . materialistic to the core.

"Ah, up to your same old tricks, I see. Man, wish we had a babysitter who bribed us growing up."

"Au pair. Or Governess, thank you." I swat Jason and go over to the fridge to get a bottle of water, take out two, and hand one to him.

* * * * * * * *

16

"And the parents? How did you get on with them? Who are they? Are they famous?"

"Oh, that's the one weird thing . . . they weren't there. I don't know who they are – I saw some pictures in the house but didn't recognise them."

"Really?" Jason looks confused. "But, isn't it strange for parents not to meet you before you start?"

"I guess they trust Kobus to hire for them. I mean, he's like the personal assistant to the mother, so he must deal with all this kind of stuff. She must be really busy, but I'm sure I will get on with them great. They are divorced or something, so it looks like I will just be working with the mother, but that's OK. Women doing it for themselves, you know, just us two ladies getting along. I bet she has a really hard time with having to raise the two girls on her own. She'll probably be so happy to have my help she will be lovely to work for."

I smile brightly with visions of long afternoon cups of tea, chatting with Mrs. Totally Awesome about the day while the children have their nap. I will entertain her with adorable stories of the cute things her girls say and she will offer me Romany Creams and tell me what a lifesaver I am and how she could never do without me, and increase my already awesome salary . . . But, even trapped in my own frilly fantasy, I can't help a slight concern pulling at the corners of my excitement.

"Well, it all sounds great, Jem. I was wrong after all, this sounds like a big step up." Jason, along with Mom and Dad, had been trying to convince me to find another kind of job, something more corporate, with the potential of growing into a career. But when I told him how this one was paying literally double what I used to get in Cape Town, he seemed willing to re-think his opinion. Especially as I had been living off him for over six months without finding any work other than doing some promotional work on the side.

"I'm glad you found this – you look really happy. It's going to suck for me though, you being away in the weeks now. Who's going to cook for me?" I throw my water bottle at him.

"One of these days, Jason, you are going to make that poor girlfriend of yours a terrible husband."

I spend the rest of the evening suffering from extreme, projectile word-vomit. I tell Jason all about my day at The Palace while I pack, re-pack and re-re-pack my bag for the first week; how all the staff who work outdoors wear white pajamas and all the in-door staff wear black tunics; how the floors are heated to just the right temperature so even though you need to leave your shoes at the door, you never get that cold-marble-under-your-feet feeling; how shoes, once left at the door, get magically removed by one of the maids, brushed, polished, sprayed with shoe-freshener and put back all shiny and new looking for when you leave. Like little shoe elves! When I'm big I definitely want shoe elves.

I move a few tops aside in my suitcase to stuff in my turquoise blue fake-fur collar jacket, for what I'm not sure – I know I will only be looking after kids so it should be as easy as a few pairs of shorts, some jeans and shirts, maybe my pink MovePretty leggings with the flamingos all over them. I'm still partially shell-shocked with being around such glamour. All over The Palace, while on my grand tour, I noticed photos of the lady of the house posing in elegant Coco Chanel style with hundreds of famous people. She is strikingly beautiful, and in all the pictures she is standing, Mona Lisa smiling, toasting on balconies, in conference rooms, at banquets, even riding a jeweled elephant. With an array of celebrities as if they are her oldest dearest friends. I spotted Prince Charles, Madonna, Seal, Mark Shuttleworth, Richard Branson, Sir Elton John, that guy who rode bikes and dated Sheryl Crow before the scandal . . . the list is just endless. There's even a photo of her standing next to a frail looking Nelson Mandela. And in every single one of these pictures, their mother is dressed like a goddess; adorned in the kinds of clothes I only see in Harper Bazar and Vogue.

Gucci, Marc Jacobs, Prada, Armani, Hermes, but mostly Louis Vuitton – not to mention the diamonds, emeralds, rubies, gold, hats, scarves, bags, sunglasses, rings . . . and the shoes. The shoes!

"Is this too much?" I ask Jason, holding up a spiked heeled pink knee-high pearly snakeskin boot. I got them at the Steve Madden end-of-winter sale last year, a glorious seventy-five per cent off! They have gleaming patent shininess, a cute trim of fur peaking round the tops, and are by far the most fancy boots I own. He rolls his eyes giving me a 'what do you think?' look and I glance down at my overflowing suitcase. I squish up my nose. "Ya, you're probably right. A bit over the top. It's not like I'm going to be going out or clubbing or anything."

I laugh at myself for getting so carried away and toss the boots aside. I'm the au pair, for goodness sake. I don't need to dress up to impress the lady of the manor. I'm the down-to-earth au pair. I can do this. I was born to do this… In a pair of low-rise, slim-cut, Guess jeans with trendy rips and diamante G on the back pocket, of course.

I add pink-tartan panties for good luck and start packing my bathroom bag when the doorbell rings. Jason goes to open up, and the loud bustle of "Helloooo Dahh-ling. Mwah, mwah, MWAH!" tells me Frederick has arrived.

"You like pink, don't you sweet-bottom?" Frederick says, sitting on the edge of my single box-bed after kisses and hugs and all the usual fuss he enters a room with has subsided.

"What gives you that idea?" I ask, innocently.

"Uh, your pink matching travel luggage. Your pink strappy vest. Your pink faux-cashmere scarf. Your pink spike-heeled boots. Your pink 'Pinker than Pink' lipstick. Your pink and pink shorty pajamas. Your pink bath towel, pink make-up bag, pink . . ."

"OK, OK! You got me. I love pink. And I am not ashamed to admit it!" I lift my chin, feigning the pride of a political activist. "Jason may think it's stupid and call me Suchagirl for it, but I will carry this colour with me to my grave." I hold up the scarf in my fist.

"Here here," agrees Frederick. "A pink casket! That would be fabulous." He laughs, grabbing the scarf and wrapping it around his head into a turban. "How's this?" he asks, posing sideways with one shoulder arched, pouting his lips.

"Like a fabulous fish, daahh-ling!" I give an exaggerated pout myself.

"It's a good colour, I'll admit." He readjusts the scarf into a sailor's necktie, turning this way and that, admiring himself; I'm sure he's wondering if he could get away with being a touch more flamboyant on a regular basis. "Such frivolity." He grins wickedly. Turning back to the mirror, he scolds his reflection. "*Vat daai ding aff! Is jy a blerrie moffie of wat!*"

I can't help laughing. It's always so strange to hear Frederick's real accent and home language. He hides it well, like nestling a potjie pot in a flurry of fresh rose petals. I keep forgetting he's as Afrikaans as I am English. I love it when he does it, because secretly I think it is way more beautiful-sounding than his day-to-day lingo. I pull the scarf off his neck and throw it into my bag.

"Pink always makes everything feel better, don't you think? It's such a happy colour. When I'm surrounded by pink I feel as though the world is a dazzling place and good things are brewing. My granny always said that's why all the best sunsets have pink in them, you know. It's the universe reminding us we all deserve happiness."

In the end my bags are all packed and I'm ready to nudge Frederick and his bright chatter gently out of the door. I intend to be well rested for my first day.

I still can't believe I got this job. All those years of working bad hours for mediocre salaries, being puked on by ungrateful kids - or worse - is finally about to pay off. I told Jason it would all pay off. My CV is super strong now, and with all the childcare experience I have, it's no wonder the royals hired me.

I've been working with children pretty much all my life. From a really early age I helped out in our church youth group. In high school I started to babysit to earn money for shoes, stationery and gifts. I babysat for friends and family, and Mom's book club buddies. Someone always needed me. By the time I finished school it kind of just stuck. But the rule at home was if we were eighteen and decided not to go to university, we would have to fend for ourselves. Jason went the studying route, but I didn't know what I wanted to study yet so decided to look after children until I figured it all out. After a couple of years it became somewhat of a comfort-zone, I guess. I took childcare courses at the local library, baby CPR at the fire department, and became an official au pair.

When Jason was offered a too-good-to-turn-down job in Johannesburg, and I found myself in a too-bad-to-keep-on relationship at the same time as being unemployed, we decided to move up to Joburg together. Our parents finally cut the apron strings, and so Jason had to fend for us both while I was looking for work. Jason would never complain of course, but he did spend six months circling jobs in the paper and printing out offers off websites for me. Mostly corporate jobs in office buildings, of course, and I did go to a few of the interviews, but secretly kept looking for an au pair job on the sly. Now I have found the one I wanted, I am so happy I can pay him back, and get him off my back at the same time.

This position feels right. Something about being a nanny – au pair, dammit! Au pair! (I really must remember my title) – resonates with me. It's the only time I think I actually do well and don't stuff everything up.

I'm due back at The Palace at seven a.m. The plan is I will join my employer and the girls for the new term welcoming at their private school. Tasanee is starting grade one, and Lola is joining pre-primary.

On the first day all teachers and parents meet for a light chatty-type breakfast, and the girls will be shown around and introduced to all their classmates. It seems to be quite a big thing in these private schools, and I'm sure there will be some champagne and orange juice going around for moms and nannies, rather than boring old tea like at the public schools I went to in Cape Town. I'm quite looking forward to it.

After finally persuading Frederick to go home with promises of a full weekend of catching up, I go through my outfit in my head again, hoping I have chosen the right look to meet the wonder woman from the photos. 'Stop being so silly,' I command myself, trying to force my eyes closed so I can sleep. 'This is all going to be perfect. You've got this!'

I am the one who was chosen to look after "royalty" after all.

I am the new caregiver for the children of a woman who knew Nelson Mandela.

I am working in a mansion bigger than most boutique malls back in Cape Town.

I am a professional au pair with the most awesome new job…

…And I am going out to celebrate!

"Jason. Get up. We're going out!" I throw my favorite jeans back on and look in my closet for a sparkly top. One should always wear sparkles when one is celebrating.

"What the–" Jason appears at my doorway blurry eyed as I hop around trying to fasten one bright pink wedge-heeled platform to my ankle in the air.

Oops, maybe he had already fallen asleep . . . But it's only 10pm and we are young and I can't sleep, so he'll just have to suck it up. "Let's go for a celebratory drink – just one!"

The very best thing about Jason is he is easy to convince. All I needed to do was call my friend Troy, and she was already out at the new Chocolate Lounge – with Frederick who didn't go home after all, so it's a done deal.

"Only one drink," I say to Troy and Frederick when we arrive at the bar. "I start tomorrow morning and don't want to be too tired. We didn't even Uber, I brought Peaches. But I couldn't sleep. Too excited! Eep!"

Jason pulls back slightly and eyes me suspiciously. "Is that one of your made-up words, Jem?" he asks, accusingly.

"No." I protest. "Eep is a word. All the kids are saying it. On Twitter."

"'S'true," says Frederick, popping a cherry into his mouth and pulling out the stem.

"See." I beam at him.

"Sure it is, pop-culture princess," he laughs, heading to the bar.

I smile again, bounce a little and get back to the celebrations. I start to feel the spirit of the moment bubble inside me. This is the new job that is going to help me change my life, grow up and be one of those more mature, more expensive shoe-wearing, better car-driving types. So here and now I decide it's also time to stop making up words, or using poppy slang.

But not tonight. Tonight we celebrate!

"Two cosmopolitans for the ladies." Jason brings over two long-stemmed martini glasses filled with deliciously ruby-pink liquid for Frederick and I. "And a double jager-bomb for the hardcore party animal." Troy takes her drink from Jason and flashes him her most charming smile. She has been flirting with my brother since the day she met him – even though she knows he has a girlfriend who currently lives in the UK. Sometimes I wonder if she's my friend because she likes me or if it's all a ploy to get to Jason. Not that she would need a ploy. I can imagine her going up to him and saying 'Alright then,' Lilly Allen style, and it'd be on like Donkey-Kong. Then again, he's a good guy, and wouldn't do that to his girlfriend, even though they are constantly breaking up, getting back together, breaking up again and so on. They are as bad as a celebrity couple.

"So tell me about this place again?" Troy sets herself down on the big white leather couch in-between Frederick and me, crosses her legs at Jason seductively, and leans back to hear my story. Troy is a total man-eater. She is tall, athletic, has rich chocolate brown hair and a glowing all-year-round tan. She does perfect smoky-eye make up, and she invented the side-glance half-smile half-pout come-hither look. Works every time too. She trumps me in every possible way.

Jason hands me a new glass and I realise I've been so distracted that my first drink is already empty. Maybe I spilled it?

"I figured you might need a bit more fuel for this story," he says. "You should have seen her when she got home today. Total basket case. She's convinced she's going to become best friends with the Queen and party with Beyoncé."

"Thanks, Jason – way to stick up for your better half," I mock glare at him.

"You two are so funny – like the Tweedle-twins," says Frederick, finishing his cosmo.

"And that would make you who?" I tease. "The Mad Hatter?"

He winks at me. "Johnny Depp? Yes please!"

Troy flicks her hair at Jason, and he suddenly seems really thirsty, chocking down his beer. "Back to the bar! Looks like we need more refreshments, and I may as well buy my sister drinks one last night before she has any money to pay for them herself."

"I can't believe it." I say to Troy, swirling my cosmo. "My life is so perfect! I have the world's greatest twin brother, the best friends," – Troy and Frederick bow their heads slightly and chink my glass in agreement – "and the most amazing new job. It just doesn't get better than this."

"Well," says Troy teasingly, twirling a piece of my blonde hair in her fingers. "Not exactly. It would only be perfect if you had this all dyed rainbow, and hooked up with Romeo over there." She gestures towards a tall Italian-looking guy, brooding in the corner. "Hey there, Sexy Bitch!"

I cringe as he looks over while we quickly duck down in the couch pretending it wasn't us, which is useless because Frederick gives it away by sticking up his head like a meerkat and swiveling around to see at whom she just yelled obscenities. "Good Gaga," he mouths.

"Troy," I hiss while pulling Frederick down, "I could change the oil in my car with all that hair grease he has going on."

"Or you could change his oil." This girl has a sick fascination with making me blush. I can feel even in the dim lights of the cocktail bar my face is glowing bright red. She knows I can't talk dirty, or handle it when someone else does. Ugh.

Frederick fights free and assesses the greasy Romeo with enthusiasm.

"What's going on?" Jason asks innocently as he arrives back at our nook with a new round.

"Oh nothing!" I say, grabbing my cosmo and waving it in front of me, hiding my face. "Oops . . . I spilled." I jump up and brush off the few drops that splashed out on to my jeans.

"Well, then, we are just going to have to get you another, aren't we?" says Troy, sashaying over to the bar. "Drink up, Working Girl" she calls over her shoulder as she goes.

"Just one drink, huh?" Jason raises an eyebrow at me as Troy comes back, laden with more cosmopolitans and a tray of green Springbokkie shooters.

"Ya," I say slowly, pushing the shooters aside, looking longingly at the cosmos. "But they are pink, and you know how much I like pink drinks . . . We can call Night Owls to drive Peaches home. Maybe, just one more?"

"Cheers to that, sweet bottom!" agrees Frederick, shoving a new glass in my hand. "And to your new-found fabulousness! Well done on getting the job." He raises his glass.

"Hear, hear!" adds in Jason, holding up his beer.

"Hear, hear!" Troy repeats, leaning in with her drink.

Ah, to hell with it.

"Hear, hear!" I shout, throwing all caution to the wind, and give myself a mental hug as four drinks clink each other in the air in swirly, topsy-turvy delight.

Chapter 3

· · · · · · · · ·

"Jemma, wake up! You're going to be late!"

"Wha . . ."

Three pink drinks – Italian – dance floor – Sringbokkie shooters – missing shoe – more pink – disco lights – clear shooters – Big Joe from that new club in town – giggle giggle giggle – tummy contest – abs – McDonald's – tomato sauce fight – socks – Chinese lantern dragon costume tom-yum – more-pink – swap-clothes-flashing-lights-egg-dianosaur-puddle-giggle-gigglegigglegiggle . . .

Oh no.

I sit bolt upright in bed. I clutch my stomach – oh no oh no – stumble out of bed, shove past Jason, and slam the bathroom door shut.

"You have just short of an hour to get there. Don't worry. I'm leaving Valoid and Myprodol at the door here." I hear a glass of water being placed on the floor outside the bathroom door. "And I'll start frying eggs. You get dressed. I'll put your bags in the car with a Red Bull."

Jason is so not my brother. He's actually an angel who was sent to earth to watch over me and help fix me when I have a Jemma moment. I manage to stand back up from releasing all the pink contents of my stomach, grab the pills and water and down them. I jump into the shower, spilling

· · · · · · · · ·

toothpaste all over the place while trying to brush my teeth, wash my hair and scrub my smeared make-up face all at once.

My legs are wobbling dangerously as I co-ordinate getting them into grey skinny jeans while hopping into one of my pink boots (yes, I decided to wear the spiked heels after all) and pull my shirt over my head. Wet hair leaves streak marks all the way down my jade top, but I don't care. I can feel the petite white pills settling in my stomach – Jemma's Little Helpers – and grab my make-up bag. Jason meets me at the kitchen doorway with a plate full of fried eggs, runny and greasy just the way I like them on mornings like this, and I see he has even managed to fry up some bacon on the side. I shovel food into my mouth while thanking him, muffled and emphatically, and stabbing at my face with brushes, sponges and finally a swoop of mascara. I step back to look at myself in the full-length mirror on the dividing wall between our kitchen and lounge.

Then I charge back down the passageway to the bathroom and lose my breakfast too. Ah well, probably better if I do this on an empty stomach anyhow. And that should have taken care of any remnants of last night's alcohol content in me.

I hear another sound at the bathroom door of a glass being put on the floor. "Round two of miracle hang-over kit!" shouts Jason. "Twenty-six minutes to go – and counting!" I don't know how he does it, but I so owe him.

Thank the lucky fairy-star-dust I remembered my sunglasses. Also, the M1 wasn't as bad as I thought it would be with morning traffic and I'm making good time. Sitting at the Grayston Drive off-ramp, I take another swig of Red Bull Jason left in the cup holder for me when something catches my eye in the rearview mirror.

"What the . . ." I swing round in my seat, practically cracking a rib against the seat belt, and stare at the back.

There, perched like it had always been there, like it belonged there, is a giant bright pink plastic flamingo.

That's right.

A pink flamingo.

The sound of hooters snaps me out of my confused moment, and I quickly turn back to the steering wheel and focus on the road.

"If only you could talk, Peaches," I say out loud to my car, reaching back with one arm and fiddling round till I find the flamingo and shove it to the floor. "Good thing we called Night Owls, hey."

It must have been our only saving grace in my state the night before – I still remembered to call the driving service out to come and fetch us, and take us, and Peaches, safely home so I didn't drive drunk.

I pull into Hollywood Drive, popping another Valoid and Myprodol for good measure (I have a stash in my handbag, put there by Jason-ala-Angel-Gabriel.) This is good. I'm actually feeling OK-ish and I still have six minutes to go. But man, that was a close one. It would have been one major catastrophe. I make a mental note to remember I look after children by day, and so should not be club hopping by night, even though I'm only twenty-four, and take another swig of Red Bull.

I sign in at the gates, slightly annoyed at the delay, and make my way up the brain-gratingly loud clinky drive, feeling considerably less enthusiastic than last time Peaches and I were doing this. "OK, Jemma," I command myself, "time to pull it together."

I park in the same spot as before and climbing out, I look around, not entirely sure what to do. Kobus said to use the staff entrance, but surely on Day One I should rather knock on the front door? I still need to meet the lady of the house, after all, and I don't want to just walk in via the staff door un-invited. I make my way to the front door, deciding that will be the best answer. Plus, it's the closest door to me and I'm feeling less than athletic this morning. There is a beautiful big Porsche Cayenne 4x4 parked in the drop-off zone in front of the house. I squint painfully at its shiny exterior, admiring its deep metallic blue as I walk around it to reach the front door. It looks like a futuristic whale!

I pause at the front door. There isn't actually a doorbell or even a knocker on a latch, so I reach up and knock softly on the frosted glass. I can't hear anything from inside the house, but it is so big all sounds would get lost before hitting the front entranceway. I knock a bit louder, wait a few moments, then knock again, leaning in close to listen for footsteps. I jump back as a shadow crosses the door. Of course I wouldn't hear footsteps, I realise – they don't wear any shoes inside! The handle turns and Suda pulls the door open a crack. She stares at me through the slim space, bewildered, as if she doesn't remember me.

"Er, morning, Suda," I say. "Nice to see you again."

Suda doesn't say anything but narrows her eyes and keeps staring at me. She looks over her shoulder to one side, then the other, leans forward and says in a sharp whisper: "What you do here? You go staff door!"

"Oh!" I say apologetically, matching her whisper instinctively. "I'm sorry. I just thought maybe on the first morning . . ."

"Suda. Who is that?"

The Voice reaches my ears, the hairs on the back of my neck standing on end. Whatever hangover I may have had has now vanished in an icy blast. I stand there, mid-sentence, barely breathing, wondering what to do. Suda is staring at me like she too doesn't know what to do. Her eyes have widened and seem to be frozen, and I notice dew forming on her brow.

"Suda!" The Voice comes again. "Who is it?" That Voice is loud yet soft, treacle sweet yet deathly cold and terrifying all in one. It oozes into your ears, fills your brain and simmers there like a bubbling volcano. I start noiselessly to shake my head at Suda while trying to creep backwards, but too late.

"It new nanny, Khunying." Suda quickly stands back, holding the door open wider. There in the entranceway to the left I see her. The most beautiful woman I've ever seen. The most perfectly formed, beautifully dressed, warmly sun-kissed, full-lipped woman. A Venus de Milo in the flesh. Sure, she was pretty in the photos, but this woman is truly exquisite! I take her all in like a diamond-blast of stormy wind. Flesh, skin, hair, eyes . . . cold eyes . . . Her eyes are gleaming at me with an icy stare.

The blue eyes dance in her flawless face as if spirits have taken residence in her body. Something about blue eyes and tanned skin has always fascinated me, like a radioactive latte. I stand staring at her, struck motionless.

There is a long uncomfortable silence. No one dares move; no one dares speak. The air sucked out of the room.

"Er," I finally muster. "I'm so sorry. I should have come round the other side of course. I – er – I . . . Lovely to meet you, Mrs Awe . . . Uh – my name is Jemma Richardson," I hold out a shaky hand in her direction. "The new au pair." When I get no response, I add: "Should I – should I go round to the staff entrance . . .?"

"Of course you are," says The Voice. "Who else would you be? Come in. Leave your shoes." And with that she turns and swishes out of the room.

Suddenly I can breathe again. That wasn't so bad, I tell myself, stumbling through the door and taking off my boots. First impressions are always iffy. Besides, she didn't sound angry. Just sort of annoyed. Or not really annoyed entirely – more like uninterested.

"Come!" Suda gestures to me impatiently. I follow her through the left passageway and into the sunroom. Standing in a stream of fresh early morning light, Mrs. Totally Awesome is gently surveying herself. She brushes down her arm with one perfectly manicured hand, then moves gracefully round and holds her skirt, looking down her front. In her perfect presence, my well-planned outfit seems like a joke. What was going to be young and hip, yet responsible and professional, now feels frumpy, cheap and miss-matched. I become hideously conscious of the streaks my wet hair left on my top, now dried to a slightly lighter colour than the rest of the fabric. Damn cheap synthetic fibres! And my fitted pale charcoal jeans suddenly feel like saggy grey sweats that look like they once belonged to an elephant. This is the difference between spending two hundred rand on an outfit and spending two thousand rand on an outfit, I resolve. I shuffle uncomfortably, not sure what to do next.

Then, hands on both hips, she turns her sapphire-blue eyes on me.

"Jemma." She lifts her chin and smiles warmly. "I am Nicole-Annella Janssens. You may call me Khunying." She holds out a diamond-encrusted hand for me to shake, but she keeps hers turned palm down, like a queen. I step forward into the pool of light and take her hand, feeling immediately warmed and more welcomed.

"My girls tell me you were very interested in the origins of my house staff?" she says smoothly, not taking her jewel-like stare off me for a second. She sits down on a Victorian armchair and lifts a china teacup to her lips, taking an elegant sip.

Crap! Tasanee must have told her I asked about Suda!

"Oh, I only wondered," I say with a nervous laugh, "because of Suda's accent, you know. It's a little different . . ." I suddenly feel like I'm being interrogated, standing there in the middle of the room while Khunying surveys me from her throne. The beam of sunlight shines straight at me - an accusing spotlight.

"Do you make a habit of exchanging inappropriate dialogue with seven-year-old girls, Jennifer, or are you working as a spy?"

Crap!

My skin is about to burn off under her stare. I fumble around in my brain for something to say, heart racing, when suddenly Khunying tilts her head back and gives a light and melodious laugh.

I laugh too, hesitantly, but still feel incredibly awkward. I look to the Cleopatra-style ottoman longingly and back to Khunying, holding my hands stiffly next to my sides. "Um, it was just, um . . ." What the hell is wrong with me? Why am I suddenly so paralysed? And where did that "um, ah, uh" stutter come from?

"Oh, don't worry." Khunying interrupts my mortification. "You will of course be learning a lot from Suda. Perhaps you could ask her your questions in future." Khunying is smiling warmly, but I want to die of embarrassment. She takes another dignified sip. "Now, what do you think of my outfit?"

She stands up and gives a small turn. She is wearing a soft cream sleeveless top with matching skirt, flowing mid-calf. The material must be silk or chiffon, I think – something that floats over her body like a haute couture drawing. The skirt has a thin panel of sheer material spiraling down to the hemline, revealing opaque flashes of sheathed thigh on every turn. I look away from her legs, a pink flush rising in my face, and focus on her feet. She has one funny big toe that curves a little too much in towards the rest. She shifts her feet and I quickly look back up to her face, feeling like I have once again done something I wasn't meant to.

"You look very nice," I manage, "Khunying," I add, feeling the need to say something like "Ma'am" after every sentence. My voice has gone up an octave again. Great. Calm down, Jemma, this is ridiculous!

Khunying frowns, though I notice she only draws her forehead down about one-hundredth of an inch. Botox.

She suddenly turns and walks out the room without so much as a word.

Did I say something wrong? Sheesh. This is the strangest first meeting I've ever had with a parent. And the most intense. I let out a long breath, realising again I've been holding it in. My headache is back, obviously revived from its initial retreat when fear and stupidity were the governing forces of my being for a while there. I put my hands to my eyes trying to soothe away everything, and decide to chance taking a seat on the corner of the Cleopatra chair.

"Jemma!" The girls come running into the room, Tasanee in a cute little powder-yellow school uniform, and Lola in a pink and denim playsuit. Tasanee bounces onto the chair her mother was sitting on, and Lola stands to her right, shyly sucking on her two fingers.

"Don't you two look pretty!" I say, forcing a smile and feeling a bit of relief at their presence. Much easier than dealing with Khunying. Tasanee swats Lola away as she tries to lean on her mother's couch. I reach out and pull Lola towards me gently by one hand. "You're going to school!" I say to her encouragingly. "No need for those two fingers anymore." She takes her hand away from her mouth and wipes it on her shirt.

"Are you going to drive with us, Jemma?" asks Lola, her sweet voice timid with hope.

I'm actually not sure what the plan is – no one has really said anything to me yet other than to be here at seven. "Let's wait and see what your mommy says, OK?" She climbs up on to the Cleopatra chair and sits next to me with her hands in her lap, swinging her legs underneath her.

"I go to real school," says Tasanee, lifting her chin with an air I can already see comes straight from her mother, and looking over towards Lola and I, challenging us. "Lola is still only in baby class. It's not real school. I am going to be doing things like Maths and Spelling and Science and stuff."

"How exciting," I say to her, though I give Lola a slight reassuring squeeze of her hand to make her feel comfortable.

"'Stuff' is not a word, Tasanee," says Khunying coldly, coming back into the room. "You should have corrected her, Jemma or do you think 'stuff' is appropriate language where you come from?"

Something tells me this is a hypothetical question and I am not meant to answer. Tasanee quickly jumps off the armchair and goes to stand with her mom.

"Sorry, Mommy," she says obediently. "Oh, Mommy, you look beautiful!"

Khunying smiles, satisfied, and tucks Tasanee's hair behind one ear. She has changed outfits. I'm quite surprised, as I really thought she looked stunning before. But now she is wearing a beige pantsuit with a choco-late-coloured camisole. I suppose this does look a bit more conservative, so maybe that is what she was going for. I have also stood up on impulse when she came in the room, and am now tugging at my jeans self-consciously.

"Do you have all your things, girls?" she asks, and the two children run out of the room, leaving me feeling nervous to be alone with her again.

"I'll just – uh – go see if I can help them," I say quickly, taking the initiative. Good idea, Jemma! Get away from the Ice Queen and look like you're doing a good job.

Khunying doesn't seem to have heard me, or doesn't feel the need to respond to me, so I start my retreat from the room. I do notice, however, she gives me a disapproving once-over as I leave. Damn synthetic saggy cheap-ass low-cost crappy clothing!

"Girls," I say, walking into Tasanee's bedroom, following their voices. "I have a little something for you. A first-day-at-school gift!"

"Oh goodie!" shouts Tasanee and she runs up to me clapping her hands, back to her seven-year-old self. Lola follows her lead and bounces towards me too. I take the two SpongeBob SquarePants Pez dispensers out of my bag and hand one to each of them. They look confused, and turn the plastic yellow figures around in their hands. "What is it?" asks Tasanee.

"You don't know who SpongeBob SquarePants is?" I ask, bewildered.

Tasanee rolls her eyes. "Duh, of course we know SpongeBob. But what is this thing? A toy?" She shakes the figure up at her ear, obviously per-plexed at the rattling sound. I show them how to access the sweets and they both exclaim out loud in excitement, pressing them open.

"Have you never had one of these before?" I ask, completely baffled. What kid, in this day and age, hasn't learnt to use Pez?

"Nope" they say simultaneously, while shoveling candy in their mouths.

I watch in astonishment for a moment, and then remember the task at hand.

"But let's put them away for now, OK? Where are your school bags? Ah, do you have everything you need?"

"We get our lists today, so we don't have to take much. Just snacks, which Jim packed for us." Jim is the chef I met when I first came to the house. I look in Tasanee's satchel and see there is a Hello Kitty-branded lunchbox and cool-drink bottle neatly packed at the bottom. She picks up her school blazer and starts towards the door. "Let's go!" she calls behind her as she leaves the room. "Last one to the stairs is a looooooser!" and off she runs.

Lola makes an attempt to catch up with her sister, but is obviously way too far behind. I see a sad look on her face as she realises Tasanee has gone on without her.

I pick up her school bag, check there is a jersey inside for her, and follow her down the staircase. I notice she still has her bunny. Before I reach the bottom of the stairs I hear Khunying's voice scolding her.

"You will not take that ghastly thing to school with you, Lola. Put it down at once! And why are you two running and squealing like pigs on a farm? You are young ladies, and this is an elegant house – not a petting zoo. Now behave the way I taught you." I see her coming through the hallway, pulling Lola a little too roughly by the hand, the other ornamented hand gripping a phone to her chest as though to muffle her parental rebukes from who ever is on the other end. The tiny girl looks scared and sad, but trips along obediently. Seeing them right next to each other, I notice Lola has her mother's full lips and radiance. She definitely inherited the beauty, while Tasanee got the killer instincts. "Right," Khunying continues into the phone after disposing of Lola's hand and shushing her in my direction. "Where was I? Yes. Yes. No. No absolutely no! What did I say before? What did I tell you? NO! I'll sue, I tell you – I'll SUE!" I usher the girls out the door and away from the scene, feeling quite rattled.

Khunying has chosen to drive, and Tasanee jumps into the passenger seat before anyone else can. Lola and I climb in the backseat, which suits me fine. I spend the journey to the school playing finger games with Lola, making small puppets out of my hands and keeping a smile on the elfin girl's face. She giggles softly every time I catch her with my imaginary hand crocodile.

As soon as we get to the school, Khunying stalks off without a word to me, so I just follow behind with Lola. Tasanee is running up ahead of us, keeping in step with her mother and chatting away about the school and teachers to Khunying. She has been in this school for two years already, starting in the pre-school class Lola is now joining, so she knows the grounds, and seems to know a lot of the teachers and students. I'm quite taken aback to see her interact with the adults, and even a lot of the older students come up to her and talk to her with big smiles. She copies her mother's aloof air, but I can see an excited gleam in her eyes every time someone gives her their full attention.

I feel a miniature hand slip in mine and look down to see Lola holding on to me, looking shell-shocked. I smile reassuringly at her and we keep following the mother-daughter combo.

Prrrr prrrr, my cell phone goes off in my pocket. I chose the kitty-cat purr ring tone because it is so cute, but now, this close to the cast-iron elegance of Khunying, I flush with embarrassment. I quickly grab it and see it's Troy. I can't believe she's awake already. I look around. Khunying is engrossed in a heavy conversation with a very peroxided-blonde school mom; I hear her say "I should sue!" in her terrifying (as is obviously the norm) voice, so figure this might be a long one, and stop behind a big old oak to answer the phone.

"Hey Troy – listen I cant really talk now–"

"OMG babe! You're still alive! I can't believe last night! What a wild party, huh?" Troy sounds as though she is still in bed and her voice is all low and husky as if she has been smoking about a thousand cigarettes.

"Ya, thanks, I mean it was cool – not feeling so great today – but I can't really talk now . . ."

"Really? I feel great! I actually just got up for some water, and now I can't get back to sleep. How's it going with the new fam?"

"Actually, I'm at the school with them all right now so can't really talk . . ."

Troy is giggling hysterically again. She must still be drunk.

"Babe, we have to do it again this weekend, I had the best time!"

"Ya, I had fun too. But listen," I see Khunying turning round. "I really have to go."

"OK, Jem, good luck today. Call me later in the week, OK? We'll chill at my place on Saturday. Bring that gorgeous brother of yours – I have a new Brazillian-cut bikini I need to try out on a man. I'll call Frederick. Bye babe!" Why does she always have to go on about Jason? Doesn't she know he's taken?

"Bye." I jab at my phone – I'm still whispering as Khunying fixes her glare on me and starts towards me like the Terminator moving in on its target with a bloodthirsty homing device . . .

"I don't pay you to have private conversations on your cell phone," she says, her ice-blue eyes burning mercury holes into my soul.

"I'm sorry, Khunying, it won't happen again." I quickly switch my phone to vibrate and put it in my pocket.

"Ah, there's my Uber Black. I'm leaving now. Here are the car keys. You will stay for the rest of the day and bring the girls home when everything is done."

She's leaving?

"Make sure the girls attend the welcoming warm-up games after the breakfast and don't just sit there, chit-chatting on your cell all day. I expect you to be attentive to them, and to interact with the teachers." She hands me the keys, and then when she sees me hesitate, a mean look creeps across her face. She seems to decide to have a last say at me. And loudly.

"And if you must go behind my back and give my children unautho-rised foods, if you can even call that no-doubt carcinogenic, MSG filled garbage you gave them 'food', please do have the courtesy to check with the chef if they are approved first. You may be OK with filling your body with toxic chemicals, but I don't want them eating anything that hasn't been looked over."

Crap.

What am I, some creepy child-poisoner? Her accusing stare says: Yes, yes I am.

Crap Crap-crappity-crap!

How on earth did she find out about the sweet dispensers so quickly? I feel my cheeks burn and look over to Tasanee, who is wearing an expression of "What?" She told her mom on me? Again? What for? And how? I was with them, or at least in hearing distance for the whole time. How on earth did she tattletale? Telepathically?

As I try to say sorry for not running the gifts by her first, Khunying puts her hand up right in front of my face, as if to silence me, and turns away before I have a chance to reply. Barely giving Lola a second glance, she walks over to Tasanee, bends down and actually air-kisses her daughter. It is the most bizarre thing to watch – a mother kissing her child goodbye like an Italian designer kissing a French model hello. I stare in disbelief, feeling as though I've just witnessed a panda bear perform dental surgery on a budgie. So unreal. "Goodbye Lola" she calls over her shoulder and walks off.

I can't believe it. I am suddenly very aware of the keys in my hand and feel daunted. I'm sure it will be fine, but she didn't even show me where the hand-brake is. I've never driven a car bigger than my uncle's old 1400 Nissan bakkie – let alone a 4x4! And a Porsche? And I wish I had paid more attention to the road coming here – I don't know I will remember how to get back on to the highway. OK, calm down, Jemma, it's all going to be OK. You can use Googlle Maps. Besides, you're in this now, so be like Dori and just – keep – swimming. Deep end is your specialty, after all.

Chapter 4

. . . .

"WHOOOOOOOO LIVES IN A PINEAPPLE UNDER THE SEA?"

"SPONGEBOB SQUAREPANTS!"

I've discovered the key to getting Tasanee and Lola to play together without arguing. We are all singing the SpongeBob song sitting in the afternoon light on the grass outside, toys littered all over the lawn around us. Our morning at the school, after Khunying's disappearing act, was actually a lot of fun. Tasanee carried on owning every group she walked past and eventually went off with some other Gucci-Grade-Oners to their classroom, arms linked on either side. Lola relaxed visibly after her mother left and was quite the clown at the school games, making a lot of her new classmates laugh. And my hangover slowly but surely subsided, packing itself away in the back of my head as nothing more than a dull, tired ache. The girls seemed to be on a high afterwards.

All the school moms took me under their wing with open sincerity. There didn't seem to be any other nannies there on their own, so maybe they felt sorry for the girls and me being stranded by Khunying on the first day. It turned out to be great fun though, and I can't help feeling it wouldn't have been as enjoyable if Khunying had stayed.

. . . .

After getting home, we took our lunch of chicken-vegetable kebabs and Appletizers outside to eat on the lawn, and Jim gave the Pez dispensers back to me on our way out the kitchen door. "These are fine," he said. "I don't know why she wants me to look at them." He seemed amused by the whole situation.

Once they finish their lunch, they start playing darts with the kebab skewers in a neatly brushed-up pile of leaves raked there by one of the men in white pajamas, and who now is scowling at us.

We spend the rest of the afternoon discussing the first day of school and playing a Hello Kitty version of Simon Says – Hello Kitty says do this, Hello Kitty says do that, Hello Kitty says jump around and act like monkeys (Lola didn't quite understand the rules of the game and spent the rest of it doing her comical monkey-dance, giggling like an adorable goggle-eyed lunatic) until the dog got out of his gated garden. We wrestled Bruno for a while (it's the only way spending time playing with the brute of a dog can be described) and then I finally persuade the girls to come in the house for some colouring-in at the dining room table, and they draw pictures for their mother. I remember one of the things I was asked to do was use time for educational activities, so don't want to slip up again. And seeing that Tasanee seems hell-bent on informing her mother of every little thing we do, I had better make sure I do things right from now on.

As soon as we get upstairs to the playroom, while looking in the book-case for appropriate books, I hear the click of the flat screen going on, and turn to see Tasanee all settled down on a bright pink poufy sofa flipping channels on the TV. Lola drops her crayon box, and jumps up to cuddle next to her sister.

"Oh, I don't think we are supposed to be watching TV now," I say.

"Oh no, it's OK," says Tasanee, not looking away from the screen. "Mommy always lets us watch in the afternoons.

I look to Lola for some sign of confirmation, but she is staring at the TV blankly, like someone already sucked her brain out of her head through the eye sockets.

"Um, alright, but just for a bit, OK? I'll be back in a minute." I go to find Suda. Better be safe than sorry and ask her what the rules around screen-time are.

I hear some music and voices coming from the kitchen so head towards it. I hear laughing, and as I come round the corner, I see Suda, Ramie, the other housemaid, and Jim all standing round the polished black granite-top counter in the middle of the room, drinking coffee and eating decadent looking cupcakes. They stop talking the instant I walk in and turn to stare at me. It's the domestic version of an old western stranger-walks-into-a-bar scene.

"Uh, hey guys," I say, trying to be friendly and relaxed. Jim is eyeing me, making me a little uncomfortable.

"Where girls?" asks Suda, using her usual unfriendly tone.

"Don't be so nasty, Toole," says Jim. "Give the fresh meat a chance before you chase her away too." He laughs and holds out the cupcake plate to me. "Can I make you some coffee, new girl?"

"Um, thanks, but Suda is right, I must get back. Actually, Suda, that's just something I wanted to ask you about? Are they allowed to watch TV yet?"

Ramie shakes her head to herself and starts making a clicking noise with her tongue. Jim emits a low chuckle.

"TV? You let them TV? No! They no TV in afternoon. They mom be very cross!"

Oh, for goodness sake. Why does it seem like there are so many rules around here, but no one tells them to me until I've broken them?

"OK, but you see Tasanee told me . . ."

"Tasanee very bad girl" says Suda. "You be careful that girl."

"What Suda is trying to say, new girl," says Jim coming towards me with a fresh hot cup of coffee, "is that you might want to be a bit careful with Tas. She is a cunning mini-version of her mother. Sugar?"

Oh, why not. I sit down on one of the barstools and accept the coffee. I survey my new colleagues, wondering if we will get along? Jim seems OK. He might be my "in" around here. Suda is tough on the outside, but I suspect she is much nicer than she would like me to believe. Ramie, though, I haven't quite figured out Ramie . . .

"Well, back to what we were saying," says Ramie, as if reading my thoughts and deciding to help me suss her out. "Jim, you say a month, I say a week. Suda, what do you say?" Suda suddenly looks straight at me, just as I take a big bite of the cupcake, smearing chocolate icing on my face.

"Maybe two. Two week."

"Alright, so for a hundred rand, Jim says Jemma will last a month. You say two weeks and I say one week."

What? I almost choke on my cupcake. They are actually betting on how long I will last in the job? This is crazy. And so rude! How can they do that, and then be so brazen about it and talk about it while I'm sitting right here. I straighten my shoulders and lift my chin, hoping to convey a look of complete what-evs!

Jim starts to laugh. "Oh, new girl. Don't look so upset. It's just a friendly game we play with all thee new babysitters." He gives me a wink. I almost say "au pair" through the chocolate, but stop myself and rather focus on swallowing. What does he mean anyway?

I decide it's time to go back upstairs, so I put the rest of my cupcake back down on the plate and leave my coffee half-drunk. I stand up and turn my back on both Ramie and Suda. "Thank you for the coffee and cake, Jim," I say, speaking calmly and politely with just a hint of bitch-slap. "I'm going to go back up to the girls now."

As I'm leaving the kitchen, I hear Ramie sniggering.

"You will understand soon," calls Jim, but I keep walking.

On my way up the stairs, muttering to myself, I suddenly hear a scream. I look up, shocked, and run the rest of the stairs two at a time. By the time I get to the room, the girls are no longer on the couch where I left them. Lola is sitting on the floor of the little terrace behind some French doors, crying bitterly. Tasanee is standing over by the bookcase looking defiant. And the TV has been switched to a music channel with some scantily-clad creature writhing all over it.

"What happened?" I ask as I pick up Lola's sobbing frame, grab the remote and turn the TV off. She cradles around me. "Mu," she sniffs, "Tasanee threw Mu." She points to the garden below. There, impaled on some rose bushes, is Lola's toy rabbit. An afternoon shower has drenched everything outside, and the rabbit is dripping and pitiful.

"Tasanee!" I look at her in horror. "Did you throw Lola's bunny out the window?"

"None of your business." Tasanee faces me with her hands on her hips. I can't believe it. She is so sweet and polite one minute, then the next pulls a stunt like this! The cheek, who does she think she is? I stare at her, taking it all in. She's small for her age, very petite like her mother. I can't help feeling the urge to laugh at her standing there, half my size, defying me, like a baby mouse stamping its foot at the local alley cat.

"Listen here, young lady," I say, trying to keep the laughter out of my voice. "I am your babysi – au pair – and you will listen to me. You will not be nasty to your little sister and you will most certainly not throw her toys out of the window."

"Or what?" she says, challenging me with a hard stare. Her face is squinted up in a shrimpy pout.

"Or I will tell your mother, that's what."

A defiant smile crosses her lips. "Is that so? Well, I bet Mommy will be much more interested in how the help put the TV on for us to watch music videos so she can go do her own thing in the house without us."

Suddenly, all amusement goes out the window with Mu. I cannot believe it. Day One and already she is trying to play me off? I can't believe this manipulative child is only seven. Seven going on sixteen. I feel heat rise in my brain. Glancing over Tasanee's rigid insolent frame, an idea strikes me.

"Hello Kitty says, Come with me." To my surprise she actually follows me down the staircase and outside the front door. Our shoes are nowhere to be seen, so we all put on the wellington boots kept in a cupboard next to the door, walk round the side of the house, and stop in front of the dripping rosebush garden.

Before I can stop her, Tasanee darts into the middle of the garden and plucks Mu from the bush he was stuck to. She brushes him off, retreats expertly and hands him to Lola. "Here he is, Lolly," she says, giving her sister a hug. "Sorry I did that." Lola smiles and wipes her eyes with a small shaky hand, clutching the toy rabbit. She has put her other hand in her mouth again, sucking two fingers.

"That was very nice of you, Tasanee," I say softly. "Very good to say sorry." I smile at them both, happy the peace has returned to the fold. That seemed easy enough, though I have to say, I'm so confused with these two. With this whole set up. Everything is so different from what I'm used to and I feel completely out of my depth somehow. But no matter. It is only the first day – I'm sure I will settle in and get used to it all.

"These are really pretty roses," I say, changing the subject. "Let's go for a walk, shall we?" Children love stomping in puddles, and this should help to calm everyone.

"These are my Mommy's Nicole-Annella Roses," announces Tasanee. "My daddy bought the species and named it after Mommy when he met her. He said she was even more beautiful than them, but they smelled sweet and made him happy like she did."

"The whole species?" I ask, awed. Once again Tasanee's grown-up front is in full swing and she raises her voice, speaking with authority. "Yes. He made them change the name in books and on the internet and everything. Mommy says it's the best present she ever got and I heard her telling Granddad if it wasn't for the roses she would have left him years ago. He's not really her type, but he does these things. So she stuck around for the romance."

Seven-year-old, seven-year-old, seven-year-old.

I'm so taken aback by Tasanee's mannerisms I take a few moments for the information to sink in.

Wow. How could anyone ever leave a man who names a whole species after you? Unless it's a Venus Flytrap or something. I snort-laugh, and try to cover it up quickly with a cough before Tasanee notices – knowing her, she would. We walk around the rest of the garden, looking at flowers and picking some to take back inside. "We can make a bouquet for your mommy," I say as the girls choose their favorites.

While passing the walkway to the maid's quarters, I spot a new face in the laundry. The door is open, and there in the midst of whirring tumble dryers and – are those my shoes? – I see an elderly lady, heavy and very grumpy looking. The shoe elf, I think to myself, smiling at her with a little wave. She scowls at me, leans forward and pushes the door closed. OK then.

When we get back to the house, Suda meets us at the door and whisks the girls away, saying something about bath time and how I can busy myself for the next half-hour. I take the flowers to the kitchen and start looking through cupboards under the sink till I find a vase to put them in. As I'm filling it with water, Jim walks out from the freezer, arms laden with boxes. He seems startled to see me, but quickly recovers.

"New girl!" he beams. "You decided to quit yet?"

"Why do you guys think I'm going to quit?" I ask, not returning his teasing smile. "I've been doing this for a long time, you know."

"Oh, but you have never been in this place" he says with an annoying knowing look smeared over his face.

"Every home is different. It just takes some time to get into the groove."

"Ah, this is no ordinary home, new girl, and your employer – she is no ordinary boss. You'll see." He stares at me while saying this with such dark intensity I feel a chill run down my spine. I shake myself and go back to my flower arranging, wondering if Frederick would approve of my amateur work. Jim shrugs and smiles. "We are just, how you say? Teasing. Playing with you. What would you like for dinner?"

A choice? "I really don't mind. Anything the girls are having, I guess. Thanks."

"Beef stroganoff it is," he says and starts to take out spices, vegetables, chopping boards and sauces. I sit on a barstool watching him, wondering what I should be doing now. Suddenly I hear what sounds like a police radio buzzing to life, causing Jim to jump

"Arrival," it says in its scratchy voice. "The Black Swan is in the building"

As if a jolt of electricity has been spread through the house, Rami comes bustling in to the kitchen, sleeves rolled up and arms laden with cleaning products, though I'm pretty sure I saw her reading a magazine with her feet up in the sunroom a second ago.

Jim has transformed the kitchen in an instant: things are sizzling and boiling and steaming all over the place. He doesn't seem to notice me anymore. I hear the front door bang and keys dropping noisily in to the porcelain key bowl on the table at the staircase. Soft footsteps are padding towards the kitchen, Jim is at his stove station, pulling a tall and ostentatious looking chef's hat onto his head, and a moment later, in walks Khunying, looking as effortlessly beautiful as ever.

"Jemma," she says when she sees me, "The girls' things will be taken to your room. You will need to cover their books for school tomorrow and pack their bags with everything on the list. I have also sent all the school mail to your room – I suggest you use your evening going over the newsletter and teachers' notes and familiarise yourself with the school schedule. Also, arrange for dog-training for Bruno. He's a menace and I am this close to selling him. Jim, have Suda bring my coffee to my room." With that she turns and walks out again, leaving nothing but a whiff of something intoxicating behind.

Her no-nonsense business manner is quite impressive. Maybe she's not so bad after all. Just very straightforward. The rest of the house staff probably don't understand her. But maybe I will. Maybe I'll be the one to relate to her – after all, we both obviously like clothes, though very different styles.

Jim takes down a china teacup, one like I saw Khunying drinking from this morning, and puts it under the spout of the trendy coffee machine. He takes a bottle of cream out the fridge and pours a drop into the cup, expertly making a swirly design. He turns to me with the cup. "Will you take this up to Suda, new girl?"

"Oh, OK," I say, realising I'm just standing there and still have the vase of flowers in my hands. Khunying was so abrupt I hadn't even thought to give them to her. I guess I can get the girls to give it to her now, which is better. I head off to take Suda the steaming cup of coffee.

Suda seems highly irritated at the coffee cup request, but takes it off to Khunying, leaving the girls to finish getting dressed with me. They have matching Disney princess pajamas, one with Princess Elsa on the front, and the smaller of the two with a picture of Belle from Beauty and the Beast. The girls smell like a very expensive bath-salt shop and have traces of glitter in their tied-up hair. I hand them the flowers, and the drawings they did in the afternoon to give to their mother, and they go running through to their mom's side of the house. I stand at the entranceway to the East Wing wondering exactly what to do, when I hear Suda shooing me out the way from behind. She is coming up the staircase with a load of what must be dry-cleaning and disappears down the East Wing hall. There are some armchairs by a huge window over to one side of the landing, so I decide to sit there and wait. Soon, Suda comes out again with both girls in tow.

"Come. Dinner time. And you meeting," she says to me and we all head down the stairs. When we reach the bottom I see Kobus has arrived and is waiting for me outside, enveloped in a thick cloud of smoke. He sees me too and waves away the smoke, coming inside. The girls run ahead to the dining room and I follow Kobus into the music lounge.

"So! How has your first day been?" he asks me, a slight concern in his voice.

"All good, thanks!" I lie, hoping it's convincing. "The girls are so lovely and Khunying seems to be happy enough so far . . ."

I trail off, seeing Kobus's pained expression. "Is everything OK?" I ask, fearing something awful.

"Jemma. The thing is," he begins nervously, "there have been a few small incidents today. Just a few, nothing too bad!" He adds a clown-face smile for good measure. I can almost picture the big painted teardrop under his left eye.

"Um, OK," I say. "But just so you know I didn't know about the TV and that bunny thing was sorted quickly and of course I will be more vigilant with their school work, you know, when they actually have school work."

"Bunny thing?" Kobus starts to ask, then shakes his head as if deciding not to bother. He takes out a leather-bound folder, opens it up to a typed-up page of notes and I see at a glance it is signed at the bottom with a very elaborate swish of a signature. He straightens out the page, draws himself up in preparation and says, "The thing is, Jemma, is that . . . well . . . Khunying has a few requests. We had our conference call, and she, uh, mentioned the car."

"The car?" I ask, confused.

"Well, yes. The car. Your car, to be specific," he adds, looking back down at the page. "She doesn't like it and wants you to get rid of it."

I pause for a moment, saying the words over in my head. She doesn't like my car, and wants me to get rid of it.

What?

"She wants me to get rid of Peaches?" I ask tentatively.

"Peaches?" he says, confused.

"Er, my car. Kobus, I know it's run down, but I can't just get rid of my car, I mean, I need my car, right? How else am I supposed . . ."

"Um, well," he interrupts quickly, looks all round him, then lowers his voice and leans in, "I don't think you should actually get rid of it, I mean, of course not!" Nervous laugh. "But perhaps you could park it somewhere she won't see it? Around the block maybe? Just . . . just try not to bring it on the property again. Maybe you could get dropped off at work instead?" His eyes are so wide with what seems like the urgency to convince me in a nice way I almost feel sorry for him.

"Right," I say, taking all this in. I have a tendency to over-react and over-think situations, so this time I'm going to be better. More grown-up. And Kobus looks so concerned that I can't let him down. So I decide to shrug it off, take it in my stride and put on a brave face. It's not too terrible so far, I decide. No complaints about my actual performance, just a bit of a . . . cosmetic glitch, I guess.

"And, uh, the other thing is . . ." OK, now he really is starting to look uncomfortable. "Uh well, the thing is, uh, she doesn't think your clothes are appropriate. Um, shorts, for example."

I look down at my long grey jeans.

"Oh, not what you are wearing now," he quickly offers, noticing my confusion. "You look lovely today. The thing is, though, is she had the maids open your bags and said she didn't think you packed the right sort of clothes."

She did what?

He breaks off, a frozen smile on his face, but I see his eyes darting around, searching the room for anything to look at but me. I knew my bags were taken to my room when I arrived, but I never imagined they would be unpacked.

"She . . . unpacked . . . my things? She went through my things?" I repeat, not knowing exactly how to react.

Is that even legal? Isn't it an infringement of my rights? And what if I had something private in there? I suddenly feel so, so violated!

"Well, she didn't unpack them, not exactly. She told Ramie to do it. She just wanted to help you settle in! You know, sort of a welcoming," he insists, laughing uncomfortably. But he won't meet my eyes. Then, looking back down at his notes, he continues, as if being dragged one syllable at a time to the dentist chair: "And, well, she also doesn't want you wearing any of the–" and here he takes a breath, clears his throat, and I see him looking back down at the page, reading over whatever is written there. "She says you shouldn't wear your, uh, make-up. And I need you to sign here saying you have been told all this and accept it."

He hands me the page and I scan it, completely rattled. Why would she be against me wearing make-up? She was wearing make-up; she doesn't seem Amish or anything. What could she have against me. . . Then I spot the sentence on the page and read her instructions word for word: ". . . will not be permitted to wear the tartish parrot-coloured war-paint she has in her call-girl make-up bag. Neutrals only." I stare at the words, and look up at Kobus. He is pressing finger and thumb to the bridge of his nose.

This has got to be a joke.

She went through my make-up bag?

She went through my make-up bag?

What's next? A strip search?

I start to fume. This is ridiculous. The only thing she should be concerned about is my nanny abilities, not my dress code or choice of eye shadow.

I stare at Kobus as he slowly closes his notes and smoothens down the front of his trousers, giving me a moment to calm down. I roll my shoulders back and take a deep breath, sign the offending page, and hand it back to him.

Just stay calm. Don't let something so fleeting and insignificant get you all riled up. And don't let the house staff scare you off – you need this job. You need this.

Maybe having my bags un-packed is a normal thing around here. Maybe the make-up was un-packed to be placed at my exquisite stage-lit make-up mirror for me. Let's not forget the exquisite stage-lit make-up mirror, Jemma. Perspective.

After all, everything else seems to get done for you. And all the other staff wear uniforms, so maybe you should consider adjusting your wardrobe. I mean, she didn't actually say "Here's your pinafore", did she? You still have some freedom. And there isn't anything wrong with matching your eye make-up to your skin tone. Neutrals still come in shimmery shades – it'll be OK.

"I suppose I will just have to wear my jeans all week then. Anything else?" I'm working really hard to keep my voice calm.

"Oh, that's all!" says Kobus, brightening up as if he's just been let off the hook after being caught speeding. He probably thought I would blow up at him. Maybe previous nannies would vent all their frustrations on him. Well, I'm not that kind of girl.

"Just one more thing."

Drat. So close!

"Not about you, don't worry! She is leaving for Italy, and would like you to take the girls to stay with some friends when you leave this weekend.

You have to drop them off on Friday and pick them up again on Sunday night. I will have the address and all the details ready for you on Friday morning of course."

"Oh, OK," I say, as Kobus gets up and gathers his things.

"Oh, Kobus? She told me to get a dog trainer or something for Bruno. Do you know what I am meant to do?"

"I suppose she's had enough of him. He jumped up on her car door earlier so I guess she figures dog training will help. I'll find a place for him, don't you worry."

"Thanks."

As I leave the room I let out a sigh. I'm suddenly feeling so tired, and I just want to get dinner over with so I can go to my room.

My invaded, make-up raided room.

With the exquisite stage-lit make up mirror . . .

As he walks out, he pats me warmly on the back and adds: "I'll take her to the airport now. Call me anytime you need anything, OK?"

The airport? What, now?

Chapter 5

. . . .

T he dining room has been set up to the max. There are silver candlesticks on the table, white napkins, and the three places are set for what looks like a five-course meal. A crystal jug of lemon water sits on an ornate silver tray, with drops of condensation running down the sides. There are large bowl-shaped wine glasses set at each place. The girls are sitting next to each other, Tasanee at the head of the table and her sister on the right, leaving the seat at the left open. I'm about to go back to the kitchen to see if my place is set at the granite-top counter when Jim comes in. He walks over to the table and starts to pour lemon water into wine glasses for the girls.

I watch the scene in amused disbelief as Tasanee takes a small stately sip of water from her wine glass. Just like her mother.

Jim looks up at me. "Lemon water?"

"Yes, please, but where shall I sit?" There are three places set here, but it's all so fancy I think obviously I'm not meant to eat with them at dinner times. He starts to pour the water into the glass by the open seat. He puts the jug down, pulls out the chair and stands there, looking at me expectantly.

"Uh, am I not eating somewhere else?"

"Is there a problem with this seat, new girl?"

. . . .

"No, I mean it looks wonderful – very, throne-like – it's just I thought . . ."

"You thought?"

I stop and look from Tasanee to Lola to Jim and back to Tasanee again. They are all looking at me, brows raised as if I've just insulted them.

"Oh, I thought maybe Khunying would be sitting there."

"She's gone to Italy," says Tasanee darkly, but takes a quick, less polished sip of her water. Beneath the brisk movement, I see it: She looks so sad, and something in my heart pings sorely

"Already?"

"Didn't Kobus tell you?" Tasanee looks up and I see her expression change. She looks at me as though she is about fifteen years older than I, seventeen levels farther than I, and I'm the new fresh young intern at the firm who knows nothing.

"Yes, he said she was going, he was taking her - but I assumed it was only later, or at least that she would say goodbye before she left . . . that maybe she was only–"

"She's gone to visit her lover," interrupts Tasanee, and picks up her napkin. She gives Lola a nod, who quickly picks her napkin up too, following Tasanee's movements as she shakes the napkin open and lays it over her lap.

"Her . . . excuse me, her what?"

"We will have our starters now, Jimmy," she says in a business-like fashion, ignoring my question.

Khunying has left already. On my first day here. Before I've slept a night in the house. A stranger to her and her girls. Before the girls have even really started school. Before she has seen me interact with them at all. Without even coming through to say goodbye. Really?

And she has a lover. Well, I suppose that is no shock – I mean the woman is a goddess – but still. It seems slightly inappropriate her seven-year-old talks so freely about it. Gotta monitor TV, that's for sure. If I even sniff an episode of Keeping Up With The Kardashians, I think I might have to ban screen-time all together. Wow, I really have a lot to get used to. I shake out my napkin too in a perplexed trance. Tasanee picks up her spoon when the starter of green soup with a glazed orange peel on top arrives, and Lola follows suit.

The rest of the dinner passes much the same. Both girls act as if this is a fine dining experience in a top restaurant. Tasanee is so poised and deliberate with every move while eating, it's as though she is putting on a Victorian-era play for me with her little understudy copying her every move. She starts making what I imagine to be her "dinner conversation". As soon as she starts to talk, she lets out so many of what must be family secrets I'm almost afraid to be in the room, in case there is a nanny-cam catching all my newly attained incriminating knowledge on film. I wouldn't even want to be a fly on the wall! I am left feeling completely stunned, and hardly eat a thing.

"So then Mommy threw Daddy out and now she has the Count and she says Daddy is good for one thing and that's to pay for her flights to see her lover," she finishes. Lola has given up on copying her sister and spent the last fifteen minutes playing cannonball with her peas in the soup and forcing strips of beef stroganoff to "walk the plank" off her knife onto the side plate. I'm so captivated by Tasanee's flapping tongue I don't even help Lola eat at least half her food before playing, as I should.

"When I'm grown up I'm going to be a businesswoman like Mommy." Tasanee changes gears, but keeps talking as if we are her own personal audience.

"I'm going to be a pirate," puts in Lola, coming out of her fantasy food land. I notice she is a lot more comical than she was earlier when her mom was home, almost as if a weight has been lifted off her shoulders.

"You can't be a pirate, stupid," says Tasanee sharply. "There are no more pirates."

Lola glares at Tasanee across the table. "Are too."

"Are not."

"Are too!"

"Are not!"

"Are too!" Lola hurls her fork, mashed peas, beef stroganoff and all at Tasanee. Gravy goes splatting in a perfect arch across the table, lining the room in sticky meaty flavour. Tasanee retaliates immediately with a handful of mashed potatoes and knocks over the jug of water.

"Lola! That was very naughty! Tasanee, Hello Kitty says, Put that down this instant. And don't call your sister stupid. Both of you, go wash your hands. Now!" I've thrown down my napkin, scraped my chair back and am standing staring at the two girls, hands on my hips. They look as if they are about to protest.

"March!"

They both jump and run off down the passage giggling all the way as if it was a big game. I shake my head in a daze. This is the craziest day ever.

When I arrive upstairs, after being assured by Jim the mess will be cleaned up and I should not worry about it at all, and then bumping into Ramie who gives me a radio-active death stare as she walks past, I find the girls standing on up-turned buckets in Lola's en-suite, splashing and laughing and playing with Barbies in a basin of water. Tasanee is helping Lola get a mermaid tail fastened on her Barbie and they are talking in funny high-pitched voices, pretending to be Ariel from 'The Littlest Mermaid'. I lean against the doorpost and watch them for a while, smiling at their happy make-believe world. They really are so cute when they play nicely together. I suppose all sisters fight sometimes; it's normal.

"OK, try not to get your pajamas wet," I say, coming into the bathroom and picking a towel up off the floor. "Come along, let's get you ready for bed."

"We only go to bed at eight," says Tasanee, as if opposing my suggestions is her new favorite thing to do.

I don't think I can take much more of this today.

"I know," I say with a sudden wave of inspiration. "You get into bed now, and I will read you a story. Then at eight you go to sleep, OK?"

Their little eyes light up. "Oh yes, please, Jemma!" they both shout and run to Lola's big double bed, jumping under the covers. "Can we both sleep in here tonight? We don't like to sleep alone when Mommy is away."

"Sure," I say, feeling the pang in the centre of my heart strike harder. This must happen quite often. To be so small and not have your mommy around to tuck you in at night must be quite hard. Well, I'm happy I can be here to help.

I choose a book that looks quite good with a few short stories in it. After the third story, Lola has fallen fast asleep, but Tasanee cuddles closer to me and asks for one more. When I am done with the fourth story, her eyes are closed. I move Lola's arm off me and try to slip off the bed without disturbing either of them.

Tasanee turns over, giving her little sister and Mu the rabbit a bit more room. "You're nice, Jemma," she says sleepily. "No one ever reads to us." She seems so much like a child again, and I feel sorry for her. She has such a tough exterior because she must have been forced to grow up too soon. Divorce is always hard on children, as they are made to understand things that parents would much rather protect them from, in a perfect world. But this isn't a perfect world. Perhaps staying unhappily married would have been worse – and harder on the kids as is also so often the case. I suppose Tasanee is a product, and her own personality and her way of coping, whilst parentless on what seems to be a regular basis, has led to this conflicted child. It just seems as though she is constantly trying to be someone she is not, and when this little girl, the real Tasanee, comes out, she is just a sweet soft urchin, like her sister.

"Go to sleep, Tas," I whisper, and pull her covers up closer around her. She snuggles down, murmuring softly, and I tiptoe out the room.

Finally! I'm in my own room, door closed, and have flopped down on the bed absolutely exhausted. What a day! I wish I was home in my teeny tiny flat with Jason. It might fit into half a wing of The Palace, and might be packed into its security complex like a mustard coloured rabbit warren, but I miss the normality. At home I can look out the kitchen window and see a vast open veld over the electric fencing, a veld that brings me back to earth when I feel stressed. Miraculously, this stretch of land has not been developed yet, and has a tiny hill sloping away from our complex, with a natural spring passing at the bottom before a mirage of twisted trees. Over the past months it has changed its facade from pastel cosmos flower carpets, swaying their heads in the wind, to golden matted grass, clutching the earth protectively in the dry winter months. Sometimes I see the Sakabula birds dance across their territorial grasses, long tails rippling below them like ribbons of black satin. Watching nature have its way with that patch of untouched land takes me to a different time, a time where lions roamed freely, where zebra may have sipped at the dampness on resilient, African soil. Now, walled on one side by multiple apartment blocks and fly-over highways, the veld is as misplaced as pink glitter on a T-bone steak, even though it was there first. The veld is the last remaining connection to a simpler past. Lying on this luxury bed, I feel just like that veld. Misplaced. Out of my depth.

I'm drained. I could stay right here like this, fully clothed, and pass out. Then I remember the school things Khunying sent to my room to prepare for the girls. I roll over, grab the list and look into the stationery packet. There are about twenty books in there. What on earth could a five-year-old and a seven-year-old do with so many schoolbooks?

I sigh and sit up, take out the paper and plastic and begin to wrap.

Chapter 6

· · · · · · · · ·

"I come bearing baked goods." Frederick is standing at the front door to Jason and my little apartment, arms laden with what looks like frosted pieces of heaven. "I present these to you: my latest naughty nibblies."

I love it when he bakes, though I've learnt not to ask questions. He's completely dirty minded with his creations. These fluffy, puffy, powder-pink cupcakes have cherries strategically placed on top to look like nipples.

"You're too sweet," I say gloomily, taking one of the cupcakes as he walks past me into the small flat. I already made explanation of the terrible-horrible-no-good-very-bad first week via constant voice notes, but it's the first time I've seen Frederick since arriving back at the apartment for my weekend break. I shuffle back to my nest on the couch and tuck my slipper-socked feet under me again, picking up a champagne glass of milk to help wash down the sugar rush and self-flagellation.

My first week has been filled with daily phone calls and disapproving letters from Khunying. Even though she is all the way in Italy, somehow she still hears of every little thing I do, and it's usually wrong. So I've spent

· · · · · · · · ·

the week apologising, signing her memos and changing my usual way of doing things.

"Oh don't look so forlorn, poppet," Frederick says, snuggling up next to me. "Muscled men in white pajamas, exotic barefoot women in black, emotionally bulimic abandoned princesses, a Cordon Bleu ringleader and a demon-possessed goddess all under one roof? This is so exciting! It's just like you live at the Rocky Horror mansion. This is the stuff the best reality TV is made of." Frederick is a nut for reality TV – the worse the show, the more excited he gets and the worse the addiction becomes. Throw in a hillbilly wedding and he might just explode.

I raise my eyebrows at Frederick's inappropriate excitement.

"I'm glad my miserable existence gives you so much pleasure." I drip monotone sarcasm emphatically in his general direction.

"Oh, it's not miserable, darling." Frederick takes my milk away from me and steals a sip.

"Actually, she is," interjects Jason, walking through the lounge to the kitchen. "She's been like this since last night. No getting her out of it. Not even jelly tots will do it."

I feel a twitch of guilt. I've been a bit of a sour-puss since I got home, and I've taken it out on my well-meaning twin, I guess, forcing him to listen to my endless accounts of how horrible it all was and making him watch Breakfast at Tiffany's with me for the thousandth time. It's my ritual. When I feel down and out, I drink milk from a crystal champagne glass like the character in the movie and watch an Audrey Hepburn. It usually sets me right as rain, but this time it hasn't worked its magic just yet. Not even the sight of my beloved veld out the window has helped. I know I'm wallowing in self-pity, and feel bad for it . . . But, I tell myself, not without cause! I groan dramatically and fall forward on my knees, covering my head with a purple throw cushion.

Frederick pats me on the back. "There there, sweet bottom. Tell me all about it again."

I re-count the events of the first week, and he acts suitably shocked at most of what I have to say, making me feel better.

"A conference call!" he exclaims when I tell him about Khunying's first criticisms sent via Kobus. "That's hilarious! And going through your stuff – that's an infringement of your rights, for Gaga's sake!"

"That's exactly what I thought!" I exclaim, perking up.

"And she threw out her daughters drawings? Is this woman for real?" I had seen the wastepaper basket when Ramie was cleaning out Khunying's wing and couldn't believe it when I spotted the drawings the girls did that first day, all crumpled up inside it.

"I don't know. I mean, she looks more like a plastic mannequin than a real person. OK, that's not actually true. She looks better than a manne-quin. Mrs. Totally Awesome has no imperfections!"

"Doesn't sound like it to me. More like Mrs. Totally Lost the Plot."

"Or Mrs. Totally Never Should Have Had Kids," Jason puts in from over the kitchen counter, taking a sip from his own (normal) glass of milk. "Who throws out their own children's drawings?"

I shrug, finishing my cupcake and licking my fingers. "I don't know. Maybe it was the maid who threw them out. I just saw them in the bin, not who put them there."

"Regardless. She phoned you three times a day just to crap all over you?" Frederick continues dousing my new employment situation with scorn to try to help make me feel better.

"Well, not exactly three times a day. But daily. And she doesn't call me directly. She sends a message via Kobus for me to call her. Just so that she can moan at me. It's like she knows if I have to do the calling, it will prolong the pain and she wants me to feel as scared and nervous of what she might say next for as long as possible!"

I hold my hand against my face, pretending to be on the phone. "Hello, Khunying? Oh how are you? Did you have a nice flight? Would you like to say hi to the girls?"

I change my voice to sound haughty and irritable: "Don't waste my time, Jemma. This is a long-distance call. Take the girls to Angelique's birthday party tomorrow afternoon and make sure you wrap a nice gift and sign the card from me and the girls."

"OK, but who is Angelique and what should I give her and where is the party?"

"I don't even know why I have to call you to tell you to do this! You should already know. Do your job! Click!" I pretend to hang up, then pick up again. "Jemma, Tasanee tells me you gave Angelique the Disney princess doll from the present closet? What on earth were you thinking! You never give the daughter of a judge a common doll! Are you some kind of imbecile? Do you know how important her father is? And you signed it from me? Now they probably think I was the one who gave her such a tasteless inadequate gift! Take the oriental collector's porcelain princess figurine to her immediately and explain your stupidity. And this time, wrap it properly!

"Jemma, Tasanee needs another school skirt. She tells me she has been wearing the same one for three days now!" (Like how the hell was I supposed to know that? The maids deal with the clothing. I just take the skirt hanging in the closet out for her to wear.) I continue to imitate Khunying's shrill disapproval: "You may not care about your outward appearance, but how you could just let a child dress in dirty clothing is beyond me. Buy her a new one at the school shop immediately! No, I don't have time to speak to the girls. You are their babysitter. Babysit!"

I stop and look at Jason and Frederick who are listening intently, looking horrified. "And I'm not even kidding. That's exactly how she said it all!"

Then I feel bad again. "I guess I should just deal with it. I'm not there to judge her parenting skills – or employer skills for that matter. I have a job to do, that's all. I'm there for the girls."

And I realise I feel good about that. Something about those two makes me warm up when I talk about them. They are truly special children.

"Thank goodness I have Kobus on speed dial to ask about everything. He's great."

"And you get to drive a Porsche!" adds Jason. "I'm Mr Totally Not Jealous At All, though, so don't think I am 'cos I'm not."

"Yea, I guess. Plus, the girls and I are getting along really well," I brighten up, accepting another cupcake from Frederick. "It was good fun driving them to school. And they love to play SpongeBob SquarePants. And Barbies." I half-smile at Frederick out of guilt.

"Good Gaga, child!" he throws his hands up in the air. "You are so faking it. You love it!"

"I guess it has its benefits," I say, giggling as Jason rolls his eyes.

"Your phone is purring," he says, tossing my cell to me from the kitchen counter.

I catch the phone and answer. "Hey Troy! Oh just hanging. Ya, Frederick's here already. He brought Cupcake Boobs. Sure! Come over."

Frederick is looking at me in disgust. "Why, Miss Jemma Richardson. You dirty-minded hoe-bag you. Those are not made to look like boobs. Sies!"

"Sure they're not," I taunt, and burst out laughing as I spot Jason noticing the cherry-nipples for the first time, a blush creeping up his face.

"Seeing you have your sidekick here to help you recover from the terrible-horrible-no-good-very-bad week, Jem, I'm going to go and call Tracy, if that's OK," he says, putting the cupcake down.

"Sure. Tell her I say hi! But it's probably best if you don't mention the boobs," I jeer as he closes his bedroom door to call his girlfriend.

"Julle is vol kak," Frederick says, critiquing our sibling banter. "You are both so prudish. He's even worse than you – and you are practically Miss Daisy!"

"I am not," I say, folding my arms around a cushion.

"Of course you are."

"You just called me a 'dirty-minded hoe-bag'! I can't be both."

"I was just being kind."

"Oh really?" I know where this is going. Frederick is forever challenging our old fashioned rigid up-bringing, telling us we need to walk on the wild side.

"OK, Richardson. If you are such a dirty-minded hoe-bag, say kak."

"No."

"Alright, what about F–"

"Don't say that word!" I shove the cushion out in front of his face to block his mouth.

His muffled laughter comes from behind the cushion. "What word? Vo–"

"No!" I cover my ears and squeeze my eyes shut, pretending to be in a state of mortal fear. "Not in English, not in Afrikaans - nether language!" Frederick laughs dismissively and brushes my arms aside.

"OK, OK. I won't say the F-word. Or the V-woord. But if I was Suzelle DIY, this wouldn't be an issue."

"Thank you," I nod, an expression of reserved agreeableness on my face, ignoring his reference to one of my favourite local YouTube sensations, who says the 'V' word quite frequently.

"Seriously though," Frederick says, shaking his head. "Why don't you ever swear?"

"I do say 'crap' and 'damn'," I say darkly, filling the teapot with water.

"Oh, you wicked girl, you."

"Speaking of wicked girls," comes a breathy voice from outside the window, "I'm in the mood for a round or two!" Troy walks through the front door and kisses both Frederick and me before picking up my latest Vogue and flopping down on our old couch.

"Tea?" I ask.

"Sure. If it comes with a splash of Bloody Marys?"

"Ooh yes!" Frederick agrees and claps his hands together eagerly. "Bloody Marys!"

Oh fine. I move the teapot off the heat and take out the tomato cocktail and vodka instead.

"Jason!" I call to my brother's closed door. "Bloody Marys!"

His door opens and he comes out his room looking dejected, but starts busying himself making us all mounds of crushed ice for our cocktails. We make a good team, I think.

"Oh, by the way, guys," I say. "Now I have all participants of last week's disastrous and mysterious late night out in the room together, do any of you know why there is a plastic pink flamingo in the back seat of my car?"

"Seriously?" asks Jason, putting more ice cubes in the crusher.

"Oh, that is too funny!" says Frederick. "A pink flamingo? Can I see it?"

"So you don't know where it's from?"

"No," they both say together. I realise only three of the four participants of that fateful night have spoken. We turn our heads as one and look at Troy, who hasn't stopped leafing through the Vogue.

"Troy?" I ask, accusingly.

"What?" Wide-eyed innocence. Somehow, whenever Troy looks innocent, I know something is up. It just doesn't come naturally to her.

"The pink flamingo?"

"Oh that. What about it?"

"Troy!"

She sighs and puts down the magazine. "You swapped it for your phone number, babe. Remember?"

"No, I did not." I'm indignant.

"OK, fine. I offered your number, but once you had your flamingo we just moved on. And before you get all huffy, you did want the flamingo. And you could do with the boy. So I got his name and found him on Facebook and told him we'd meet him tonight. In like 20 min's, so you should probably get ready." Jason and I both stop making cocktails and stare at her.

Frederick is grinning from ear to ear. "Devious!" he whispers in awe. "I love it! Troy, jou onnooslike ding!"

I'm going to kill her!

"No! No, no, no, no, no, Troy, no! I don't want to meet some slimy greasy club guy!"

Troy waves my concern aside as if we are making a mountain out of a molehill. "Oh relax, I approved him for you. He's clean as a whistle. Great abs, tallish…has blonde hair. You like blondes, don't you? The whole Corporate Thor vibe? Or was it brown?"

"Troy!"

"Blonde. Definitely blonde."

"Troy!"

"What? Don't you want to meet your tall dark handsome stranger? With beautiful black hair? Definitely black. Now I remember."

Oh, for goodness sake. I raise my hands in exasperation.

"Er, I hate to interrupt your meltdown, Miss Daisy, but shouldn't you change if you are about to meet Prince Charming?" Frederick starts handing out the Bloody Marys and nudges me towards my room. "Not that I don't just love your housewife look of course. But go. Change. Wear the sexy jeans and a plain pink vest. Simple is always best."

I glare at Frederick, then glare at Troy, and then glare at Jason for good measure. He hasn't said much to defend me, and now just shrugs his shoulders at me, taking a sip of his Bloody Mary.

As I huff off to my room and pull my leggings off, I can't help but feel a sparkle of excitement. Not that I will ever give Troy the satisfaction of knowing that.

Once my make-up is done and I'm happy with my hair, getting dressed only takes a few seconds. I pull on my jeans and a bright pink frilly nineties Britney Spears-style, medieval-come-pirate ensemble on top in an act of defiance against Frederick's suggestion of simple. One pink cardie and bright yellow and black polka-dot Minnie Mouse baby-doll shoes later, I'm all ready.

Troy has been making it her sole responsibility in life to get me "back on the horse" (or to be more specific, back on as many horses as she can round up) since my fateful brake-up in Cape Town eight months ago. Everybody mutually agrees he was Bad For Me. He spent most of our relationship belittling me (to make himself feel better about his secret homosexual tendencies, of course, according to Troy – no offence, Frederick), but so subtly I didn't realise what was happening until it was too late and I found myself an insecure pile of mush, drunk on left-over schnapps I scavenged from the back of the cupboard, and on the phone at two in the morning begging him to reconsider. Even though I had caught him cheating on me the day before.

Jason tried to psychoanalyse me, saying I only ever chose guys who I knew were total jerks and would mess me around so I would never have to be disappointed in love. His reasoning, mixed with the schnapps, hurt my head and I decided to stop making him watch Sex and the City and Girls marathons with me after that. Besides, he's been in a long-term relationship with Tracy for like ever, so what does he know.

The truth is I don't exactly have the best track record with relationships. Well, they haven't all been with total jerks, but I am currently single, therefore proving I'm as yet unable to make one work. I'm not totally against giving it another go, but with my new-found job and subsequent maturity, I was thinking of giving it a break for a while - rising above the carnal need, so to speak.

Troy, on the other hand, can barely contain her excitement. Oh, she's playing it all cool and calm, but I recognise that gleam in her eye. The one when she is super chuffed with herself for pulling off one of her devious plans successfully and getting exactly what she wants.. Well I'm not putting all my eggs in her sneaky pink flamingo basket.

As it turns out, the club guy, Ryan, isn't all that bad. He has mousy brown-hair and does resemble Thor after all. A bit bulky in the chest department, but he smiles a lot, and even though he talks about CrossFit non-stop, he seems to be quite sweet. And drunk-Jemma seemed to like him, so I should give him a chance. Turns out he just moved here a few months ago from Port Elizabeth, so we have that coastal hometown thing in common. He obviously doesn't have any other friends in Joburg yet, other than the people at his CrossFit – but why he would want to hang out with people from the gym, I don't know. I catch him smoothing out his hair and flexing his muscles under his too-tight shirt in the reflective surface of the bar, making me snort-laugh to myself. His eyes droop a little, which I thought was a bit of a sexy bedroom look at first, but realised after a while actually his eyes are just dopey like that. I can't write him off as a total jerk or even a loser just yet, but reserve my right to suspicions. And I'm not getting any butterflies just yet.

"He is delectable! Say you like him!" Troy demands the second we take a girl-break to the bathroom.

"He doesn't speak about anything other than deadlifts and thrusters, so I don't know," I half lie. He is quite cute in a doofus kind of way, but I don't want to give her any positive affirmation for the bad thing she has done. Training your friends can be such hard work.

"Oh, come off it, babe. You're smitten. You were certainly into him the night of the pink flamingo! And he is acting very interested in you – staring at you the whole time. He hasn't noticed one other girl in the place."

"He's not staring at me, he's watching his own reflection in the window behind me. Anyhow, fixated obsession does not a relationship make."

"And totally being ignored by your idiot ex-boyfriend does?" she retaliates, reminding me of the way my ex used to treat me. I look at her standing there, wincing slightly at the memory.

Sigh. I guess she's right. I may as well give this one a try. After all, I am the new, more grown-up Jemma now. The one with the well-paying job and the new-found life experience. So what's to say I won't be in a better space to date?

"Fine." I hold out my hand. "Hand me the Cherry Monster."

Cherry Monster is what Troy and I call this amazing lipstick she got from INGLOT. It's kiss proof, and the colour just makes men go gaga. We use it as a secret weapon whenever we are 'on the hunt', as she puts it. Troy beams at me triumphantly and hands over the applicator.

Back at the table, I slide in to the booth, sitting a little closer to Ryan than before. I smile at him prettily and ignore Frederick's excited head tilt when he spots my freshly applied lip colour. As Troy sits down opposite Jason, Frederick twitches even more and I look over at Troy to see what all the excitement is about. She is also wearing the lipstick. And thick. And she is pouting at my brother. I try to hide my annoyance by pretending to be amused by something Ryan said about muscle-ups. Ya right, Troy. You can try but you're chasing the wrong conquest. Jason is a taken man.

Frederick sparkles at me like a champagne bottle that has been shaken up and is bursting to pop. He's such a sucker for romance! I giggle at his palpable enthusiasm. Maybe it's the power of the Cherry Monster, or maybe it's because I'm surrounded by friends and with the possibility of a new romance in the air, but I feel all the worries of the week begin to melt away.

. . . .

Chapter 7

. . . .

It's Monday morning, and I walk both girls to their classrooms, as is the required protocol, according to the faxed, elaborately signed memo shoved under my bedroom door at The Palace. I notice there are a few other nannies in the drop off zone too, but still lots and lots of moms – peroxide-blonde moms. What is it about these snooty schools and bottle blonde hair?

Once the girls are safely in their respective classes, particularly Tasanee, who tried her luck with complaints of a fake cough (she's done this most mornings), I make my way back to The Palace, wondering what to do next. When I lived in Cape Town, I would go to the beach with a book while the kids were at school, or busy myself with doing courses or baking muffins for the kids' afternoon snack. But Jo'burg is still pretty new to me, and I'm not exactly free to use the kitchen, so I decide to spend the morning in my room chatting with Jason, checking Facebook. Troy has already put up photographs from our drinks sessions with Ryan, and tagged me in a very intimate-looking shot, which is just fluke really – he was leaning over me to grab the salt. But Oh-So-Instagram worthy!

After two hours of hiding, I get tired of sitting in one place. I get up and decide to go see if I can make myself a cup of tea. As I pass the entrance to Khunying's wing of the house I can't help feeling the allure of seeing what is

. . . .

in there. I stand at the top of the stairwell for a few seconds wondering. My feet are itching to walk over and have a peek. The thing about being told you are not allowed to do something is it becomes the only thing you want to do. But I resist the temptation and start to head down the stairwell. I'm a responsible, professional employee. Not a snooping babysitter. Maturity is my new mantra. I keep chanting it to myself as I take one step after the next.

Success.

Halfway down, I stop.

Well, I did have good intentions. And she went through my stuff. My curiosity is getting the better of me. I look back up, across the hallway, past the top of the staircase and down the enticing passageway into Khunying's wing. The house is deathly quiet; not a sound of movement anywhere. I tiptoe up the staircase again, pausing for another long listen just to be sure, and brashly march over the forbidden threshold. I stop on the other side of the entrance, my heart pounding. I know I'm not allowed in here, and I don't even know why I'm so curious. But something in me is dying to see. I look around me. The passageway leads off with two sets of closed double doors, one single door, and then a turn at the bottom of the passage leading to the left.

The first door closest to me is a single dark wood one. I take a deep breath and turn the handle. It creaks open ominously, revealing a large walk-in linen closet. I tiptoe in, looking at the shelves of linen and blankets. There are hundreds of packs of toiletries – the complimentary ones you get on international airline flights. I pick up one deep maroon bag and look inside, getting taken away by my snooping self. She looked in my bags, I tell myself again. I'm just returning the favour.

I open the bag and see it is filled with Yves St Lauren face products in mini-sizes, and some very nice silk navy blue eyeshades for sleeping. I pull out the toothbrush, looking at it from all angles. This stuff must be all first class – it's better than anything I've ever been given on a flight. I pick up another cream-coloured travel bag and look inside. That one has Clinique inside, and a miniature bottle of perfume too. She must have at least fifty of these all stacked up on the shelves. I wonder why anyone would keep all this stuff? If you go on one or two flights the bags could come in handy at a later stage, but to keep every single one? And to just stock pile them and not use anything . . . it all seems a bit excessive!

The opposite wall has shelves full from bottom to top with magazines. Most of them still in the plastic. I pick up one that is open, a Fair Lady, and see there is a post-it sticking out the side. Turning to the marked page, I feel a cold chill run down my spine. The eyes! Cold and fixed on me. There, in a full two-page spread, Khunying is staring out of the magazine, her icy blue eyes unmistakable. I drop it and look all around as if I've just been caught out. I let out a silent embarrassed laugh. Why am I so jumpy? I take a breath again, feeling stupid for letting a picture un-nerve me and pick up the magazine again.

The picture is followed by a three-page article, all about how successful she is and a mother too and just generally what an amazing power woman she is – an inspiration to us all. Remembering what Kobus said in the interview, that she is a 'silent partner' in all the firms, I wonder if her success was something given to her by an obviously rich husband? He could have bought her a spot on all the companies she brags about in the article – not exactly a sweat-off-my-own-brow story. And given the way she's treated me over the last week, I recon she has loads of free time on her hands. I skim-read until I see her quoted: "My girls mean the world to me. Everything I do is for them." I snort out loud to myself. Not likely. Everything she does is for herself first, and then maybe they get a bit of left-overs.

Another magazine, also with a post-it, catches my eye. Then another. There are about six different issues of glossy magazines, all featuring articles about Khunying. The pictures of her are a bit strange. She is prettier in real life, I realise, looking at the frozen, posed images. Something about the camera actually makes her seem dull. Fake. More put on. There isn't the slightest inkling of the natural glowing skin I saw sitting sipping her coffee on that first morning, nothing to show the way her clothes float over her perfect frame. These pictures are just of some Gauteng princess, dressed in her Louis Vuitton, talking about her take on Manolo Blahnik shoes and Hillary Clinton.

I pick up a bundle of un-opened magazines. That's funny. It's a stack of about ten of the same Fair Lady issue that had the article of Khunying in. And that stack over there is all of the Marie Claire. The whole wall is lined with dozens of copies of the same issues. So she stockpiled these magazines too? Very strange. I wonder what for? Probably to give to people or sneakily take out and leave them in waiting rooms at various hotels or plastic surgeons' chambers . . . I laugh again, seeing a mental image of Khunying walking into a doctor's office, dressed in her Chanel coat and Jackie-O glasses, sitting down and when the receptionist is not looking, quickly taking one of her issues out of her designer handbag and placing it open at the article about her with the rest of the magazines on the table. Doing her own undercover PR, that sort of thing.

I put the magazines back and make sure they all look exactly the same as when I picked them up, then, looking up and down the tower of Ode to Self one more time, I back out of the closet and close the door. Peering back towards the passageway to make sure I am still alone, I tiptoe a bit further in. The double doors on the right lead to a small study complete with black leather office chair, shiny mahogany desk and shelves and shelves of books. I scan the titles and see Khunying is addicted to romance novels. There must be every Mills and Boon under the sun in this room. I wonder if she's heard of Kindle yet, or if she just likes to keep it old school.

There are also a lot of other books I recognise, mostly recommended bestsellers, the kind of thing I imagine Oprah would endorse. She sure does read a lot. Maybe that's what she does with all her time, while not looking after her kids, not being a wife, and not working at the offices she claims she runs. I shake my head, feeling a twinge of bitterness. I know it's not right and I should never judge her or be spying on her, but somehow the more I learn about her, the more I see, the less I like her. It's the kind of life people would expect you to envy, but seeing it from the inside it just makes me feel pity and distaste. I hope never to be like this. Then I remember I'm the one snooping around someone else's personal space, and reproach myself silently.

But I've come this far. I may as well go the full haul and so with shoulders pushed back, I head straight for her bedroom. I pass her bathroom without much interest (at a glance I can tell it's pretty much the same as the rest of our bathrooms, just bigger.)

A mother of a bed covered in luxurious charcoal silken sheets stands in the centre. There is a strange arrangement of crystals, rocks, mini African statutes and a big Buddha on the side-table. It looks a bit out of place next to the rest of the room, sort of like a hippy-corner in the middle of a glamazonian lair. I laugh softly, spotting a deck of angel cards amongst the precious stones. There is also a dream-catcher hanging above the bed – like a leering speck tarnishing an otherwise Elle Home-decorated room. She must have a bit of a hobby . . .

A door leading off on the other side of her bed calls to me and I head straight for it.

The walk-in closet!

I go inside and . . . the shoes! Oh, the shoes! It's absolutely filled with gorgeous things, jackets, hats, scarves, dresses – but above all, shoes! I run my hand over the expensive Italian leather and feel a pang of jealousy. Although most of these shoes are a little too old for me, the styles a little too straight-laced, I can tell they are all of the highest quality and are beautiful. I pick up a peep-toe beige pump – Jimmy Choo. I thought Jimmy Choo only made crazy wild shoes? I guess those are just the ones I saw on Sex and the City– never actually having been in a Jimmy Choo store. A row of black Louboutins is arranged backwards, so you can see the red soles. I've always thought if only they were pink. I step back and take the whole shoe-shrine in. One day, I tell myself, one fine day. It's admittedly amazing, but would be better if so many of them weren't beige. Come to think of it, looking around here, a lot of her clothes and accessories are beige too.

I look down at myself, my baby-blue and pearly-pink teardrop patterned fifties skirt and purple V-neck tank top looking a lot more tatty next to these fabulous creations than it did when I put it on this morning. A touch more circus carney than what I was going for.

Different tastes, I guess.

I tear myself away from the shoe racks and pull open a drawer on one side. A light goes on inside the drawer as it opens – that's cool – and I see inside is a whole bunch of lingerie. She definitely has a taste for the more raunchy side of night attire. Suddenly I feel a little creepy about going though another woman's underwear and decide to quit while I'm ahead. No one has caught me yet, and no point in hanging around tempting fate. Also, I am not sure why I was so interested in seeing all this stuff anyway.

I walk out of the closet and have a quick look around the room.

There is a large TV cabinet between two bay windows facing the bed. I decided to have one last peek, and go over to look inside. I want to see what movies she likes to watch. I start to pull out the DVDs, completely engrossed, and see she has some box sets, Life of Pi, the extended version, and . . .something hard and cold. A wooden box. I pull it out, tempted by its cold, shiny finish. I wipe a hand over the top and feel around for the clasp. Rats. Locked. I wonder what could be in here? Putting it back I pull out a few of the box sets to see what she's in to. Downton Abbey, Greys Anatomy and – oops. I drop a disk case by mistake and it pops open, the DVD's spilling out. Crap! I hope nothing got scratched. I pick them up, dust them off and wipe them gently on my shirt before replacing them. Then I notice something else – a small key taped to the inside of the box. I wonder. . .

I un-tape the key and pull the wooden box back out. It fits! An imperceptible click unlocks the lid and I open it, intrigued.

Wow! If I thought the rest of the house, the cars, the grounds were impressive, this takes the cake! I lift a jeweled, intricate tiara out of the box. Light catches the precious stones and reflect in my eyes, prisms of awe. I turn it this way and that – it must be real – it's really heavy. Slowly, in a trance, I lift the tiara up to my head and place it gently, the delicately combed arms resting at my temples. It fits perfectly! Not too tight, not too loose – if I was Goldilocks then this piece of princess headgear was just right. I stand up, unable to resist the urge to look at myself in the dresser mirror. This is the moment in movies when Fairy God Mothers appear. Or when simple damsels realize they are royalty. Or scattering sparkles of magic float up from the floor and spiral round the plain girl, spinning faster and faster as her clothes transform from rags to bedazzled gowns. . .

Oh. My...

My heart stops. Ramie is standing in the doorway, looking at me. I'm caught red-handed, standing in the middle of the room, surrounded by DVD covers, and the open wooden box, a priceless tiara on my head.

Crapcrapcrapcrap Crap! Hello Kitty says: What the hell were you thinking coming in here, Jemma?

Ramie's eyes meet mine and I am frozen. My cheeks are burning. I can feel the sweat begin to seep out of my forehead, like a damp sponge being squeezed. She has a bundle of what must be clean laundry in her hands. Neither of us moves. Then Ramie slowly walks over to the closet room, goes in, and comes out again, hands empty. She looks my way one last time, a strange expression on her face I can't read, and then without saying anything, she walks out the room. I cannot believe it. I cannot believe I've just been caught with... with... with this! Crap!

I fumble to take the tiara off. Placing it in its box with shaking hands, my heart racing, I lock the lid and shove the box back in the cabinet. After returning everything where I found it as fast as possible, I jump up and back away, staring at the cabinet as if fearing it is poisoned. I turn and run out the room, down the passageway and straight to my room, not entirely sure what to do.

After what seems like hours I've managed to calm down again. I decide to face my doom and go down to the kitchen. Maybe Ramie will keep it to herself. She didn't say anything – she didn't even look at me for very long. Maybe she isn't that surprised – maybe all the nannies do this. And after all, I didn't do anything that bad. I just took a little peek into Khunying's room – that's all.

Or maybe I could say I smelt smoke or something and was going to see if there was like a hair straightener left on. Lying seems like a much more attractive option right now.

I take a deep breath and head down the stairs again.

I don't find any of the maids in the house. On my way back from the kitchen, I pass the music lounge and see the grand piano, gleaming in the streaming late morning light. Piano. I've always loved the piano. As a child I would tinker on my mother's upright all the time – and as a teenager, whenever I was upset, only playing the piano would soothe me.

Without thinking about it I walk over to the beautiful grand and run my fingers over the closed top. In a moment I'm sitting in front of it, opening it up, and have my fingers resting lightly on the elegant shiny white keys. A grand piano is my favourite. Truly a beautiful piece of artwork. I've never actually seen one in real life before, and here I am sitting at one! It has gold engraved writing on it, "Khun Chain". I am mesmerised as I feel the keys under my fingertips, not daring to press any for fear of breaking this awed silence. Then, just as I'm about to play a note, Kobus walks in to the room and I jump out of my skin.

Not again! Caught twice in one day! I could kick myself.

"Kobus! Oh, I'm sorry – I didn't see you there – er, I mean I didn't know you were coming – er, I mean, I'm sorry if I wasn't meant to touch the . . ." I feel my face flush bright red again. What is it with this place? It's like living in a museum, and I'm the china-shop bull.

But Kobus doesn't seem too worried about me touching the piano. He crinkles his eyes at me and laughs. "It's OK, but I wouldn't be caught by Khunying playing that thing. Or any of the staff for that matter – you never know who tells who what around here." I have a vivid flashback of Ramie standing in Khunying's doorway while I am sporting her precious crown, I stand up abruptly and paste a smile on my face, trying to dismiss the memory.

Kobus is smiling, but I get the distinct feeling I'm being warned. "Do you play the piano?"

"Oh, only a little," I say and quickly move away from the evidence.

"Well, here's a tip," says Kobus, hushing his voice. "If you really want to play, why don't you get the girls to practise, and you can help them."

"They play piano?" I ask, feeling a jolt of excitement. I could help them with their scales, which means I could play, which means I could play a grand piano!

"Yes, they both take lessons. It's all in here," and he holds up a folder.

Turns out the school schedule was not the only one I needed to study. The second week of school is when all the extra activities begin, and Kobus hands me an extensive daily schedule to go over, with activities, addresses and phone numbers included. It smells faintly of cigarette smoke and I wonder how long it's been in his briefcase. There are horse riding, swimming, art classes and music lessons.

"Wow, the girls have more of a life than I do!" I joke.

Kobus smiles kindly, and I suddenly notice he is looking at me with a bit of a gooey expression. "You know, I think this is going to work out just fine, Jemma," he says. "When the other nanny quit I was terrified, but Khunying hasn't even seemed to notice. You are doing great!"

"Other nanny?" I say, a bit confused. Jim walks in with a tray of tea, and Kobus doesn't say anything until he leaves the room again. "Not sure about that one," he whispers, gesturing after Jim's leaving figure, then carries on.

"Well, when I interviewed you I told you there were a few young ladies we had seen for the job. I short-listed your CV to Khunying right away, of course, but she said she didn't want a hippie looking after her children."

"Hippie?" I ask, bewildered.

"Capetownian. She thinks all coastal people are hippies."

"Oh," I'm guessing she thinks 'hippie' is synonymous with 'dirty' too, but I don't say anything more.

"Anyway," he continues, "we hired another girl. Needless to say she lasted half a day. Khunying said I may as well call you and here you are." He looks at me with a triumphant expression as if to say he single-handedly saved my life by getting me the job. Well, I guess I had kind of let on in the interview how badly I needed it . . . and considering the salary with this position, I guess my enthusiasm was somewhat over-expressed.

"Uh, well, thanks Kobus," I say, feeling awkward. He shouldn't be telling me this stuff, should he? But it seems as if he needs someone to confide in, or simply to talk to around here.

"Now, on Thursdays," he suddenly changes the subject, "you will need to get Jim to pack lunch early so you can take the girls straight to horse riding from school. You must also take their bags with the clothes for them to get changed into – Suda or Ramie will give you those."

I realise Ramie is in the room, dusting in a corner. My head is prickling with the humiliation, and fear of what she knows. She must have just walked in, which is why Kobus is being so business-like again. I get the distinct feeling nobody trusts anybody around here.

For the next half an hour, Kobus puts on a bi-polar show for me. One minute he is going through the rest of the girls' schedule and a few other rules whenever a staff member is in or close to the room. But as soon as we are out of earshot, he changes character instantly and starts to fill me in on all the family gossip. He's worse than Tasanee!

It started with him telling me about the piano. It was a gift from the Queen of England, but was given specifically to the father. The father studied classical piano right through his schooling career, while Khunying didn't have a musical bone in her body. When they separated, Khunying locked her paws on anything and everything of value in the house. "She pretty much stole what she could," he says, lowering his voice to almost inaudible depths. "He had an antique perfume bottle collection, she took it. He had her wedding tiara in a safety deposit box for safe keeping, but before the divorce papers were even done with the first draft, she got hold of it and hid it somewhere. No one knows where – it's worth millions and is an heirloom on his side of the family. Pity to have lost it to her." I feel shame burn right through me. I swallow hard and try to look interested and surprised, as though I never even knew such an adornment existed, or that I in fact knew exactly where she hid it. I focus all my abilities on appearing interested in Kobus's explanation of the messy divorce, but it's hard. I think of the girls, which helps shift my focus.

Though Khunying doesn't have full custody of the children, the father travels so much for work he doesn't see the children that often, and Khunying has forbidden him to come to the house. He could get the courts involved but doesn't seem to want to fight and so gives in to her demands. He does see the children when he is in town, though.

As I suspected, Khunying's success story is one of the gifts handed to her when they were in love. He bought her businesses, put her name on boards but ultimately she doesn't do anything in any of the companies other than draw dividends – and go to a lot of parties. The rows and rows of Louboutins make a lot more sense to me now.

I ask Kobus what the father is like. He sounds like a decent person, some big-time Thai businessman. He travelled a lot and met Khunying on one of his business trips to South Africa, fell in love and swept her off her feet. He earned the title of Lord Khun Chain just before he married Khunying, the title she was given as his wife, and they sounded like a high-powered couple. She is definitely power hungry, but doesn't seem to have an actual career, or job, or do any work for that matter other than have conference calls with Kobus about nannies. Kobus doesn't seem to like her very much, and keeps telling me to watch my back and not trust any of the house staff. "Skelms," he calls them. It's quite a lot to take in for the second week, but I'm glad to have a friend around here. I take the opportunity to ask more about what I am and am not allowed to do and find the pool is off limits to me if the girls aren't swimming too. Other things that are off limits include the Jacuzzi house, the steam room, the tennis courts, the maids' quarters and the laundry room, along with Khunying's bedroom wing, of course.

I feel the blush rise again and quickly cover it by pretending to be fully engrossed in the printed-out schedule Kobus gave me earlier. Kobus doesn't seem to notice and carries on about the restrictions, and I remind myself I'm here to work, not live it up in a five-star hotel. I am also presented with a credit card to use for errands or emergencies.

"Can I buy Boggle and the Memory Game for the girls with this?" I ask. "It's just I'm meant to play educational games with them, but the only games I could find are Monopoly and Scrabble. Might be a bit heavy for the kids . . ."

"Sure," he says. "That's a great idea! You know, Jemma, you really are the best nanny we have had so far, and you've only been here a week! I'm so glad the girls have you now. It's hard on them, living this life. So yes, buy the things you think will enrich their lives. You're doing a great job. Just keep the slips."

Kobus seems like such a nice guy. I wonder why he works for someone like Khunying, especially since he doesn't seem to like her that much. Then again, I work for Khunying, and I like her less and less too. And I don't even know her! But the money is good. Maybe he gets paid really well – after all, he's been here long enough. No wonder he smokes so much.

I look at his kindly smile and listen to all his secretive, whispered gossip about the family, and I feel an urge to tell him I know where the tiara is. But I decide it's best not to confess the snooping incident just yet, even though I'm tempted to after all the confiding he's doing in me. I'm dying to tell him. But I decide to wait for him to mention anything more about it when I'm a bit more settled in. Till then, it's going to have to be my (and Ramie's) dirty little secret.

Chapter 8

· · · · · · · · · ·

After my meeting with Kobus, I'm feeling quite spirited. Now I have an actual manual, I definitely will not be stepping out of line anymore and will be able to get on with my job happily. I start to plan an exciting afternoon with the girls – they only begin their extra-curricular activities tomorrow so we are free today.

I'm twenty minutes early, waiting in the school drop-off zone along with the other au pairs and moms. Just as I'm getting into a friendly conversation with one of the more social moms about the benefits of Woolies' pre-packed snacks for school lunch boxes, my phone purrs.

I look at the screen and see it's Frederick. Excusing myself politely, I walk away and answer.

"Hey cupcake," I sing. "Have you calmed down from your cupid aneurism the other day yet?"

"I don't know what you are talking about," Frederick says, pretending not to remember his obvious glowing, foaming-at-the-mouth demeanour the afternoon we all met Ryan. "But seeing that you bring it up, how are things with lover-boy?"

"He's alright, I guess," I say non-committedly.

"What? You two were getting so cozy! And I saw that photo Troy tagged of the both of you canoodling on Facebook"

"That was a fluke photo and you know it."

"Oh alright. But you did make a cute couple. So why no bows and arrows, Katniss?"

Friends are always so well meaning when they try to set you up with someone, or even when they are present for a set up like in Frederick's case. But the thing is, you can never really tell if the butterflies will be there or not. And friends most certainly can't tell.

"I don't know," I sigh. "It all works on the outside, and he is very good looking, but…"

"But?" Frederick presses. I think for a moment. I like Ryan, I do. But somehow I'm not about to jump up and down on a couch for him.

"No magnet," I say simply.

"You and your magnet." Frederick sighs loudly into his receiver and I giggle.

"You know me, I have to feel a magnet between us. If there isn't a magnet right from the beginning, where do we have to go from there?"

"So you didn't have fun with him?"

Thing is, we did have a lot of fun – out – and after drinks at the club. I even started enjoying his obsession with fitness, cheering him on when he began doing handstand push-ups on the dance floor. His cute smile made up for the fact that he droned on and on and on about Crossfit this and Crossfit that. "I did," I confess slowly, "But does that mean. . ."

"Up to you, sweet bottom. Just remember, not every guy you date has to be the one. Sometimes having a little fun is ok."

I think about my last boyfriend. He had the magnet. A magnet so strong I was convinced he was the one. But all it ended in was humiliation and silence. A free-fall precipice of nothingness filled with the invisible emotional trauma he put me through. It whistled through my head day and night, night and day, for weeks. Sure he had the magnet, but what started out to be deep, warm and enveloping turned misty, dishonest and filled with pain. Just thinking about it has that feeling in my stomach returned instantaneously. That feeling you get after a horrible break-up – where the butterflies used to be, but now all there is in the pit of you is hollow pain. "Maybe you're right," I say. "After all, I'm the new, more mature Jemma – shouldn't I do something mature in my love life too? Like take a lover. If Khunying can do it…" Frederick laughs, clearly on board with the idea. The school bell rings and I look up at the magnificent building. Hogwarts in the Sunshine, I think.

"Listen hun, I have to go. Thanks for the chat – I'll be taking a lover and you'll be tickled pink, naturally.

"Naturally, darling!"

We say our goodbyes, and I head up to the kindergarten classroom to collect Lola, feeling lighter than before. Taking a lover. I could do that! I could so do that. Who needs a magnet when you have abs!

Lola is playing catchers with some other children and I watch them for a while thinking how happy she looks. When she sees me she comes running and starts babbling all about her day. This kid is going to love school, I think while laughing at her cute tiny-toothed chatter. We collect her schoolbag and lunchbox from her locker, then go to find Tasanee. Once I manage to tear her away from all the Gucci-Grade-Oners – these girls are such little socialites – I bundle them towards the car so we can start making our way home. They are competing for airtime, excitedly talking over each other about their day at school and all the things they did. I try my best to listen and pay attention to both of them at the same time.

"So, how would you like to stop for a treat on the way home?" I ask with a twinkle in my eye. The screaming and clapping that ensue is three times louder than I could possibly have expected, and I'm so pleased to see the eager anticipation dancing on their faces as they jump into the car.

This is the greatest day ever!

. . . .

I stop at Hyde Park shopping centre, which is the fanciest mall I've ever seen. I've driven past it on Jan Smuts Avenue many times before, but never ventured in. Historically it's the oldest enclosed shopping center in South Africa, being built in 1969, and the inside is decorated with exquisite mosaic artworks by local artists. "Now you both need to hold on to me, OK?" I say and each girl takes a hand, walking along either side of me.

First we stop in at a restaurant for some ice-cream boat floats. It's something my dad used to do when I was young as a special outing and I will always remember how special it was to go out for the yummy banana-chocolate ice-cream treat. It seems to be working the same magic on them. The girls are shoveling their spoons in and out of their tiny mouths so fast I'm worried they may chip a tooth.

"Oooowwww," says Tasanee, dropping her spoon and holding her hands to her head.

"Brain freeze?" I ask, and they both collapse in a pile of giggles.

"Lola, no!" I say in hushed horror as the petite girl lifts her bowl to her face and starts licking it. When I see a big smear of ice-cream on her nose, I can't help laughing too, and let out a loud snort while trying not to. This only makes things worse as the two girls start trying to laugh through their noses to get the same effect. But all they end up doing is get ice-cream through their noses.

"Shh," I say, in-between spluttered giggles, but in no time at all, all three of us are sniggering so much people in the restaurant keep turning to look at us. "Sorry, sugar rush," I say to the waiter when he brings us the bill. He just looks at me as if we are crazy, which sets the girls off again.

Finally we manage to stop laughing and peel ourselves out of the restaurant. I take the girls' hands again and walk with them to a bookshop. Once inside, they go gaga over all the books and both want to choose some to look at. "OK," I say, "but don't get any pages dirty, OK?" The girls agree and start picking up and putting down books excitedly. I start leafing through Harry Potter en die Kamer van Geheimenisse. Could be useful later, when they have to start reading in Afrikaans . . .

I look up and realise I can't see Tasanee any more. "Where's your sister?" I ask Lola, but she shrugs.

"Tasanee?" I call. "Tasanee!"

I can't see her anywhere. I feel a panic rising. "Are you sure you don't know where she is, Lola?"

"No. I don't know?" she says, looking scared.

I start looking around the shop, between shelves, even around the corner of the Gruffalow display in the window – she is nowhere to be seen!

"Tasanee! Tasanee!" I call evenly, but nothing. "Excuse me, sir," I say to a shop assistant, trying not to sound hysterical. "Did you see the other girl that came in with me?"

"Sorry," comes the apathetic answer. He doesn't even look up. Not the best advertisement for a children's bookstore. I vow never to come back here again. I search everywhere in the store again, but don't find her. Now I'm really starting to freak out. I put my shopping basket down on the floor and, holding on to Lola even tighter, leave the store scanning the corridor. I don't see her at all.

"She likes to go off on her own. Mommy says she's going to get stolen by bad people," Lola's voice is uncertain. I look down at her wide-eyes.

"Don't worry, Lola," I try not to let my voice shake. "She's here somewhere. We just can't see her. I bet she's playing hide-and-seek with us." I fake a small laugh. Lola doesn't answer but grips my hand even tighter till the skin on her knuckles goes pale.

Oh no. What if she has been kidnapped! I have heard of it. And these kids are practically royalty! Oh no, what if I've just managed to get the child I am meant to look after kidnapped by money-hungry thugs who are going to call Khunying with a ransom? How would I explain that?

I start walking, scanning left and right and up and down – where on earth could she have gone? I walk faster and faster until Lola can't keep up any more, so I pick her up and put her on my hip. Back out in the corridor I keep searching till I'm out of breath. How could I lose a child! In the second week on the job! I start to feel like I want to cry. She's been kidnapped! Mongolian warlords have taken her and all we will ever get from her is an ear in the post telling us they have our girl.

And I will be so fired!

I put my free hand to my face, my mind racing, when I hear a small sob in my ear. "Lola! Don't cry. It's OK," I put Lola down on a bench and crouch in front of her, pushing the hair out of her face. She has put her fingers in her mouth and is sucking and crying and snotting all at once. "Lola," I say, finding a tissue in my bag and wiping her eyes and nose. "Listen to me. It's all going to be fine. We are just going to look for a nice security man and ask him to help us find her, OK?" Lola nods her head, but I can see she is still petrified. I look around and see a security guard. Taking Lola by the hand, I ask him to help us find Tasanee, and he immediately starts speaking into his walkie-talkie.

"Is she wearing a yellow school uniform and has long black hair?" he asks.

"Yes, yes! Do you know where she is?" I shout, almost clapping my hands in relief.

"Ya, I think so. A little girl of that description is at the information desk right now. She's asking for someone named Jemma."

"That's me! Oh thank you, sir! Thank you thank you thank you!"

I run in the direction he is pointing, poor Lola jogging at my side to keep up. As we come round the corner, I see Tasanee standing at the information desk, looking pale, and crying.

"Tasanee!" When I get to her she throws her arms round me and hugs tightly while sobbing into my neck. "Where did you get to?" I ask, still trying to keep my voice calm. Her face is white as a sheet and she has tearstains all down her cheeks.

"I... I... I saw a bird and followed it and... and... and when... when I looked I... I... I couldn't find you." She is hiccoughing while trying to speak, her voice rising with every sob. "And I didn't know what way I walked and, and I... I... I couldn't see the shop and I didn't know where I waaaas!" she cries.

"This is a very clever young lady," says the woman in the booth. "She went into one of the clothing boutiques and told the assistant she was lost, so they brought her here. Not a lot of young children can think clearly like that when they get lost. She must be very bright," and she smiles kindly at Tasanee. Tasanee smiles back and wipes her eyes on the back of her hand.

"Thanks," she says, calming down visibly and sniffing. I give her a tissue and hug her and Lola together.

"Oh, I'm so glad it's all OK!" I say, secretly adding, I'm so glad you weren't sold into the slave trade, to myself. I'm suddenly feeling completely worn out from the scare. "Let's go home, OK?" I walk, lost in the aftermath, my mind heavy while taking them back to the car. I want to call my mother to offload! And Jason. Even though I'm trying to keep a smile pasted on my face for the sake of the girls, my insides are a jumbled knot of nerves and panic. If I could just take a moment to phone my mother . . . but no. I'm the new Jemma, the Jemma who will take a lover. I'm going to have to learn to cope on my own.

"I'm proud of both of you," I say to the girls when we get back to The Palace. "Tasanee, you were so clever to find a grown up woman to help you, and Lola, you were so brave!" Both girls have taken my hand again as we walk in to the house and I give them each a squeeze.

We get our lunch from Jim – smoked chicken salad with blue cheese dressing – amazing what these girls eat – and take it out to the garden.

Once the shock of the mall scare subsides and the two girls are laughing and playing again, I declare homework time, trying to keep their minds as far away from the incident as possible, and feeling quite proud of myself for diverting all attention without any help. I don't need to phone a friend. I've got this.

After getting Tasanee started on her sums, I help Lola open up a photo folder on the computer to find a few family pictures for a collage she needs to do.

We go through the photos and I see what an incredible life these two have had so far. There are pictures of them in all sorts of beautiful foreign lands. There's one of Lola, from not too long ago I'm assuming, grinning in front of the Eiffel tower while pretending to have the tip of her finger pressed up against the leaning side of it. One of them is with a tiger – a live tiger! Both girls are wearing tiger-coloured hoodie jackets with ears sewn on the top, growling at the camera excitedly. It's too adorable for words.

There's one photo where they are both about two years younger, wearing oversized sunglasses on their baby faces, pointing to the pyramids in the background. And one of Tasanee at about age four in a mini pink ski-suit next to a very blonde instructor. There is even one of the two girls riding an elephant, just like the one of Khunying framed in the sunroom. Strange how she chose to frame the one of herself rather than of her kids. I see some photos of a very elaborate eastern-looking wedding, Khunying glowing under rich traditional dress. My eyes go straight to her head and there, in all its glory, is the tiara. I feel my guilt flaring up and shoot a glance at Lola, as though she knows. Then laughing at myself silently, I take a deep breath and keep scrolling through the pics, determined to calm down. I see their father for the first time – an older man with the same wide round face as Tasanee, and a big kindly smile. Lola definitely looks more like her mother. Looking from the photos to Lola's cute dimpled face and back again, it's as clear as day, and Tasanee is one hundred per cent her dad.

These girls have had such an amazing life, and I almost had one of them kidnapped and chopped up for ransom! This has not been a good week. First I get caught snooping, and now I almost get Tasanee killed. What on earth is wrong with me? I pat Lola's head, lost in my own thoughts and she cuddles up next to me, leaning her small frame against me while looking at the photos. Such a sweet child. I'm going to be extra careful from now on. No more incidents, at all!

When it's bath time and I get shooed away by Suda, I go to my room and check my phone for messages. There is one from Kobus telling me Khunying wants me to call her again. I feel a sudden wave of panic.

She knows . . . She knows I lost her child! She knows about the Mongolian warlords and how Tasanee almost got kidnapped and got chopped up and had her ear posted to us . . .

How could she know? No, she's just checking in. That makes more sense. One of her usual 'you-are-so-incompetent' phone sessions.

I get off the bed, take a deep breath and march myself down to the kitchen. By the time I've dialed the number correctly (these foreign codes confuse me) I've calmed down quite considerably and actually think this is going to go well. She can't know, and everything will be fine.

I hope.

"Hello, Khunying. You asked me to call?"

"Jemma," The Voice. She sounds much colder over the phone than in person, if that is even possible. "I hope everything is alright? Are the girls settling into school well?"

"Oh, y-yes, everything is fine thanks," why does her voice always make me so nervous? "We did homework today and Lola needed some photos for a collage so I helped with that. I asked Suda. I hope that's OK?"

"That's fine. OK, well, if that's all . . ."

She doesn't know! Oh happy day! Not fired after all!

But... I know I have to tell her.

If there's one thing I've learnt in the past ten days, it's that she may not know right now, but she will know soon. Tasanee will tell her for sure. It will probably be better if I just bite the bullet right now and tell her myself first. I take a deep breath and close my eyes.

"Actually, uh, well there is something else. Something I need to tell you."

"Yes,"

"I, um, well, you see, I took the girls for ice-cream, sort of like a back-to-school celebration. Don't worry, I checked it with Jim, and they did eat proper lunch when we got home. It was just a little treat – and I made sure it was whole milk, organic, refined-sugar free. . .." I stop briefly to try re-group, stop babbling and sum up my courage.

"Go on."

"Uh, OK. So when we were at the shop, I took them to buy some games. Educational games. You know, like Scrabble and stuff."

For goodness sake, Jemma, don't say stuff!

"Er . . . I mean, like ones like that. Nice ones, a bit more at their level, you know. Like the Memory Game. Do you know it?"

I can sense Khunying's irritation, drumming her fingers on the other end of the line.

"Anyhow. Um, then we were all looking at books, and, uh, well you see, Tasanee sort of followed a bird out of the door. She was obviously amazed at seeing a bird inside a mall. You know how strange it seems when you see that. I know I'm always a little like 'wow' when I see a bird inside a shopping mall, I always sort of stop and go 'There's a bird indoo' . . . Uh . . . anyway, so she followed this bird and sort of, well, she sort of, got lost. Butwefoundherrightaway . . ." I pause, waiting for a response. But Khunying says nothing.

"Um, so it's OK though. So don't worry. She was really very good. She went straight to a lady in a shop and they took her to Information and called it through to all the security guards and we were already looking for her and, so, well we found her. But it's all fine. She wasn't even missing for that long. It was probably only ten minutes in total, even though it felt like forever – I mean, well, that is to say, it was a little scary. But not so bad actually. And she is fine. Really. And I'm very happy she is so clever to have gone to that lady in the shop. But she is all fine, so you don't need to worry about anything. I just thought you should know."

I wish I had an off-button. I force myself to stop speaking and with my eyes still squeezed closed wait in dread for Khunying to say something.

Silence.

I can feel it burning in my eardrums, making me strain my hearing in case she is talking but the line is too soft and I can't hear her. But Khunying is definitely not speaking. She sounds like she may not even be breathing. I wonder if I lost the connection . . .

Just as I am about to start talking again, I hear The Voice clear as daylight.

"Well, Jemma. It sounds as though you handled the situation. Thank you for letting me know." And she puts down the phone.

I've been gripping the receiver so hard my hand hurts. I unlock my iron-tight fingers and put the phone back on the hook. My palms are sweaty and I feel like I need a drink.

"You lost Tasanee?"

I jump and see Jim standing behind me in the kitchen. Damn this no-shoe policy – people keep sneaking up on me!

"Looks like you might need a cup of coffee, new girl," he hands me a steaming hot cup.

"Thanks, Jim." I accept it gratefully. "Don't suppose you added any whisky?" I joke, awkwardly, and take a sip. It's not whisky, but it will do. "It's all OK though, she wasn't lost for–"

"I know, I heard it all. How did Khunying sound?"

"Um, I think she's fine with it. She said thanks for handling it or something."

"Really . . ." he says slowly. He looks at me for a long time as if trying to decide something. Then he claps his hands together, turning to the oven and taking out a large red Le creuset roasting pan, steaming and delicious smelling.

"Dinner's ready!"

Chapter 9

· · · · · · · · ·

The rest of the week goes by relatively smoothly with no major drama. Bruno seems to have figured out how to unlock the door to his kennel and keeps bounding up on us and trying to hump everything in sight whenever we are out in the garden, despite the dog-training lessons, and Kobus's usual 'Voetsek! HOND! Jou bliksem!' But other than that, all smooth sailing. Thank my lucky fairy-star-dust!

Suda is leaving me alone with the girls for longer and longer periods, not appearing until bath time. I get the sense she is starting to trust me, and so I don't take her lack of presence as an insult but rather as a compliment. Also, she really struggles with her back, I can tell. So I'm happy to take as much pressure off her as possible.

Ramie, on the other hand, is not making herself scarce at all. She always seems to be leaning on doorframes, coming round corners or leaving rooms when I am around. It puts me on edge. I can't help feeling she is watching me and it is thanks to our perchance meeting in Khunying's wing of the house. But something tells me she isn't watching me out of concern for the privacy of her employer. I can't figure it out exactly, but she makes me feel very uncomfortable.

· · · · · · · · ·

Even Jim, who is openly friendly and not too threatening, has been making me feel uncomfortable. He's just a tad too familiar.... I decide maybe I'm paranoid and feeling the weight of a guilty conscience, so I'm seeing things a bit more sinister than they really are.

Khunying doesn't speak to me on the phone again, amazingly, but I do get three more signed memos to sign, instructing me to do this, not do that, and for goodness sake pay more attention to her children and try not to get them killed. Well, they never said that exactly, but I'm reading between the lines here.

I resolve to spend my alone time working on a new folder of all the day trips and outings I am going to take the girls on. I work on it like a dedicated teen working on a massive school project, with beautiful colourful pages and cut-outs, cleverly collaged and all bound together in a booklet labeled "Educational Outings and Fun Days". When Khunying gets back I will show her this to remind her, and myself, that I'm doing a great job and the girls are in good hands.

On Thursday evening, after dinner, Kobus has arrived and is waiting for me outside the bay window in the music lounge, surrounded by his usual grey cover of smoke. I take the girls up to their rooms with some books to read in bed, then go back down to meet with him.

"Jemma, I need to chat with you quickly," he says, reaching into his briefcase and pulling out some papers. "Will you be able to take the girls to friends again this weekend? Khunying has decided to stay away a bit longer than planned."

"Oh really?"

I wonder how often she goes away like this. And if it's always for this long. Lola lost a tooth this week, and is starting to get freckles on her nose that weren't there before, and her mother is missing it all.

"Sure, I'll take them," I say, feeling a wave of pity.

"Thanks," he smiles at me. "Another thing, though," he pauses uncomfortably, shifting in his chair. "I, uh, I'm meant to give you this." He hands me a sheet of paper, not meeting my eye. It is very formal looking – more so than the usual memos I get, and this time with a company logo on the top. Then I realise what it is.

"I'm getting a written warning?" I ask, shocked. Kobus seems to really feel bad he has to be the one to do this. He frowns sympathetically and nods his head.

"I'm also meant to tell you that you cannot take the girls out any more. Just the extra-curricular activities in the folder, and anything else she asks. But no malls or anything."

I sink down onto the sofa, looking at the offending sheet of paper in disbelief. There goes my Educational Outings and Fun Days plan.

"She said you were shopping for clothes and left the girls to wander around on their own–"

"What? Kobus, that is so not what happened! You can even ask Tasanee!"

"I know, I'm sure it's not what happened. But you know what, don't worry about this. If you sign it I will just file it away and you can get back to things and not worry about it. It doesn't even really mean anything, trust me. She has me hand these things out here all the time – I can't tell you how many of them Ramie and Jim have signed – she never even remembers. I'll just put this in the 'Where did it go again?' file," he smiles at me gently. "It's similar to how she is always going on about suing people – but she almost never does. The cases always fall apart." I stare at him in horror, making him laugh out loud. "Oh don't worry! This is nothing like that. It will all be fine. You'll see."

Sighing deeply I take the pen and sign. A written warning! This is ridiculous. But I suppose, looking at it from a mother's perspective, the girls are in my care and if anything did happen to them . . . I rub my face trying not to think about it. Kobus puts down his folder, sits next to me and gives me a 'siestog, skat' kind of look.

"Why don't you tell me what really happened?"

I relay the events to him, not leaving out a thing. When I finish he grins at me. "You shouldn't have told her about it, you know."

"But I had to! If I didn't, Tasanee was bound to say something. You yourself told me she tells her mother everything."

"True. She is desperate to please Khunying. Well, at least it's over now. No need to dwell on it. Come on! Let's get a glass of something to soothe the pain, shall we?" He walks over to a cabinet on the wall, pushes a button and a long panel automatically opens up to reveal a blue illuminated bar. Glasses, bottles, ice buckets, decanters and every other kind of drinks-accessory you can think of are all lined up on neat glass shelves. "I'm having a Brandewyn. What would you like? Wine? Champagne?"

It's like a scene straight from an old Bond movie. I half expect masked henchmen to burst through the doors and windows, shattering glass everywhere.

"Am I allowed to drink? I mean, on the job?"

Kobus grins broadly and laughs. "Jemma, you need to loosen up. You are tiptoeing around here all day like a scared bokkie." He pours coke into his glass, and I watch the sweet, amber liquids mingle to form the cultural drink called 'Klippies en Cola' "Don't worry," he continues. "You won't get into any more trouble. Not for this. Everyone round here knows I'm in charge when she's away, and I say you deserve a drink! Besides, it's after dark, the girls are in bed – you can relax now." He's right, the big boss isn't in town, so why not? What could go wrong?

I nod. "OK, wine please." I can't help remembering the way Kobus looked the first time he met me here at the house, a bit like a deer in the headlights. Could it be he also relaxes and comes to life when Khunying is away?

Kobus pours me a glass of wine, and holds up his glass. "To written warnings!" he says, and we clink before settling back down on the couch. We spend the next twenty minutes sipping our drinks and chatting. He is such a neighborly man, very warm and friendly and seems totally to understand how I'm feeling. He tells me about his life with Khunying, how his wife is constantly worried he is going to have a heart attack one of these days. He has a good sense of humour but I can tell he takes his job very seriously.

"You're one of the good people," he says to me as we take our glasses through to the kitchen. "You have such a pure quality – raised right. Your parents should be proud – you are a good, good person. This family needs that, you know?"

I feel guilty, and am tempted to tell him about the tiara incident again. But then he would know I'm not one of the good ones. I decide not to rat myself out yet.

After I go to bed I lie awake thinking about what he said. This job is hectic and I just can't seem to settle in. But the girls . . . What about the girls? I've never felt more needed by any of my other employers' children before – maybe it's because they have such an unconventional life. Showered with luxuries and anything their little hearts desire, but no full-time mother or father living in their home. They are raised by staff. The way Lola has been latching on to me, and even Tasanee seems to want me around all the time, and wants to impress me with her schoolwork and anything else she does. I found being a nanny can be really rewarding, allowing the children special places in my heart, but this is the first time it scares me. They need me a little too much. And I could grow to be too attached to them.

And 'Surrogate Mother' was most definitely not in the job description.

I can't sleep. Maybe a glass of milk will make me feel better. Even if I don't use a crystal champagne glass. I get out of bed and pad down to the kitchen. The house is dark and even though the under-floor heating is on, I feel a shudder as I walk through the deathly quiet passageways.

My eyes adjust to the dark and I can make out samurai swords leering at me from their perched positions, and heavy, ancient paintings pressing down from the high, unwelcoming walls. By the time I reach the kitchen my heart is pounding and my whole body has gone rigid. What am I doing here? Living in this, this museum? A house where nothing lives. Nothing breathes! I'm never going to fit into this kind of life – it is just too different from what I am used to. No family has ever been like this before – parents so detached from their children's lives. No household has felt so clinical, so cold. And who am I becoming, snooping around? What was I trying to find in Khunying's room anyway? Shoes? Do I really need to be crossing boundaries for the sake of a glimpse of someone else's Louboutins, no matter how fabulous they are?

I feel a small splash on my hand, holding my glass. Then another. Why am I crying? What is it about this place that makes me feel so inadequate? Maybe the reason I keep trying to work as an au pair is because I can't do anything else. Maybe I'm useless and will never grow up. I look down at my pajamas – pink shorts and a top with miniature Betty Boops blowing kisses all over it. I'm afraid to grow up. I'm just the girl who used to look after the toddlers at church, because I was older than they were, and they all looked up to me no matter how small and insignificant I was. But now, when I finally get an opportunity to be the ultimate au pair, I can't even do that right. Jason has all this faith in me and keeps telling me I have so much talent and passion, but all I can do is look after children, and clearly, not even very well! And when I'm not watching the children, I end up going off to spy on my employer. For what?

I'm never going to achieve anything in life. Of course I could never get a real job or make something out of myself in the real world – I can't even do this job right!

Just as I'm about to crumble in self-pity completely, I hear a small voice. "Jemma?"

It's Lola. I quickly wipe my eyes and turn to see her standing in the kitchen doorway, clutching Mu close to her.

"Lola? What are you doing awake, sweetie?" I ask, putting down my glass and going over to pick her up. Once on my hip she puts her head on my shoulder.

"What's wrong?' I ask softly. "Couldn't you sleep?" She sakes her head and puts her fingers in her mouth. "Neither could I."

I pour the raven-haired princess a glass of milk too and sit her down at the kitchen counter where we both sip silently. After a while, Lola wipes her mouth and says: "I dreamt Tasanee was gone. So all that was left was me alone. And it was all dark. And I was scared."

It hits me like a thousand knives. I stand up, go over and pick up her small frame and hug her with everything I've got.

"I'm here with you now, Lola. I won't go away. I won't leave you.

Chapter 10

. . . .

"Oh man, it feels good to be home! Sometimes I wish I didn't have to live in that horrible place!" I have flopped down onto our hideous sofa. "I love you, old green couch! I love you, battered coffee table! I love you, veld!" I shout, feeling such overwhelming relief to be in the poky flat again.

"What are you talking about?" Jason says, picking up my bags, which I abandoned at the front door, and taking them through to my room. "You live in The Palace and have shoe elves and a chef. Why on earth would you want to stay here with all the mismatched furniture and chipped mugs instead?"

"Because I can put my feet up here! Anywhere I want. And I love that our coffee mugs are n bietjie rof" I sigh. "Over there I feel like I'm constantly being watched," I say, only half-joking. "Here I never get into trouble. At least here I know where my boundaries are." Jason doesn't reply, but I can sense he is not really listening to me as he fusses over the messy trail I am leaving in my wake. "Helloooo," I call down the passage.

"Ya ya, I know, your life is so bad, you have to drive a Porsche blah blah blah," he comes back into the lounge and sits down on the armchair.

. . . .

I sit up and look at him, my most grave expression summed up and pasted on my face. "Remember that time I almost drowned? When we were six? You could swim, but I couldn't and I just wanted to be like you and do what you could do. I went under and no one even noticed till you realised I wasn't coming up and jumped in to save me. Remember how awful that was? Well, these past weeks, I've been underwater the entire time. I can actually breathe here. Look! I can reach my room from the sofa!" I throw a couch cushion across the room, down the passage and in through my bedroom door. I giggle, feeling the tension releasing already, and kick off my shoes.

"I've been underwater a bit myself too. Things are weird with Tracy – the long distance – I don't know. Lately it just feels a bit more 'distant' than usual."

"Oh, I'm sure it's fine. You two have been together for so long, this is just a phase. Before you know it she'll be back here and you will be kicking me out so you can shack up together. Your problems are not real problems," I half smile at him. "My problems, on the other hand…Fukushima!"

"Oh, come on, it can't be so bad," laughs Jason. "And don't think there aren't rules here too, you know. Don't start throwing things around and leaving your junk all over the place." Jason has always been a neat freak, and I the chaotic one. As twins we couldn't be more different. My closet usually looks more like a price-off bin than shelves of clothes, and I pretty much never make my bed. He gets annoyed with me when I leave my mess loitering through the flat, but I can see a good-natured glint in his eye as he scolds me.

I slip off my chunky bubble Perspex bracelet and put it on the coffee table, then take out my pink glass studded earrings, suddenly feeling the need to be free of all accessories.

"Seriously, it's like the walls have eyes over there! And nobody trusts me. Did I tell you about Ramie coming out of my room the other day? I caught her in the act, but she just walked past and never said anything. I should have asked her. I still don't know what she was up to . . ."

The truth is I wouldn't ask Ramie what she was doing because I'm too scared she might say something about me sneaking around in Khunying's room.

"Oh, and did I tell you about the elephant photo? Khunying puts up one with her in it, but just leaves the one–"

"With the kids in a folder on the computer. Yes, you told me."

"Oh. Well. I think that's horrible."

"She's a horrible lady and you don't know how she can leave the kids for so long and she doesn't even phone them every day and she alienates poor Lola and yes yes, I know, Jem. You haven't stopped talking about her. Can we take a break from work-talk for a bit, please?"

I look over at Jason feeling bruised, but decide maybe he's right. I do talk about work and Khunying a lot. It must be annoying for him.

But the gossip is just so juicy! It's as if I'm addicted or something. I've tried not to look for advice – the new me can handle things on my own – but that doesn't mean I can't keep him updated on the craziness. I can barely wait to get on the phone with him every time something happens at The Palace.

I don't tell him about how much Lola has started clinging to me though. Or how Tasanee has started climbing into Lola's bed every night, even though I put them both to sleep in their own beds.

"So the other night was fun," I say, changing the subject. "What did you think of Ryan? Really."

"Nice guy, I guess. Plus he needs a group – sucks to be in a city like this with no drinking buddies," says Jason, rummaging in the freezer to get more ice. "And anything to get you to stop thinking about that loser ex is fine with me."

"I guess. I might see him more."

"Well you certainly looked cozy enough in that photo Troy put up –"

"Troy seemed to be getting really cozy with you, too – better not let Tracy find out," I tease, trying to lighten the atmosphere. Jason meets my eyes for a moment, and then looks away.

"You know Troy . . ." he waves a hand dismissively, scouring cupboards for something else. I wonder what he means? What about Troy? That she's generally quite touchy-feely, or she's a man-eater and seems to have a thing for him? I wonder if things are actually worse with Tracy than I realised. Besides tonight, he hasn't really mentioned her for a while – or has he? I can't remember. I've been so focussed on my own problems.

"Hey, Jase," I say as he drops something in the cupboard and mutters angrily under his breath. "Is it really that bad with Tracy? The distance, I mean?"

Jason doesn't re-surface from the cupboard, but keeps busying himself shoulder-deep in the shelves. A few more muffled obscenities later he answers me. "Ag, you know," he says, his voice drowned by the clinking and clanking of bottles as he moves things aside. "It's weird . . ." he pauses and straightens up, not turning round to face me. "You're probably right though. It's..."

While he speaks, I go over to my handbag to find my earring box – something I keep with me all the time. It's a small gold and emerald jeweled antique cocaine box my grandmother gave me. It's a family heirloom and she told me it was actually used to carry and sniff cocaine back when nobody knew how bad it was, and everyone had these tiny snuffboxes. I always loved this one from when I was a very little girl, playing in my granny's vanity drawer, puffing powder all over my face and smearing on rouge lipstick. When I started growing up she gave me the gold box as a gift and I've kept it close to me ever since. I keep earrings in it now, because I'm often late for appointments and only remember things like earrings after I've left home and am rushing to get to my destination. So this way I always have a few small select pairs handy to put in while I'm on my way out.

But right now, I can't find it. Jason has been talking about Tracy, but I'm not listening. I keep rummaging through my bag, searching, turn the bag out all over the kitchen counter and shuffle through everything, but it's not here!

"Jemma, are you even listening?" Jason sounds hurt.

"Jason, it's not here!"

"What's not there?"

"My earring box! Granny's snuffbox! I can't find it!"

"Really? You can't find something in that jumbled mass-mess of yours? I can't believe you ever do find anything . . ."

"This is not funny, Jason – its is gone!"

"Are you sure you didn't take it out and leave it somewhere?"

"No, I never ever take it out. Ever! I always keep it right here in my handbag because I want it to be on me all the time. I never take it out!" I start to panic. I search every bag, go through all my cupboards, the bathroom. I look behind cushions, under the couch, even in the fridge. After rushing out to the parking area, crawling through Peaches looking under every mat and between the back seats I finally give up, completely exasperated and covered in orangey felt-dust from Peaches' crumbling upholstery. Tucking the pink flamingo under my arm, which was still stuffed down behind the seat, I slump back up the stairs to our apartment.

"It's not here!" I flop down on the green couch, putting the pink flamingo next to me. Jason looks at the flamingo, but doesn't say anything about it.

"Maybe you left it at The Palace. I mean, that's possible, right? Why don't you phone them?"

"I don't have the house number," I say, realising this for the first time. "And besides, they aren't there this weekend. No one is."

"Don't worry, you can look when you get back on Sunday. Come on, let's order pizza and find something to watch on Netflix."

I sink as far into the couch as possible. I want to cry. I can't lose my grandmother's snuffbox! It's my favourite thing in the world, and one of the most precious memories I have left of her. Feeling huge tears well up in my eyes, I take a few big gulps of air and I try to calm down. I have to stay positive – Jason is right. I could have left it at The Palace. As hard as I try, I just can't remember taking it out of my handbag, but maybe it fell out in my room. I'll just have to wait till the weekend is over to find it.

"Don't worry, Jem," says Jason, handing me a champagne glass of milk. "It will turn up. It will come back to you or whatever that airy-fairy stuff is you keep saying. Try not to think about it anymore tonight, OK? Now what do you want on your pizza?"

I accept the milk and succumb to comfort food.

"Sooooo," Frederick lowers his sunglasses and bores into my eyes with inquisition. "Have you taken your lover yet?"

"Frederick," I hiss, looking over to the bar to make sure Ryan didn't hear. Not that he could have, over this throbbing music. He sees me however and waves, his board shorts showing off the most ripped legs I've ever seen on a man. I smile and wave back, lie down on my deck chair again and turn to Frederick who is adjusting himself in the sun, grinning at me knowingly.

"Aw, look at that. You have a puppy."

"Oh shut up," I giggle. "He's here for all of us, not just me. Needs friends, remember?"

"Oh yes, I remember. I take my civic duty very seriously. Getting him in to the group and on to you is top of my priority list."

"Shhh!" I blush insta-red. It was Troy's idea to come to Zoo Lake today. The new Tiki bar is the latest thing and a great addition to the well-loved picnic and boating spot for those of us trapped in the urban jungle, which seems to be a lot because there are semi-clad bodies in the hundreds! It's

seems to be a lot because there are semi-clad bodies in the hundreds! It's lucky we got these deck chairs when we did, like securing a VIP booth in a popular club.

"So no shenanigans yet? Good Gaga, child, you are slow. Look at that body! If he was mine, I would –"

"No one needs to know what you would do if you had the chance, thank you," I hold my hands up, laughing. "Besides, when would I have had time for any shenanigans? I've been trapped at The Palace all week."

"Snap chat?"

"You know I'm more old-school than that."

"Phone sex then? Oh, don't blush! You Richardsons – honestly!"

I try to cover my pink cheeks by re-applying sunscreen and pulling the brim of my panama hat lower. Then remembering my vow to be the new me, I lean over to Frederick surreptitiously and whisper, "He did send me a video clip of him doing some bizarre thing at CrossFit though. Muscles – EVERYWHERE," I widen my eyes over the tops of my glasses, and start swiping through photos on my phone to find the video clip as Frederick leans closer eagerly. "And he was all hot and sweaty and – "

Frederick stiffens. He is staring just past my head, and as I turn I find myself face to crouch with – yep, of course –

"Ryan!" I say, jumping up and guiltily dropping my phone. The crowd surges, bumping him forward, and he slams right up against me.

"Well hello there, little lady," he says with a huge grin. I am suddenly very aware of the fact I'm in my pink polkadot bikini and pressed up against his bare chest. Nothing about this feels like taking a lover. It feels more like being way too close and personal with a stranger. I grit my teeth into a smile and slowly begin to peel myself off, just as Troy and Jason appear through the chaos, protectively cuddling a few glasses in their arms and giving me a good enough excuse to step away.

"Drinks!" Troy announces and she starts to pass the glasses round. "Sorry, Ryan, I didn't know you had arrived or I would have got you something."

"That's ok," he says holding up his bottle of water. "I got this already. Not drinking alcohol this weekend. It's test week at the box next week and I'm planning on PB'ing my way up the grid by at least 20%." We all stare at him, not entirely sure what he just said.

"Er. OK. . .Isn't this place great?" Troy is the first to break the awkward silence.

"Kind of like a mini festival," I say, trying to seem cool while wrapping my sarong around myself consciously, as Ryan's exposed skin keeps brushing up against mine, "except without any live music." I glance over at Frederick who has not missed my cat-like move. Of course he wouldn't. Would he be terribly disappointed in me if I give up on the lover idea altogether? Is this the way it's meant to feel? I'm not sure, because I've never done such a thing. Maybe it's meant to be all strange and unfamiliar. Maybe it's something you warm up to – like getting into a cold bed and shuffling around, kicking and tucking things till you feel all snug and warm. To be perfectly honest, things haven't been going as well as I'd hoped at The Palace, or with my new life, at all; so perhaps this is one thing I could enjoy. I survey Ryan's tousled dusty blonde hair and glistening abs once more. He certainly looks like the kind of person who could warm up a cold bed in no time. . . I decide it's too soon to give up on the new me.

Sunday afternoon finally arrives and at four-thirty I'm back at The Palace to park (or rather hide) Peaches, pick up the Porsche and fetch the girls. I give my room a quick once-over looking for the gold earring box again, but still can't find it. I will have to ask Suda when we get back, I think, turning into the driveway of the house where the girls have been spending the weekend.

After being taken into a waiting room by the housekeeper, I hear a loud thudding coming down the stairs. Lola and Tasanee come flying into the waiting room and both hug me at the same time with huge smiles on their faces. "We missed you, Jemma!" they shout.

"OK, OK," I laugh, almost falling over with them hanging onto me. "Come on, let's get your things in the car and we can go home for Sunday Night Surprise!" I wiggle my eyebrows at them.

Their eyes widen. "What's Sunday Night Surprise?"

"Ah, well it's a surprise obviously! So I can't tell you. Hello Kitty says 'Go say goodbye and don't forget to say thank you', and?"

"And thank you very much for having us," they say in unison. These two sure do learn fast when they know there's a reward on the other end of whatever it is I tell them to do!

Once we get home and have the bags brought upstairs, I open up the girls' cupboards, and the hundreds of drawers of clothes to start the evening's planned festivities. "Now for this surprise, we need to be dressed in a special way," I say, pulling out a purple sarong and some daisy-covered beach hats. "We need to look like we live on a tropical island. What about this green skirt? Or the pink shorts with the yellow flowers?"

"That doesn't go!" shouts Tasanee in gleeful horror.

"Doesn't go? Doesn't go?" I protest in mock outrage. "My dear girl, how could you not see the glamour, the beauty, the sheer style in – this?" and I produce my pre-chosen outfit. Standing up, I hold up a lime-green mesh off-the-shoulder top and luminous orange spaghetti-strap sun-suit together to my body. It was quite a thing finding this outfit myself – I had to get the sun-suit from Troy and the mesh top is one of those things I never wear but can't bring myself to throw away. You know, in case I ever need it. Like now. I've also brought the pink flamingo along to complete the outfit, and tuck it under my arm as if I'm taking it to the beach.

The colours are hurting my eyes, but I start posing like a model and making ooooh, aaah noises for the girls. Once they are giggling and laughing their way through their own wardrobes, I unpack their over-night bags and take their dirty things to the laundry basket.

That's strange. There's something small and hard in Lola's jean jacket pocket. I reach into the pocket, and feel something solid and cold. My heart stops. It's my gold box! I pull it out quickly and stare at it. She took my box? She went into my handbag?

Like mother, like daughter. I can't believe it.

"Is it time for the surprise yet?" The girls, both dressed in shocking holiday colours that would put even the worst Hawaiian shirt to shame, have run into the bathroom. I quickly hide the gold box in my hand and hold it behind my back. I actually don't know what to feel right now. Relief at finding it, or anger at Lola for taking it. Mostly relief, but I'm dumbfounded. I can't believe she stole from me.

"Uh, yes. Um. Let's go downstairs. The surprise is there," I slip the box into my pocket and lead the girls down to the kitchen.

"And the surprise is . . ." I announce like a circus performer, "SpongeBob Night! And we will be making our own . . . Crabby Patties!"

"Crabby Patties! Yay!" shout the girls, jumping up and down clapping. "Whoooooooooooo lives in a pineapple under the sea! SpongeBob SquarePants!" they start dancing around the kitchen, laughing and singing and squealing in excitement.

I rented the new SpongeBob SquarePants movie for the girls to watch, and decided to make the cartoon's famous Crabby Patties for dinner together. I arranged it with Jim when picking up the car to fetch the girls, and he left us ingredients for Thai crab cakes. He actually seemed really happy to be getting the night off, practically skipping out the door the second I suggested it.

Once the girls are immersed up to their elbows in bowls of the mix, squelching crabmeat, herbs and breadcrumbs through their fingers in delight, I stand back and watch. Lola is giggling wildly and smears a glob of mayonnaise on Tasanee's cheek, who retaliates with a puff of flour on Lola's nose.

I still don't understand why Lola took my grandmother's snuffbox. She's such a sweet angel girl. So innocent! I will have to ask her about it later. I can't ignore something as serious as theft. But I won't do it in front of Tasanee, and we definitely won't be telling Khunying about this one. She's hard enough on the child as it is, from the little interaction I did see between them.

When the food is all ready, and we are settled down in the projector room to watch the movie, I let the girls snuggle up on either side of me the way they seem to like to when I'm reading to them. "It's just like being at the movies, isn't it," I whisper to them as if we are in a real theatre and have to be quiet.

"We haven't ever been to the movies," says Tasanee distractedly, staring at the screen and throwing popcorn into her mouth. "Mommy calls it 'Mass Market Middle-Class.'"

I stare at her in disbelief. That is actually a little funny, but terrible. She's raising them to be such snobs!

"Mommy doesn't like being with so many strangers. She says strangers are dirty and smelly and sitting with them in a small space is something we pay not to do."

Well, that explains a lot.

Once I've persuaded the girls to sleep in their own rooms, and I've put Tasanee in her bed and turned the lights out, I go into Lola's room and sit down next to her. She isn't asleep yet, but is playing with her bunny in the air. She puts it down when I come in, and I tuck it under the covers next to her. "Lola, I need to talk to you about something," I say, dreading the conversation. "I found my earring box in your jacket pocket. Did you go into my bag and take it?" Lola instantly sticks her fingers in her mouth and starts sucking. She looks down away from me and doesn't answer.

"Lola, it's OK. I'm not cross with you. But you can't do something like this again, OK? It's not good to take something that doesn't belong to you. You won't do it again, will you?" I brush her hair out of her face gently. She looks up at me, small tears spilling out of her eyes.

"I'm sorry, Jemma."

"Oh, Lola, don't cry. It's OK. I told you I'm not cross!" I lean down and give her a big hug. Wiping her eyes I smile at her. "But why did you take it?"

"I saw you with the box in your bag when you had it in the car," she tells me in a small voice. "And then I was scared to go away this weekend and I didn't want you to go home. So I took it to keep with me when you were away. I was going to give it back. Please don't sue me."

I stare at Lola, painful thoughts crashing through me. Sue? That's insane! She must have been listening in on her mother's phone conversations over the years and concluded that when adults get angry they sue. This little girl needs love, so much love! As for the earing box, she must have seen it a few times, when I would take it out to use. She only wanted a piece of me to keep while I was away. I totally get that now. I keep it close to me for the exact same reason. To feel like I still have my grandmother close to me, even though she is long gone. I give her another huge hug, then tickle her till she giggles.

"I'd never sue you – besides, it's illegal to sue an angel."

"Really?" she says, her sweet face clearing in wonder.

"No more crying, OK?" I say gently. "Mu is worried now. He wants you to be happy. He needs you to be strong for him, you don't want him to cry too, do you?"

"No," she says, smiling and cuddles her bunny closely to her.

"Tell you what. Tomorrow, I'll find something special for you. Something of mine – I'll give it to you so you can keep it close all the time. Does that sound good?"

"Yes please, Jemma." I kiss her on the head as she closes her eyes, her tiny lips pouted in a sleepy bow.

After I go to my room, completely emotionally depleted, I feel the urge to call my mother.

"Hello?" I hear the nervousness in her voice. If I ever call my mom after 8pm she automatically thinks something is wrong.

"Mom, hi, it's me."

"Oh, Jemma, what's happened?"

"Nothing, Mom, nothing's wrong. I just wanted to call."

"Are you sure? You sound hungry. Are you eating right? Are they feeding you right? You know, you always were a problem child with your food. . . ."

"Mom. Please. I'm eating very well. Can we talk about something else?"

I hear my mother humphing at being cut short, but she stops the nagging, thankfully, and lets me speak.

"Sure, honey. What's on your mind?"

"Mom, when I was little, did I ever take anything of yours to keep with me when you were going away or something? Like a memento. Did I ever want a trinket or something of you to keep with me?"

"When you went on your first Brownies camp, you asked if you could take our wedding photo album along. Of course, I couldn't let you take it – it would have been ruined. And it was too big and heavy for your tiny bag anyway. But we gave you a small photo of us coming out of the church, one of the spares. You kept it long after that camp till it crumpled and fell apart in your little red Cherokee jacket pocket, remember? So sweet. Is that what you mean?"

Of course! I suddenly remember the jacket – the smell of it, the warm fluff that seemed to envelop me like a cloud. I remember that camp too - being so scared about going away from my parents I wanted a picture of them to look at so I wouldn't forget them. I would take it out every night with my torch and stare at it before I went to sleep. I even made the photo kiss me goodnight on the forehead, pretending it was my mother, not just a black and white photo of her on her wedding day.

"I think that's exactly what I mean, Mom." I decide a photo is the perfect idea – I'll take a selfie with Lola in the morning and print it when she's at school. "Thank you, that really helps. Things have been, well, they haven't been great."

I tell my mother all about the earring box and Lola taking it. I tell her about my midnight conversation with Lola, about her dream of losing Tasanee and being left alone. I tell her how the girls love to hug me and never used to be read to at night. How Tasanee seems to be so grown up and mature sometimes, but then just a young girl the rest of the time. Once the floodgates open, I can't stop. So I tell her about losing Tas at the mall, the written warning and how I'm not allowed to take them anywhere now. She listens and doesn't say anything till I've spoken myself raw.

"Well, darling," she says softly. "It sounds to me you are doing so much more than a job there. You were meant to meet those girls. You are in their lives for a reason, and you just need to figure out what that reason is."

"I suppose," I say, my voice tight. "I'm just so in two minds though. I want to stay and at the same time I want to run! But I can't. Maybe it's just the newness of it all." I breathe deeply a few times, the phone line crackling with comfortable silence. My mother, even a thousand miles away in a different part of the country, makes me feel so at peace. It's something I am grateful for and would never wish away, not for all her nagging and worrying!

"Thank you for listening, Mom," I finally say.

"Of course, dear. Just . . ." My mother pauses, and I can tell she is unsure of how much she should say. "Just be careful. That's all."

"I will."

But I don't know if I can.

Chapter 11

· · · · · · · · · ·

It's Thursday morning and I'm preparing for a fun afternoon with the girls. Since I can't take them on outings any more, I figure we can have "outings" at home. Today they are going to dress up like bunnies.

I head down to the kitchen to ask Jim to prep lunch according to my bunny-food menu. Ramie is sitting in the sunroom as usual, her feet up and reading some glossy gossip magazine. She has one of Khunying's special china teacups in her hand, and sipping as if she is trying out for a part in the royal family. I laugh to myself, but sneak past as quietly as possible – I still don't know how to act around her.

After searching the kitchen, pantry and walk-in freezer, I go outside to see if I can find Jim. I hear some music coming from the Jacuzzi room below the pool deck, so I follow the sound, the beat getting louder and louder as I come closer, and finally knock at the door. No one answers but I hear laughing and loud voices coming from inside. After three more knocks, I put my head in. "Jim? You in here?"

I've stumbled onto what can only be described as a 'when the cat's away' situation. The room is littered with pool-party paraphernalia including a hula skirts, a giant blow-up dolphin and bright cocktail umbrellas in empty glasses. Jim is in a pair of Bermuda trunks, lounging back on the

· · · · · · · · ·

side of the bubbling Jacuzzi, along with a man I don't recognise, and a woman in a black string bikini. The strange man sees me first and nudges Jim, who turns and after the slightest hesitation beams at me.

"New Girl! Come in. Join the party." He jumps up, dripping all over the floor and hands me a ready-poured cocktail from a tray in the corner.

I'm sure this is against the rules. Dead sure. But Jim seems to be completely oblivious to the tensing up of my body and my uncertain voice.

"Er, actually I just wanted to talk to you about the girls' lunch . . ."

"What? Speak up, new girl!"

My voice is being drowned out by music blaring from the plasma screen. I carefully put down the cocktail that was forced on me and shake the spilled drops off my hand uncomfortably.

"Don't look so worried," he laughs at me. "It's fine! We do this all the time. That's Eugene over there, my brother. And that's Felia, one of the housekeepers from next door. Her bosses are also overseas, eh Felia?" he throws a beach ball at the scantily clad woman. She gives me a hostile glare of recognition, then turns to wade further into the giant Jacuzzi. I notice with embarrassment she is wearing a G-string. And then immediately I feel stupid and childish for being embarrassed. After all, it's not my rear end in there, flailing around in strategically placed dentil-floss!

"Jim, can we please speak outside for a second?" I say, pushing my way back through the French doors.

"Sure," he says, following me. His bony legs are dripping with water, making the black spindly leg-hairs stick to him in a tapestry of patterns. It's strange to see him in anything other than his usual Chef attire. Once safely outside I turn around and look at him quizzically. "Aren't you worried you'll get into trouble?" He laughs dismissively, and folds his arms, waiting for me to speak again. But just as I'm about to ask him about making carrot sticks and chopped up celery for lunch, one of the security gate guards appears through a row of trees, running and waving his arms at us. By the time he reaches us he is so out of breath he can barely get the words out.

"She – here – back – early."

As it dawns on Jim I can almost see a sheath cloud over his casual friendly demeanour. His eyes widen and his face pales. "Why didn't you call me on the intercom?" he splutters.

"I've been trying! No one was answering! She's here! On her way up now!"

In less than a nano-second, Jim turns and starts streaking across the lawn back to the house. He looks like a brightly painted animal running away from its big hungry hunter. Instinctively I follow suit, and start towards the house too. Looking back over my shoulder I see the security guard dragging Eugene and Felia's wet, hardly clothed bodies out of the Jacuzzi house, their things all bundled up between them, in a panic to get out.

Back in the house, everyone is suddenly busy – and visible! For the past week I've hardly seen any of the staff, but now they all seem to be polishing, folding, or preparing something. I almost get knocked over as Ramie flies past me in the kitchen, taking a big package Jim throws at her and rushing out the door towards the staff house. I realise I have nothing to do myself, and contemplate making a break for my room, but too late. I hear the front door bang shut, and the sound of Khunying's keys in the bowl. One by one her shoes drop to the ground, making a hollow echoing noise on the marble that ricochets all the way down the passage to the kitchen. I hold my breath – and I'm pretty sure the rest of the household are all doing the same – but don't hear anything more. I am frozen, straining my ears, but still can't hear a thing. I look over at Jim who has thrown a chef's uniform over his Bermuda shorts and he looks as strained as I do. After what seems like hours, Ramie creeps into the kitchen. She shoots me a belligerent look, and says to Jim "She went to her room" in a hushed voice.

The shrill ring of the phone makes me jump out of my skin. Seriously – I'm pretty sure I shed at least one layer of epidermis. Jim grabs the ringing receiver. "It's Khunying," he says, placing the phone back in its cradle, "wanting her coffee brought to her wing by Suda."

Shaking myself free of the panic-stricken mood I allowed myself to get in, I walk slowly towards the main entrance. Kobus is stumbling through the front door, weighed down by suitcases, handbags and a few shopping packages. He is so out of breath I worry he's about to have a heart attack. I rush over to help him.

"Hi!" I say brightly. "Let me help you there."

"Thanks, Jemma," he says wheezing, as I take some of the packages away from him and put them down on the table. "There're some things in there for the girls, but I will get Suda to unpack and put it all in their rooms. Aren't you meant to be fetching them from school?"

I look at my watch, suddenly realising the time. I'm actually thankful to be able to leave the house and get away from my guilt, seeping down from Khunying's room, through the floors, down the walls and finding its path all the way up my legs and into the pit of my stomach. I'm positive she will be able to tell I went through her things and touched the tiara . . .

I say goodbye to Kobus and head out to fetch the girls, taking deep breaths all the way and telling myself she won't find out.

After getting back from the school, Khunying still hasn't emerged from her Chanel-scented lair, but I hear her distinctive voice ricocheting from her wing. "Are you mad? I'll sue! SUE, I tell you!" I get Tasanee changed out of her uniform and Lola into a clean sundress, abandoning the bunny plans for now, and once the threats of suing whoever she's talking to or about have subsided, let them both go through to Khunying's side of the house to say hello. Standing at the entranceway, I feel a little bit better about everything. She couldn't possibly find out, and now the girls are home I feel more like I belong here too, and less like a criminal, ripe with the stench of "snoop".

I notice once I told the girls their mother was home, Lola started sucking her fingers again, and instantly lost all her spark. But Tasanee swelled with self-importance, a puffed-out-chest in her yellow school dress.

Late afternoon, a weary-looking Khunying sashays into the sunroom, her silk Japanese gown flowing round her body like liquid. She places herself elegantly in her favourite armchair, and, as we have just finished up with homework and some colouring-in, I suggest the girls go in to spend some time with her. After all, they haven't seen her for over two weeks. I stand at the door as they tiptoe into the room, ready to call a retreat if she seems upset at all.

She looks up when Tasanee approaches her, and, as if a whole other person takes over her body, she smiles sweetly. Warmly. Kindly, even. She calls the girls to both come and sit with her. Tasanee squeezes into the chair next to her, but Lola opts to sit on a cushion at her feet. She reaches down and strokes Lola's hair maternally while resting her head on the top of Tasanee's briefly. "I missed you girls. Did you miss Mummy?"

Maybe I was too quick in judging this woman. Maybe the distance and the phone calls kind of put a bad slant on my take on the situation, but now I see her here again, in the flesh, interacting with her girls, it all looks very different. She seems to love them. Her life must be so different to anything I could imagine – no wonder she doesn't have time for the nitty-gritty of child-rearing. But when it matters, here she is being a mother. I lean back, out of view so as not to interrupt.

"We always miss you, Mommy!" insists Tasanee, adding in a luscious laugh. Khunying smiles weakly at her daughter and suppresses a yawn. "Are you tired, Mommy? You look so tired. You must have had a long trip. Was the plane OK?"

"Oh, it was awful. I didn't sleep a wink. Some ghastly woman had her ogre of a child on the plane and it didn't stop bothering me once on the flight. Inconsiderate brat. You are such good children. You know how to behave on aeroplanes."

Tasanee smiles triumphantly at her mother, as if she has just won a prize.

"After that flight I swear I have twenty more wrinkles. Do you think I look older, my darling?"

"Oh no, Mommy," gushes Tasanee, "you are the most beautiful woman in the world!" Khunying smiles to herself, seemingly satisfied. She turns to look at Tasanee straight on. Her forehead crinkles slightly, and she takes the young girl's round face in both her hands.

"My angel. When you are eighteen we will get your eyes fixed. Slant them the right way."

What?

"And your nose, it has to be thinned out. You have your awful father's bulbous nose. Not your fault, but something we need not live with forever, thanks to Dr. Smit." She turns Tasansee's face from side to side, scrutinising her.

I am horrified. Telling your seven-year-old she needs plastic surgery?

Tasanee seems to not notice. She keeps gleaming pearly white teeth at her mom and soaks in every suggestion of facial alteration. "And I want your blue eyes, Mommy," she says, mesmerised by all the individual attention. "You have the prettiest eyes in the world!" Khunying smiles again – that is a smile she must practice; it has 'Mirror mirror on the wall who is the fairest of them all' written all over it.

Suddenly Khunying seems to bore of Tasanee's face and reaches down for Lola. Lola stands obediently and faces her mother. I can't see her face, but I can see her shoulders are slumped down so far she looks like a long-haired Benjamin Button.

"You don't need much work done, Lola. You were more fortunate than your sister – you got much more of me than your father."

Tasanee, being moved over to the side, narrows her eyes looking at her little sister. But she doesn't say a thing. She stands, staring, her smile faltering.

"Your horrible gums – I would do something about those. Yes, your mouth is far too wide and I can always see your gums when you talk."

She's five, and she's only got baby milk teeth. Of course you can see her gums. I want to walk in there and stop the madness, take Khunying by the shoulders and shake her till she stops planting seeds of insecurity in her young children. But I'm frozen, rooted to the spot. Like standing at the scene of a horrific accident and knowing you are not a paramedic and can't help. Khunying is handling Lola's perfect face a bit roughly. I see the baby girl wince slightly as her mother's talons tighten on her cheeks.

"Yes, definitely bad gums. So ugly! They will have to go. Fortunately we can start working on your face early. Dental surgery is considered ethical no matter what your age. And what on earth are these ugly things? Freckles? You are not wearing sunscreen, Lola! We will have to get fading cream asap – I will not have my child's face permanently scarred. Disgusting."

How rude. I have freckles and I love Lola's tiny sun kisses. Freckles are adorable! Everybody thinks so!

But Khunying doesn't seem to be much like anybody I've met before. She pushes Lola aside. "We will fix that face starting first thing tomorrow. Tasanee, however, you are going to have to wait a bit longer, my darling," she reaches over for Tasanee again, clearly done with Lola. Lola stands for a moment while her mother coos over Tasanee, and then slinks off to another chair. My heart is breaking for her. For both of them. What kind of mother talks like this? This has got to be in a book somewhere – Parenting 101: What NOT to do!

I make a mental note to tell the girls how perfect and beautiful they are just the way they are as often as possible.

"Jemma. Is there any particular reason why you are hovering in the shadows?"

Oh crap!

"Are you spying on me or would you like to come in and join in my family catch-up with my own girls whom I haven't seen in ages?"

Her sarcasm claws into me, dragging me into the room and I stand there, not sure how to handle the situation. Of course I didn't mean to spy, but if she knows I was standing there the whole time it must look like . . .

Crap!

A guilt tsunami crashes over me as images of me sneaking around her room flood my brain again. When did I become such a horrendous person? I better come up with a reason as to why I was eavesdropping, and quick.

"I'm so sorry, Khunying, I didn't mean to pry. I was – uh – just–"

Think, Jemma, think!

Khunying waves a crimson-dipped hand at me. She laughs suddenly, catching me by surprise.

"Oh, Jemma, I am only teasing. Do you think I was about to invite you to sit on my knee?"

Tasanee laughs loudly, over-emphasising how funny she finds her mother's jokes.

"No, no, I was just teasing. Jemma, seeing that you are here I have some things to discuss with you. Firstly, what are you wearing?"

"Um," I look down at my clothes. I'm wearing blue skinny jeans, yellow sandals with big bright daisies on the front and a pink tank top, covered by a very loose sheath in yellow and white. The sleeves come halfway down my arms and the bottom of the shirt ends in a long V-point halfway down my thighs. I thought this would be something she would approve of – I mean, I'm not showing any flesh at all!

"Yellow? Pink? Daisies? Really Jemma, you are in your twenties, not four. I would expect Lola to put something that chaotic together, not a grown woman."

I don't know if I'm meant to respond, but fortunately she moves right along.

"You will take the girls to lunch after school tomorrow. Kobus will call you with the details in the morning. Their . . . father . . . is in town and wants to see them." She spits the word 'father' out venomously. "Just please don't lose the girls this time."

So never going to live that one down. The remorse washes over again, a fresh wave choking me. She sits there, staring at me as if she's waiting for me to apologise again and just as I'm about to she waves her hand in the air, dismissing me.

"You may leave us."

I rush out, not asking questions, thankful to get away. I go straight up to my room, close the door and press my back up against it as if trying to keep the 'bad guys' out.

As I walk over to the closet to change, I suddenly stop. What did she say? I'm going to meet the father?

The father.

The father!

The one who named an entire species of roses after the love of his life. The man who made all this possible with his alimony money. The man to whom the freaking Queen of England gave a freaking grand piano. The man whom Khunying seems to detest so much.

The father! This should be interesting.

Chapter 12

．．．．．．．．

Sure enough, soon after leaving the girls at school the next day, my cell purrs. It's Kobus, giving me the time and place arranged for the girls to meet their father.

"You will need to stay with them for the whole lunch, of course. Just try not to say too much about Khunying, her travels, or your daily routines with the girls. If it gets back to her she'll . . . well, you know."

I wonder why I can't speak about the girls' lives to their own father, but I don't argue. I've learnt things go a lot smoother if I do what he suggests and don't ask questions. So after school, I take the girls past the house to get changed, and head off to the restaurant. I feel a prickle of anxiety as I park the car.

Meeting the father. This is exciting!

Wait a minute. This could be quite nerve racking. What if he is as unfriendly as Khunying? What if he is even more hostile?

Oh my word – all those samurai swords! Maybe he is cold and unfriendly and has an unhealthy obsession with sharp antique killing instruments. He could be a monster! And come to think of it, the girls never really talk about him – they don't even seem too excited to be seeing him today. Now I really am nervous.

We walk into a beautiful, open courtyard filled with circular tables set with crisp white tablecloths and large crystal wine glasses. The silverware glitters in the sunlight and soft jazz floats over the open-air space. I've never been to a restaurant as fancy as this. I look around, mesmerised by all the sparkly things. I bet this is where the twenty years of hand-me-down cutlery Jason and I have at home dream of coming to when they die. They probably have a whole perfectly-folded-linen-napkin religion dedicated to it.

The girls walk next to me as if they are quite used to eating out in such style. It's fascinating to me a parent would choose such a pristine setting to have lunch with their small children. A bit of a change from Spur or McDonald's at any rate. I ask for our table and a waiter checks the booking list.

"Ah, yes. Lord KhunChain's party. The gentleman has arrived already. Please follow me."

He leads us to our seats and I see a tall man at the table waiting for us.

I eye him, intrigue mixed with suspicion, as we walk over, taking in his appearance. I wonder if he could possibly be any of the things I imagined? Something about this man doesn't exactly scream old billionaire royalty, or masked villain. He is clean cut and close shaved. He's built tall and straight, and looks right at home in a pair of jeans, no label visible, but expertly fitted. A very basic white T-shirt sets off his sepia skin, and a pair of John Lennon sunglasses give him an air of open simplicity only very comfortably stylish men seem to have. And it sort of makes him look trustworthy. He looks like any well-to-do middle-aged man, but with a certain something; One who looks after himself, I can't help but notice. He has broad shoulders, with a slight definition of biceps peaking out from beneath his t-shirt sleeves. He has lovely smooth forearms with very fine hair on them – sexy forearms . . .

Sexy forearms? What on earth is wrong with me! He is their father, and Khunying's ex. That is all I need to know and that is all I need to think. I give myself an imaginary slap, and try to come back to reality. I fix a smile on my face, a professional smile, not too warm or alluring, and guide the girls through the tables towards him.

My lips suddenly feel dry and I have to lick them. I wonder if I have some of Troy's Cherry Monster lipstick in my bag?

As we come closer I can see his hair is very neat. A lovely rich blue-black colour with no trace of a receding hairline, but with a dusting of silver beginning at the temples. It highlights his creased brow, which has clearly been worked heavily in its time. And just as with most older men, it makes him look even more attractive.

As he sees the girls, he stands up waving and smiling brightly. A big wide grin I recognise as Tasanee's, but somehow more manly and – goofy. Goofy, inviting and fun. And sexy.

Dammit, Jemma! Do not think of the father as being sexy! What am I, a pent-up old nympho who just got out of prison? It's Ryan I'm interested in. Ryan. Troy must be having an evil effect on me. Man, would Troy get a kick out of this guy. She would flirt her designer day-glow right off at him in a second.

"My angels!" Mr Totally Hot calls warmly in a slight accent, increasing his hotness by a thousand points, and picks Lola up, squeezing her affectionately. She giggles and squirms, but stops laughing as soon as she catches a glance from Tasanee.

"Hello, Bruno," says Tasanee, formally, holding out a hand.

Bruno? Isn't that the name of the dog? I can't keep up with these people!

"This is Jemma, our new nanny," she moves her hand towards me as if she is presenting a new car at a show. Ever the hostess. Seven going on thirty!

"So nice to meet you, Jemma," says Mr Totally Hot, I mean, Bruno, I mean Lord KhunChain.

As he turns to look at me, I feel a wave of nerves take hold of my sanity, and suddenly am aware I have automatically put my hands together in "prayer position" and bowed my head the way the girls showed me they do in Thailand. It's almost as bad as if I had just curtseyed.

"Sa-wat-di-kap," I say, remembering the word for hello, unable to stop myself. Here he is, dressed down in jeans and a T-shirt, and I'm bowing and curtseying and fumbling my way through foreign introductions! Well, there's something he has in common with Khunying, I guess. The ability totally to rattle me just by his presence.

He laughs, takes my hand in both of his and shakes it warmly. "You are looking after my children well. I hear you are highly qualified."

"Oh! Thank you," I say, suddenly feeling a lot more at ease under his encouragingly open gaze.

"Kobus filled me in on your previous work, and on how well you have been doing since starting here with these two. Are you enjoying your position?"

"They are wonderful girls," I say. "So easy to look after, really. A delight! We have a lot of fun together." I smile at the girls while we all take our seats.

"Well, I can tell you are doing a wonderful job. Thank you."

"No, thank you, Lord Kh–"

"Oh please, call me Alak," he interrupts apologetically, putting his hands up as if trying to push something away from him. He laughs a great big booming hearty laugh, and sweeps his hands from side to side charismatically. "None of this Lord KhunChain nonsense. Unnecessary formality. It's just me, Alak. So tell me, girls, how is school? You must be very pleased to be in school with your sister now, aren't you, Lolly?"

I notice Lola seems to be torn between laughing with her father and shying back under Tasanee's surveillance. Tasanee has adopted a protective air, one that says 'I am not a little girl anymore and you are nothing special to me'. It's worrying to see her treat her dad like that, and I wonder if Khunying has manipulated her in any way against her father. I bet she has. But he seems to be undeterred by Tasanee's attempts at snubbing the conversation.

"Diving, hey Tas? That sounds dangerous. Not something you got from your old man – I can barely even swim. You have always been brave!" He is leaning forward with a hand on his chin, looking completely engrossed in her every word. Nice move. Tasanee can't resist any form of attention, no matter where it comes from. I watch the chit-chat – Lola being playfully cute with her father, and Tasanee visibly trying to be aloof, but slowly slipping into enjoying herself. And I can't help but notice the familiarity with which Alak is treating me. Every time one of the girls says something adorable and I laugh, he looks over at me, and I swear he winked at me a few times.

We proceed to have a lovely lunch. The girls order sushi and show me how good they are at using chopsticks. I in comparison didn't have sushi till I was nineteen and couldn't use chopsticks at all. We all laugh as Lola loses patience with a piece of California roll she's having trouble picking up, and drops the chopsticks, picking the sushi up with her hands and shoving it in her mouth, licking her fingers clean afterwards.

"Oh Lolly!" laughs Alak. "This one has the face of her mother," he adds, lifting his eyebrows at me, "but the manners of a barnyard animal! Not her big sister though. Tas is the perfect gentle-lady, aren't you, my dear? Could teach your old man a few to-dos, couldn't you?"

"I could teach you, Bruno," agrees Tasanee. She seems to ease up quite a lot while the rest of us are all chatting and laughing and having a really wonderful time. Alak is the most relaxed, inviting man I've ever met. He speaks calmly and softly, like the low rumble of a lion. His big round face is so open and friendly, and he is slightly off-centre kooky – I can't believe he was ever married to Khunying. Maybe opposites attract. Or maybe her beauty bewitched him!

But Alak seems like a good guy. He doesn't seem like the kind to be fooled at all. I sit watching him with his girls, and wonder how he ever fell for an emotional graveyard like Khunying.

He keeps making silly dad jokes, and the girls laugh despite themselves. It reminds me of my own dad, how he always goofs-off to make me laugh, and I feel warmed. It's so sweet to see the girls come out of their shells; I'm really glad we had this lunch. Both of them have a glow about them, with happy pink patches on their cheeks.

Eventually Tasanee forgets herself and begins to tell Alak everything. "And then Bruno jumped up on the table and took the glasses," she giggles, telling her dad all about how their dog had destroyed my sunglasses earlier that week, "and ate them! Jemma had to take him to the vet and the vet told her he found all sorts of things in his tummy! Stones and toys and Jemma's glasses . . ."

"They found a fork in there," I add, nodding away Alak's disbelieving expression, and popping a salmon rose into my mouth.

"Is he going to be OK?" he asks, sounding more amused than concerned.

"Oh yes," says Tasanee. "The vet says he will take it all out, and it won't be too hard."

"It's a very small procedure," I say, trying to add clarity to the whole story. The girls are still giggling. They found it extremely funny that Bruno, the dog, ate my sunglasses.

Suddenly I feel awkward. We have been speaking of Bruno, the dog, in front of Alak . . . the other Bruno. But he doesn't seem to notice or mind. I decide to try change the subject matter though, just to be on the safe side.

After what feels like hours, and the girls excitedly having given Alak a complete educational rundown of exactly what SpongeBob SquarePants is, I finally make apologies and get the girls ready to leave. I thank Alak for the delicious lunch and hold out my hand to shake his goodbye. He looks down at it comically, then laughs and pulls me in for a hug.

. . . .

I'm a little stunned, and very aware of his aftershave. I try to re-compose myself quickly enough to say something normal, like "Goodbye, nice to meet you, thank you for the lunch" or anything even remotely similar. All that I seem to be able to come up with, though, is "Jolly good".

Jolly good?

Troy would be so ashamed. And Frederick would disown me! I decide not to tell them this version of the ending, but make up something else. To Jason, I'll tell the truth, though. Only because he's made from the same stem-stuff as I am and will know instantly that I'm lying.

"By the way, Jemma," Alak says, lowering his voice covertly. I lean forward, feeling as though I am being invited into a secret club. "You greeted me by saying 'Sawatdikap'?"

"Yes," I whisper, feeling unbelievably embarrassed but hoping as hard as I can he found it charming that I tried using his own language to greet him.

"Well, Jemma, that basically means you are a man."

I start to blush. "What? Oh, sorry! I thought it meant 'hello'!"

He smiles kindly, and I find myself laughing at myself, suddenly feeling familiar and happy instead of being embarrassed. "You are right," he continues, "it does mean 'Hello'. But you only say it that way if you are a man. If you say 'Hello' and you are a woman, you say 'Sawatdi-Kaa', not 'kap'. See?"

"Your dad is very nice!" I say to the girls emphatically while driving home. "Did you have a good time?"

Neither of the girls speaks. Lola nods at me, looks to her sister and doesn't say anything. Tasanee is simply staring out of the window ignoring my question.

"Hellllooooo. Earth to Tasanee! Did you have a nice time with your Dad? Lolly? Tas?"

Lola sticks her fingers in her mouth and starts concentrating really hard on sucking. Tasanee looks over to me, a small smile crossing her otherwise worried face, and then quickly looks away and out the window again.

"Tasanee?" I ask pointedly. "What's going on? Is everything OK? I thought we had a wonderful time?"

"We did have a nice time, but we aren't really supposed to speak about our time with Bruno," she says, not looking away from the window. "Mommy doesn't like it. We can see him when he's here, but Mommy says we aren't allowed to talk about him."

"Oh. OK. But your mother isn't here. It's just us."

Tasanee looks at me, calculating in her child mind, but I can tell Khunying's influence runs deep. She frowns and stares out of the window again.

This is just so wrong. I start to fume internally, feeling all the injustice of the situation. Alak is such a lovely man, and he is their father. They should be allowed to talk about him, to enjoy his company, to love him!

The car is filled with a screaming awkward silence. I hear every automatic gear change. Every click of the indicator. The soft whistly-wet-noise coming from Lola sucking on her fingers.

"Well, can I ask one thing, please?" I blurt out eventually, breaking the silence. "Then I promise I will drop it."

Tasanee turns towards me expectantly, and Lola takes her fingers out of her mouth.

"Why on earth do you call your father Bruno? You nick-named your dad after a dog?"

There is silence for a moment, and then they both burst out laughing. "Bruno is Daddy's nickname. We always called him that. We named the dog after Daddy," Tasanee says, wiping her eyes with her sleeve. "When he left and we got a dog, we named him Bruno because we missed Daddy. We

· · · · · · · · ·

133

didn't name Daddy after the dog!" And she crumbles in convulsive giggles again.

When we arrive home I take the girls in through the front entrance, still giggling, and we all stop to take our shoes off. I notice a small trinket hanging from the inside handle of the front door. Bright red with gold flecks on it and a tassle. Not exactly the usual taste of the place, but interesting.

After we are done with dinner and homework, I play Barbie Mansion with the girls until their bedtime. I get to be the blue-haired Barbie today from the Fairy Princess range. I've named myself Dory, and am personifying the cute blue amnesiac character from Finding Nemo through the Barbie doll.

"But I don't know who you are!" I say, moving the doll aggressively away from Lola's black-haired rocker Brat Doll. "Why are you following me?"

Lola is laughing so much she can barely speak. "Because . . . you are . . . my best friend . . ." she splutters, making her doll jump after me. "And my . . . sister!"

"Yes, but who is my sister? And who are you!"

"Lunch is ready!" shouts Tasanee, her chosen classic blonde Barbie dressed in black high heels, a purple jumpsuit and a pink frilly apron. I can't help but notice how much that one resembles their mom. Right down to the perky plastic boobs.

"Our daddy is taking us to lunch, come with me!" she makes her Barbie say.

That's an interesting twist to the game. She's not allowed to talk about her dad in real life, but something tells me this Barbie is about to have a wonderful lunch re-enactment after today's events with . . .

"Isn't this game a bit juvenile for you, Jemma?" The Voice interrupts my thoughts. Real-life perky plastic-booby Barbie is standing at the door, looking at me through a funnel-vision of contempt.

"Oh, Khunying!" I say, startled. I stand up quickly, dropping my doll and smoothing down my hair.

"A word," she says coldly and glides off.

Crap-crappity-crap.

"Sorry," I whisper to the girls while stepping over the pantyhose high-way and round the throw-cushion Hollywood hills. "You keep playing till I get back, and Lola, you do me, OK?" I add as she picks up my Barbie.

"Oh, who are you?" I hear her saying to herself in a high-pitched voice as I leave the room. "I'm your best friend. No, you're not. Yes, I am. Stop following me!" She's so cute.

I find Khunying in the music lounge waiting for me. She has one leg elegantly crossed over the other, her perfect French pedicure complete with a tiny diamond on the second toe, bobbing up and down impatiently. The diamond confuses me slightly. I always thought nail art was considered tacky by people like her. But there it is, twinkling on her toe like a tiny spot of shiny mildew re-appearing on a freshly re-painted wall. It reminds me of the tatty dream catcher in her bedroom.

"And how did it go today with their father?" she says disdainfully as soon as I walk in. She is peering at me with a mix of superiority and the need to possess something I have . . .

"Oh, uh, good, thanks," I say, trying to fight the inevitable rising temperature in my face. I breathe in deeply, hoping she doesn't notice my fear.

"Just good?" She is getting impatient.

"Um, well, it went really well, thanks. They seemed to have fun."

I'm sweating again. Why can't I just be a normal, cool, calm and collected grown-up around this woman? She un-nerves me, obviously – but I need to not give in so easily. I try to remember the positivity I was feeling at lunch today, and how happy Alak was with my interaction with the girls. But I can't remember the happy feelings any more – I'm just dying to get out of here. I can't breathe around this woman!

She narrows her eyes at me and I watch as the calculations tick behind her eyes. She looks just like Tasanee when she does that! Keep breathing. She isn't as scary as she seems. She can't do anything to you.

"Did he try to find out about my holiday in Italy?"

"Uh, no . . . he didn't mention anything like that–"

"Did he try to get you to tell him about my staff here? Or did he ask about the garden?"

"No, no, nothing like that at all, Khunying. He just spoke to the girls mostly about school and their riding and, just stuff – I mean – just general . . . topics."

"I see."

Another long silence. There is an itch behind my left ear. I dare not scratch it.

"Well, I, uh, I better get back to the girls."

"One more thing. The chef tells me there is some meat missing from the freezer. About six fillet steaks. Do you know anything about that?"

"What? Oh, no, I mean, no, I don't know anything about that."

"Are you sure you didn't – see them?" She peers at me accusingly.

What on earth? Is she saying that she thinks I would steal steak? For what reason would I steal steak? No, don't freak out. She is just asking. She is not accusing anyone of anything.

"Sorry, Khunying, I haven't seen them."

"Yes, well," she says, looking at me slowly up and down, like a futuristic laser beam scanning my entirety. I suddenly wish I hadn't changed out of the sundress I wore to lunch. Or that I had changed into my darker jeans rather, the ones with the better fit – and a shirt that didn't have a picture from Alice in Wonderland on the front, all oversized arms and legs and head coming out of the little house windows and chimney. I feel like a child around her. A bad and poorly dressed oversized child, with arms and legs and heads coming out of the windows and chimney. Can't miss me!

"Jemma, I would like to speak to you privately."

"Um . . ." I say, looking around me uncertainly. We are alone; we are talking – I thought we were talking privately?

"Please close the doors."

I fumble around to find the back hook of the door, locking it to the wall, and finally manage to release it and close the door behind me. I notice there is another one of those strange trinkets hanging from this door handle too. The door bangs a bit louder than I intended as it closes and I give a startled jump.

"Sit down." She has that friendly smile again. She is actually quite human looking. And she is patting the sofa next to her!

I gulp quietly and slowly sit down next to her, my back as straight as if I had a metal rod sewn into it. I'm enveloped in a cloud of expensive-smelling perfume. Up close I can't help being mesmerised at her beauty once again. Her face looks like it was constructed by angels, so that old, tired, trodden, beaten, thirsty men could gaze upon it and be filled with such awe their spirits would be revived . . . I realise I am staring, and clear my throat, pretending to be very interested in an imaginary speck on the wall across the room, and sit up even straighter.

"Jemma," she coos, "I am very thankful for the work you are doing here. You seem to handle my girls very well, and I see they have already grown quite attached to you."

Really? Wow. Didn't see that one coming. But what about the Mongolian war lords and almost getting one of them killed? Surely she hasn't really forgotten the written warning already? But she is being so nice all of a sudden, all friendly like. I want to say thank you, but can't find my voice. I manage a small strained smile instead.

"And I am sure there won't be any more incidents involving silly out-ings where you get my girls lost."

There ya go.

"But now that I am sure you will be with us for a while, I think it is time to let you in to the inner circle. Fill you in on some of the more important family needs. The girls' needs." Her voice is washing over me like honey. Sticky honey. I can feel it clogging up all my vents and holding me down in a thick, sugary mind-numbing pool of goo. I start to feel fuzzy. Maybe this is it. Maybe this is the part where she snaps out of suspicion of me as a new employee, and welcomes me in with open arms. I feel the sugary fizz start to fill my head and it's making me giddy. I broke through . . . Cracked the shell! I'm in!

I wonder if I'll get a raise. There's a pair of Italian boots I saw at Sandton City . . .

"The girls' father," she breaks into my thoughts, smoothing down her cream pants elegantly, "is not to be trusted. He was awarded dual custody by a short-sighted judge, and so I have no choice but to let him see them when he is in town. And you handled today's lunch very well." Here she pauses and places a hand on my shoulder.

Holy crap. Contact! Her hand is warm, but after all the indifference, all the coldness, all the nasty comments, and now the friendliness, it just feels weird. She smiles directly at me and I feel myself being sucked into her beautiful clear blue eyes.

"But I believe, Jemma, he is plotting to kidnap them."

What? Wait a minute. What?

I feel her grip tighten on my shoulder. She's serious. This woman truly believes Alak, sweet, funny, lovely Alak, is planning the kidnapping of his own daughters. "I know you may be shocked, as was I when I came to real-ise his plan. But you must be vigilant now. Keep your eyes open at all times. Make sure no one follows you when you are in the car."

"Um, why would he want to kidnap–"

"Do you think I would make this up?" she flares up instantly, like the gas fire was just turned from level two to eight. "I was followed home today! I have all the security on extra surveillance and I am increasing the manpower at the gates. Do not be fooled by him. Evil lurks in corners. Bad spirits. That man is capable of anything."

I don't know what to do. I don't believe her for a second. She is obviously living in one of her books – a romance-thriller by the sounds of it. Crazy-ass woman hunted down by sweet, world peace type. From naming roses after her to kidnapping his own children?

Whatever.

"Uh, OK. I will be careful," I say, not entirely sure what she wants from me right now, but wanting to end this conversation as soon as possible. This woman is clearly insane . . . I can see the Italian boots disintegrating. After looking me over again, she seems to be done and lets go of my shoulder.

"Thank you. I am sure you will. And you will report all interactions with him to me, of course." That is a clear order, but almost as fast as the words come out of her mouth, I hear a voice in my head – the same voice that keeps calling Alak sexy – saying: Oh no you won't.

"I'll see you Monday." She stands up and walks over to the door, opening it and holding it for me. I follow awkwardly, feeling a little odd having her open a door for me. Surely I should be the one doing any form of manual labor? Well, at least she's dismissing me! Kidnapping conversation over, thank my lucky fairy-star-dust.

"OK. I'll just get the girls to bed, before I leave . . ." I start towards the staircase.

"Oh, don't worry about that tonight. You go on home. I will get the maids to deal with them."

I feel torn. I'm sure they won't read the girls stories in bed or recite silly poems. But I can't exactly argue.

. . . .

"Oh. OK. Thank you, Khunying." I feel more as though she has taken something away from me than granted me something pleasant, but at the same time I'm desperate to get out of here.

"And remember," Khunying says as I'm about to leave the room, lowering her head and staring at me so intensely it makes my skin crawl, "vigilance."

Chapter 13

· · · · · · · · ·

I decide to go to Sandton City on my way home, to kill some time. I need to start looking for something for Jason for our twenty-fifth birthday. It's still over a month away, but I like to be prepared with these things, and better do it before I spend on my emergency credit card. After all, I haven't actually had a pay cheque yet – it's going to be a while before I can splurge.

However, Khunying's dress code is proving to be more limiting on my wardrobe than I realised and I need a few basic items to help keep up a look she will approve of. But not beige – I will not buy anything beige. I browse around for some white and grey tops and maybe some grey formal pants. Ooh, and that really cute purple beret hat with the adorable sparkly baubles on top, but that's it. Nothing else.

OK, maybe just these pink and white tartan shorts with the matching pink and white tartan-trimmed tennis socks. I mean, I may decide to start playing tennis.

And that's all. Nothing else. I will not use my credit card – again.

But I must just get this Hello Kitty toothbrush bag – for Tas of course. She will love it.

And something for Lola . . .

But that's all. Really.

Oh crap, Jason's gift! OK, one more credit card swipe for this bottle of Kouros – his favorite. The gift set. Its only R160 more, and has a cool money clip in it.

And wrapping paper. And a bow. And ribbon.

And a card.

But nothing more.

Sellotape.

Gum – I need to make some change for the parking garage after all . . .

As I stop at a clothing store with fluffy waistcoats in the window and contemplate going in, I spot a pair of beige capri pants. Those would be perfect. They will go with a lot of the kinds of things she wants me to wear. And those ballet flats will match them nicely too! Beige, but with white polka dots. Polka dots are a good compromise.

Suddenly I hear a friendly voice calling my name. "Jemma! Jemma! Oh, how nice to see you again. I'm a lucky man, bumping into you twice in one day."

I turn to see Alak striding towards me, his smile gleaming like a movie star. Mr. Totally Hot! I feel my face flush but try to act cool. When he reaches me, he gives me a warm hug as if we are old friends, and my shopping bags bunch out at funny angles while I try to hug back or not hug back or what ever it is I am trying to do. When he lets go, I can feel my hair is a mess and suddenly remember my Alice in Wonderland T-shirt. What am I, twelve? I vow to get rid of this t-shirt – it's caused me enough humiliation for one lifetime. Twice in less than a twenty-four-hour period!

"Oh, hello Alak." I shift the bags around so I can get one hand free to smooth down my hair. I wonder if this is something that falls under the "forbidden" section in my handbook at The Palace. Am I allowed to talk to Alak when I'm on my own? Outside of the responsibilities of work?

"You doing a little shopping?" I ask, trying to sound casual, while internally wondering if bumping into the so-called kidnapper could be grounds for another written warning. With Khunying, anything is possible.

"Yes, I needed razor blades." He holds up a Checkers shopping packet as proof. He shops at Checkers? I thought billionaires were only allowed to shop, like, abroad or something.

"And I was going to grab a cup of coffee. How about you?" he says with a playful smile. "Looks like you have done some shopping yourself. Or are you stocking up for the winter?"

"Oh, no, it's just . . . this is just . . . Khunying sent me home early so I . . . Uh." I cut off, noticing Alak is trying not to laugh at my fumbling.

"I was – just – teasing," he says, smiling. "I am fully aware of a woman's right to shop – and I support it! Do you have time for a coffee with me? I'm flying to Hong Kong tonight, and won't be back again for a few weeks. It would be lovely to get to know my daughters' au pair better before I go."

Something resembling a catfight breaks out in my innermost being. A Jemma-shaped angel, complete with pig-tails and pair of goodie two-shoes is standing on one side, shaking her head saying, "Remember what Khunying said: Vigilance". On the other side, a devilish Jemma in a skin-tight black leather cat suit with a bright pink pitchfork is smiling seductively, saying, "Go on, Miss Daisy. Put on your best Cherry Monster and show us what you've got".

And the latter, as so often is the case, wins.

Sitting across from Alak at a coffee shop in Nelson Mandela Square, surrounded by cobblestones, I soak up the late afternoon sun in the courtyard. Beams of light soak into the towering, 20ft bronze statue of Nelson Mandela, giving it a fatherly quality. If an inanimate object could convey tenderness, strength of conviction, and the biggest heart possible all at once, this sculpture does just that. I feel relaxed as I order a latte. There are no formalities with Alak. We have been chatting about the girls, and all my feelings of flustered childishness have long since bid me au revoir.

He tells me about their last trip to Thailand as a family, and, I notice, doesn't say a single bad thing about Khunying. He barely mentions her, in fact, other than a few times here and there while describing parts of their holiday. Also, he never calls her Khunying but rather uses her real name, Nicole. It sounds weird hearing someone call her Nicole – almost as if they are dishonouring her indirectly. I feel a tiny flinch in the back of my brain each time he says it, like she's bugged my head and will know.

Alak also tells me a bit about what he does for a living (seems to do a lot of things really, but at the moment, freight shipping sounds like it's the number one priority).

His open, friendly nature is completely infectious and I find myself lost in time. A cup of coffee turns into two cups, then three, and then into a piece of blueberry cheesecake with a glass of water to wash it all down. I tell him about Jason, my new life here in Joburg, and even about Troy and Frederick. I'm amazed at how well we get on, given I'm just a nanny, probably about twenty years younger than he, and he is a powerful, important man with a title.

After a while, he leans back, stretches out his legs under the table, and folds his arms over his chest, looking at me quizzically. "So," he says, tilting his head to one side. "Tell me what you really think of the job."

Up till now, he has been just this big booming presence of carefree conversation. We weren't talking about the job, so I could pretend he isn't my other boss. But I guess I knew it was bound to come up eventually.

"I love it," I say, carefully. "Really. I mean, I love the girls, they are so–"

"I know you love the girls. I could tell that instantly. But what do you think about the rest of it? I didn't want to say anything in front of them at lunch, little mice with big ears those two, but . . . " He pauses, looking at me with such intensity I start to feel slightly hot under the collar. "How are things at the house? Are they treating you well?"

"Um, well. Kobus is great. He really has taken me under his wing."

I start to feel the catfight act up again. Angel Jemma is telling me to zip it and not say anything at all for fear of incriminating myself. After all, I've only just met this man. I don't know him. I don't know if this is a trap or not. I don't know how much of what Khunying said could hold some truth. But Devil Jemma is saying: "Khunying? That psycho? She deserves whatever I have to give her! Tell him all about the crazy house staff. Tell him about Khunying's mental mean streak. Tell him how awful she is to the girls. Tell him about the pictures the girls draw and she throws out! Tell him . . ."

I take a gulp of water, biding my time.

"And how about Suda?" prompts Alak.

"She's, well . . ."

Alak starts to laugh, and all the tension fades again. "Ah, is Suda being an old battle axe again? Oh dear. She can come across quite stern, but is a sweetheart underneath. I'm sure you will soften her up over time. She's been with the girls from the beginning, you know."

"Really?" I say, suddenly drawn back into the easy flowing conversational style from earlier. "And she came from Thailand?"

"Yes. She worked for my mother back home. Helped run a health spa at a five-star resort."

So she was a hot-stone masseuse! I knew it!

"But when Nicole fell pregnant with Tasanee, and my mother was selling the salon, I asked if Suda would like to come over here to help us out. It was a bit of an adjustment for her. I mean, she used to be the manager of the spa, overseeing all the treatment staff, cleaners and so forth."

OK, so not a masseuse after all.

"But she agreed to come here to South Africa and be our night nurse. She was their first nanny, but she seemed to be much more at home managing the house rather than playing with two rowdy toddlers. A lovely woman, but not all that 'child-friendly', if you know what I mean."

I nod, even though I don't really know what he means. Suda is stern, yes, but she is very good with the girls. Strict, but fair.

"She was my nanny growing up too – did you know that?"

How old is this woman? She has aged well.

"No, I didn't! That's nice, you have your own nanny looking after your kids now."

"Yeah, that's why I asked her. I trust her. Even back then I got the feeling Nicole wasn't going to be . . . well . . ." He looks awkward for the first time, and after a pause, changes the subject.

"Anyway, Suda was getting on in years. So we brought on the other staff."

"So, now that there is Ramie and all the others working for Khunying, doesn't she want to leave? Doesn't she miss her home?" I can't help feeling sorry for her.

Alak thinks a while. "I don't know for sure, but I sometimes suspect maybe she feels a responsibility to Tas and Lola. To me." He pauses and looks down at his hands for a second. Is that a flicker of guilt? He looks back up, right into my eyes as if opening up something very private. "I can't be around all the time because of my business. And even when I am in South Africa, it's not that easy to maintain a relationship with the girls with Nicole's – influence. But she isn't around all that much either, and they need stability. Most au pairs don't last very long, so I think Suda has stayed for them."

That makes sense. Suda has that mother hen thing about her, no matter how cross and bothered she seems. But I think about Lola and her feelings of aloneness and wonder if Suda is enough.

Alak smiles again, as if reading my thoughts. "Something tells me you are different from the others. I'm sure you won't be leaving any time soon, will you?"

I try to sound as casual as possible. "No, I don't have any intention of quitting." I decide to open up too. "I must admit, it can be a bit hard sometimes. It feels like I've been on a rollercoaster ride, without a seatbelt. Very scary on the downward spirals!"

Alak throws his head back and laughs again with his hands pressed to his stomach. He straightens up and smiles at me broadly. "Don't worry, you will work out how to deal with Nicole. Her bark is worse than her bite, trust me. When we were married I learned that about her. When she feels as if she isn't adding value, isn't contributing to this world, or at least when she feels people are seeing her in that light, she bites back. She used to have so much ambition, ready to rule the world! When she was helping at our corporate real-estate company, she seemed happier. After a while, she just gave up. Too many society parties, too many shopping trips to Italy. She's lost in life, I think, and so takes it out on those around her."

I'm so drawn in to the warmth of Alak's confidence. I know I shouldn't say any more, but can't help myself. He seems to be the only one who really knows what's going on. Something about him makes me trust him instantly. So I take a breath and say: "If she doesn't have a job, and doesn't really do anything with her time other than – uh – travel, why doesn't she want to spend more time with her own children? They would add value – caring for them is very rewarding. I think if she just spent more time with them, she wouldn't feel so lost. She would realise she is their mother, and that in itself would open up a world of opportunity to her feelings of self-worth. Missing out on them growing up – the daily interactions – that is something truly special and it makes me sad that she misses it all."

Alak is quiet for a while again.

Have I said too much? Crap. I've probably overstepped the boundary now. What was I thinking, talking about my employer like that? And to her ex-husband! I hold my breath and wait for the worst.

He is just looking at me. There is a softness to his expression, and he is smiling, his head tilted slightly in thought. He reaches over the table and pats my hand.

"You, my dear, are going to make a wonderful mother one day."

Then, thank goodness, he lets go of my hand and calls over the waiter to ask for the bill.

"It was lovely seeing you again, Jemma dear, but don't let an old man keep you away from your youth. You must have lots of fun things on your agenda for the weekend and your brother will be wondering what's keeping you."

"Oh, don't worry about that," I say, but start to gather myself to leave too. I offer to pay for my drinks, but Alak laughs and pulls the bill away from me. He slips some cash into the folder and hands it back to the waiter. "You have been very kind to keep an old man company. The least I can do is pay for coffee."

He is so chivalrous! Like my dad.

We discover we are parked in the same area, so he offers to walk with me to my car. I resist the urge to link arms with him.

On our way we pass a sunglasses store, and Alak pauses to look in the window. I stop with him, and look over the bright diamond-sterile displays. They seem to be using a water theme, and have bowls of bubbles, vases of shimmery liquid with sunglasses suspended in them, and splashes of glittery dewdrops all over the place.

"Wow, those are great," I say, pointing to a large D&G pair floating in its vase.

"You like them?" says Alak. "Let's go look inside."

"Uh, OK, sure," I say, following him inside. This is the part I don't like about shopping – when I see something I love but could never afford. Still, it's fun to look, and a man who is willing to window shop? Bonus!

Alak strides right over to the sales assistant like he owns the place. "Can I see that pair over there in the window?" The assistant brings out a pristine white box and opens it up to show me the glasses. They are really beautiful. A little on the Jacky-O side, and very classy. I put them on and look at myself in the mirror. I look good! Maybe investing R3000 in a pair of sunglasses isn't the worst idea, if I had it . . .

"You like them?" Alak asks me again. I turn to look at him through the lenses. The whole store has gone dark and he is filtered in amber. They are so much clearer than any glasses I've ever owned – they even feel smoother resting on my nose. I smile at him and strike a pose.

"What do you think?" I say, realising I may be behaving too familiar. Oops.

"I think they look lovely," he laughs good-naturedly. "You look like a one of those actresses from Gossip Girl. Suits you."

I laugh, imagining myself wrapped in something chic and exotic, smiling at the flashing cameras through my D&Gs. "You know about Gossip Girl?"

"I spend a lot of time on planes," he explains. "They all have re-runs on the in-flight." He smiles at me, admiringly.

Suddenly feeling hot and awkward under his surveillance, I reach up, take the glasses off and fold them up carefully, handing them back to the assistant. "Thank you," I say to her with a rueful smile. "They are beautiful, but we're just looking."

"Actually," says Alak, taking the glasses back from the assistant. "I think we will be taking these."

What?

"Uh, Alak?" I say.

"You need new sunglasses don't you? You were saying so at lunch."

"Oh, ya, I do. But, well . . ."

I'm too embarrassed to say: I can't afford these and will just be buying something cheap and nasty from a dude at the robots on William Nicole Drive. So instead, I say: "I just wasn't going to buy any till the end of the month."

There. That sounds like a normal mature response.

He just grins at me and puts the box on the cashier's counter. "You're not paying for them. I am."

"Oh no, Alak, that's very kind but I couldn't possibly–"

"Of course you could. My dog ate your old ones, after all. I need to replace them."

"Yes . . . but–"

"Resistance is futile," he says, waving my excuses away gallantly and handing over his credit card. "I owe you, and I always honour my debts."

I stand there feeling helpless. Resolutely deciding to blame it all on an out of body experience, I watch in slow mode as Alak's gleaming black card is swiped, and he signs the little white slip that says they're all mine. The sales assistant places the glasses into their beautiful white box, slips it into a silver embossed sleeve, and puts the whole package with receipt into a crisp white paper carrier bag, handing it to me.

I turn to Alak, still not knowing what to do or say. I smile shyly. "Thank you. So much".

"You are most welc–"

Ah, to hell with it. He was the one who broke the personal space boundaries in the first place. I jump at him and give him a huge hug.

"Thank you thank you thank you! I promise not to get these eaten or cracked or scratched or dirtied or–"

Alak laughs, steadying me at arms length. "This was fun," he says. "We should do it again."

"For sure!" I agree, eagerly. "I mean, the coffee, of course," I add quickly; I must sound so materialistic.

As we finish the walk to the car, I can't help beaming like a child on Christmas morning. Not only is Alak a wonderful, forthcoming man, but he's also so generous!

But, as they say, all good things must come to an end. No sooner than I've put the D&Gs on my nose, even though it's dark by now, and driven Peaches out of the parking lot, my conscience begins to prickle with something a little less comforting than expensive labels.

Chapter 14

"You're a lot more chirpy today than the last few weekends, Jem?"

Jason and I are fighting for mirror and basin time in our humble bathroom. I'm getting ready for my first date with Ryan – well, the first date we are having just the two of us. I'm trying to do my make-up while Jason is trying to shave. This place is so damn cramped – I never really noticed it before, but now it seems way too small for two people.

"I am?" I nudge him over so I can compare my eyes and make sure I've matched the shadow on both sides. I've tried something a tad less colourful than usual tonight, settling on charcoal eyeliner and smudging a shimmer grey into the creases of my lids.

"Ya, like you're happier. Did something good happen at work?"

"Not really." I'm not ready to confess to my newly obtained treasure. "But it was an interesting day. I met their father."

"Really. The father, huh? And? What's he like?"

"Um. Nice."

Jason stops shaving, hand halfway down his face, and opens his eyes wide at me in the mirror. I try my very best What? expression and avoid eye contact.

Jason narrows his eyes. Drat. He knows me too well. I've been dying to tell him all about Alak the second I got home, but have been hoping it would kind of slip out, nonchalantly, so he doesn't ask too many questions. Questions that make me ask too many questions. Like is Alak really trustworthy? Is he safe? Or can I become his friend, sort of, while keeping it away from Khunying? Jason would bring out all those questions and I'm not ready to face them just yet.

But clearly my plan is not working.

"Jemma," he says accusingly. "What do you mean, 'nice'?"

"We got on really well, and I think we could be friends."

"Jemma! For goodness sake. He's their dad! Not some new buddy to hang out with. You work for these people. You need to keep it professional. And didn't you say he and Khunying weren't on good terms?"

"I said she wasn't on good terms – he's totally different. Really sweet."

Jason rolls his eyes and picks up his razor again. "Ya, ya, whatever. Just don't start dating the guy."

"What? I'm busy getting ready for a date with Ryan, dumb-ass!"

"Could be dating two guys at once," he teases. "Wouldn't put it past the new you."

How rude.

"I would not!" I say, swinging from denial to protest in a dramatic loop. "Ever heard of the word platonic? Besides. I would never date Khunying's ex. She'd probably put a hit out on me."

"Or sue you."

Make-up done, I head into the kitchen and pour two glasses of wine. While I wait for Jason to finish shaving I stand in front of the dividing wall mirror in the hall and double check my outfit. Dark skinny jeans, and a long silver-grey three-quarter sleeve top. The grey make-up matches my top beautifully, and I turn sideways, making sure my butt doesn't bulge out too much with the low-hanging shimmering fabric reaching just below it. My socked feet stick out at the bottom of my jeans in pink knits with white hearts on them and I wiggle my toes in the reflection. I peer around the side of the mirror and over to the front door where I left the black knee-high boots I will be wearing tonight. Yep, they will go nicely with this.

Jason comes down the passageway, and I hand him his glass. "Cheers. Where are you off to tonight?" I ask.

"Just drinks with Troy."

"Troy? Alone?"

"Ever heard of the word platonic?" Point taken. I do wonder though. If Jason tells Tracy about her? Or if Troy even cares he's in a long distance, long term relationship? We are all friends, so I guess it could be harmless flirtation, like between Frederick and me, but it's not quite the same. It bothers me, but I try telling myself it doesn't mean anything. Or at the very least, Jason is a big boy and can handle his own affairs. I wrinkle my nose, defeated, and take a sip of wine.

"Alright, tell me about the father before Ryan gets here," he says. "I promise I won't tease you."

I tell Jason all about the lunch with Alak and how different he is to Khunying. "And, oh my word, Jason! You won't believe it!" I say, building myself up to a grand finale. "Get this, she believes Alak – nice, sweet, kind Alak, is actually planning to kidnap them!"

"What?"

"I know – nuts, right?"

"Well, I don't know, is he?"

"No, of course not! I keep telling you, he's really, really, really nice!"

"Really really?"

"Don't make me hurt you!" I glare at my brother, one hand on my hip and pointing a finger close to his neck. Jason laughs and takes another sip of wine. "I think he misses the girls, but definitely not in the way that would drive him to try steal them from her. He wouldn't hurt a fly, trust me."

Jason shakes his head and laughs. "Do you think she's a pot head? Like paranoid?"

"No, she could never be a weed smoker," I snort. "She's way too skinny. Definitely never gets the munchies."

"So then she's just living in her own soap opera."

"Ya – and these are the 'Days of her Imagination'!"

I wonder if I should tell him more – like bumping into Alak at Sandton City and the designer sunglasses – but my thoughts are interrupted by the doorbell.

This is why us millennials don't date anymore. We do the whole social gathering 'hang-out' thing till someone is familiar enough to pair off with. It's way less stressful than this date. First, he takes me to Sandton City to watch a movie, but walks me right to Nelson Mandela Square for a before-movie drink. The 20ft bronze statute looks quite different at night, bearing down on me with a questioning eye. Do I mention I was here earlier today with Mr Totally Hot? Of course not! I try to invoke the stoniest poker face known to man.

"Are you ok?" asks Ryan

"Huh?" I snap back to the present and realize a pink cocktail is in front of me – the waitress must have brought it while I was caught up in my inner struggle.

"You look – er –" he's obviously uncomfortable, and I don't blame him. I shake my head and laugh guiltily.

"Sorry! Just thinking about something at work. You know. Boring au pair stuff – I'll spare you. Anyhow. How was your day?"

Phew, he seems to buy that. He starts to talk about his day at the office, but switches gears quite quickly with "and then at the box, after work, I killed it with Karen…" Huh? Who's Karen? Oh, he's talking about CrossFit again. The next 20 minutes drag on as he rambles, and I can't help wondering back to the coffee non-date I had with Alak a few hours earlier.

"So would you?'

Crap! He's looking expectantly at me. I've no idea what he said, but he's clearly looking for an answer to something he had been saying. Snap out of it, Jemma! You're on a date for goodness sake!

The movie doesn't go much better. I let him choose because it's the least I can do to make up for not paying attention earlier, and he picks the most typical skop-skiet-en-donder available. Plus he refuses to get coke and popcorn – forbidden fruits for the fit, it would seem. Apparently his 'carbs' for the weekend are all being taken up with the one beer he had earlier. I mean, come on. The only reason to go to the movies these days and not just stream something, is the coke and popcorn! And now all I can smell is hot, fresh popcorn. Probably dusted with butter salt. Or the vinegar shake – mmmm, yea, that one is good. Or the –

Ryan takes my hand. I get such a fright I pull it away with a force that makes him jump. If we did have coke and popcorn it would have gone all over the place! Now I don't know what to do. He's sitting staring dead ahead, I'm trying not to breathe, my heart racing. What the hell is wrong with me? This is so not how to take a lover! And now it's been a few minutes at least. Each second that passes without explaining or apologising creates a cavity, a rip in the space between us. Tick tock tick tock, concrete buildings begin to topple and fall into the giant void, ground giving and the devastation growing. By the time the movie ends, I'm hot with humiliation and Ryan is avoiding catching my eye at all costs.

"So, uh, good movie," he says

"Ya." This is horrific. Worst date ever! I have to do something. "Listen, Ryan," I'm just going to have to take the bull by the horns. "I'm sorry. I wasn't expecting that. I kind of just – I guess I just – freaked out. It's not you. I, uh, I'm kind of shy…" I must sound so pathetic. I mean, I sat on his lap the first night we met! Well I didn't, drunk Jemma did – but still. She used my body so saying I'm shy must be the lamest excuse in the book. But magically, it's working. He peaks a look at me, and one side of his mouth turns up in an awkward smile.

"You pulled away so hard, I was impressed!"

"Impressed?"

"Yea, that strength! I was like – Woah chick! You'd be a beast at the box!"

Oh for the love of –

But I stop and consider for a moment. He's turned to me now, and looking at me with something more intense in his eyes. Respect? Admiration? It's nothing like the look Alak gave me when I was trying on the sunglasses, but still makes something inside me warm.

"Lets get another drink. Why not! I'll go for a 15k tomorrow morning to work it off. It's a Friday night after all. Is this ok?" He hooks an arm through mine and leads me back towards the square and I follow, a bit stiffly, but relived at the change of topic. Once again, Nelson Mandela looks down on me. Berating me. Telling me I'm a good girl deep down, and should try be a bit better to those around me…

Ryan, clearly encouraged by my willingness to be led by the arm, slips his hand down and gently grasps mine. I dare not pull away, but can't quell the indecisiveness inside me. How am I supposed to do this? I can't even hold a hand properly, let alone take a lover! What was I thinking… It's all Troy's fault. Troy and the Cherry Monster lipstick. Just then my phone chimes and I see a message from the devil herself. A thought occurs to me. If Troy is to blame, Troy is going to hold my hand through it. My other hand. "Feel like joining my brother and friends for a drink instead of here?" I ask innocently, showing him the text on my phone.

"Sure!"

I can't believe all of this is really happening. After meeting up with Jason, Troy and Frederick, one drink may have turned to four – and a couple of shooters – each one making the idea of Ryan all the more appealing. I can do this. I'm the new me! I have a great new job, well, it's ok I guess, but it has great pay, and I can feel myself maturing almost daily. I mean, buying beige pants? Who would have thought! The night starts to take a spinney sort of turn, and I realise I've had way too much to drink. Ryan seems quite liquored up too, swaying and drooping his eyes, which, admittedly is very cute. I can see why drunk Jemma was totally into him. But he begins to really put on the moves, and I have to dodge kisses and ass-grabs while still trying to stay on track for the new me.

Finally Ryan goes off to find the bathrooms and I drag Jason aside.

"What's 'm I goin' nu do!" I ask, swaying on my feet and spitting while I speak. "S-orry," I add, wiping my mouth.

"Do about what?" asks Jason, taking my drink away and handing me a glass of water instead.

"'Iss! 'Iss. Kh . . . iss. He is trying to kh-iss me!"

"Well, what do you expect?" he says, all brotherly. "You flirt with him all night and then you expect him not to try get some sugar?"

I scrunch up my nose. "Don' say that," I giggle. "You're my bwotha."

Jason laughs, and looks over to where Troy is dancing and seems to spend a long time thinking. Or maybe not so long, I really don't know any more. The room is totally spinning now and I hold on to his shoulder to take a break from all the standing on two feet I've been doing. He turns back to face me. "If you really don't like Ryan, you shouldn't be leading him on like this." Troy, as though sensing Jason was watching her, spots us and sashayes our way. She drapes a tanned, toned arm over my brother, and the other one over me, still swaying her hips to the music.

"Sealed the deal yet, babe?" she asks me with a wink. Suddenly I'm taken over by a wave of irritation. Who the hell is Jason to tell me not to lead Ryan on while he stands there, practically one with Troy. Just friends? Platonic? I'll give him platonic…

"s'nice of youuu to. Um. To. S'nice you think I'm leading…" my finger is out in front of me, jabbing at the two of them with a mind of its own.

Jason frowns. "You look really drunk," he says with concern.

"I doo?" I say, opening my eyes wide to show I'm not that drunk. "I don't. I don." I'm about to protest more, but give up, realising the roof now looks like the floor, which looks like the walls.

"And you're acting funny." His expression is wobbly, but I'm pretty sure it's not approving.

"Why are you drinking so much? You're usually fine. Suddenly tonight it's like you're a bottomless pit with a desperate thirst for tequila! You never drink tequila!"

"Yea, babe. You don't look great," Troy lets go of Jason and touches my cheek. "Such a light-weight. I'll get you a Red Bull. Sort you right out." She disappears and I squint up at my brother, who is staring at me expectantly. What does he want from me? I feel queasy and don't want to talk about this here in a loud club.

"What's really going on, Jem?" he asks again. Something flares up inside me.

"Tracy!" I slur, completely frustrated.

"What about Tracy," Jason looks taken aback.

"Tracy annn, an, Troy. You have sooooooo much to sh, shay 'bout me. Me. But you."

"Oh not this again. Troy is a friend, Jem. OUR friend. What's gotten into you? Trying to turn this on me to avoid having to feel bad for leading some guy on…"

"I'm not!"

"You are! You come here, all cutesie with him, and spend all night flirting while giving bat! It's quite a show you've put on."

"Really. Then why, is been long sinsh, shins, since I last heard you saying 'I love you' to her. To your grrrrl-freeeend," I elongate the word meaningfully. "But YOU an an, an TRO-"

"Stop!" His face seems to close up, and he speaks slower, lowering his voice dangerously. "Jemma, you're drunk. I don't even know what to think. What the hell is wrong with you? What's your plan?"

This is escalating quickly. I'm aware of a feeling I don't want to fight, I don't want to say the things I'm saying, but I can't help myself. Why is he being so awful and mean? My head really is spinning now. Why is he making me explain all this, in my delicate state! Horrible nasty brother. "If Tracy knows – knoooows," at the mention of Tracy's name again, Jason stiffens and his mouth sets in a stern line. But I keep pushing on.

"You knows," I jab at his nose, leaving a light scratch mark down the side. "Sorry – s'orry, I din mean," He steps back, folding his arms tightly. The move lures me, like the whiff of blood to a shark. I shout louder. "YOU knows what you doing with hers and her. An her… I'm jus' nervous an' an' I DO like Ryan…I DO like -"

His face thunders. "Oh really? So you need to drink half the bar just to prove that? No. You're shamelessly leading on a guy you have no feelings for. If this is the 'New Jem', I'm not impressed."

Wow, that was direct. Even in my drunken state I get the venom of his words. I look at Jason, feeling hurt by his rigidity. He usually isn't this horrid. But his face is completely clouded over with something so dark I feel a sharp pain in my chest. The dronk-verdriet starts to settle in and I feel tequila-tears well up in my eyes, stinging them.

"What's 't to you anyhow?" I begin to shake. I can feel all my defenses stand on edge, like a porcupine spine up in the face of an inquisitive dog.

Jason sighs and unfolds his arms, visibly trying to calm the conversation. "Jem, I'm sorry. I didn't mean to be - "

"Whatev'!" I shout and storm over to a couch, falling down into it and closing in on myself.

"Jem . . ." he says, following me. I don't look up at him, I don't answer. I just look away, out into the blurry lights and moving bodies. "Jem!"

"No! You don' und'stand! You don't know what 'ts like t' be me! You never got your heart broken." All my emotion starts to ramble out, fueled by the alcohol. Even the room stops spinning briefly and a moment of clarity takes hold of me. "You're inna perfect relationship wi' a perfect woman an' hav' a perfect job an' you make perfect money an' you hav' a perfect life an' you don't hav' to deal wiv' any thing! Ev'thing always works for you, but I'ma, a mesh. Mesh. MESS. You have no idea how hard 'sis with Khung –khhhung-ynynyning, in The Palash – doesn't matter where I go or wha' I do, shomeone is there to screw with me! 'N you have it - all togev'r! You don' know whatsh feels like being me, or new me! An' you've always been grown-up, grown, UP – you don't know what's like! You just don' know. An you don' care!" I realise I'm crying now, splurting out everything I'm feeling, even though I know none of this is Jason's fault. He looks quite surprised, taken aback by my sudden outburst, but I keep going.

"And you, you have a c-career an' I'm jus, I'm jus – I'm justa babysitter!" I bury my face in my hands, crying bitterly and feeling very sorry for myself. I'm not entirely sure why I'm feeling so awful; I mean, this started out as a particularly awkward evening, a laughable date I should be giggling over with my brother and friends about, I don't know why I brought all that other stuff up about the job. I shove his hand off my shoulder and look up. I'm as surprised as he looks. Do I really feel this way?

Troy suddenly enters my vision and I look hard at her, trying to get her to stay in one place as the alcohol haze takes over my eye sockets. She says something to Jason, but I'm not sure what. It sounds like "your face".

"Wha'?" I say, putting my hands to my own face.

She shoots me a glance, looks up at Jason again and leans closer. "Babe, what happened with your face? Is that a scratch on your nose?" I glare at them and Jason turns to see me screw up my eyes fiercely towards them.

"OK, time to go," he announces, pulling me to my feet. "Where's Frederick and Ryan?"

"I'll find them," says Troy, looking worried. "Meet you outside!"

"Troy! Wait, no, Troy! We'll just text!" Jason calls after her, but she gets swallowed up by the crowd.

A moment passes, as though he is trying to decide something. Then he makes up his mind. He lets go of me and says something about me sitting down again and waiting while he goes to find Troy. How could he abandon me when I feel like this? For her? For Troy? I slump back, suddenly feeling really tired, and I close my eyes for a second, trying to block out the spinning flashing lights. When I open them again, Ryan is sitting next to me, one arm around me and leaning in close.

"Hey there, sexy!" he says, grinning goofily. Wow, his chin is huge. He looks part-Neanderthal this close up. Behind his blurry face I can see Jason. Without thinking I lean forward and squish my face right up against Ryan's. My nose is completely bent sideways, blocking all airflow. My eyes are squeezed shut so tight they hurt. My chin feels instantly bruised by the hard protruding mound that makes up the bottom of his face, and his stubble burns into my skin. But I am determined. My lips find his and I kiss for all I'm worth.

Chapter 15

· · · · · · · · · ·

Something has changed. Ever since the fight, I have been feeling an overwhelming sense of gloom. As for Jason, even though the hang-over breakfast and miracle helper kit that awaited me when I woke the next morning made it clear he had forgiven me, I still can't pin point exactly how I feel about it all. Something is not right. Things aren't much better at The Palace. Khunying never seems to notice me, or if she does, it's only to give me a look that says, "Please don't inflict your presence on me, pond scum." The effort I'm putting into my clothing – no frills, no clashing colours, no pink – is falling on blind eyes. Unfortunately she's back to her normal, unapproachable self. Her attempt at winning me over with friendly confidence in the study after lunch with Alak was short lived, clearly just a one-off special.

I keep trying to convince myself I'm just reading into things and being too sensitive. But I've also noticed the girls fight more too. It became very obvious to me it was in fact the presence of their mother that threw a span-ner in the works. If she wasn't at home, they would play nicely together most of the time, run around outside with Bruno, squeal and laugh out loud and just generally behave like happy children.

When Khunying is home, though, everything changes, vividly and suddenly. Tasanee becomes more alive (though in a manner that is much

· · · · · · · · ·

too old and mature for her age), and both Lola and I seem to have the life sucked from us. Khunying is our kryptonite – a death-ray fun-sucker! If she comes into a room or walks past while I'm with the girls, whatever we are doing, Lola, who is usually a ridiculously adorable and bubbly clown, sidles up to me silently. She goes all sullen and quiet and sucks on her fingers, looming around close to me till her mother is gone.

But I keep trying to tell myself not to judge.

Besides, I've enough to worry about what with the disastrous effect that infamous night out had on everyone. Since that fateful weekend, I've had to screen calls from everyone, even Frederick, knowing he wanted to know what happened, hoping it would all just go away, kind of like the ostrich-head-in-the-sand tactic.

After getting the girls started on their homework and going back downstairs to get a few cooldrinks for us all, I pass Khunying in the sunroom; she is in her pink silk gown, pacing up and down shouting into the phone. I expect to hear her shouting about suing people, as is her usual mantra, but my interest is piqued when I hear her mention her children. "I don't care about the girls – they can stay behind. I will not fly cattle class! With all the peasants? Is that what you think of me? My flights are already booked and I am flying first class, you hear me?"

She turns and stares, her icy blue eyes boring into me. "What do you think you are looking at!" she screams, and I quickly run to the kitchen, almost falling over Jim as I come through the doors. I nearly knock a stack of boxes out his hands.

"Whoa, new girl! What's up?" He steadies me and laughs.

"Oh, hey Jim," I whisper breathlessly, gesturing for him to speak softly so Khunying doesn't hear us. "Sorry I, I just . . ." I feel completely panicky again. My nerves are shot, and after my recent drunken meltdown, I'm suddenly a lot more aware of the doom and gloom in this job situation.

"Don't worry, it's OK. You need coffee." He starts to busy himself at the espresso machine. I can still hear Khunying screaming on the phone through the closed doors, so I move to the far side of the kitchen, closest to the staff entrance. Or exit, as the case may be.

"I need to get some drinks for the girls," I say, explaining my presence but also biding my time before heading back past danger-zone-Khunying. I look up at the windows wrapped across the back of the kitchen. I never noticed how much like prison bars the grids on them look. I glance at Jim again, feeling a bit like a cell mate, and wonder how he has stayed here for so long. Maybe he just works the system. Ever since that day when I caught him in the Jacuzzi house, I've wondered how much of a good idea it is for me to be friendly with him. But at the same time, he is really nice to me and I'm glad to have a friend on the inside. Sort of. He brings over a steaming cup of coffee and I accept it with a smile.

Just as I take a sip, Khunying bursts through the door and I almost choke on the hot brown liquid. So it is possible to drown in a teaspoon of water, after all. I splutter and cough, trying desperately to catch my breath again while jumping up and grabbing the juice boxes Jim put out on the counter for me. Khunying scans the room, but her eyes thankfully fall on Jim. "Have you done the shopping yet?" she demands.

"No, Khunying. Not yet. I'm waiting for Ramie to finish cleaning the bathrooms."

"Well, don't waste time! Take Jemma instead. Go!" We both jump at the bark in her voice.

"Um, but the girls . . ." Khunying turns on me, her face hard. "They are upstairs doing homework . . ."

"So leave them there! You don't think I can deal with my own children? Go with Jim, they will be fine without you for half a second. Honestly!" She throws her hands in the air and storms out of the kitchen again, her silk gown flowing behind her like an angry sea monster, bringing the night sky over the day.

. . . .

165

"You drive, new girl," says Jim, tossing the keys at me and heading out the kitchen door. He leads me down the garden path to the garage at the bottom of the property and opens the door to reveal an old black Merc. It looks very stately, though a very old model and rather brick-like. Driving a new car would have stressed me out before, but now I'm used to it. I climb in to the driver's seat with ease and make the necessary adjustments while Jim packs something into the boot.

"I'm not new anymore, you know," I say as he gets in, while starting up the engine.

He turns to look at me, narrowing his eyes as if contemplating my situation. "No, I guess you're not. You have lasted well! I'm impressed."

"Thanks," I say while putting the automatic gear into Drive. From here I can smell him; a mixture of boiled spinach, sweat and too much cologne. "So how long have you been working for them?" I'm trying to sound like I'm just making small talk.

"About three years, Turn that way!"

"What? But I thought we were going–"

"Just turn! We are making a stop."

I turn down the road he is pointing to and follow as he directs me through more roads, into another fenced off village, around huge properties and finally we pull up outside a house that is not on as big a plot as The Palace, but the house itself looks just as spectacular.

"You wait here," he says, and jumps out the car before I can protest. He opens the boot and takes out the pile of boxes he was carrying earlier. Another man in a chef's uniform opens a side gate and I recognise him as Jim's brother from the Jacuzzi. Jim says something to him at the gate, and they both turn to look at me. They burst out laughing and disappear into the house.

After we get home from doing the shopping, I help Jim unpack the bags from the boot of the car and try to sneak past the sunroom just in case Khunying is still in there. I don't hear anything - she must be upstairs with the girls. I'm halfway up when I hear a door banging and Khunying shouting from below.

"Jemma! Jemma!"

I jump, turn around and run down the stairs again as fast as I can. I find her standing at the front doorway dressed in a fitted black polar neck and black skinny jeans. She is kicking off her platform heels, and I can see she has had her hair done so a sweep of sleek blonde hair falls over one side of her face. She must have gone for a blow-wave while we were out shopping.

"Jemma. That imbecilic Jim forgot to get me cream for my coffee. I just passed him now and he told me. Go buy some and bring it back to him."

"Oh, uh, shall I take the girls–"

"What's wrong with you? Go. Be quick!"

"OK, yes, Khunying," I say quickly and grab the car keys.

"Take my car. I need petrol. Make sure they fill it up properly this time."

"Yes, Khunying." I switch the keys for her Porsche 911 and grab my handbag and the petrol card from the hallway drawer. She keeps all the petrol cards and some extra cash in there for emergencies.

Once at the petrol station I look at the time. There is no way I can fill the car, make it to the store and back home in time to finish the girls' homework and get them ready for bath time and dinner. My phone purrs and I see mother's face appear on the screen – I can't take it now. Ignoring the phone, I look up and see the electric doors of the garage shop open and close. There is a fridge at the back of the store with fresh goods in it, and from here I can see milk and cheese through the opening doors. I jump out and go look for cream. Perfect! They have the one Khunying uses! I climb back in the car just as the petrol attendant is bringing my card and slip back to me to sign and give him a coin from my own purse as a tip. Khunying never lets me tip the petrol attendants with her money when I fill her car.

I rush back to the house, driving as carefully as I can in a hurry, and give the cream to Jim. "I got it at the petrol station," I say, while rushing back towards the staircase.

After getting the girls ready for their bath, I go back down to take Bruno for his daily walk around the grounds. I'm just getting his lead down from a cabinet in the kitchen when Khunying walks in. Her face is still red, probably from shouting so much. Jim looks up at her from behind a chopping board, but keeps working on dinner without saying anything. She walks over to the fridge, opens it up and takes out the tub of cream. She turns to face me, locking me in a death stare. I feel cold shivers running down my spine, and start to breathe a bit more shallowly.

"What is this?" she demands.

"Uh, it's cream, Khunying."

"And where did it come from, Jemma?" Her voice is coming out in a seething hiss, like a snake. I look over at Jim, but he is acting as though he can't hear a thing.

"Um. The shop. You asked me to get you some just now–"

"What. Shop."

"The shop at the garage. I got it while filling up your–"

"Did I tell you to buy the cream at the garage?" She is now rounding the kitchen counter in the middle of the floor and I start to back away against the wall of the scullery. I swear I can actually see steam coming out of her nostrils!

"No, you didn't. But I didn't have time to go to Hyde Park and fill the car so I –"

She hurls the tub of cream at me full force. I duck just in time as it hits the wall behind me, splattering cream all over the place. I feel the cold wet cream dripping in my hair and down the back of my neck as I crouch there, frozen in horror. Jim stares at me from behind Khunying, but turns away quickly and starts rolling out pastry.

"WE. DO. NOT. SHOP. AT. THE. GARAGE! WE. ARE. NOT. PAUPERS!" Her voice echoes all through the kitchen and windows actually shake. How is she screaming this loud? She has actually lost it. I am terrified. Her face is shadowed with pure evil and the malice with which she is spitting out the words is petrifying. She is standing there, roaring at me like a banshee, shaking her fist at my face and I think I'm going to pass out. This is completely insane! Firstly, doesn't she realise things at the garage cost more, so the word "pauper" just doesn't make sense. Secondly, what the hell just happened? It's like something just snapped!

"Khunying?"

She swings round. Kobus is standing at the staff entrance, staring at the scene in confused shock, a fresh cigarette still dangling from his lips. I scurry up and rush over to the sink, wiping cream from my face. This is it. I'm out. I am out!

"In the study, Kobus. Now!" Khunying barks, storming off.

Kobus disposes of his cigarette, passes Jim, eyes wide, staring from my cream-streaked face to the wall and back to me again. "Juslik! What the hell happened?" he whispers hoarsely.

"I have no idea!" My hushed voice is shaking and I'm desperately trying not to cry. "I bought her cream at the garage and she just went nuts!" No wonder he smokes so much . . .

"OK, OK, I'll talk to her. You go get cleaned up in your room." He scurries off after Khunying.

Oh, I'll go to my room, all right – I'll be packing my bags and leaving!

As soon as we are alone, Jim rushes over to me and starts mopping at me with a towel. I swat him away, not sure if I should be mad at him for just standing there when it all went down, or embarrassed he witnessed it.

"I'm so sorry! I mentioned you got the cream at the garage – I didn't think she would do this!" He starts to wipe the wall down as I clean off as much of the cream as I can from my face and arms.

Suda walks in and stares at the aftermath of the attack. She locks a gaze with Jim I can't interpret, walks up to me and silently wipes at a few streaks of cream I missed on my face. "Girls ready for you," she says gently, but doesn't comment any more.

I take a deep breath and head back upstairs. I will go and attend to them, but then I'm going to go pack my bags. I will leave tonight. There is no way I'm sleeping another night under the same roof as that psycho bitch from hell. She might try to kill me in my sleep next time! So I'll do what I need to get the girls ready for dinner and then I'm packing my bags and I'm out of here.

Hah! I said "bitch from hell", even if it was only in my head. Frederick will have to retract his Miss Daisy nickname now!

Yep. That's right. I said it. And if I can say the b-word, I can quit this job too. This is completely unacceptable. I don't need to be treated like this. I'm out!

I walk into Tasanee's room fuming, but my thoughts of an early AWOL are interrupted by sniffles. I find the two girls sitting on the floor hiding behind Tasanee's bed. They both look up at me, their baby faces scared and worried.

"Is mommy going to sue you? Are you fired?" whispers Tasanee, her eyes as wide as the comical plush kitty on her bed. They must have heard all the screaming from the kitchen.

"No, of course not!" I say, trying to force a laugh. There's no point in making it worse. I'll just calm them down and explain why I need to leave. A bit later. They look really upset right now – even more so than me, if that's possible. "I'm not fired, promise," I say again, trying to comfort them. All that seems to do is make things worse. Lola bursts out crying and Tasanee throws her arms around my waist.

"We don't want you to go! Why is Mommy so bad? We don't want you to go!"

"Shh. Don't worry. It's all fine."

But it's not fine. My heart is still pounding. That look on Khunying's face is still hovering in front of me, burnt into my eyes. She looked so angry – as if she was going to kill me! I hug both girls to me, trying to calm down my breathing. I take them to the playroom and distract them with some paper dolls. As I watch them dress the dolls, I glance out the window into the drive-about where I see Jim carrying some suitcases and then Khunying and Kobus come out. She climbs into the car and Kobus leans in at the window talking to her. As soon as Jim slams the boot shut, she drives off, leaving nothing but the dust of the unsettled cobblestones billowing behind.

"Play here for a little bit, OK? I'm just going to go, uh, see what time dinner will be ready." I go down to look for Kobus and find him sitting in the music lounge, his head in his hands. He hasn't even bothered to finish his cigarette outside, and it is still lodged, smoking, between his yellow fingers. "Kobus?" I say tentatively as I come in, hoping to talk to him about wanting to quit. In time. I need his advice about how to leave the girls. He looks up his face stops me from saying anything. It's as drawn and sallow as I've ever seen.

"Close the doors, will you?" he asks while walking to the drinks cabinet. He stubs out the cigarette, takes out another one, lights up, then pours himself a double brandewyn and gestures to me with his hands clamped over the burning therapy. "Shock treatment?"

"No, thanks. I'm still busy with the girls."

Kobus sighs heavily as he sits back down and takes a deep swig of the brown liquid. I sit next to him, feeling my whole body relax for the first time. Kobus is the only one who can make me feel comfortable in this place. He understands me, seems to understand how I feel all the time. He takes another sip, puts down the glass and turns to me.

. . . .

"I'm going to resign," he says resolutely.

"What? No! Why?"

"Why?" he laughs once, then again. Then he throws his head back and starts laughing maniacally. "Why? Liewe kind! You are jagging me right? Have you met Khunying?" He can barely speak he is still laughing so much. I stare at him in horror.

"Yes, but, but Kobus . . . You can't leave me!"

"Oh, you will be fine," he says, patting my hand. "She likes you." He downs the rest of his drink and gets up to go pour himself another.

"What? Did you not see what just happened earlier? She threw cream at me! I thought she was going to attack me and cut my throat with the empty tub!"

"Jemma," Kobus laughs, coughing as though he has inhaled all the contents of a burning building. He leans on the counter and surveys me, his eyes sketchy and a bit mad. "There is so much more going on than you realise. The divorce. The expenses. The lawsuits. Even the company is – well, it's not your problem. I shouldn't even bring it up." He sighs and takes another swig. "Everyone is under a lot of pressure. But, believe it or not, she likes you. She's mad at you because you are the only one she trusts around here. Sort of like hurting what's closest to you, you know? She feels most comfortable with you, so attacks you when she's feeling stressed." I stare at Kobus bewildered. I cannot believe what I am hearing.

"Kobus, she's been nothing but nasty and vicious with me from day one. She can't possibly like me!" I can't help feeling a pang of guilt about the tiara incident.

"You're still here, aren't you?"

"Yes, but–"

"Jemma. Let me tell you a little bit about Khunying and the staff round here. Have you not noticed how everyone has a uniform? Not you. Yes, yes, I know, she doesn't let you dress the way you normally would, but you still get to wear your own clothes. You are different in her eyes. Trustworthy and more on her level. You are the au pair – before it was all just 'servants'. She used to have night nurses and day nannies. They were all Thai. Six of them. She had them all working here like dogs, living in that maids' quarters out there, sleeping on the floor! She made their lives a living hell, and one by one got rid of them. Three were fired for various things, giving the girls juice in their bottles instead of iced-tea, taking them for walks in their prams dressed in the wrong jackets. She found the most ridiculous things wrong with them all the time and then one of them would do one tiny thing and they would be gone! Two of them quit on their own. They couldn't take the pressure. She kept replacing them, of course, but no one lasted very long. In the end she didn't bother to replace them. Suda is the last one left."

Oh. There seems to be a lot more to the story that Alak told me.

"And after Suda took over as head of the house staff, and stopped being the main nanny, Khunying fired the drivers and started hiring au pairs like you. Not a single one of them lasted. You are the first to stay this long. She likes you, trust me."

I take all this in feeling completely at a loss. Is Kobus telling me the girls have never had an au pair last longer than I have? And I've only been here for under two months! I can't quit now? I can't leave them too.

"She may make you bleed once in a while, but at the end of the day she is happy you are here with the girls. She trusts you. You and Suda. And me, I guess." He comes over to sit with me again.

"Makes me bleed?" I snort sarcastically. "More like wants my complete destruction."

Kobus laughs and smiles at me. "I used to work for Alak. He was a great boss - I was his PA at the head company here in SA. It was after they split up that she stole me from him. He is such a gentleman and doesn't like to fight. He gave her everything she asked for, including me.

"But I can't take it anymore. My wife can't take it anymore! She thinks I'm going to kill myself with all this smoking – you know I used only to smoke socially? Now I'm up to two boxes a day. Anyway, after the last incident where Khunying called me at home at 11pm, screaming about something I could in no way help her with, I decided to call Alak and have a chat. He has agreed to re-hire me in a new company where he is a silent partner. She won't know he's involved. If she found out, well, she would go bos." He laughs, uneasily.

"But then who's going to help Khunying?" I ask, finally finding my voice. "Who's going to help me?"

"She will find someone, no doubt." He gives me a strange look. "You will be fine. She's very impressed with you, you know. All the extra stuff you do for the girls. The way you bought those educational games and you've been walking the dog."

"Well, I didn't exactly have a choice." I rub my face, feeling completely overwhelmed.

"She probably would have had Bruno put down by now if you hadn't helped so much," he reinforces. He smiles at me, nodding, and then looks away, staring blankly at one of the elaborate collector art pieces on the wall. "I'm going to do it at the end of the month. But don't worry, I have to give her notice so I won't be gone that soon. I'll break the news to her as soon as she gets back." He says, still nodding his head as if needing to convince himself.

"Where has she gone?"

"Italy. She's gone for another ten days with her boyfriend."

"But . . ." I start doing calculations in my head. "But it's Lola's birthday on the twenty-fifth. Next week – she won't be here for that?"

How could she? How could their mother be so cold? How could she be such a bitch! And of course, now I can't leave them, not now. Not with a life like this.

· · · · · · · ·

174

"Oh, thank you for reminding me!" he says, snapping back out of his daydreaming head-nodding trance. "She wants you to stay here over the weekend, and to organise a birthday party for Lola too. Nothing big. Nothing like Tasanee's birthday in January, she said. And she doesn't want you using the credit card. You can use the money in the hallway drawer."

She normally only leaves about a thousand rand in that drawer. That won't even cover the cost of the food. "That doesn't seem fair? The girls told me all about Tas's party; they hired a whole zoo, practically, put up a circus tent, and had animals running all over the place – Lola was ecstatic and I know she will be expecting something just as great. How can Tasanee have such an elaborate one and then a few months later, Lola be thrown nothing but a, a dry scrap of a party? A bone! You know that will hurt her, she's smart."

Kobus sighs and pinches the bridge of his nose, squeezing his eyes closed for a moment. "I know it doesn't seem fair. But those are Khunying's instructions. She won't be here, and all she will want to know is how much of her money, well, Alak's money really, we spent. I have faith you will take what you have and make it into something special for Lola. You have a unique connection with that little girl, even more so than Tasanee. You will know what to do."

He opens his blood-shot eyes and looks at me again, a kindly grin spreading over his weary face. "And I will contribute to the party so Khunying won't need to know how much you spend."

I smile back at Kobus, but feel myself skirting along the edge of the sinking hole developing in my stomach. Poor Lola. Poor girls! No nanny lasting for longer than six weeks?

Well, I will be here and I will be the best au pair ever. They can count on me. And as far as Khunying is concerned? Forget her! And forget her puny budget for Lola's birthday party, too. Maybe I will use more money than I'm allowed, maybe I won't. Or maybe . . . maybe I'll just call Alak myself and ask for some more money. I'm sure he won't mind. It's his daughter's party, after all. And if I'm going to be sticking around, I'm going to find my own support here. Kobus is leaving. Jim is creepy, and seems to like to "tell" on me too. Suda is, well, Suda. Ramie . . . has way too much dirt on me.

But Alak is cool. He listens when I talk about work. He understands. He will be more than happy to help me out. And to help his child out for her birthday. Yes, that would be a good reason to call Alak.

Chapter 16

· · · · · · · · ·

"Please Jason! Pretty, pretty, please!"

"No! You've got to be kidding me. There is absolutely no way in hell I am dressing up as a giant yellow sponge!"

I hang on to my cell phone as if for dear life, pleading into the receiver.

"But you have to! I don't have anyone else who can do it. I can't hire anyone; I don't have enough money. And that woman left poor Lola with nothing for her birthday and I can't let her be disappointed. Please?"

"You've actually resorted to begging? For people who could afford to buy my whole life twenty times over?" I can hear Jason is trying really hard to take a moral stand, but isn't immune to my persuasion.

"I'll steal if I have to," I say darkly. "Don't force me to become a criminal."

I decide to leave my conversation with Alak out completely. No need to let Jason know I called him, and he was more than willing to put some cash in my bank account for the party. I didn't want to go overboard, though, so I only asked for money to pay for the materials I'm going to need to make decorations, a wonderful cake, and money to rent the SpongeBob SquarePants costumes.

"Pleeeeeeaaase, Jason!"

· · · · · · · ·

"Why don't you do it? It's your party. You dress up and parade around like an idiot!"

"I can't! They know my voice; they'll know I'm not the real SpongeBob."

"These girls will know it's not 'the real SpongeBob' no matter who's in the suit. There is no real SpongeBob!"

I gasp at Jason as if he's just broken the news to me that Father Christmas isn't real.

"Why don't you get your fake boyfriend to do it?"

"Ugh. Please don't bring that up." Jason's reasoning did get through to me and I realized I should not be leading Ryan on till I was sure of how I felt. But I kept on putting off having a talk with him, and then he went and sent me a "girlfriend" request on Facebook. I mean, isn't that a bit presumptuous? We're hanging out, not dating. Well, not since that night. I've been busy. Troy hasn't helped matters either, and has been eagerly provoking the cupid mania in him, making sure he doesn't give up on me even though I hardly see him. But in a twisted way, I'm starting to get used to having Ryan as part of my life. I answer his messages now, and strangely, we have some very pleasant conversations. As if we were friends. It's just when he starts trying to add some kind of cutesie thing in that I remember I'm supposedly dating the guy and need to end it. But it's so ridiculous! I mean, a fake break-up for a fake boyfriend?

"Jason, you do the perfect impersonation of his voice," I say, trying to get back to the point. "You would be such a great SpongeBob."

"I knew I should never have showed you that. Damn tequila!"

Jason listens to my pleading a while longer, and I can almost see his arms folded resolutely across his chest. I keep talking, ending with a thousand please please pleases until finally he gives in. "Fine!" he yells. "I'll wear the suit, but I am not, I repeat not wearing the yellow tights!"

"Oh thank you thank you thank you! I'm sending you a phone hug – imagine I'm flinging my arms round your neck and jumping up and down!"

"OK, where is this SpongeBob monstrosity. How do I get to the fancy dress store? I want to see what I'm getting myself into. And I suppose I may as well pick up the rest of the costumes for you then too."

It's Saturday morning – party time – and we have successfully transformed the first level of lawn and the pool deck into a magnificent, brightly coloured underwater sea world. I've been making giant cardboard cutouts of starfish, sea horses, sharks, bubbles, jellyfish and seashells all week long. It's been a fantastic distraction from my double life as a girlfriend-on-the-run. I feel some contrition that I haven't actually sorted everything out as I promised Jason I would, but, well, I wouldn't know where to begin, and don't have time to deal with anything else right now. I don't have time to worry about my ever-blossoming pseudo-romance; I have a Bikini Bottom underwater world to create!

The party has been a hot, hot topic, with phone calls flying back and forth between Frederick and I planning the whole thing. He has some amazing ideas, and I even manage to rope Suda in to help me build and paint a five-foot pineapple we have taped to the front of a table borrowed from the laundry room. We have covered the table with a huge yellow sheet and put a bunch of throw cushions under, as well as Lola's pink tea-party chairs and table set. It looks just like SpongeBob's pineapple house and the children can't get enough of going in and out of the cutout door, taking turns to sit inside, under the yellow-drapes.

I look around, feeling a huge sense of relief that it worked out so well. With all the help from Suda, Jason, Troy, Frederick and even Kobus, we have created the most incredible replica of the SpongeBob SquarePants TV world in the garden. And I spent so little! The paint was cheap at the Chinese store in Newtown, and I found a pack of ten thick black poster pens for twenty rand. I was so ecstatic to have managed to stay in my budget I did a victory dance right there in the store, making a bunch of strangers look very concerned and uncomfortable.

The food was easy too. I got Jim to bake mini-burger rolls, and defrost five kilograms of mince from the stockpile in the freezer to make some delicious homemade bite-sized burgers. He is now all set up at the Weber, grilling them under a big sign I made saying "Crusty Crab's Diner". Jim is dressed in a red velvet suit – who knows where he found it – and I made him big crab pincers to staple to his sleeves. The effect is perfect!

The most expensive thing was hiring the SpongeBob and Patrick costumes for the day, but it was totally worth it, I think, watching Jason and Frederick stumble around in their big foam suits. Children are running everywhere, screaming while chasing each other with butterfly nets and blowing bubbles. I found plastic fish-shaped bubble blowers at the Chinese store and bought a bucket load for practically nothing, so each kid got one on arrival as a party favour. And the butterfly nets were a steal.

The parents of all the girls I invited were really supportive too. When they heard I would be hosting Lola's birthday party and that Khunying was out of town, most of them offered to help supervise. I was so grateful because I was worried about having so many children running around the swimming pool. It's turned out to be the perfect sunny Johannesburg day, and everyone brought their bathing suits. It's all going so well! Swimmingly, in fact, I joke to myself, and laugh out loud. I am giddy with pride at a job well done, and when I see Lola's lit-up face, shining with delight as she comes out of the pineapple for the fifteenth time, I know it is all worth it. Her swimming armbands stick out from just below her shoulders making her look like a raven haired angel, glowing with a huge smile.

In fact, the only person who doesn't seem to be having a great time of it is Jason. I walk over to his ridiculously yellow square form and whisper: "Hey, how's it going? You doing alright?"

"I don't know what to do!" he implores, swinging his huge foam body round to face me, almost falling over in the process. "They don't seem to get my jokes. I'm not funny to them. They hate me – they love you but they hate me! I knew this was a bad idea, I don't know how to make kids laugh!"

I think for a second, and an idea occurs to me. "Just make a complete fool of yourself! Kids like that. It's the easiest and fastest way to get in with them. Go!" I trip him up purposefully as I push him away. Two little girls close by burst out laughing as he grumbles trying to get up in the giant square foam suit.

He turns to look at the girls in astonishment, and shakes himself comically going "Whoa. I think I split my pants! Oh, how embarrassing!" and sticks his hands behind himself, pretending to cover an imaginary rip in his pants. The girls shriek delightedly and a few more come over to watch as he mock sews up his pants while still covering up, going round and round in backwards circles. "Don't watch! This is embarrassing! It's private! You bad girls! How can you watch?" He falls over again backwards, kicking his legs up in the air as he rolls around on the ground.

By Jove, I think he's got it.

I watch, smiling as his awkward dance gathers a crowd. Behind him, I spot Troy over at the cool-drink table in her Squidward costume. She is leaning against a tree and scrolling through her phone. She isn't paying the slightest bit of attention to the children coming asking for drinks, but keeps reading, yawning and swiping, as if bored out of her mind to be here. Well, I guess she is in character.

I've hidden paper cutouts of the character Plankton all around the lower garden. The child who finds the most plankton and brings them back to me wins a secret prize (more cheapies from the Chinese shop). Frederick is gathering children, sweeping them all in the right direction with his enormous puffy pink starfish arms. "Hustle, girls!" he is shouting from inside his costume. "Shake those tushies! That means you, missy!" The girls follow him, giggling delightedly.

When it's time to go, all the children leave blowing bubbles and carrying balloons laughing. Once the last mother and child leave, Troy, Frederick

· · · · · · · ·

and Jason help me and the rest of the house staff clean up, going round the garden picking up pieces of balloon or cardboard or half-eaten cake and throwing them all away in big black bags. Troy and Frederick say their goodbyes and head home, but Jason lingers behind as I throw the last of the black bags onto the growing pile. His hair is all matted to his head, and he looks a bit exhausted.

"Do you want a coffee and maybe a tour of the house?" I ask him when we are all done.

"Would I? That would be awesome!" Jason says, eyes lighting up happily. He gets a new surge of energy in his step as we head up to the kitchen.

It's only after Jason leaves, and I see Ramie taking a black bag of something up to the maid's quarters, that I realize she had been in the house, as I took Jason around. Now I see the black garbage bag in her hand, I wonder what she was up to. She can't be moving trash in there; it makes no sense? Come to think of it, she takes things up there quite often. I won't ask her about it though – the last thing I want to do is rock the boat with Ramie. She's the only one who knows about my little indiscretion of snooping in Khunying's bedroom. I try to suppress a pang of guilt remembering the tiara. Tiara trumps trash of course. Every time.

Chapter 17

· · · · · · · · ·

I take a deep breath. Then another one. Then another. She gets back today – she is due to arrive any moment and I'm waiting for her, as instructed by Kobus. She told him she wanted to see me as soon as she got back. She's going to scream at me, I think. Or throw things. The last time I saw her was that day she went wild and threw the cream at me. Just thinking about it now makes me break out in a nervous sweat and my breathing becomes shallow. My phone purrs and I dismiss the call immediately – I can't chat to Frederick right now. My nerves are shot.

Deeeeeep breath, Jemma, deep breath. I'm sitting at the kitchen counter, freshly changed into clean colourless clothes, and am trying to focus on a spot on the kettle to keep my nerves calm. I look over at Jim who is scrubbing a big heavy pot.

A crackly voice comes over Jim's walky-talky, making me jump. "Big Bird has landed."

Breathe breathe breathe . . . I think I might start to hyperventilate any minute now.

I hear the front door bang closed with its usual thud. Then the familiar jangle of keys dropping into the porcelain bowl on the entranceway table.

· · · · · · · ·

Then a few seconds later, Khunying is standing in the kitchen doorway. I turn to face her, a strained smile plastered to my face.

"Jemma," she says, a strange pleasantness to her tone. "Let's have a chat in the sunroom, shall we? Jim, I'll have my usual coffee, and bring something for Jemma too, will you? Come along, Jemma." I am totally thrown. She's smiling, being nice, friendly even. I follow her into the sunroom and take a seat as she settles lightly into her favorite chair.

"Ah, it's good to be home," she says, closing her eyes and lifting her perfect chin, breathing in the air.

"Did – ah – did you have a good trip?" I'm not sure if I should be making small talk or not.

"Oh, well enough, thank you," she says, smiling at me as if I'm a long-lost friend. Jim comes in with the coffees on a silver tray, gives Khunying hers and hands me a cup.

"Thank you," we both begin to say at the same time. I quickly stop and look at her, as if I've interrupted her. "Sorry," I say.

Khunying laughs lightly, shaking out her perfect hair and taking a conservative sip of coffee. Something about her is suddenly so diplomatic – I'm almost more nervous than when I thought she would be flying at me in a fury. "How are you, Jemma?"

Is this a trick? Or maybe the Invasion of the Psycho Employer? Or is this a dream? I realise I've been opening and closing my mouth like a cod, but still haven't spoken.

"Um . . ." I manage eventually.

Khunying laughs again, her mystical charm filling the air like audio perfume. It's getting up my nose, making me want to sneeze. "Well aren't you the loquacious one today," she laughs. "Let me help you. I hear you threw quite a lovely party for Lola."

"Oh. Yes. Yes, I did. Well, not just me, everyone here helped out."

"I look forward to seeing the pictures."

I start to relax. Something about her smile is making me feel calm. I take a sip of coffee and allow myself to settle into my chair. Khunying is surveying one of her perfectly manicured hands, then places it delicately in her lap and looks up at me again. She keeps the same, inquisitive expression on her face, studying me. I suddenly feel really self-conscious and lift a hand to my face. Is something on my chin? Did I spill?

"You know, Jemma, you should dye your eyebrows. I do. It lasts weeks and really opens up the eyes. It could do wonders for your face. In fact" – she reaches for a notepad on the side table – "here is the name of the salon I go to, and the name of my therapist. She's the best. Give her a call and tell her I sent you, OK?"

I take the piece of paper from her outstretched hand as if in a trance. Keeping up with Khunying is a full time job! "Uh, thank you."

She sits back again and smiles at me. "You have now been with us for three months. I don't know if you remember but your contract had a probation period for three months, so it's time to talk about what comes next.

"So, I was wondering if you would like to talk about your future here with me and the girls?" She actually sparkles at me. Like a Disney character! I am dumbstruck.

Oh, of course . . . The light goes on in my brain.

She is only being nice because she wants me to sign a new contract! This woman is incorrigible. I nod my head slowly, processing. If I want out, now is the perfect time. I can just say I'm really thankful for the opportunity, and the past few months have been wonderful but I feel it is time to move on to the next chapter in my life and respectfully decline a renewal. Easy. Clean legal break. Jason would be screaming it in my ear right now if he knew – in fact, I think I have a miniature something sitting on my shoulder right now. It's the devil-clad Jemma, hot-pink pitchfork in hand pulling on my ear: "Run! Run! Think of yourself!" But at the same time, on my other shoulder, there is a little angel. Two little angels, actually. Dark-haired and bright round faces with beautifully slanty eyes. I have to stay for them.

But I may as well bring up some of the things I've been thinking about while we are here.

"Well," I say, smiling nervously at Khunying and taking a big breath, "Er, I would like to stay, but will we be looking at making any, uh, changes?" Like overtime pay, I think to myself, but don't say it out loud.

"Changes? Oh, of course!" she says, happily. "Anything. How would you like access to the Jacuzzi and pool?"

I can't help laugh. Quickly covered up by a fake cough. Even though she is being desperately nice right now, I still can't help feeling the complete ridiculousness of the situation. It feels as though we are in a play, just going through the motions. None of it is real. It doesn't actually even mean anything if I get her to agree to paying me for my extra weekends and overtime. It won't change how she treats me. She will get what she wants and I will just do what I'm told. She still has all the power, and could dis-embowel me with one look if she wanted to.

"Um, that's great. Thank you."

"Good, then it's settled! I will have Kobus draw up the new contract and you can sign as soon as it's ready." She starts typing something into her iPad. "We will make this one a six-month contract, shall we?"

I nod, a sinking feeling in my stomach. "Thank you, Khunying. I will be happy to stay on."

"Good," she smiles back at me. "Now, I have been invited to a royal affair at Sun City this weekend and will need you to accompany us. Please make sure you sign the contract with Kobus before then, and make sure you pack appropriate clothing." She has returned to a less-friendly demeanor. Business style. "And I need you to take the girls to have dinner with their father tonight. That is all. You may go now." She goes back to typing on her iPad.

"Alak is back?" I ask before I can stop myself. Her head snaps up immediately.

"Alak?"

She is staring at me, her eyes flaring, like she's burning into me, clawing away at my brain and extracting my every thought.

"Uh, I mean, Lord Khunch–"

She lifts a hand and stops me. After a long silence, she finally drops her hand and lifts her chin.

"Have you . . . been speaking to my ex-husband?"

"Oh, no. Er, no. I mean that is to say I saw him at that lunch when you told me to take the–"

"And that is all? You have not had more contact with him after I warned you of his intentions of kidnapping my children?"

"No! No, of course not!"

"And you still refer to him as if he is a friend of yours?" She says this last line sarcastically, as if someone like Alak could never possibly befriend someone like me.

"He, he told me to . . ."

"You will not refer to my ex-husband by his first name. It is unforgivably inappropriate." She stands up and starts to pace back and forth, raising her voice with force. "I've no doubt he told you to call him that," sweeping talons through hair, "the insufferable Mr. Congeniality that he is," muttering to herself, then she swings round to face me, one long pointy finger held up in my face. I jump back an inch and clutch at my chest, fearing my heart just jumped right out of it.

"I'm sorr–" I try in a tiny voice.

"But know this," she leans in, her nostrils flaring, "he is a wolf in sheep's clothing. Not to be toyed with."

"Really, I didn't mean to," I say, trying to inch away from this whole mess. I shoot a glance at the door. It looks so open, so invitingly wide! If only I could just . . .

Khunying holds up a hand, standing back and dropping her shoulders, and presses the other hand to her forehead as if feeling faint. Wow, this woman is dramatic! She should have perused a career in acting. She takes a deep breath, and then slowly lets it out and opens her eyes. Her look has changed from one of a cruel and crazy judge passing an accusatory sentence and has softened to a manicured sympathy.

She puts her head on one side.

Really?

"It's OK, Jemma. I will forgive you this time. Please just remember what I have told you. It will be better for us all that way."

"Yes, Khunying," I say, wishing none of this had happened. Why did I have to go and let that slip? Ugh. She stares at me for a while longer, then finally smiles and sinks down in her seat again.

"I am only trying to protect you," she says. Hah! "Now, shouldn't you be off to get the girls?"

"Yes Khunying." Finally.

The second I'm out the door my excitement returns and starts to bubble over. Alak and Sun City. Alak and Sun City!

As soon as I'm in the car pulling out the driveway, I speed dial my brother's number.

"Jason!" I shout excitedly as he answers the phone. "Guess what? I'm going to Sun City! To the Palace! Not The Palace as in where I work . . . The real Palace! At The Lost City."

"Jemma?" his voice is somewhat nasal as if he has a bit of a cold. But I'm too excited to ask about it.

"Yes, it's Jemma – who else? I'm going to Sun City! I can't believe it! Just when I was starting to think maybe this job isn't the best thing after all and maybe I wasn't cut out for it and maybe I shouldn't sign the new contract, just then, things get better. I mean, I've never been to Sun City before. I've never even stayed in a hotel before. This will be my first time, and I hear The Palace is one of the best hotels in South Africa."

"You signed a new contract?" His voice is stern.

"Oh, Jason, please don't be such a kill joy. Come on. Sun City!"

"Ya, OK, fine. I know. Sounds awesome. So why are you going?"

"Khunying is going up for some royal thing, and she wants the girls to come with her so I have to look after them. Next weekend! How cool?"

"Very cool." He goes quiet and I wait to see what else he is going to say, but all I hear is a somewhat muffled mull of office noise in the background.

"OK, fine, ask me about the contract," I say, sighing loudly. Honestly! My brother can be so serious sometimes. Way too rational ever to have any fun.

"Have you signed a new contract yet?"

"No, not yet. She spoke to me about it, saying my probation period is over and she wants me to stay on. She's going to get Kobus to draw up a six-month one this time."

"Did you ask for some changes?"

I knew he would do this. He's so concerned about the negotiation process. He has been going on about my extra weekends at The Palace and not being paid for any of it for ages now.

"Yes, I mentioned changes. She's going to look over it and–"

"So she agreed to the changes we spoke about?"

"Well, not exactly . . . But before you go on and on about it, please can't we just be happy for a moment, about my trip to Sun City? Please can't we just enjoy this for what it is? Just this once?"

Jason breathes in loudly. "OK, fine. Enjoy the moment. While it lasts."

"Thanks Jason!" I squeal, my voice once again filled with delight. "So what do you think I should take with me to wear?"

The girls and I are all dressed up and ready for dinner, and so here we are, standing in the front entrance hallway, putting our shoes on at the front door. I see lights shining along the drive-about, and seconds later a beautiful black Bentley rounds the fountain and parks in the valet section.

My nerves, which have been cocooning all day, suddenly rush to my tummy and a flurry of butterflies takes over my insides. Suda is fussing over Lola, who doesn't want her hair brushed. She has been chasing the raven-haired girl since bath time with a big ornate-looking brush, swatting away as if trying to groom a wild pony. "You must look good for young Alak!" she keeps shouting.

Alak opens the car door and leans over the top, looking at us all congregating as if waiting for the sighting of some hot celebrity. His dark eyes and wide smile emanate from his face like the painting of a saint. I can almost see the halo glowing around his head!

"Ladies!" he shouts warmly. "Aren't you a sight for sore eyes. What a lovely scene for a tired, over-travelled man." He was flying in today, so must be pretty bushed. It's so sweet of him to insist on seeing the girls tonight, even though he knew he would be jet lagged.

"My girls," he smiles, crouching to hug Tasanee and Lola. They both hug him with a lot more enthusiasm than last time. I smile to myself. This is more like it.

Alak is wearing a crisp white button-up shirt tonight, paired with dark jeans and a lovely dark charcoal dinner jacket. Which kind of matches my chosen outfit, I think with secret triumph. I chose to go with a dark grey fitted dress I used to keep as a back-up funeral dress, but suddenly looks extremely chic and Victoria Beckham-ish to me. It has a scooped square neckline and is hemmed just below my knees. Instead of my usual bare legs, I've paired the dress with sheer dark grey stockings and patent black Mary Jane shoes. I had to colour in the scratches and scuff marks with black permanent marker, but if you don't look too closely they look OK. I hope. My hair is straightened to perfection, and I'm wearing charcoal, shimmery grey and dove-white colour on my eyes. I'm hoping this look is more elegant and mature than my usual attire. No more Alice in Wonderland t-shirts for me. Especially around Alak. Kobus told me we are being taken to one of Jo'burg's fanciest restaurants, so I feel like Cinderella waiting to be taken to the ball! If old Cindy was a nanny and had two kids tagging along, that is. And her suitor was just a friend twenty years her senior.

Alak turns to me and smiles. "Ah, Jemma. You look absolutely beautiful." He leans in and kisses me on each cheek. I feel them flare up immediately and thank my lucky fairy-star-dust we are standing in the dusk outside with the light behind us.

Alak moves on to Suda – she is actually smiling! I don't think I've ever seen her smile. "Suda," he says, taking her by the shoulders. "My Suda! I have saved the best for last! So good to see you!" He wraps her up in a huge heartfelt hug. I feel a tweak of something resembling jealousy but shrug it off immediately.

"Young Alak!" Suda smiles. "You are so big!"

They switch to Thai and speak for a while, holding each other's hands the whole time. It's very sweet to watch and I stand on the side quietly, with both girls next to me, a hand on each of their shoulders.

Finally, after kissing Suda and hugging her about five more times, Alak swings back toward us and opens his arms wide. "Shall we go?" he says, his broad chest accentuated in the porch light. As we get to the car he bounds forward comically and opens the back door. "M'ladies," he says, tipping an imaginary hat as the girls climb in giggling. Before I can open my own door, he steps forward and opens it for me. I thank him, feeling a little embarrassed, and slip in, making darn sure to keep my knees closed the way Mom taught me!

The dinner goes by like a beautiful song being played by the most exquisite orchestra ever. Every single thing is perfect. The food is amazing, the table is immaculate, the conversation is fun and free flowing and the four of us laugh and talk our way through all five courses like a happy family. I forget myself a few times, feeling so familiar with these people I need to remind myself that I work for them. Alak offers me a top up of wine and I accept graciously – after all, we are both grown-ups here and I'm not driving. The girls sip their Appletizers from wine glasses like proper little princesses and I can't help laughing at their table manners. Tasanee is of course as poised and polished as ever, but Lola keeps making mistakes, like knocking over the salt and dropping her fork on the floor. A stuffy waiter rushes over every time she does something and corrects it in such a flash we start to whisper that we should keep doing things to see if he keeps it up all night!

After the final course, Alak leans forward and lowers his voice. "Who would be interested in ditching this restaurant and going to Monte Casino for some ice-cream?" he says in a secretive half-whisper.

"Oh me, me, me!" squeal Lola and Tasanee together, bumping the table and causing a huge crash as Tas's glass falls to the floor.

"Oops," she says, her eyes wide and her mouth in a small O shape. Lola bursts out giggling as the ever-ready waiter arrives at Tasanee's side, picking up the pieces of broken glass and actually apologising to her, as if it was all his fault.

I take Tas and Lola off to the bathroom as Alak sorts out the bill, making sure we are all cleaned up and ready for part two of this wonderful evening. I look in the mirror, smiling at my reflection – I still look sufficiently grown up, though my cheeks are a permanent pink colour thanks to all the smiling and bubbly feelings. Maybe the wine has added a glow too . . .

A tall blonde woman is washing her hands at the basin next to me, and I see her smiling at us as I pick Lola up to help her wash her hands.

"Your daughters are beautiful!" she says, taking a rolled up towel out of a basket on a side table.

I turn and look at the woman, speachless. How could she possibly think they belong to me? They don't look a thing like me! I'm about to say, "Thank you, but they are not mine" when another woman bustles in, cutting me off.

"Debs!" she says to the blonde woman, "We have a situation. Trevor says you are thinking of going skiing in Argentina this year rather than in Italy!"

The ski crisis is far more interesting than my answer, so I don't bother trying to correct her. I take the girls by the hands and lead them back out the bathroom.

"A lady thought Jemma was our mommy!" says Lola to Alak as soon as we get to him. I think my face is going to burn right off. Awkward!

"Really?" says Alak, cocking his head on one side and looking at me, seemingly filled with amusement.

"I, uh, I tried to tell her I'm not," I stammer in quick explanation. Alak laughs and waves it off.

"You are very nurturing and loving with them," he says. "It's no wonder she thought you were their mother."

A wave of pride fills me and the glow expands all the way to my toes.

When we reach Monte Casino, the girls go running off with their ice-creams into Game Cave next to the movie house. Alak and I follow behind, looking up at the magical indoor sky painted on the roof, and slowly eating our own treats. I chose a frozen yogurt scoop in a cup with hundreds-and-thousands sprinkled on the top, and Alak went for a chocolate brownie. We walk in silence for a while; a comfortable silence, I think. It's amazing how easily we get on. He reminds me of an old movie hero. I enjoy his company so much.

When we catch up to the girls, Lola is trying to bop gofer heads down with a giant red sponge mallet, while eating her ice-cream at the same time. We laugh as she knocks one of the gofers down, takes a desperate lick, knocks another one, takes another lick, knocks, licks, knocks again.

"She's amazingly coordinated tonight." I say. "Usually she can't get a hand to her mouth without spilling something on herself along the way."

"True," agrees Alak. "But I guess the ice-cream is too good to waste by spilling. Well they are going to be busy for a while. Shall we go and sit down?"

"Sure." I look around. "Where should we sit?"

"How about there." Alak is pointing towards a snug corner in the game cave where some cushy-looking couches are scattered round a big TV screen, showing cartoons. I settle on one of the seats happy to get off my feet. These Mary Janes may look wonderfully grown-up and sophisticated, but man do they hurt my feet.

"This has been a lovely evening," says Alak, choosing a giant green beanbag and stretching out on it. He looks completely comfortable and at home. Here is this amazing man, so mature and established – a Lord for goodness sake – and he is sitting in a children's play centre on a poufy beanbag! I laugh to myself, thinking about my meticulously planned out-fit for tonight – the one that was meant to convey the message of 'I am a woman, not just a nanny' – and here we are lounging around in the Game Cave watching Finding Dory.

"What's so funny?" Alak asks, a hint of tease in his voice.

"Oh, you know," I say, trying not to sink too far down on the cushions in my fitted dress. "This."

"What 'this'?" he says, smiling sleepily. "Did I spill something?"

"No!" I laugh, feeling completely at ease. "It's just strange how we ended up here – in the Game Cave! I mean, I never expected you even to know about this place."

"Are you kidding me?" Alak leans forward. "With those two around?"

"So you do things like this often?"

"My dear, I know you are the professional here, and can pull a SpongeBob SquarePants birthday party out of your magic Mary Poppins handbag at a moment's notice, but I'm not so out of it myself, you know." He winks at me.

"Oh really?" I raise an eyebrow.

"For an old man, I know a lot about fun places for kids to go." He pretends to count off on his fingers. "I've done Gold Reef City, WildWaters in Boksburg, Loop-de-loop Land out Randburg way, Build-a-Bear at Sandton City, the . . ."

"OK, OK," I laugh, putting up my hands. "You got me! I never expected it, but you definitely know the inside-outs of kid world!"

"The truth is," he says, leaning even further forward and gesturing for me to come close. "I have a little secret."

"You do?" I say, lowering my voice to match his.

"I do indeed. You see, deep down, under this terribly boring exterior, I'm still a kid myself."

I laugh. How is it possible he was ever with Khunying? "Well, you're the biggest kid I've ever seen."

Alak throws his head back and laughs heartily. "Ah, Jemma, you are a delight. And you have just reminded me." He takes out his BlackBerry and starts to type into it. "I wanted to put some money in your account for these kinds of things."

"Oh. What do you mean?" I'm feeling awkward. Money in my account? He already gave me money for the birthday party, but that's over now.

"To take the girls on outings. When I can't be around."

"Oh. Well, actually," I start to explain, feeling bad for having to confess, "I'm not allowed to take them on outings." I decide not to tell him the reason why, as I have not mentioned the whole Mongolian warlord incident to him yet.

"Because of losing Tasanee at Hyde Park?" he asks, stopping typing and looking at me, a small frown on his forehead.

Crap. He knows!

"Well, yes. Khunying forbid me to take them anywhere after that."

Alak shrugs his shoulders. "Their school holiday is coming up soon, and I'm the one who pays your salary. And I am saying you are free to take them where ever you want. Five-thousand rand should do it?"

"Oh!" I say, processing all this information. So he pays me? He is actually my employer? Which makes Khunying just my sort of manager? I like the sound of this! He finishes tapping on his BlackBerry and puts it back into his pocket, leaning back in his beanbag and putting his arms behind his head. I hear my phone purr in my handbag, signalling the transfer going through. I decide not to look at it right now in front of Alak.

"Thank you," I say instead, leaning back too. "I will make sure they have a wonderful holiday!"

Alak smiles over at me. "I know you will. And there is a little extra in there for you to enjoy too," he says. "Would you look at that fish! It's the funniest thing!" he adds, looking at the screen and ending the conversation.

I accept he doesn't want to talk about the money anymore and settle back to watch some of the cartoon with him. After a while he shuffles in his seat.

"So tell me, how have things been since I last saw you? At the house, I mean. Any better?"

I wonder how much I should tell him. We are getting along so well, as though he were a friend rather than an employer, so I decide to let him in on a few of the things that have happened. Eventually, completely encouraged by the flow of our conversation, I decide to tell him about the cream attack in the kitchen. He doesn't look shocked at all, and I'm slightly surprised at how normally he takes the news.

"But you are OK? She left it at that?"

"Well, yes," I say, feeling guilty about my thoughts of quitting that day. "But it was a bit of a shock."

"Of course," he says, but doesn't offer any more comment. After settling back down in the poufy seats again, I peak at him out the corner of my eye as we both watch the screen. I'm completely intrigued by this man. I wonder how it is he never says anything bad about Khunying. He must know how crazy she is; he must have experienced some of her most insane moments first hand. They are divorced, after all! There must have been a reason. Eventually I let my curiosity get the better of me.

"So, Alak," I say, plying bravely with my words. "How is it that you never say anything bad about Khunying?"

He looks at me for a while, then over at the girls playing their games. "Positive energy is not something that comes easily. But it is the only thing that keeps things in balance. So I work for it in my mind, all the time. And with my words. Do you understand what I mean?"

"I think so," I say, not entirely sure.

He seems to read the underlying confusion in my voice and continues: "You see, Jemma. Many good things have happened in my life. I worked hard for them, but at the same time I was in a fortunate position. All that together gave me a life most men envy. But I started to let it all go to my head, started to become arrogant." He pauses, as if thinking hard about what he is saying. "I thought I could have it all, that I deserved it all – like the Kennedys." He looks at my blank expression and adds, "Or the Obamas." Ah, ok. "When I was studying at Oxford, I admired these kinds of power families. They had everything. Power. Money. Family. I thought to myself I would have that one day too. The perfect family and the title and the success. I took it when I saw it, for the wrong reasons.

"Perhaps it was my arrogance that attracted negative influences to my life. My ego led me to places where I didn't find happiness, but ended up finding. . . When I left, I knew I had to accept my mistakes and move forward. I realised even though they would always be a part of me and they would always make up parts of my life story, they were now over. I had to let go. I could not let them keep eating at me, or I would find one day I would have nothing left. Not possessions, but the important things. Love. Freedom. Happiness."

I listen to him speaking, his voice lulling me; calm and clear like a Buddhist monk teaching me the way of life.

Then he shrugs his shoulders, his voice going back to its usual confident self. "So if I speak bad things, and think bad things, I will be feeding the bad pasts with my attention. Not a good use of my energy. So I try to feed only the good."

I actually get that. Maybe it was the third glass of wine, but somehow I totally understand what he means. I'm nodding my head slowly while listening, lost in the trance of it all, and then realise he has stopped speaking.

"Oh, you don't feed the trolls," I say snapping out of my introspective thoughts. Alak bursts out laughing, and I cant help but return his smile and laugh too.

"Well," he says, smacking his hands to his knees and standing up. "I think we should probably get these two home, don't you? It's long past their bed time, I'm sure."

"Oh, yes," I say, getting up too. "Yes, it is."

On our way out of Monte Casino, the girls decide to make a chain with both Alak and me, standing between us and linking hands. As the four of us walk along, there is a strange something in the air between us, as if enjoyment and happiness is crackling between and all around us like positively charged electrons in a lightning ball . . . Or how ever that thing works.

Just as we come around the corner, heading towards the parking garage, I see a face I did not expect to see tonight. The last person on my mind! Ryan.

He sees me too, and comes straight for us, a big smile on his face. Oh no. Not now.

"Jemma!" he says, disentangling my hand from Lola's with a big unwelcome hug.

"Oh, hi, Ryan," I say, stepping backwards and releasing myself. Ryan looks at the girls stupidly as if not knowing who they could possibly be.

"A friend of yours?" he says to me, his eyes falling on Alak at the end of the hand-holding train.

"Oh, uh, actually . . ." I begin.

"Alak," says Alak, stepping forward with one hand outstretched.

Ryan looks skeptical, but takes his hand, shaking it gingerly. "Ryan." He says. "I'm Jemma's–"

"Friend!" I say quickly. "Ryan is my friend, uh, and I should just, uh," Ryan looks at me, confusion all over his face. "Ryan, these are the girls I look after," I say, trying to ward off questions and hurry things along. "And Alak is their father. We are actually just leaving. Pretty late for the girls to be out, you know," and I start to edge away, taking Lola by the hand again.

"But," says Ryan.

"Chat soon though! I'll text you, OK?" I call and move us all towards the parking and away from Ryan.

As soon as he is out of earshot I apologise to Alak: "He's just this guy I know – a friend of a friend –" I laugh, nervously. I really don't know why I didn't just say he's someone I'm seeing. That would have been a very grown up thing to say.

Alak looks at me curiously, but fortunately doesn't say anything more about it. Thank goodness! I do not want to explain this one to him.

After putting the girls in bed, I go to my room and take out my phone. A few messages came through during the evening but I didn't bother to look at any of them, not wanting to seem rude around Alak. Now I see there is one from Frederick demanding a full account of the invitation to Sun City, one from my mother worrying that I haven't called her in forever (even though it hasn't even been two weeks), one from Ryan saying he doesn't know why I ran off so quickly and didn't want to speak to him but he guesses I was working and will chat to me soon, and one from the bank. Oh yes! The transfer! I open the text message and look at the screen.

Wow.

Chapter 18

A s the week goes by and I don't hear anything more from Khunying, so I wonder if things are settling to a level of normality in The Palace. The girls and I see Alak twice more for daytime visits while he is in town, but Khunying doesn't try to get me to give her any more information about him. I see another swishy signature memo has been placed on my bed. Even though I saw her car parked out front, and heard her shouting at someone on the phone down her wing as I walked past. Honestly, she's not away on a trip overseas, she's right here! Couldn't she just call me or wait to talk to me when she sees me like a normal human being?

I pick up the memo, dumping my handbag and cell phone on the bed, and flop down to read it. It's a list of things I can and cannot wear on our trip. My phone purrs so I grab it and answer.

"Hey Frederick!" I say, while resting back on my pillows. "Sorry I never called back before. Just been really busy."

"Good Gaga, child. Hardly important in light of the news I hear down at the docks. You are off to live it up with royalty at The Real Palace this weekend?" he asks. "I hope you have your camera ready. I want a picture of Prince Harry!"

"Yes, I'm off to The Real Palace. Though I don't know that Harry will be there. But who cares about Harry – I'm going to The Real Palace!" I sing. "In fact, I'm looking at my list of things I can and cannot wear as we speak."

"Your what?" Frederick loves a scandal more than life itself. I roll over and flatten the memo out on the bed so I can read a bit to him.

"Bare midrift tops will not be permitted," I read from halfway down the page. "I mean, I never wear bare midrift tops at work, why would she think I would suddenly start wearing them?"

"It's Sun City. Makes people do crazy things," he offers.

"Absolutely NO cleavage. Underlined three times! OK, trying to make a point there, Khunying. Got it."

"And why no cleavage? What's the point of being female if you can't flaunt some button-popping bosom every now and again?"

"Well, she underlined it three times. So whatever the reason, I better cover up like a good little Amish au pair."

"Well, you do know how to wear a decent Amish hemline . . ."

"Pha!" I spit in mock protest. "Oh, get this!" I say, reading further down the memo. "No make-up unless it matches your natural skin tone perfectly."

"What is her thing with you and make-up?"

"Oh, and my shoes need to be un-scuffed, and tire-track and lace free!"

"Lace?"

"Tire track?" I can't hide my incredulity.

"I'm guessing that's the long and pompous way of saying no sneakers. Or military boots with laces."

"Ah, ok. I see. But it's as if she half-expected me to pack as though I'm going on a camping weekend! Of course I won't wear boots. We are going to Sun City. It's going to be super hot! I'm only packing my slops . . . oh wait . . . no. Nope. Scratch that."

"What?"

"Point number twenty-four: No Slops."

After sufficiently exhausting the topic with Frederick, I say goodbye, hang up and dial Jason's number to start all over and complain bitterly to him about my dress code restrictions.

"Anyhow," says Jason a few minutes and complaints later, "so you won't be here at all this weekend? Not even Sunday?"

"No, we are only driving back late Sunday, I think. So I may as well stay here. How come?"

"Troy wanted to meet up with us. But I guess I'll tell her you can't make it. Maybe next weekend."

Why didn't she just message me? "Oh. Ya, tell her sorry. Next weekend."

"And what about your fake-boyfriend?" Drat. I really wish that would all just go away! I better come up with a story for Jason quickly.

"Actually, I bumped into him this week. While out with Alak and the girls."

"You didn't tell me you went out with Alak?"

"Oh, didn't I? Must have forgotten. Anyhow, I bumped into Ryan while we were out, and kinda told him I don't want to date him anymore. So I think I'm just going to kind of let that settle for a while."

"You did, did you?" he says, disbelievingly. Damn Jason! How does he always know what I'm up to, even when I don't tell him?

"Yes," I lie, defensively. "Anyhow, back to this letter from Khunying."

We are all packed and ready for Sun City. Khunying has decided to/ drive, so I sit in the back with Lola as Tasanee has naturally already claimed shotgun. Khunying drives like a bat out of hell, and I try my best not to notice all the chances she takes with oncoming traffic every time another car dares to be in front of her on the road and she must take over. Not even the beautiful surroundings, as urban turns to rural, and sub-saharan land-scapes open out across the horizon, work to calm my nerves.

Thankfully, we arrive at the promising gates of Sun City in one piece. The sound of beating drums fills the air with African welcome and the jungle-like greenery gives way to reveal The Palace, Jewel of The Lost City. When she finally stops in the drive-about of the hotel, a red-coated door-man runs up to let me out of the satanic blue death trap. I step out of the back seat with wobbly legs as Khunying sashays around the car, handing the keys to another red-coated man. "Do give it a wash, will you?" She sounds as though she has marbles in her mouth, faking a posh accent. "Dreadful journey up here. So dusty."

She says the word, almost in accusation, as though it's all his fault. And what's with the sudden accent? Is that meant to be British? While we wait for our bags to be off loaded, I look up at the golden and tan-zanite domes glinting in the sun. I remember once hearing of this being part of Africa's Golden Triangle. Lola and I follow Khunying and Tasanee into the enormous front entranceway – I can't believe I'm standing in The Palace – The actual Palace, at Sun City! Lola clings to my hand as we are led to the check-in desk where we are greeted as if we were their most esteemed guests. We hover next to a zebra skin sofa trimmed in gold while Khunying goes off to the side with the concierge and speaks to him quietly for a moment. I notice the body language. The flick of hair, breezy smile, a light laugh. And then contact – the foolproof touching of the arm while asking for the thing she wanted. Damn, she's good.

We are taken to our rooms – Khunying has rented two suites on the top level. She pauses at the door of my suite and directs me. "Change them into those adorable new outfits I bought them from Italy, and make sure Lola brushes her hair." She glances over at Lola sternly. "And for goodness sake, wash the child's face! I don't know how you get so dirty, Lola, you are a disgrace!"

Lola is expressionless, a blocked-out nothingness she has taken to using when her mother speaks to her like this. I put my hand behind her back and give her a warm squeeze, drawing her a bit closer to me.

"Oh, Tas, you won't disappoint me, will you?" Khunying has adopted the air of persecution. "Now go and get ready. We are all going to meet the Prince! I've been told he will be arriving shortly and we are going to be down in the lobby ready to greet him."

A prince? Oh, so that's what this is all about! I actually think I just saw a girlish smile flash across her face. It wasn't clear, and so quick I would have missed it if I had blinked, but I'm ninety nine-percent positive I just witnessed Khunying displaying an emotion other than cool indifference or spitting anger.

If it's Prince Harry I will have to somehow get a photo for Frederick. I wonder how I'm going to do that, but Khunying interrupts my thoughts with an impatient "And hurry!" as she slams the door behind her.

I rush to get the girls dressed, wash their faces and brush their hair. I've just enough time to give my own hair a brush and put on a quick coat of gloss

"Oh, don't you two look adorable!" Khunying gushes at Tasanee and Lola as she opens her hotel room door when we knock, ready for our inspection. I can't believe how much happier and nicer she suddenly seems. A hotel room at Sun City must be good for her. "Come quickly now, Prince Edward will be here any moment!"

Prince Edward. Which one is he again? I rack my brains, running through all my knowledge of the British royal family, trying to remember how he fits in. Darn it, where is Frederick when you need him – he knows them all backwards!

We rush back to the elevator and go down to the lobby. I can almost feel the prickles of electricity coming off Khunying. She has freshened up beautifully as usual, but somehow has a certain extra sparkle to her this afternoon. I can't quite put my finger on it, but it's almost as if she is star-struck, itchy to speak to the prince.

We follow her out to the drive-about where she lines us up to stand next to the valets and bellboys. "You keep them in line, Jemma, but don't speak to anyone. Do you understand me?"

"Yes, Khunying," I say obediently.

It's a bit embarrassing watching Khunying behave like this. It feels stupid, but I brush down the girls' clothes one last time for good measure and double check that my plain beige T-shirt dress has not crinkled either. I stand up straight in the spot allocated to me by Khunying. I get the distinct feeling of being on a stage and the director is calling "Places! Places everybody!"

Let the show begin.

We stand there for a while, not daring to move a muscle, while Khunying stands this way and that, trying to get the perfect pose for when the prince's car arrives. One or two vans drive through dropping people off, but no prince. After clearly getting restless, Khunying leaves her post and stalks inside again, most certainly to speak to the concierge. She comes back out a minute later looking agitated, but goes back to waiting in her spot on the curb. We must look so random, lined up like toy soldiers. Surely royalty get enough of that with the guards at Buckingham Palace, and we don't even have any big fluffy black hats!

Finally, a dark van pulls up and Khunying jumps to life. The van is blocking my view so I can't really see who is climbing out, and a few big, scary looking men in suits surround the group with expert precision. In no time at all I hear Khunying's fake-posh voice singing out: "Oh, Prince Edward! It's been too long! And Sophie! How lovely to see you again."

I look at the girls, wondering if I'm meant to take them over to where Khunying is no doubt blocking the prince's pathway to freedom. Tasanee looks up at me, clearly as confused as to what to do as I am, and so we just stay there, all three of us huddling closer together.

"You must meet my girls! Where have they got to now? You know we only just arrived, and I looked up and saw you coming down the drive – ha ha – isn't that so funny. So I thought we could wait a few moments to greet you."

She is such a groupie. I can't believe my ears as she continues to gush over this man and his wife. It's hilarious; I'm actually laughing inside – I want to snort! It's pathetic really. But then they start coming towards us – Khunying, Sophie and . . . and . . . and I find myself face to face with The Prince.

Hilarious? Not so much anymore. All of a sudden they are standing right here in front of the girls and I . . . I can't speak. This is the real Prince Edward! And Sophie! I am standing in front of the real Prince Edward! And Sophie!

"Ub," I start to say.

"This is my eldest" – for once I'm thrilled to have Khunying cutting over me and completely ignoring my existence – "Tasanee. You met her when she was just a baby."

"A pleasure," says the Prince, shaking Tasanee's hand elegantly. Tas has her toothy piranha grin on and is checking to be sure her mother is getting all this. I see Khunying give her an excited nod of approval behind the royals' backs.

"Oh yes. Look how big you've grown! Into a real little lady too!" Sophie has a different mannerism from the Prince, and comes across charmingly loud and fun. "And who are you, little darling?" She beams at Lola, who seems to be as frozen as me. Lola opens her mouth, darts a scared look at her mom and quickly closes it again.

"Yes, this is Lola, my baby. She is quite shy, I must apologise." Khunying stumbles over herself to block Lola. But Sophie puts her hand out for Lola. Lola takes it timidly and looks as though she is about to fall over when Sophie gives her a hearty shake.

"I simply love your trousers! Such pretty seams. Look at this! Lovely. And you too, Tasanee. Lovely trousers, yes. Would you turn for me please?" Lola giggles and I just know she is laughing at the word 'trousers' – something we don't say much in South Africa.

We all stand there for a few seconds after Tasanee obediently turns around (with a flurry and a twirl) for Sophie to admire her outfit, but now no one is making the next move. I've snuck back a little through it all and am standing a way behind the girls now, hoping not to be noticed. Just as I think the thought, Sophie stands up and sticks her hand straight out at me.

"Sophie. Pleased to meet you," she says, all expectant smiles.

"Uh . . ." I manage to find my voice and movement in my right arm, take her hand, and reply: "Hello. I mean. Good day. Uh . . ."

Smooth, Jemma. Real smooth.

"Oh, this is the nanny," says Khunying, waving her hand dismissively and taking the prince by the arm to steer him towards the door. But he stops her mid-turn. The guards shift ominously in one smooth but tense moment.

"Excuse me," he says to her politely, taking his arm back and stepping over to me. "How do you do?" he says and holds out his hand. I shake it, feeling as though my entire body has suddenly become carbonated, like one of those soda streams. I am completely star-struck. So this is what it is like. I'm just as bad as Khunying!

"I'm Jemma. Uh. How do you do – too – I mean? Uh, I mean, uh . . ."

"What a lovely young lady!" He laughs heartily.

"Oh Edward, you are making the poor girl blush," says Sophie kindly and swats him playfully on the shoulder with her handbag. Am I blushing? Oh crap, yes I am! I can feel the heat in my earlobes. Ugh.

"Well, let's all go in then, shall we." Sophie takes charge. "No point in standing around jabbering away like this! What will the neighbours think?" They all laugh.

Once inside, the prince and his wife successfully break free from Khunying's clutches, I hear Sophie parting with an invitation to sit with them at the brunch held in the courtyard the following morning. "And bring that delightful au pair of yours too," she adds, twinkling in my direction. I like her. I can't see Khunying's face, but I know she is seething. I wasn't meant even to speak to them and now here they are inviting me to join them for breakfast! Khunying says goodbye and comes over to where the girls and I are standing. We all travel up silently in the elevator again and walk down the corridor to our rooms without speaking. Once in our room, Khunying finally turns to me. She looks pleasant again, as if she is a different person somehow.

"Now, you will be able to order whatever you want for dinner through room service, you may as well stay in the room. I will not be available tonight as I am attending the royal ball. I will collect you all at eight tomorrow morning – please make sure the girls are properly dressed for breakfast with the royal family."

"Yes, Khunying." I'm feeling relieved that we are going to be locked up in the room. For all the excitement of staying in such a classy hotel and meeting such high profile people, I'm exhausted and am looking forward to playing some UNO with the girls or watching a movie.

About two hours later, Khunying is back at our door looking phenominal in a dangerously shimmery black dress with a slit up her thigh. She has diamond-encrusted heels on, and her neck, wrist and earlobes are dripping in diamonds too. And she's wearing – oh wow. It's the tiara! My eyes take in the vision with a mixture of awe and guilt, and in an instant betray me. I know my face has given it away – I've seen this tiara before. Like a bird of prey, she spots it. Or does she? A moment passes between us and I try to read her. Is it suspicion? Is she merely sizing me up for the task of keeping her children safe in a hotel room all evening? She lifts her head regally and the tiara twinkles under the artificial hall lighting.

"I've just come to kiss my angels good night," she says guardedly. "And to give you this." She hands me an ice-cold open bottle of Moet and a champagne glass. I'm almost too surprised to take it. "It was left for me, obviously as a guest of the royal family they wanted me to be well treated, but as I am on my way to the ball now anyway, you may as well enjoy some."

"Oh, thank you, Khunying," I say, quickly re-composing myself and taking the bottle. "Wow, thank you, this is really kind. I will just have one glass of course. The girls . . ."

"No, don't be silly! It's French! You will have at least two glasses, Lola may have one sip, and Tasanee may have a quarter of a glass."

"Oh, OK. Thanks. Thank you, Khunying. Thank–" I realise I'm saying thank you too many times. This friendly, gift-giving Khunying is so strange. It's as if Hitler suddenly threw on a Father Christmas suit one day.

"Well!' I say to the girls as soon as their mother has left the room. "A champagne sleepover – aren't you girls lucky!" I can feel the happy mood has spread. Tasanee climbs up on to one of the beds and starts jumping up and down.

"Yay!" she squeals, pulling her little sister up to jump with her. "Come on, Jemma! We always do this in hotel rooms!"

"No, no!" I laugh. "You can't do that! You'll break the bed!"

"Not me, I'm light as a feather!"

"Well, I'll break the bed, then. I'm as big as a buffalo!" Tas and Lola collapse on the bed laughing and making grunting noises. "What on earth are you doing?" I ask, looking for the room-service menu.

"We're making buffalo noises," giggles Tas. Lola is too busy laughing, snorting and trying to squeeze out grunting noises to say anything.

"Don't be silly! Buffaloes don't grunt. Do they? Oh Lola!" Lola has just rolled off the bed with a soft thud. Tas and I have both gone deadly quiet, but in a flash Lola's pink face pops back up from behind the bed, giggling and spluttering. She lifts one hand in the air and gestures just like in the movies shouting: "I'm OH KAY."

Oh, thank goodness. The last thing I need is the girls sustaining minor injuries when they are locked up in a hotel room with me. Khunying would probably sue me. That would be one sure way to end this bizarrely enjoyable trip.

We order chicken burgers and start flipping through the movie channels to see if there is anything to watch. There seems to be a Dora the Explorer marathon on so I decide that would be safest. Then I pour myself a glass of the champagne.

"Would you like your sip now or later?" I ask Lola.

Lola screws up her nose in disgust. "Ew, no. I don't like champagne," she says, frowning at the glass of bubbly golden liquid.

"Well, that's good, I suppose. What about you, Tas?" I really am not too comfortable with allowing the girls to taste alcohol, but their mother had specified . . .

"Nope. I also hate it. I only drink some when Mommy wants me to. Also, I don't like Moet. I prefer Verve Clicquot."

For once the children are wiser than the adult. Amazing, though, how such small girls can already have discerning tastes, and have already had experiences in their young lives that allows them to have formed an opinion on French Champagne. I take a sip of the deliciously crisp liquid and feel all the bubbles sparkle on my tongue luxuriously. This sure isn't J.C. le Roux. This is quite a thing, staying at The Palace, drinking champagne – even if it is while spending the night watching cartoons on TV.

Chapter 19

．．．．．．．．．．

The next day is gloriously sunny. They don't call it Sun City for nothing, I suppose. I dress the girls in matching floral denim playsuits with half-top jumpers that tie in front. They look beautiful, Tas in her lilac jumper and Lola in pink. I've chosen to wear my knee-length black and blue sundress, even though it is a bit open on top, though not around the bust area. I'm willing to take the chance with showing my shoulders.

"You look so pretty, Jemma," says Lola sweetly, looking in the mirror at me as I'm brushing her hair. "Just like Mommy." I realise the girl hardly ever sees me in a dress or with make-up on. I'm usually in jeans and a shirt, running around after them.

"Thank you, Lolly, and you look lovely too." She squishes her face up in a smile.

Khunying arrives at 8am sharp and we all make our way down to the courtyard for breakfast. "Did you have a nice evening?" I ask her, trying to break the usual uncomfortable silence in the elevator.

"I did, thank you."

"This is the first time Jemma has stayed in a hotel," says Tas suddenly.

Khunying looks at me in surprise. "First time?"

"Er, yes," I admit, feeling a bit stupid.

"Well! You really have been sheltered!" she says condescendingly. But then she laughs and adds, "How wonderful that your first stay in a hotel is at The Palace." I can't make out if she is new spritely-happy Khunying today or if she is miserable disturbed suspicious Khunying. I decide to keep my own persona as neutral around her as possible, just in case, and smile without answering.

After breakfast I take the girls for a walk around before we get changed into our swimming things and go down to the pool. I see Khunying sitting under an umbrella with a small group of people when we walk out to the pool, but she doesn't acknowledge our presence. So I find a spot close by and we settle down.

"Please can we swim, Jemma?" asks Tasanee eagerly.

"Sure, let's just get you out of those caftans."

"And you must swim too," says Lola as I pull her white cotton caftan over her head. "Pleeeeaassee?"

I look over to where Khunying is sitting. She isn't looking in our direction at all. It should be fine, I guess. After all, the rule at home is I can swim with the girls, so this should be the same. I take my own dress off and we all wade into the wide shallow pool. It's slightly warmed, and I feel the gorgeous water lapping at my skin in the hot sun. Tasanee and Lola start splashing immediately and try to see who can get the other girl's hair wettest first. When Tas soaks Lola with a particularly big splash and I see her gasp for breath, I decide it's time to end the game.

"OK, that's enough, Tas. Why don't you show me some of your swimming styles you learn at school?" She is only too happy to show off and starts a breaststroke expertly across the water. "Do you also want to swim like that, Lolly?" I ask, seeing Lola watch her sister longingly.

"I can't," she says, and puts her fingers in her mouth to start sucking.

"Well, I can help you," I say, gently taking her hand away from her face, pulling the other hand too and swishing her through the water. Her whole face lights up and she smiles over to her sister. I tow her round the pool for a while, and then hold her up in the water by her tummy while she makes frog motions with her arms and legs. Tas has decided to come help and is showing her sister some movements, circling round us in like a baby shark.

"Jemma."

"Oh, Khunying, sorry I didn't see you standing there."

Khunying is at the side of the pool. The sun is streaming directly into my face so I can't see her very well. "Make sure you re-apply sun block to the girls every half-hour, and I don't want them swimming for too long. It will make them go pruney."

"Yes, Khunying," I say, lifting Lola to stand again.

"Mommy, did you see me swimming!" says Tas excitedly.

"Yes, I did, my baby. You were doing very well! But not too much, OK? I don't want you getting silly strap-marks from that bathing suit. You know how quickly you tan, and strap marks are so ugly. So common."

"Yes, Mommy," Tas smiles up at her mother politely.

Lola is definitely the third wheel in this dysfunctional family, and Khunying hardly ever shows her any positive attention. Even now she doesn't look at Lola once, and Lola keeps dead quiet as Tas and her mother speak happily as usual.

"Lola is swimming very well, too," I say, not being able to bite my tongue. "If I help her float, she keeps her head up really well and does all the right arm and leg movements."

Khunying stares at me. She knows what I've just done –I'm trying to force her to praise her youngest child too. I see a smirk form at the very corners of her mouth, but before she can say anything, a tall, grey-haired man strides up to her.

"Nicole," he says in a deep booming voice. "Are these your girls? You never did introduce me – my, my, they are beautiful!" I can't tell from here, but something about this man gives me the distinct feeling he drinks a lot of whisky and smokes big fat stinky cigars. He smiles broadly at us, showing slightly skewed teeth. Khunying has gone into groupie mode once again.

"Oh, your lordship, yes, these are my daughters. Tasanee and Lola." She gestures to each of the girls with a delicately jeweled hand. I start to usher the girls out of the pool to go over to meet this man and re-apply sunscreen.

"And who is this lovely creature," he asks as we all climb out. He is staring right at me, a huge grin on his porous face. I suddenly feel very exposed, standing here in my swim suit.

"Oh, she is just their nanny," says Khunying, a slight edge to her voice.

"Well! Your nanny has an exquisite body! Good thing the man of the house isn't around anymore, eh? Bwahaha!" he ogles my dripping skin while guffawing. I feel instantly degraded and completely naked. I instinctively look to Khunying for guidance, but her eyes burrowing into me even harder.

"Gin and tonics, everybody!" he suddenly shouts, and walks off to find a waiter.

"Cover yourself up, Jemma!" Khunying hisses at me. "There are royals around here – and you walking around like some cheap tart. It's a disgrace!"

"Sorry, Khunying," I say quickly and scurry to get a towel over me, only feeling too glad to be covering up. I sit for a while, ringing out my hair, watching Khunying fuss over Tasanee again.

After we head back to the hotel room, it isn't long before there is a soft knock on the door. I open it up, and to my surprise, Alak is standing there!

"Daddy!" Lola shouts, and runs to give him a hug.

"My goodness, Lolly," he laughs. "You almost knocked me over! Tas, come give your father a hug hello."

As it turns out, Alak is here for the 'business side of things' this evening. "But I want to take my girls to the Valley of Waves first, and then maybe to the toy shop…" he says, lifting Lola squealing into the air. "Come along. Before your mother changes her mind."

As we all leave the room, I see Khunying hovering at the door to her own suite down the hall watching us leave. Arms folded under her chest, she nods, but turns and shuts the door with a thud when I nod back in reply.

Just before dinnertime, Alak takes us back up to the room, the girls' arms loaded with all their spoils of the day. From stuffed animals to candifloss bags, he bought them everything they laid their eyes on. I have to say, the level of things this man gives his kids is a bit extreme. No matter what they ask for, they get it. The things keep piling up in their arms, and I see them being lost in a giddy air of spoils. It troubles me – and I speculate this is a short-lived substitute for a solid home life, but I see how much Alak laughs with them and hugs them, and I tell myself to stop concerning myself with the lifestyle. Just because it is different from what I'm used to doesn't make it wrong.

Almost seconds after we say our goodbyes and close the door behind him, there is a loud knock. I open the door again to see Khunying standing in the hallway, looking irritable and edgy.

"The girls can stay with me tonight," she announces. "Pack up their things. I will have a bellboy move their bags to my room just now. Come Tasanee. Come Lola." She takes a bewildered Tasanee by the hand.

"Oh, Mommy, can I please bring some of the things I got from Bruno – look at this beautiful rhino doll." Khunying's eyes fall on a half eaten bag of bright pink candifloss and she glares at me. Crap! The no un-authorized sweets rule!

"No. Come now," says Khunying sharply, pulling her daughter out the room behind her. Lola hasn't moved yet.

"Go on," I say, nodding at her encouragingly. "It will be fun. A whole day with your daddy and now a whole evening with your mommy." I try to smile convincingly at her, but she clearly doesn't want to go. I pick her up and carry her across to Khunying's room instead. Khunying and Tas are already inside and they have closed the door behind them, as if not waiting for Lola at all, as if forgetting her. I knock on the door and wait for Khunying to open, her cold expression evident.

Once back in my room, I'm just about done with packing up the girls' things when the phone rings.

"Lola will stay with you tonight. Send over Tasanee's things, and I will send Lola back to you with the bellboy."

"Oh, OK. Yes, Khuny–"

"And don't pack any of that junk they got from their father. Throw it all away."

Click.

Chapter 20

. . . .

D ays go by and I manage to continue my expertly planned movements around the house to avoid bumping into Khunying. She
seems really scarce herself since we got back from Sun City.
Unfortunately, though, she is my boss, and as in most jobs, no matter how
unpleasant, there are times when you just have to face the boss. The letters
and school notes have been piling up, so I realise it's time to talk to her
about everything we need to discuss.

I decide to look for her to chat while the girls are at school. She tends to
get up at about 10am, and likes to sit in her gown in the sunroom drinking
coffee and reading the newspaper for about half an hour every morning.
Then she usually has scrambled egg whites, goes for a dolling-up session
in her wing of the house, and disappears for the day. Sometimes I hear her
in the afternoons shouting at someone on the phone, but usually she isn't
around much.

I decide to catch her when she comes for breakfast, to get it all over
with nice and early. I'm waiting for her in the dining room, my arms full
of school letters, birthday-party invitations and horse-riding updates.
I've even made extra-specially certain I'm wearing something she would
approve of: a crisp white button-down shirt with the beige Capri pants and
some very sensible plain white flats.

. . . .

When she comes in for breakfast, she looks at me, indifferently, and sits down at the table.

"Good morning, Khunying!" I say brightly, trying to be as natural and breezy as possible.

She takes a long time to settle in her chair, lets out a sigh and looks up. "Can I help you?" she says curtly, folding out her napkin slowly.

"Yes. Er – I'm sorry to bother you like this, but I need to go through a few things with you." Khunying accepts her plate from Jim without thanking him, sprinkles salt over her eggs and gives me a small irritable wave. "Go on," she says, not looking up, and taking a negligible bite of scrambled eggs. Her mouth barely moves as she chews. Must be to avoid wrinkles – or calories.

"Um, thank you. Yes. Well I have a few school letters that came home with the girls these past few weeks. Uh, Tasanee needs to fill in this form for a school day trip . . . Lola's teacher would like us to choose time on the schedule for bringing the class hamster home for the weekend . . . um, and–"

"Why are you telling me this," interrupts Khunying, putting down her fork.

"Oh, uh, well I thought you would want to know–"

"Don't I pay you to take care of my children?"

"Yes." My voice has gone up a pitch. "Yes, Khunying, you do. Of course. But–"

"Well then. Take care of it. Do your job. I am a busy woman and my life is filled with much more important issues than the life-and-times of a pet rat. Is it too much to expect you to do your job?"

Once again I sense this is a hypothetical question.

"And if you can't figure something out on your own," she continues scornfully, "some basic detail, well then, speak to Kobus. Is that all?" she sits staring at me expectantly.

Sheesh. Someone woke up on the wrong side of the luxurious, extra-length king-sized bed this morning!

Her icy lock-vision induces a cold sweat on my forehead. Dammit! My hands always seem to be clammy when I'm around this woman.

"Oh. OK. I will. Sorry. I just needed to ask about, um, the piano lessons?"

She doesn't reply, so I carry on: "Well, as you know, they both started together, but the teacher thinks we should give Lola extra lessons because she has really taken to it. You should see her play! She's a natural! Tasanee has a lot of other things on the go, but Lola only does a few things and this would be something she could excel at. And she loves it!"

Still no response.

"OK. I'll speak to Kobus about that too?"

What is she going to do when Kobus leaves? Or, rather, what am I going to do? I know he gave his notice a while back, so it's only a matter of time now before he's gone. And then who will I go to?

"You may go," she says with a sweep of her hand. Did that mean she just dismissed me? Am I dismissed? But I really, really need to ask her about my upcoming birthday . . . Oh, and the girls' party invitations! I've opened them all to check dates, but most of them fall over weekends when I'm off-duty. I take a deep breath and resist the temptation to shield my face from her death stare.

"Oh, thank you, but, well, actually there is – um – so long as I have you here. Uh – well here . . ."

I quickly step forward and place the birthday-party invitations on the table in front of her and step back again. She stares at me for a long, long time, then looks down at the pile of brightly coloured envelopes on the table. There are shimmery pink ones, glitter purple ones, ones with embossed unicorns and even one with yellow daisy paper cut-outs stuck all over it. There are a lot of girls at this school, I think to myself, and they all seem to want Tas and Lola at their parties.

Khunying doesn't pick up the envelopes, but just keeps staring at them.

"They are, uh, um, birthday party invitations . . . For the girls. I thought seeing that you are back in town you might like to – uh – accompany the girls – um – and one of them is actually tomorrow after school so it might be nice if you could–"

Khunying still doesn't say anything, but takes another miniature almost non-existent bite.

"Some of them have specifically invited the mothers too, you see. They have drinks and cakes and canapés for the adults, I think, while the children–"

She fixes a look on me that makes me burn with apprehension and I stop speaking. I shuffle my feet a little, dart my eyes down to the stack of envelopes, back up to her, and back down to the envelopes again, and then decide it's best if I take them away – for now. I move forward, uneasily, and pick up the invitations from the table.

"You will accompany the girls tomorrow, and to all the rest of the birthday parties," she says, finally, speaking to me as if I am an idiot. "I really can't believe I have to be burdened with explaining these things to you. You have been here long enough to know what to do. Now. Is that all?" She puts down her fork tellingly.

I know I should probably just give up and walk away. I should just run all these things by Kobus and not bother telling her anything. But it is so wrong! A mother should want to know about her daughters' lives! She should go to the birthday parties with them. What is Khunying doing that is so important she isn't even willing to listen to me talk about them? And also, I need a night off…

· · · · · · · ·

I decide to try one last time. I have to! The whole reason I wanted to speak to her about all this today is I need to ask to get the night free for my birthday. If only I could use "Hello Kitty says listen to me!" on her.

"Is. That. All," she repeats, slowly, as if talking to a child.

"Yes, well, no, well," I say, pathetically. "No. Um, no, actually," I quickly say at high-speed before losing heart, stumbling over my words. "Uh, I wanted to ask if I could possibly go home Thursday night this week. I will only leave after the girls are in bed, of course, and will be back Friday morning in time for the morning run. It's just it's my birthday and I would like to–"

"Fine. Make sure you get a leave form from Kobus, and tell him to be sure to deduct the time from your pay," she says, ousting me, and goes back to eating her eggs. Typical! She will make me stay over weekends and work as many extra hours as she pleases without it ever reflecting in my pay cheque, but the second I need an evening off . . . Oh well, I guess I should be happy she said yes. I take my cue, thank her and hurry out as fast as I can.

This job is clearly a roller-coaster ride, with its occasional ups and extreme downs, where I have to tip-toe around, avoiding doing anything else wrong, holding my breath every time Khunying is in the house, but then I get French champagne and hugs from the girls and genuine pleasantries in the most unexpected of places from time-to-time…so I've learnt to enjoy the highs when they present themselves.

A beautiful warm glow grows inside me. I'm going home for my birthday! Yay! I merrily pull out my phone and see I've had another missed call from my mom. Rats, I forgot to return her last missed call. Oh well, I'll call her back later – just want to get this sorted before Khunying changes her mind! I dial Kobus's number.

Chapter 21

. . . .

"No, no, no! " I push Troy's hand away from my face. She is holding up a tiny lethal-looking drink in a shot glass, trying to force me to take it. Our birthday gathering is in full force at our cozy flat. "I'm not drinking with you people again! You get me into trouble. I need to be back at The Palace first thing tomorrow morning, so it's teetotaling for me tonight–"

"Tee-quila it is then! Come on, it's your birthday. Ryan, hold her down, will you?"

"No!" I laugh, trying to make light of my instinctive swatting away of Ryan's arm round my shoulders. He has been quite happily playing the perfect couple all night, and I know exactly why! When he arrived, he took me aside and told me Troy spoke to him and he understood I've been having a hard time at work. And he forgave me for taking it out on him and ignoring him, avoiding him, etc. Plus he was partaking in some charity thing that involved his abs somehow, so he had been preoccupied himself, and then he ended it all off by saying because it's my birthday, he's going to give me another chance. So now here he is, sitting next to me, smiling stupidly while Troy tries to force-feed me shots. I paste a smile on my face.

"No, Troy! I can't take any chances of a repeat performance. I swear if that woman catches a whiff of a hangover on me, she will–"

"Sue? Oh babe," laughs Troy, one hand on her hip. "Look at you! Running scared like a stray kitten. Come on, she can't be that bad. Have some fun!"

Jason laughs and takes the glass away from Troy. She pouts at him and crosses her arms. "Spoilsport!" she mutters. Ryan slips his arm over my shoulders again, and I shift uncomfortably – but he takes my move to be snuggling into his "nook" and smiles brightly, pulling me closer.

I give up. His cologne alone is enough to knock me out. If I try put up a fight I might just pass out from the extra inhalation needed.

"Oh, come on, Troy," Jason laughs. "Let the poor girl be. She is having a hard enough time at work as it is, and remember what happened last time you got her to drink just one on a school night . . . remember? You Pink Flamingo'd her. You Pink Flamingo'd us all!"

Troy giggles devilishly, looking over at the Pink Flamingo, which is now stacked in the bookcase next to the TV cabinet. She turns to me. "You know I love you, Jem. But I just want my Jemma back. My tequila-drinking, crazy make-up wearing, pink-obsessed, fun Jemma. But if 'new-and-improved' Jemma is going to insist on being such a wet blanket – at her own birthday party," she adds pointedly, " – well then you, dear Jason, are going to have to drink this on her behalf. Can't let it go to waste!" She leans over to Jason seductively and hovers the shot-glass at his lips. "You are also the birthday boy, after all." she adds softly, and winks as he opens his mouth so she can trickle the potent, golden liquid in. The whole display is disgusting. I wonder suddenly if Tracy has wished Jason yet? What is the time difference between London and South Africa? She usually sends me a message and phones him if she's not here for our birthday, but come to think of it, I got nothing from her today. I'm about to change the subject and ask him when Frederick speaks.

"It's too late, we have lost our Jemma to the body snatchers," he laughs. "New-and-improved non-pink-wearing Jemma has already adopted the girls. Didn't you know?"

Do they really think I've become boring? Just because I want to be more responsible and serious about my job? I mean, sure I've kind of toned down my look a bit, but only because I'm getting used to not being as outrageous with my colour scheme so I fit into Khunying's expectations better. And I quite like my new look. It's more down to earth. And I'm twenty-five now! Time to grow up. I look down at my plain blue jeans and black fitted sweater with matching black baby-doll shoes. What is she saying anyhow? I look good. Alak would like this outfit.

"Just go and look at her bedroom wall," Frederick continues, "lined with pictures drawn by the children. It's all so cute, all crayon and colouring out of the lines. There's Tas, Lola and Jemma as mermaids, Tas, Lola and Jemma as princesses, Tas, Lola and Jemma . . ."

"Hey!" I protest. "Those pictures are cute! And they draw them for me, what am I supposed to do? Throw them away?"

"Uh, yes," says Ryan, attempting a neck nuzzle which I dodge with skill.

"You wouldn't know. You're not a moth . . . An au pair."

They all stare at me. They noticed my slip up and no one is speaking. Oh dear, maybe Frederick is right. Maybe I've crossed the line! I don't think of myself as their mother, of course, but the lines are definitely starting to smudge. It's just I feel so bad for the girls. I feel I need somehow to give them the guidance and love a mother should. They won't get it from Khunying, that's for sure. She's only interested in how they look.

And Alak, well, he's great and all, but he's not around that much. Khunying won't let him be. So it's the girls, once again, who suffer because of her.

"The thing is, Jem," Jason breaks the awkward silence, "you should leave that stuff at The Palace. Stick the pictures up on your bedroom wall there by all means, but bringing it back here – well, we are just a little worried you are losing the ability to separate your real life from your working life. It's a job, remember, just a job."

So far I'm not enjoying this birthday party at all.

"I can't put them up at The Palace," I mumble. "It's against the rules. Not allowed to stick things on the walls. Not even in the playroom or on that ginormous fridge door . . ." I trail off; no one really cares. A wave of emotion fills me.

"Look, I do know it's just a job, but you don't understand. If I don't put the drawings on my wall, no one will. Khunying just throws them away! I mean what kind of mother…" I can feel another anti-Khunying rant coming on again, and I know my friends are getting sick of them, but I just can't stop myself. Anyway, it's their fault for bringing this up in the first place. "She's a monster! She won't even go to birthday parties with them. It's so sad when I am there, standing around with all the other mothers, and I'm the only nanny. Even Lusanda, who is partner at her law firm and has a full-time au pair, still comes. She says she understand the importance of outings with her children. Unlike my employer."

"Lusanda?" says Troy. "Is this one of your new friends?"

"No, she's just another one of the mothers. But I speak to her whenever I see her . . . and she's really nice. She understands what I go through with the kids."

"And I bet she dresses in beige too." Troy adds, rolling her eyes lazily. I'm quite sick of her attitude actually. So what if I'm friends with one of the other mothers? I am allowed to have other friends, aren't I?

"You know what," I say, turning coldly to Troy. "Lusanda listens to the problems I have at work. She understands how hard it is to raise little girls, and how frustrating my situation with Khunying is. And actually, yes, she does wear a lot of beige. And she's gorgeous."

"I think Troy was just saying we are your real friends, Jem," interrupts Jason, looking worried. "You complain about work all the time, in fact it's all you talk about. When we actually do get to see you. So we are just concerned."

"Well, you don't know what I'm going through. You don't know how awful it is! Every day is a rollercoaster – every day is a, a contradiction!" I can feel my voice start to shake. I'm trying to stay calm, but I really just want to shout or cry or run away and never come back. Ryan takes my hand gently, and for a moment I am placated.

"I get you're under a lot of pressure. She sounds tough - quite a contradiction with all her organic food and rules, but then doesn't want to spend time with her children, and her high life clothing, expensive shoes, and then doesn't want to spend money on Lola's birthday party…"

"Thank you!" I say, amazed and turning to him, grateful for some kind of sympathy.

"But we all are a contradiction these days, aren't we? I mean we do Burpies-for-Bursaries and give five rand coins to the petrol attendants, but then we buy smart phones made by children and stream everything under the sun rather than paying for authentic art." Wow. Besides the usual confusing crossfit reference, he surprised us all. I had no idea Ryan had a socially aware side! "So I guess, her being a contradiction is to be expected. But if it's so horrible, why don't you quit?" I pull my hand away from him, annoyed.

"I'm not going to quit! What about the girls? They need me!"

"They just met you a couple weeks ago." He's clearly affronted by my body language.

"Over four months," I say pointedly. "That's almost half a year – ages in a child's life."

Ryan folds his arms, agitated. "Whatever. All I'm saying is I'm sure they have had nannies before and I'm sure they will have nannies after you.

I mean, it's not like you are going to do this job for the rest of your life. If this woman makes you so nervous all the time, and I don't blame you, she sounds awful, but why don't you just call it quits?"

"And go back to being yourself," adds Troy.

I think for a minute, looking over to Jason for some indication of what he thinks. His face is closed, as though he's miles away, obviously not listening. What is wrong with everyone tonight?

Frederick seems to pick up on my discomfort and smiles at me. "Ah, Jem. You know we love you. We miss you. We don't want you to disappear into a black babysitting hole is all. Let the fabulous Jemma in all her fabulous pink flow!"

"Yeah well, I just, I just need," I get up, "I just need to get something," and I escape to my bedroom.

My wall is lined with all the pictures Frederick was talking about. I stare at them, first smiling at the cuteness and how sweet it is seeing the childish writing spelling out my name in purple crayon. I look around and realise maybe they have a point. I took off my Audrey Hepburn poster to make space for the drawings, and my overnight (which I've already packed for tomorrow) is filled with beige, grey and brown clothing. No bright colours. Nothing sparkly. Nothing shocking at all! I don't even remember when I last wore my frilled-out mesh tutu skirt. And it used to be my favourite.

Frederick comes in and stands next to me, slipping one arm around my waist. "You know, I don't think I've seen you much lately. I miss you, silly girl." He squeezes me kindly. I stay silent, still looking at the pictures on the wall.

"You doing OK, skat?" he asks.

"You don't really think I've been taken over by the body-snatchers, do you?" I ask, tentatively.

"Ag, siestog. Sorry, Jemma. We kinda ganged up on you there. Didn't mean for it to come out like that. We are all concerned – about all these changes, but no. I don't think you've been body-snatched."

I turn to look at him. His expression tells me he is distressed. It's nice to know my friends care, but I'm still bothered none of them seem to understand what I am going through. I decide to put these feelings aside, though. It is my birthday, after all. Time to get back to the party.

"Thanks." I smile to show I'm not as upset as I actually am. I pick a very pink scarf from the bundle hanging over my stand-up mirror and pull a pair of apple-green leopard-print ankle boots out of my wardrobe. "These will be going with me to The Palace tomorrow." I put the things next to my bag. "And this," I add, choosing a sequenced Alice-band with a giant bow on the side and putting it on my head, "will go perfectly with tonight's outfit."

As I'm posing for Frederick's approval, my phone bleeps in my pocket. Frederick raises his eyebrows at the sound.

"What?" I say, defensively. I changed my ring tone when we were at Sun City, feeling rather embarrassed at the cat purr in the presence of all the royals. Also, I didn't want Alak thinking I was a child. So I switched to a normal, grown up "bleep".

"Nothing," he says.

I look at the screen. It's a message from Alak!

I'm slightly taken aback. As much as I like him, we definitely have boundaries, and I usually only hear from him in relation to the girls. I read the message, trying to cover up my surprise so Frederick won't see.

"A little bird told me it was a special someone's birthday today . . . Happy Birthday, Jemma! I hope you have a wonderful day, and may this year be truly magical. Many warm wishes, and hope to see you soon, Gossip Girl. Alak."

Frederick gasps, reading over my shoulder. "Scandalous! What will Ryan say?"

I shove the phone in my pocket.

"What?" I say again, pretending not to be stunned by the message myself. It was really sweet of Alak to text me. How this guy was ever married to Khunying just blows my mind!

"Come on," I say, ignoring his arched brows. "Let's go make some pink drinks." Linking my arm in his, and steering clear of Ryan, I walk him back to the kitchen, straightening my shoulders and feeling cheered.

Maybe it's my new-found positivity or my friends just bore from the Jemma-bashing theme of the night, but everyone seems to chill on the whole subject of my job and we have a good time chatting, laughing and going back to the way things used to be. So much so, that at midnight we decide to Uber to Chocolate Lounge for a nightcap.

"I'll get first rounds," says Ryan flatly.

"You know, you really do need to end this now, Jem," says Jason once out of earshot. I turn around and see Ryan standing at the bar, shoulders slouched. I feel a pang of guilt, but shake it off.

"Agreed. I'm beginning to feel sorry for the poor guy. You shouldn't string him along," says Troy, following my gaze.

"But Troy. You are the one who keeps encouraging him!"

"I'm just looking out for you babe."

"Well, please don't."

"Look," says Jason, the voice of reason. "I don't want to harp on about it, but you don't want to date him. If you like him, sort of, just let him down as easy as you can and try stay friends. He's OK, he probably won't mind being friends with a girl who has just kicked him in the–"

"Jason, I will let him down easy! You know I won't be horrible. I'm always very nice to him."

"It's not very nice stringing him along for so long."

I sigh loudly. "Ya, I know. I feel bad. I'll do it tonight. And I'll be nice. I'll give him a well-explained, well-presented break up."

"Uh huh," says Jason, disbelievingly.

"I will!" I say emphatically, but can tell by the general non-response no one believes me. I'll show them. I adjust my sparkly headband and start planning the break-up speech in my head.

When Ryan gets back, he hands out drinks and a passion fruit and soda water for me.

Jason, Troy and Frederick all make themselves scarce almost immediately, so I take a deep breath and decide to get it over with.

"Ryan, can we go sit somewhere?" He looks at me blankly for a moment, then a gruesome grin spreads over his face.

"Oh, you want to go 'sit' somewhere," he says, winking knowingly and flexing his muscles under his shirt while reaching over to put an arm around me.

Ugh.

"Uh. How about there?" I turn and quickly head towards a small cozy-looking table in the corner. I sit down on the couch at the back, but instead of taking the chair opposite me, he slides in right next to me.

"Oh!" I say, jumping as he shuffles up and puts a big hand on my thigh. We must look so ridiculous. I mean, there is so much space here in this corner, but he has chosen to squeeze in next to me on a chair that is most definitely only meant to be for one. I take a big gulp of my soda, trying to wriggle my body mass into a corner a fraction of my size. If only I could will my body to seep through the pores of the plaster on the wall! That would be really good right now; pull a bit of an X-men escape. But sadly, Ryan's looming body, pressing up closer to me, squishes all the air out of my fantasy.

I try to turn enough to face him, getting ready to give the speech.

"So, birthday girl," he says before I can open my mouth, putting an arm around my shoulders, his face dangerously close to mine. "Isn't it time I gave you your birthday present?"

A present? Ooh! I mean, a present? Oh no. He better not have got me anything. That will just make this all the more awkward. But I wonder what he got me? No, Jemma! Stay focused. Break-up speech. Now.

"Ryan . . ." I try to pull my head backwards far enough to talk without my eyes squinting or our noses bumping. My head presses up against the wall, and I realise Ryan's face isn't any further away. In fact, it's coming closer! He's closing in for a kiss! I pull my head back so fast I bump it hard against the wall. Ryan jerks back and looks at me puzzled.

"What did you do that for?" he laughs. "I was just trying to give you your birthday present," and he starts to move forward again. Ugh. Typical! What kind of present is that anyway? A cheap one, is what it is!

I shove my elbow into his side as hard as I can and push his face away with the other hand. "Ryan!" I shout, feeling frustrated. "I'm trying to talk to you!"

He looks completely baffled as I shove him back and wriggle out of the corner, practically climbing over him in the process. I straighten myself up for a second, taking another breath and then sit down in the seat opposite. He stares at me as if not having a clue what just happened.

"Ryan," I say again, trying to sound less irritable. "We need to talk."

"OK," he says, starting to smile. What is he smiling at? Doesn't he know what "we need to talk" means? For goodness sake!

"The little lady wants to talk? Oh, OK then. The little lady gets to talk. What, do you want to do the 'where is this going' thing before doing any-thing more with me? You girls are so sweet. Always wanting us to make a commitment—"

"What do you mean? And don't call me 'little lady' or 'you girls'. I am a woman!" I'm getting all flustered again. He's really annoying me now.

"Sorry, sorry," he laughs, locking his mouth closed with an imaginary key. Then he pulls one of my hands over the table and pretends to put the key in it, closing it and holding it closed with his own hand. I can see laugh lines next to his eyes, and he smiles stupidly at me with his lips pressed firmly together. All it does is make his oversized chin look even bigger! I stare at him in disbelief. He actually thinks I'm playing games with him? That I want him to say he's my boyfriend or something before I kiss him again? What is wrong with him! He has got to be the stupidest person alive! Or the most big-headed – not ever believing someone could not want to be with him. 'The most incomprehensible thing in the world to a man, is a woman who rejects him.' I'm sure I read that somewhere.

"No! Stop touching me!" I pull my hand away out of his grip with more gusto than I meant to. Sitting with my hands shoved safely away in my lap, I take a deep breath and try to ignore his shocked silence.

"Jem, baby, what's wrong?" he says after a while.

"Look. Ryan. I'm sorry, I didn't mean to snap." He looks at me in blank confusion. He really doesn't have a clue. "It's just that, I just. Well, the thing is." Do I really have to say it? Can he really not tell what is going on? I mean after all the weeks of avoiding him, not responding with any cute texts to his incessant messages, not letting him get too friendly with me, not kissing him again since that stupid night at the club. . . Does he really believe we are dating? Sure Troy keeps making excuses for me, but seriously. Where is his self-respect!

He just looks baffled. "Are you tired? If you are tired I understand." He starts getting up. "Let me take you home." I feel a sudden anger rise up inside me and I can't stop myself.

"Seriously, Ryan? You don't know what's going on? Really? Really? You are such a, a, a . . . Argh! Can't you tell I don't want to talk about a commitment, about our relationship? There is no relationship! And kiss you? Not only are you . . ." I stop, gulping back my words.

"Calm down, Jemma. If you want me to be your boyfriend, that's cool. We don't really need to talk about it. I was just teasing you, saying you are the one who wants a commitment. I feel the same way, don't be so mad."

Argh!

I stare at him, not sure what I feel like doing more; beating his stupid head against the table or just patting him on the head saying, "There there, the men in white will be along shortly".

"No, you are not listening. You don't get it. I want to talk, because, well, because I don't want to do this any more."

"Well, Jemma, you were the one who said you wanted to come out here. I said let's get you home. I offered. You don't have to do this, we can get out of here." He gestures around the club with his hands, looking completely bewildered.

I slap a hand to my forehead. Never try break up with an idiot. "Not this," I say, opening my arms and sweeping my hands wildly. "This!" I point back and forth between him and myself, trying desperately to convey what I am saying. "This, Ryan. This. I don't want to do this!"

Ryan is staring at me, an idiotic expression on his face. "Jem, baby, where is this all coming from? I get you're strung out with work and all, but . . . Oh, I get it. Is it that time of the month?"

"What? What! No, you misogynistic prat, it's not that time of the month. It's not me. It's you!" I slam my hands down on the table, completely exasperated. "I don't want to date you!" I stand up, my voice a lot louder than I meant it to be. "Maybe you'd understand if you spent time on anything other than those stupid muscles, but you are the dumbest human being I've ever met! I mean, do I really have to spell this out for you? What the hell! Not interested! N. O. T. I. N. T . . ."

It's bad. Really bad. I hear myself rant on, wondering where all this came from, but can't stop myself. It's like an exorcist experience, where a psycho bitch from hell takes over. But he makes me so mad, constantly being there where he doesn't belong. In my life where he wasn't invited. Not really.

"Good Gaga, Jemma?" I hear Frederick's voice behind me. I swing round and see him standing there, holding two cosmopolitans. He is frozen, his eyes wide and disbelieving, and behind him a lot of people have stopped and are all staring at the scene. Including Jason and Troy. "I, uh, just brought this virgin cosmo over for you . . ."

Oh no. I've gone too far. Where did that all come from? I can't believe I shouted at Ryan, and called him all those names! I turn back to see Ryan slowly looking around, with realisation, embarrassment and a very sad expression on his face. Finally, he gets it. But now, seeing him look so sad, I feel terrible. I can't believe I just said all those things.

"Ryan," I start, softening my voice again.

"No, it's cool. I'll leave," he says in a voice almost too low to hear, and starts walking past me.

"Ah, Ryan, I'm sorry . . . I didn't mean to be so harsh. I just – well . . ." But he walks on, through the crowd and heads towards the exit.

"Nice, Jem," says Frederick, "been getting some bitch lessons from your boss?"

"I," I don't know what to say. I have no defense. I look past Frederick and see Jason and Troy, who are frowning at me in obvious disapproval, and Troy whispers something to my brother. Instantly I feel my insides burn.

"Listen," I say, barely keeping the tears at bay. "I don't have to explain anything to you people, O.K? I don't have to answer to you. So spare me the lecture."

Frederick's face grows even more solemn. "I've changed my mind. Looks like you've been taken by the body-snatchers after all," he says, and I can feel the disappointment reverberate through me. I look back to Jason and Troy again, but they have already turned their backs.

Chapter 22

I arrive at The Palace on time, and somehow manage to force myself to put on a pseudo positivity. I am a new woman with a new attitude. I'm starting over. I've got rid of Ryan now, granted, not in the best way, but I did it. If the people around me don't like it, well, that's too bad. It needed to be done.

It is what it is.

I feel a certain amount of remorse, but more importantly, I feel free. Therefore, I feel fantastic. Well, as fantastic as one can be so early in the morning after an all-night birthday party that ended in disaster.

While driving up the cobbled bricks, I feel a fresh wave of guilt. I still can't believe I shouted at Ryan like that. That's not me. Maybe all the stress of the job just finally got to me. But I need to get in control of my feelings, not take it out on people like that.

I look around me at the monstrous house, looming in the moonlight. Suddenly it looks terrifying. No, I must change my attitude and be positive. Awesome. That's what I'm going to think of it as. Awesome, not terrifying. This place is truly awesome and I am lucky to be here. To work with someone so established, someone semi-royal, even, is an honour.

Not to mention the girls. I do love them. They are uniquely special to me. It's been so easy to grow attached, and I don't think that's a bad thing at all. It's good: it shows we have a connection.

Everyone's comments last night come back to me. They are all wrong. I may have lost my way momentarily, but after last night, I'm back to myself. Not body-snatched in the least! I have my apple-green leopard-print ankle boots on, and a candy-stripe long pink top over jeggings. I adjust the sparkly clips in my hair, and head up the last stretch of driveway to the house with new-found determination.

What the . . . ?

Coming round the corner of the driveway, I see Khunying's sports car parked in the bushes. It doesn't look like there is any damage, but sure enough, the car is sitting in a pool of moonlight, happily parked in the middle of green shrubbery and a flower patch. A thousand thoughts crash together in head-on collisions in my mind.

She went out last night, when I wasn't here. She left the girls alone, unless she got Suda to watch them. But I know for a fact the maids are not allowed to sleep in the house, not even Suda. I left after the girls were already in bed. So when did she go out, and who watched the girls? Or did she take the girls with her? She couldn't have been entirely sober, or sober enough to get her car all the way up the drive and into the garage when she came home. Which means, if she took the girls out with her after I had put them to bed, she drove home dunk and crashed with them in the car, or she went out and left them all alone in that big house all night!

I park and rush inside to make sure the girls are OK. They are in bed, as cozy and in one piece as they were when I left them. Thank goodness! I wonder how Khunying is, then? I take my bags to my room, and there on the bedside table is a small package. I pick it up and read the dainty name-tag attached. 'To Jemma. Happy Birthday. Love Alak.' It's gorgeous: silver wrapping with a black silk ribbon tied elegantly into a bow on top. I pull the bow and ease off the wrapping, filled with anticipation. Butterflies soar in my tummy as I pull out the glinted box. It's perfume. 'Diamonds' by Gorgeo Armani. Wow! I stare at the expensive perfume. I've never had anything this exquisite, all to myself! Besides the D&G sunglasses, of course. But the extravagance of this gift! It's the most romantic thing I've ever been given. I remember what Kobus said about Alak having a thing for collecting expensive perfume, so realise this is nothing more than him being sweet and giving me a lovely gift from the kindness of his heart. Nothing romantic about it. I take out my phone and send Alak a text. "Thank you so much, I don't know what to say! This is the best birthday ever." I spray on a quick, glorious mist before I go get the girls ready for school.

On our way back down the driveway leaving for school, Tasanee sees her mother's car in the bushes. "Oh, Mommy must have gone out again last night," she says with yawn.

"Does she go out often like that?" I ask, chancing the prying question. "When I'm not here?"

"Sometimes," she says, shrugging her shoulders. "Not so much anymore, now she has the Count. She says she prefers socialising with him in Italy because all the people here in South Africa are common and boring."

"And Daddy came over last night," says Lola. I look at her in surprise. I got the distinct impression Khunying wouldn't let Alak on the property, not without supervision at any rate. In fact, that's what Kobus told me, isn't it? But that makes sense now – that's how the birthday gift found its way to next to my bed.

"Your father?"

"Yes, he phoned us and we told him Mommy was out, so he came to visit and we had a midnight feast!" Lola is still sleepy, but she is smiling warmly and I feel a lot better, knowing at least Alak was there with them while Khunying went out. I wonder how he dealt with the drunk ex-wife when she got home. He must have seen her creative parking before he left.

"He's gone away again now – he's flying back home to Thailand today," Lola continues, her sleepy head leaning against the window. We drive for a while longer in silence and I feel a palpable gloom in the air. I can't let my bad feelings get to the girls. I need to do something to change the vibe in here fast.

"Last day of school today, girls!" I try change the subject and cheer everyone up. "Aren't you excited? Kobus told me you are going away with your mommy on holiday too?" I so need this break. Even though I'll miss the girls, it's just for a week and it will be so nice to have time to myself again. Finally. It feels as if I'm always at The Palace, always under scrutiny, always fighting a losing battle in giving the girls some form of stability and positive influence in their lives.

"We're going to Grandad's farm," says Lola gloomily. "But I don't want to. I hate the farm! I wish you were coming with us, Jemma. Then we could play."

"Ya," echoes Tasanee. "We would rather be here with you than go. It's always boring there. Ever since Bruno left, Mommy just leaves us with their maids and they are no fun. They never let us play Barbie house because they say we make too much mess, and we aren't allowed to play with any water and we can't go out into the garden on our own but the maids never want to take us. We hate it on the farm."

"Well, it's still going to be nice to spend some time with your mommy, isn't it?"

"Mm," says Tas, not sounding entirely convinced. That's strange – she's always keen to spend time with her mom. Lola doesn't say anything but keeps staring out of the window. I decide to leave it alone and we spend the rest of the journey in complete silence.

After we get to the school and Tasanee has rushed off to her swimming class, Lola and I sit in the car listening to radio. I take out my usual flask of coffee and pour myself a small cup. The windows on the Cayenne start to steam up as we sit in there, snug and warm against the crisp Autumn morning air.

"Do you want some juice, Lolly?" I pull Lola's school bag towards me and open it to find her juice boxes inside. While rummaging around, I find the selfie we took together that I printed out for her. It's already starting to fray on the corners, which makes me smile. I put it back neatly and keep looking for the juice. My fingers find something cold and trinkety. It's a small gold statue – beautiful and jewel-encrusted. I don't know for sure, but this gold looks real.

"Lola, what's this?" I hold it up, but she looks at me blankly, rubbing her sleepy eyes. "I found it," she says simply.

Oh no. Don't tell me she's stealing again.

"Where did you find it?" I ask, ill at ease.

"At school."

"Lolly," I say, breathing out a sigh. "Oh, Lolly, why did you take it? I thought we spoke about this."

Lola looks confused. "I didn't take it," she says. "I told you, I found it."

"Yes, but why is it in your bag?"

"I don't know?" she says, setting her cherub mouth in a quivering pout.

It's too early to deal with this – my brain isn't even fully awake yet! I look at the pristine miniature statue in my hand. It's really well crafted, and very expensive looking. What would something like this be doing at a kindergarten class at school?

By the time I get back to the house, the car has been moved out of the bushes. I don't see Khunying all day, though, and even when it's time for me to leave, she still doesn't make an appearance. So, Khunying got pink-flamingoed – that must be one mother of a hangover. I know she is in the house because Suda keeps taking cups coffee and some gruel-looking smoothies through to her wing of the house. And a plate of bacon. I'm quite surprised by that one. She normally never eats anything fatty, but there goes Suda, undeniably with a plate of fried bacon, greasy and dripping, into Khunying's wing.

So the woman is human after all.

* * *

I take a sip from my water bottle. Jason and Troy are lying on towels drying off next to the pool at Troy's apartment block. I have my big floppy sunhat on and am trying desperately to get some sun on my pale legs. I stretch out on one of Troy's deck chairs, willing the rays to soak into my skin faster, despite the factor 50 I've applied. Everyone seems to have forgiven me for my blow-up-break-up with Ryan. Or at least, forgotten about it. No one has said anything to me about it since, and I'm really thankful. It's only been a few days, so I guess the lecture still might be coming, but for now we are all playing nice and not mentioning it.

"So explain the stolen trinket thing to me?" Troy says, sitting up and re-applying tanning oil to her already perfectly bronzed body. Some girls have all the luck. Oil would burn me to a cinder.

"They weren't stolen, that's what I thought at first. Turns out they were actually put there by Khunying."

"Because?" she says, raising her eyebrows and handing Jason the tanning oil. He takes it obediently and starts working some into her back. I wonder what Tracy would think of this. She's still in the UK and Jason is still with her, even though it's been ages since he saw her. Since he mentioned her either, come to think of it. Hmm. Oh well, I won't get involved in his love life; I've enough worries on my own plate.

"Because she's convinced someone is going to kidnap her children. I got the teacher to ask all the girls to whom it belonged, and none of them said it was theirs, so she gave it back to me." I felt penitent when the teacher gave the trinket back to me. She told me when she held it up and asked the class who it belonged to, only Lola put her hand up. She told her, as she had said to me, that she had found it and so it was hers. When pressed, we figured out she had actually found it in her school bag, so I realised someone else had to have put it there. I asked Jim and Suda about it, and they knew exactly what it was.

"Jim told me Khunying got these weird good-luck trinkets from some white witch she's been seeing, and put them in the girls' school bags. To protect them. I checked, and found an identical one in Tas's bag too."

"But why did you think the little one stole it in the first place?" Troy stretches her beautifully sculpted arms above her head and leans back again.

"Oh, I once had an incident with Lola when she took something without asking. So when I found it, I thought maybe she took it from another student at school."

"The poor kid! Guilty until proven innocent, huh?" says Jason, putting some sunscreen on his own shoulders after finishing with Troy.

"Well, I didn't accuse her or anything. I just wasn't sure."

"What, she wasn't wearing a child-sized black cat-burglar suit to help you crack the case?" Jason is playing with me, but I sense a tension in the air. He must be really mad at me for being so nasty to Ryan.

"Don't be ridiculous. I didn't actually think she was stealing. I was just confused. Also, stuff has been going missing in the house – food and CDs and things. So I didn't even assume it was Lola, I just . . . It just . . ."

I'm filled with remorse. I did jump to conclusions, and Lola was perfectly innocent. I'm turning into one of those horrible suspicious people! And poor Lola, she has a hard enough time with Khunying being so cold with her. She doesn't need me to start suspecting her of things she didn't do.

"Detective work isn't your strong point . . . I would suggest sticking to your day job, babe." Troy nudges Jason and they both seem to be suppressing giggles. I realise they are laughing at my worried expression while thinking about the whole thing.

"Oh come on, guys!" I shout feeling flustered. They both burst out laughing like a couple of schoolgirls. Honestly, all day! They have been whispering round corners and making private jokes all day long, and I'm pretty sure it's about me. It's exhausting! I guess I should just be happy they are teasing me and not flat-out confronting me about birthday night, or calling me body-snatched. I don't have the energy for that.

I give up trying to defend myself. I suppose The Palace can sound a bit crazy from the outside. But things are getting weirder than usual around the house. A lot weirder, if that is even possible. And it's totally unnerving me. Especially over the last few days, Khunying has been on a mission. She's had this team of greasy-looking lawyers round, going through papers to protect every inch of the estate. I hear them saying things like "six million for repairs", "accountable for damages" and "travel expenses" from behind closed doors. And of course, the word 'sue' comes up a lot. Kobus told me in the divorce settlement she was awarded the estate and contents to the value of fifty million, and that Alak was paying her an exorbitant salary along with child maintenance every month. He said Alak gave her a lot more than he ever should, but she was still going after more. She even kept his grand piano, the one that was a gift to him from the Queen! She wanted to try to take a few of his businesses too, and from what I can gather, started spreading rumours about her former husband to sabotage the businesses she couldn't get her claws into. She's even had the white witch come round to cast out any evil spirits, and got a priest to come and do the same.

The woman is clearly crazy. She is too nuts to be taken seriously and I should not be so scared of her. After all, I have sanity on my side – how can I let her nuttiness get to me? When I'm away from the house, it feels as if the sun comes out and I can see things more clearly. I start to laugh too, and pivot over to sun my back.

My cell starts to ring from under a magazine. I thought about switching back to the purr ring after my birthday, an act of defiance against the accusations of losing my identity, but decided some things are better the new way. Wiping my hands quickly on a towel, I grab the phone and look at the screen.

It's Frederick. I feel a tiny flip in my stomach as I answer the call. We haven't spoken since birthday night, and he was the one who looked most distressed when I shouted at Ryan.

"Hey!" I say, trying to sound bright and breezy, but sounding more shrill and desperate for affection.

"How's my little cloud-covered ray of sunshine doing this fine week-end?" I don't hear any meanness in his voice, just less of the usual zest, but still a bit of a light-hearted tease. Seems like he's going to let it go too. Thank the fairy-star-dust!!

"Oh, all good, thanks. Survived my last day at work but only barely."

"So you're a free agent now?"

"As free as can be for the next week!" I say, relaxing again and enjoying the mood. "I'm free as a bird. Free as a lipstick in Glamour magazine. Free as an added thirty-three per cent in a Woolies value bottle of milk. Free as the calories in a bowl of steamed broccoli, free as . . ."

"As a 'But wait, that's not all' Verimark ad? For gratis?"

"Exactly!"

"Well, then. If you are that free, I say we do something tonight."

"Sure! What did you have in mind?"

"Well, what I really want to do is go trawling the docks for wayward sailors, but I guess I would settle for some Asian food and a bit of a catch up in a sparkly, cheesy corner down in Chinatown?"

"The Game?" I ask, eagerly.

"Is there any other way to eat Chinese?" The game is something we do every time we go eat out in Chinatown. We dress up and act like different people – roll playing for platonics.

"So who should we be tonight? German tourists with small bladders? We can go to that restaurant where we have to get a key to the bathroom, then ask for the key every ten minutes."

"Or what about the town mouse and the country mouse? I have ears and tails and minute suitcases we can use,"

"Nah, we did that last time. How about snooty intellectuals just back from the World Carrot up the Butt conference?"

"You know I can never do the special walk right," I giggle. "Why don't I wear my tiny baby-doll cherry blossom dress with those black stripper heels and be your 'un-named escort' for the night?"

"And I'll smoke stinky cigars and be all manly like. And say things like 'Babe,'" he deepens his voice here quite convincingly.

"And we'll order things we can't pronounce and wait to see who gets food poisoning first?"

"And finally lose those pesky three kilograms I've been trying to get rid of!"

I smile into my phone. "Sounds perfect! I couldn't think of anything better to do tonight. Troy and Jason are here with me, should I ask them to come too?"

"Of course! But only if they agree to dress in character and play the game." Troy and Jason usually say no, that we are childish and behave like idiots and they don't want to be seen in public with us when we do it. But this time they agree quite quickly. Must be the sun getting to their brains, making them more pliable than usual.

"Troy says she'll be Miss Scarlet in the boardroom with the candlestick, and Jason is going to be whatever I decide to make him, OK?"

"Perfect, darling! Now get out of the sun before you go all pink and match that cherry blossom on your dress! Nobody wants a wrinkly old handbag for a date."

I hang up and sigh to myself. I'm so glad everyone seems to be letting birthday night go and the start to my break is going to be spent dressed up in Chinatown.

Happy!

Before I can put it down, my phone rings again in my hand.

"That's weird. It's Kobus. He never phones on weekends." I answer again. "Kobus? Is everything OK?" Jason and Troy look up, interested, as my eyes widen. "What? That's terrible! Oh my goodness! Is she? . . . And the girls? Oh. OK. No sure. That's fine. I will be there right away!"

"What?" Jason demands as I snap the phone shut. "Did they get kidnapped?"

"No," I say, feeling shell-shocked. "I need to go. Khunying's been in a car accident.

Chapter 23

. . . .

By the time I get to The Palace, Kobus has called me three more times with updated information. The girls were not in the car, they were left at home with the maids, rather than spending quality time with their mother, I can't help but think. But a good thing this time, as it turns out. Khunying is banged up pretty badly and will be kept at the hospital overnight for observation. Kobus isn't sure what happened, but there seems to be no other car in the accident, just Khunying's sports car. They don't think she was wearing a seat belt, which is why the airbags didn't deploy on impact, a feature I never knew about. She hit her face on the steering wheel, so the doctors want to make sure there is no swelling on the brain. I'm to keep the girls occupied and stay with them till she is released, and Kobus is dealing with everything else. I'm so thankful he is still around when this happened, even though his notice is just about up and he will be leaving soon. For now, he's been amazing with filling me in, organizing the rest of the staff and making sure the only thing I have to do is be with the girls.

When I get to the house, both girls come flying out of the front door and throw themselves at me, hugging me tightly. I crouch down on my haunches to look them in their tear-stained faces.

"It's going to be OK. Your mommy is fine, she's just fine. No need to cry." I try to force a smile as sunny as I can muster.

. . . .

"We know," sniffs Tasanee, her gruff voice cracking. "Kobus said. But it was so scary!" I give them both another tight hug. "I know, sweetie . . . But it's OK now. The doctors say she's fine, and I bet she will be home first thing tomorrow!"

"She was supposed to watch our new DVD with us today, and we were leaving for the farm tomorrow," says Lola, wiping her eyes with her toy rabbit and going back to sucking her fingers.

"You only care about your stupid DVD," Tasanee shouts at Lola, suddenly pulling away and staring at her sister in fury. "Mommy could be dead! And you only care about your DVD?"

"Not true!" shouts Lola, her voice quivering.

"Yes, it is! You don't care! You would like Mommy to be dead, wouldn't you!"

"Tas, come on now. Stop it. Lola didn't mean that. That's not what she was saying at all." Lola is staring at Tasanee, her face as pale as a ghost. Then she bursts into tears and buries her face in my neck. "She promised," she whispers through sobs. "She promised."

"Girls, you are both scared and that's OK. You show it differently, but come now, you are sisters and you both love your mother. Let's not fight, OK?"

Tasanee folds her arms and stares savagely at Lola. "You said you wished Jemma was taking us away instead of Mommy," she growls. "Its your fault. You made the accident happen!"

"I didn't!" cries Lola, stricken with fear. I hug her tightly again.

"Oh, come on you two. It's all going to be OK, I promise! Your mommy is fine, and she will watch your DVD with you another day. Saying you wanted me to go with you didn't cause anything. It was an accident! Just something that happens by accident. All that is important is she's OK and we are all sending her a lot of love and get-well-soon thoughts. Right now,

I bet she knows how much you love her, and I bet she wants us to have a nice day together while she gets better."

Both girls remain quiet.

"I know!" I continue, thinking of a plan. "Let's make a sleep-over party! Just the three of us. Come on, it will be fun. I'll make popcorn and maybe Jim can make us pizza?" I stand up and take each girl by the hand, strategically placing my body between them. Tasanee drops her death stare and follows my lead back into the house. She huffs loudly while taking off her shoes, and then marches off to the kitchen, her bare feet padding determinedly. It's an act that mimics her mother exactly. Lola and I follow her, and when we come into the kitchen she is standing at the back door, staring out of the glass panels. I walk over to her and put my hand on her shoulder.

"Promise she's OK?" she says in a tiny voice.

"Of course, Tas." I say gently. "I pinky swear," and I hold out my hand with my pinky sticking up in the air. Tasanee turns and looks through wet eyes at it for a moment, smiles and curls her pinky around mine. Lola takes my other hand and slips her pinky through mine too. Then Tasanee takes Lola's free hand. We stand there in our little pinky-swear-circle, just quietly holding each other's hands. I feel tears threatening and quickly blink them away. I pull the girls towards me for one last hug, and then start tickling them for all I'm worth. The girls both squeal happily and run away. I chase them, shouting: "I'm the Tickling Monster!" while following them all the way up to the playroom. I know I should probably let Frederick know our role playing dinner is canceled, but I have too much to worry about with these two. I'll leave it to Jason to tell him – I'm sure he'll understand.

Khunying arrives home the next day, her face so badly swollen and bruised on one side I barely recognise her. She disappears into her wing and the girls rush to take her gifts of flowers and the glittery get-well cards they made yesterday. I stand at her entranceway in a daze. She looks like she's been in a bar fight! I can just see her, in a dark concrete basement somewhere, teaming up with some big biker chick, The Real Housewives Fight Club crowd gathered round cheering as the fists fly and trickles of blood splatter her Gucci handbag . . .

"Jemma!" I hear her call down the hall. "Come in."

In her room.

In her wing of the house.

For the very first time.

I hesitate, afraid to step over the once-forbidden boundary line. "Jemma!" she calls again, and I follow her voice. I pass the closed magazine-shrine cupboard and feel a shiver as if the walls are watching me. I swear I hear rustling books, whispering they had seen me before, coming from her study as I inch past. Then the familiar enormous bathroom, and round the corner to guiltily enter the giant master bedroom suite. I feel the guilt grip at my throat, remembering how I had gone snooping in here when I first arrived. I realise my eyes have darted right to the TV cabinet where the tiara was hidden, just like the night at Sun City when I saw it on her head. Darnit, Jem! Way to give yourself away! I tear my eyes away as quickly as possible and pretend to admire the room as if I had just seen it for the first time.

Khunying is sitting on an antique chair in one corner of the room, holding her china teacup. She has changed and is wearing her soft pink silk gown. She looks over at me, the damaged side of her face falling into a frame of sunlight, and I gasp. In this light it is even worse!

"Oh, I'm so sorry Khunying" I say, unable to hide my horror. I've never been able to look at others people's wounds – just seeing them makes me physically ill. I suddenly feel the blood rushing from my head, as a flood of pity for her replaces it.

"You two may go now," she says weekly, gesturing to the girls.

"What happened?" I ask hesitantly.

Her swollen face darkens and her eyes flash. "Someone pushed me off the road. I told you it wasn't safe. I crashed into a wall and light pole. The airbag didn't deploy, so this," she gestures at her face, "Is the result. I will be suing, of course."

Of course.

"If there's anything I can do . . ." I begin.

"You believe in God, don't you? I remember seeing you had done a lot of work in a church on your CV."

Uh, OK. Didn't see this one coming. She actually read my CV? "Um. Yes, well, yes, Khunying, I do. I don't go to church or anything anymore, but I do believe in God."

"I want you to pray for me."

I am dumbfounded. Is this woman, this crazy, beautiful, beat-up, terrifying, insanely confident, just plain insane woman actually asking me to pray for her?

"OK," I say, not sure what else to do. I shuffle on the carpet uncomfortably, silently begging to be let out.

Khunying stares at me, not saying a thing, each second thickening in my head like concrete setting. I hate it when people stare without speaking – I feel so . . . interrogated! And her turning that distorted face on me is like something out of a horror movie! Suddenly she leans forward, giving me a fright. Her usual composure is taken over with a desperation I've never seen on her before.

"Why is this happening to me? Am I a bad person? Why is my life so persecuted? Dark forces are out to get me, and I don't understand why?" Her normally steady, cold voice is shaking slightly and I see something behind the bruises – an expression I don't know how to interpret. It is so foreign to me.

"The money is thinning out. That ex-husband of mine is not paying what he should. There are problems with the businesses – plural! All of them! Gone! I have to fire some of my staff now. First it was the driver and nannies, and I had to replace them all with you. But now I need to get rid of some garden staff and maybe even a housemaid too. Even Kobus is going."

She shakes her head and continues down her path of self-pity. "I had to book a holiday to my father's farm because we don't have enough money to take the girls overseas this year. The farm! What will all the girls' friends think of us? And be sure their mothers will all be talking! I've come to my wits' end! Alak won't pay any more. And now this! My face! I don't even know if it will ever be the same again. Do you think Giorgio will want me now? I can't go to Italy looking like this! I'm disfigured! Probably for life!"

Apart from a foam neck brace and a few white tape stitches, I can see no permanent damage. Kobus filled me in on the doctor's final report. She is badly bruised, and has mild whiplash, but there won't be any lasting injuries. But I decide not to disagree with her about anything right now.

"Oh. I'm sorry, Khunying."

"So pray for me. Pray to what ever god you have. Lord knows I need an entity on my side."

"I will," I glance at the dream catcher above her bed, pinkening.

"Why is this all happening to me?" The earnestness in her voice startles me. "I am cursed. Someone has put a curse on me. Everything is being taken away from me. I have nothing left. I once had jewels and crowns and now, now I have nothing." Her eyes pierce through me for a burning moment, then it's as though the wind is taken out of her sails. She adjusts herself in her chair, takes another sip from her china cup and goes back to staring out the window, as if the sudden display of weakness, of humanity, went back to where ever it came from. As if nothing ever happened. She is quiet for a long time and I'm not sure what I am meant to do, but her words have struck a chord. Nothing? Of course she doesn't have nothing.

"Um–"

"You may go." She waves a thin hand without looking at me.

I start to walk out the room slowly, but just before I get to the doorway I stop. I want to say something – I feel it tearing through me. I don't know if I should, but I feel I need to help, and the words are cliff-hanging from the tip of my tongue. I take a deep breath, close my eyes while turning back around and swallow. She doesn't look up at me.

"Um, Khunying?"

She sighs, and then finally breathes out slowly. "What?" her voice is far and distant, steeped in self-benevolence, and I can tell she is preoccupied and no longer interested in talking to me.

"I just. Well, I just wanted to say. Um. That, well, it's not all that bad. Your life. It isn't all that bad."

"Excuse me?" her head slithers round dangerously.

She doesn't look happy. Her eyes flash, and I can feel my cheeks redden with alarm.

"What I mean to say is, you do have something left. Something good. You have two beautiful daughters. Two amazing little girls who are the most special children I've ever met, and who love you wholly and completely, no matter what your face looks like."

For what seems like ages, she just sits there staring at me, hand midway to her mouth with the china cup. I wonder if I've gone too far. Then all of a sudden, she seems to soften. "Yes. I suppose you are right. I do have the girls."

Wow.

* * *

I stay with the girls for the rest of the day but need to go back home to collect fresh clothes for the new week. The holiday on the farm has been cancelled, and therefore I've obviously also lost my week's break. When I'm about to leave, Suda meets me at the door. With her usual bossy demeanour, she tells me I am to sleep at my home tonight after all. "Girls stay with they mom tonight. She say she want time with girls, she look after them herself for tonight," she says to me, gesturing up the staircase towards Khunying's suite. I follow her gaze and stare up the gleaming marble staircase wondering if it had been I who caused the sudden change of heart. I feel a gentle fog of happiness creeping in to my chest. I wasn't sure if my words had penetrated at all. She agreed with me in the end, but I couldn't help wonder how deep that platinum-coated cast-iron crust went? But maybe my words had an effect after all.

I arrive back at The Palace the next morning at 7.30am. No need for crack of dawn wake-up call during school holidays, I think happily to myself. The house is dark and quiet within. Obviously everyone is adjusting their routines accordingly.

The staff entrance door opens with an unfamiliar jingling I haven't heard before. More trinkets, like the ones that showed up in the girls' school bags and on the other doors, have been tied to the door handle. I guess Khunying is being extra thorough with her purging of evil spirits or what not after the accident. I wonder how last night went with her and the girls. I'm so happy I said what I did – maybe it resonated and helped her see what is truly important in life. If nothing else, she spent the evening with them alone and I know the girls will have been thrilled to have their mommy all to themselves again. They need a little alone time, I think. As I round the corner in the passageway, I suddenly stop dead in my tracks.

What on earth . . . The grand, normally white marble staircase is black!

I stare at it, completely gobstruck. The skylight is letting in a stream of the first glimmer of early morning light, right down the stairs, which usually spirals like silver stones leading from the top floor of the house. But now, every step has been covered with black garbage bags, taped down with masking tape. The effect is startlingly ugly, so out of place in the usually perfect house.

I pause at the base and think for a moment.

Am I supposed to be walking on here? Was there some repair work booked I didn't know about? But there couldn't have been – I was here yesterday, and it was a Sunday. Workmen don't come out on Sunday evenings, do they? I look at the staircase again, noticing how tightly the masking tape has been wrapped around the ensemble to hold it together. It looks OK to walk on, I guess, if I'm really careful.

I start to walk up slowly, cautiously placing each foot on the rustling black plastic, and holding on to the banister as tightly as I can. It is very slippery. Plastic on marble doesn't exactly stick, no matter how much tape you use.

When it's time for the girls' breakfast, we take the stairs painstakingly slowly, me in front so if they slip I will break their fall. And hopefully not fall back on top of them! Oh, this is too much stress to deal with. I quicken my pace, feeling the plastic shift dangerously under my feet. Better I fall on my own, not crushing the poor things.

Finally we reach the bottom safe and sound. A slight sweat has broken out on my forehead, thanks to all the concentration and deliberate footwork. Once at the breakfast table I finally decide to ask Tasanee about the black deathtrap.

"So tell me? Why is the staircase covered in black bags?"

"For the demons." Tas looks completely convinced this is a sufficient answer and shoves a stack of blueberry flapjacks and syrup into her mouth.

"I beg your pardon?" I ask. "What 'demons'?"

"Tho they wonth come inth the houth," she explains through her breakfast. I wait for her to finish before asking for more clarity. This is crazy.

"Say that again?"

"So the demons won't come in the house," she says, taking a sip of her orange juice to wash down her food. "That lady Mommy hired to cast out the evil spirits came last night, and she told Mommy spirals in the home are an entrance-way for evil spirits. So it had to be made black so the spirits can't see it from spirit land. That's why Mommy made Suda and Ramie stick black bags to the staircase last night."

"I helped," says Lola, smiling through her flapjacks.

"That was very good of you, Lolly," I say, patting her on the hand, then turn back to Tas. "So the staircase is going to stay like that? I mean, till your mommy thinks the . . . demons . . . aren't going to attack any more?"

"Yep!" says Tasanee brightly. "And I got a special demon catcher in my room over my bed like Mommy's!" Ah, the dream catcher doubles as a demon catcher obviously. "Me thoo!" says Lola, and spits some food out of her mouth by mistake.

I wonder if I should tell the girls it's not demons at play here – that their mother is just superstitious and they are in no danger of anything other than maybe falling down the stairs now that a crazy person has strewn it in plastic! But looking at their faces, they seem really excited by the whole thing.

I sigh and dab at Lola's messy face with a napkin. "OK," I say, deciding it's probably best to change the subject. "Besides all that, did you have a nice night with your mommy?"

The girls start to tell me all about their evening, but I can't stop thinking about the blacked-out staircase. It just seems so extreme! To plaster a marble staircase with something as crass as garbage bags is just nuts! I mean, isn't it?

Chapter 24

. . . .

"She did what?" Jason's voice comes through my phone speaker, riddled with disbelief.

"Yep. The whole thing. Black plastic bags!"

"Unbelievable. You have to take pictures!"

"It's a great big spirally monument to 'she's-officially-lost-her-mind'!" I emphasise my words like a ringmaster at the circus freak show, introducing a three-headed dog.

"That's for sure. Sheesh!"

"And it's so slippery to walk on. If I fall, I swear, I'll sue!"

"Haha, now you sound like her!"

"Ya, well."

"So, you can't come home for a break after all, huh. That sucks."

We had barely finished breakfast earlier when Khunying had appeared at the doorway, the bruise on her face a deep shade of blackish purple with yellowing edges and a green tinge. She kissed the girls goodbye and disappeared again without any explanation to me. Kobus informed me later she had booked herself into a 'healing spa' for the week, and would be flying straight to Italy afterwards, to see her boyfriend the Count or Earl or whatever he is. I wonder, is a title a prerequisite to dating this woman? I guess her quality time with the girls was short lived. And I am once again Palace-bound.

"It's not so bad. I don't mind it here when she's not around. And I have quite a few outings planned."

"I thought you weren't allowed to take them out on outings?"

"Ya, I guess not, but Alak says–"

"Alak?"

"The father." I still haven't mentioned Alak to Jason again. I specifically avoided the subject of the extra money he gave me, and hid the perfume. Jason just wouldn't understand.

"Oh, right. When did you talk to their father again?"

"Well, uh, I just saw him, like, you know, when he came to see the girls. Anyhow, he told me I could take them out. And he's my boss after all. He pays my salary."

"I don't know, Jem . . . Are you sure it's a good idea? I mean, with every-thing that's happened, do you really want to chance pissing off the crazy lady again?"

"Don't worry," I say, trying to get off the subject. "It'll be OK. So what are you up to?"

"Actually, there's something I've been meaning to tell you." Jason's voice sounds weirdly serious. "It's about Tracy."

"Oh yeah?" Suddenly, I hear Lola.

"I'm not ugly!" she cries.

"Yes you are, ugly!" Tas's voice is taunting, "You have ugly gums! Mommy said so!"

Oh dear. "Jason, I'm so sorry," I interrupt him. "I have to go."

"What?"

"It's an emergency. So sorry! I'll call you right back."

"Jemma…" Lola's crying has reached the point where it sounds like it might break glass soon.

"I have to go." I hang up the phone on a still protesting Jason, take a deep breath, and run through to the girls' room.

"Girls, girls! Hello Kitty says stop fighting!"

Khunying doesn't return from her trip all school holiday long. The girls and I've had a wonderful time but I've never been happier than now school has started again. I love the girls and it has been an enjoyable bonding experience, but I'm exhausted! I haven't been home in what feels like weeks, and I really just need a break from Barbies and fairy gardens and Bruno the dog. How on earth my mother ever did this with Jason and me as kids, I don't know - which reminds me, I need to call her sometime. It's been a while.

After dropping the girls at school, I return to The Palace and see Kobus's BMW in the driveway, and Jim carrying Khunying's luggage into the house. She must be back. About time!

I park the Cayenne in the usual 'wash' area of the driveway so it can get its daily soap-down treatment, and walk across the cobbled drive to the house. Khunying's SLK is parked in the drive-about, ready for her to take out for the day. Her sports car still hasn't come back from the garage, and I suspect it may be a write-off. The Merc's silver surface is gleaming in the early morning sunlight like a crisp sheet of ice, catching the first rays. Before I pass the drive-about to head towards the staff entrance, I hear the front door open and Khunying emerges from the house, looking like she just stepped off the pages of Vogue.

I wait for her to see me, then lift my hand in a small wave and greet her politely. "Good morning, Khunying! Welcome back! Your face looks amazing, healing so well!" All the swelling has gone down, and I can only see a slight bruising under her eye. "Beautiful day, isn't it? You must be very happy to be back." I am going for all smiles and neighborliness. Well, courtesy at any rate.

Khunying looks up at me and pauses, Fendi handbag and car keys in hand. She nods obligingly.

"Hello, Jemma. Thank you. I guess it will be nice to be back once I've done something about this hideous hair-do of mine and get a massage. Long flight." I look at her hair and think it looks just the same as always, sheer perfection. She continues, her drawl sounding bored and forced: "I trust you had a good holiday with the girls?"

"Oh, yes, thanks. We did."

"Well, good. One of their friends wants to visit tomorrow. I've told her she can come after school. Please make sure she is welcomed."

"Oh, of course! What's her name? Is she at their school?"

"Taylor. And no, she doesn't go there. She's the daughter of a very dear friend of mine, a South African celebrity. The girls haven't met her before."

"Oh, OK. What time will she get here?" I wonder if I was meant to jump at the 'South African celebrity' comment and ask who that person is – Khunying seems to love the self-importance that goes along with knowing famous people.

She glares at me and I guess I played it all wrong. Again. "After school – as I just said," she bites, and opens her car door agitatedly. "Ask Kobus any more tedious questions." Back to the old battle-axe I see. I smile apologetically and quickly make my retreat before the old angry Khunying comes out fully. It was nice not having her around. I miss not having her around.

I rush to find Kobus. It's not going to be the same without him here, especially since he won't be around to buffer any more. With this being his last week I feel almost tearful at the thought of going on without him. Partly because I will miss him, of course, but partly because I have no idea how things are going to change with Khunying. No more palming me off on Kobus. No more getting Kobus to administer memos and written warnings. No more drinks with Kobus after another of her crazy outbursts. I try to put the thought out of my mind.

Taylor turns out to be a really sweet blonde girl with a very soft voice and freckles on her nose. She's the same age as Tasanee, but is much more timid - similar to Lola. The dynamic between the girls is complicated at first, Tasanee starts off being kind of mean, but after a few "Hello Kitty Says" from me, and she calms down and has fun with the other two. They play dress-up 'Princesses', and I make them headdresses, royal pendants (cardboard cut-outs wrapped in tinfoil) and a great big crown Tasanee insists on wearing the whole time. She claims the title of "Queen Princess" even though I try to explain to her she can't technically do that.

When it's time for Taylor to go home, I take her downstairs to wait for her father. He was meant to arrive at 5pm to pick her up, but doesn't pitch for forty-five minutes. Just when I'm about to phone, a loud bang on the front glass door announces his arrival. We rush to the door and all start putting our shoes on to walk Taylor out. Her father bangs on the door again, even louder than before, rattling me.

"Taylor!" he shouts from outside. "Taylor!" I look at her while opening the door, wondering why this man is being so impatient, and get a shock at the expression on her face. She looks petrified. All afternoon she has giggled and laughed and has had a sweet smile dancing on her face, but suddenly she has frozen in fear and looks as though she is trying to shrink in size. I stop my hand on the door handle and stare at her.

"What's wrong?" I ask in a whisper. She looks up at me and shakes her head. "Taylor," I whisper, going down on my haunches to face her, "Are you OK?"

"I – I – I think I left my school jacket upstairs," she says in a quivering voice. Tasanee, the ever-aware, strangely mature child that she is, picks up on Taylor's fear almost instantly. She takes the blonde girl by the hand and whispers "I'll help her find it" to me, while leading Taylor back up the plastic-covered staircase. Lola follows them, and I stand up again, bewildered.

The banging on the door is getting so bad the glass is reverberating! Khunying appears at the door of the piano lounge, looking highly irritated. "Who on earth is that!" she demands just as I start to open the thudding door.

As I release the latch, the door flings open, almost knocking me off my feet, to reveal a tall, gruff-faced man in his mid-forties, wearing a button-down business shirt untucked on one side and sticking out of his formal grey pants. His tie has been loosened and is hanging limply above his bulging beer belly. And he reeks of alcohol.

"Taylor!" He shouts again, looking right past me with blood-shot eyes and scanning the room.

"Sir? Taylor is just fetching her school jack–" I start, but he pushes past me into the room. Lola, who is always more cautious and therefore slower going up the stairs than Tasanee now the black bags are making it so slippery, is almost at the top of the spiral, and the man sees her before she disappears down her passage after Tasanee and Taylor. He plunges forward and starts to blunder up the staircase, slipping repeatedly. I'm aghast, not sure exactly what is happening. I look over at Khunying and see she is as shocked as I am.

"Go! Go after him!" she orders, finding herself a bit more quickly than I. "I'll fetch Jim."

Obediently I stumble forward and start up the stairs after Taylor's father. Once in the girls' room, I see him grab his little girl by the arm away from Tasanee who jumps back as he yanks his daughter towards the exit. She has started to cry, Lola has ducked down and put her hands over her head to block out the shouting, and I suddenly feel myself switch to protect mode.

"Sir, you may not take Taylor," I say, blocking his way at the door. He laughs, a big toxic breath of booze hitting me right in the face.

"Saysh who! You? Hah!" He is leering at me, holding Taylor possessively. But he doesn't try to go past me. I have my arms bent firmly at my hips and legs spread and set so I am blocking the doorway. He looks so scary! So red in the face! I wonder if he will hit me, but he doesn't seem to know exactly what to do. He rocks back and forth, shouting obscenities at me, but doesn't touch me. I look past his shoulder, and see Lola and Tasanee are holding on to each other, their eyes wide with fear.

"Sir," I say, firmly. "Please let go of Taylor this instant and leave."

"Leave! Are szhou telling me stso leave? You wantsh to kidnap my daughtzer?" He shakes a fist in my face, and I feel alcohol-laced spittle hit me as he shouts. What is up with these people, always thinking someone is out to kidnap their kids! I pull my head back an inch to get out of his pungent-breath zone. There is no way this drunken idiot is taking Taylor in the car with him! Not if I can help it.

"We will arrange for her to be taken home," I start to say.

"You have gno righst!" he shouts, slurring his words angrily, "to tsake mygirrl! I'm leeeaving!" Suddenly lunging forward, he crashes into me, knocking my breath out as he shoves me up against the wall while pulling Taylor along with him. Where the hell are Khunying and Jim? How could they leave me to deal with this deranged drunk alone?

I shoot a petrified look at the girls who are still frozen in their spectators' horror, while clutching my chest where he pummeled into me and catching my breath. "Stay here!" I shout and run back out of the room after the drunken man. He has managed to get to the bottom of the staircase without falling and breaking all his and his daughter's bones, though for the life of me I don't know how. I cling to the banisters while going down as fast as I can, and slip a few times, knocking my legs and elbow hard into the marble sides as I keep my grip and find my footing again. When I get to the bottom of the stairs, Jim almost slams right into me as we both run out of the house. I see Taylor's father pushing her into the passenger seat of his car and slamming the door.

"Taylor!" I shout. "Taylor! Climb out!" She peers at me through the glass, terror-stricken and immobilised.

"Sir. Sir!" Jim says, rushing towards the front of the car. "Sir, please will you step away from the car." It's like a scene from a cop movie!

Jim reaches the car and grabs the door, stopping Taylor's dad from climbing in to the drivers seat. I run over and pull the passenger door open, helping Taylor out just as a scuffle breaks out between Jim and her dad.

I look over the top of the car, as Jim grabs the car keys away from the brawling drunk, and Taylor trips, stumbling on the cobblestones. The man leans over the car door, catching his breath. His eyes fall on me, picking Taylor up on my hip, and I freeze.

"You will – NOT – tsake – my dsaughter!" he shouts between heavy breaths, narrowing his eyes and stumbling around the car towards us. I run as fast as I can out of his reach, past Khunying who is now also outside, stalking towards the car with her phone at her ear. I don't stop, but run around the fountain and into the house with Taylor clinging to my neck. I put her down at the foot of the staircase, and hold her hand tight as we make our way up the death trap again. All the way I can hear Khunying screaming at the man outside.

"I HAVE CALLED THE POLICE, YOU DRUNKEN LUNATIC! I WILL SUE YOU! YOU DO NOT COME ON TO MY PROPERTY AND THREATEN MY EMPLOYEES AND YOU WILL NOT DRIVE WITH TAYLOR IN YOUR CAR DRUNK LIKE THIS, YOU SCUM BAG! YOU BRUTE! YOU F–"

I slam the girls' bedroom door and lock it. Tasanee and Lola are hiding behind the bed again, and I take Taylor to join them. After hugging the girls and shushing them for a bit, I open the French doors and step outside, leaning over the edge to see what is happening below me.

Khunying is running circles around the fountain, waving the phone above her head, her very best blood-curdling voice shouting: "I'LL SUE! I'LL SUE! JUST WAIT TILL YOUR WIFE HEARS OF THIS! SHE'LL

FINALLY DIVORCE YOU, YOU BLITHERING IDIOT! I'VE CALLED THE POLICE! I'LL HAVE YOU LOCKED UP AND I'LL SUE!"

The great big oaf of a man only runs faster, chasing her, waving his fist in the air, shouting: "Good! Brrring the polishe! Yous are kidngnapshing my daughshter! I wantsh the polishe! They will take onnne look a'your fashe, you bish, and see you'rge gettinnin fisht fightsh and andz are no' the kind of woman tsho be washhing over my little gil . . ."

"I WAS IN A CAR ACCIDENT, YOU MORON! YOU ARE THE DRUNK HERE, COMING TO FETCH YOUR DAUGHTER LATE FROM SOME BAR SOMEWHERE! I HAVE HER SAFE INSIDE WITH MY GIRLS, I AM A PROTECTIVE MOTHER AND DON'T YOU MESS WITH ME, YOU FILTHY–"

"I don't needz tso take thish from you, you bish! I don't need to stake anyfing from a dirty, bimbo, golddigger!"

Khunying freezes in her tracks, obviously shocked to a standstill. I pull my breath in and put my hand over my mouth, even more shocked. Did he just say what I think he did?

Suddenly Jim joins the madness too, this time with a broom in his hand. Khunying breaks away, and I hear the front door slam behind her. If that door doesn't break today it will be a miracle.

Jim holds the broomstick up as if it is a baseball bat, and squares off Taylor's dad, who has finally stopped running. He glares at Jim, wavering in his drunken state. So much dust has been kicked up from around the loose stones with all the commotion it's like watching an old western movie, the Sherriff facing the town vandal in the dusty sunset. Although it's already quite dark and I can't make out exactly what's happening any more.

I hear a sniffle behind me and look round at the girls again. I go back inside and close the French doors, blocking out the noise and going back to sit with the frightened creatures behind the bed.

A short while later, we hear police sirens in the distance. Taylor looks up at me with big anxious eyes. "Don't worry," I say to her. "You will be safe here. They are just going to help your daddy drive because he is drunk and will crash his car. I'm sure they will let him come home in the morning when he's sober again."

"I want my mommy," she says through a fresh wave of tears.

I wait a few more moments until I hear the police car come all the way up the drive and stop at the top. Then I get up, telling the girls to wait, and go down to find Khuyning to ask if we can call Taylor's mother and find out what is happening. I go outside again and see another police car arriving. Jim is talking to an officer and another officer is standing between Khunying and Taylor's father, trying to get the story out of them. "Arrest him!" Khunying is shouting. "Arrest him for drunken driving! For kidnapping! For battery! He assaulted my au pair! He assaulted me!" They are both shouting over each other and the poor policeman looks very frustrated.

Another cop climbs out of the second police car and comes over to me after having a few short words with one of her colleagues, while the fourth officer takes Khunying aside to speak to her alone. After giving the officer my account of what happened, still confused myself as to exactly what did happen, I see Taylor's father being taken and put into the back of one of the police cars. He suddenly looks very ashamed and downtrodden. Maybe the shock of the cops arriving sobered him up.

Just then a luxury sedan car pulls in to the parking, and out climbs a plumpish, weary-looking woman, her brows heavily knit. She glances at the father in the back of the cop car, glaring in his direction momentarily, and walks over to Khunying, exchanging air kisses. This must be the celebrity, though I have no idea who. Don't recognise her at all.

When Taylor's mother has taken the girl away, and Khunying's flock of greasy lawyers has arrived, one of the officers asks me to come with him to give another statement. We go sit in the dining room, and I accept a glass of chilled lemon water from Jim thankfully.

"I don't understand," I say. "I already gave my statement to the lady cop."

"I'm very sorry, ma'am," says the policeman, opening to a fresh page in his book and readying his pen over the blank page, "but there seems to be some, uh, discrepancies between your and your employer's statements."

"Oh." I told it exactly how it happened. There shouldn't be any discrepancies. I mean, I know it all happened so fast, and I don't understand why it all happened, but I definitely told it like it is. Was. "Well, maybe Khunying just told you stuff I didn't see when I was taking the girls up to the room?"

"No, not that part. It's the parts where you both gave an account of the same thing that is a problem. Your employer tells us you were assaulted?"

"Oh, well, no, not actually. He did push me against the wall, but he didn't actually hit me."

"And she says he assaulted her too."

"Well, I didn't see that happen, so I'm not sure about that. Maybe it was when I was inside?"

"No, she says he assaulted her when you were still standing outside, carrying the girl."

"Oh, uh." I rack my brains. No, that's not what happened. Khunying only came out after I was on my way back in. Why would she lie about something like that? I wonder if she expects me to back her story. But I can't. It's the police – I have to tell the truth. "No," I say falteringly. "No, I didn't see anything like that."

"And her eye?"

"Her eye? Oh, she was in a car accident a few weeks ago."

The cop sighs and looks down at his page again. "OK, Miss. Would you care to tell me exactly what happened again please?"

I recount the horrific incident while he scribbles down words on his paper. Every now and again he stops writing and looks up at me, saying, "And you're sure about that?" as if doubting what I'm telling him. I assure him I'm saying everything truthfully, and when he is finally done with me, walk out with him. Khunying, her lawyers and the rest of the cops are all standing around outside in a big group talking. I decide not to join as the officer walks towards them, and break away at the spiral staircase to head up to the girls' room instead.

"What's happened!" Tas demands when she sees me. They are being toweled down and dressed by Suda, both smelling like soap.

"Is Taylor going to be OK?" asks Lola, her voice still shaky.

"She's going to be fine," I say, smiling encouragement.

"And is Mommy going to sue that man?"

"Or put him in jail?" adds Tasanee.

"I don't know," I say, truthfully. She always shouts about suing people, though I never know if she ever goes through with it. Kind of like her written warnings. She did seem to be quite adamant about having him arrested though.

Jim has brought some dinner up for us on tea trays, obviously guessing we don't want to go back downstairs, so we eat our food in the playroom silently.

"It's been quite a day!" I say eventually, packing up. "Why don't you brush your teeth and I'll read to you. You can both sleep in Tas's bed together tonight, OK?"

Once the girls are tucked away and have managed to wrangle an extra four storybooks out of me, I eventually turn off the light and head back down to take the dinner trays back to the kitchen.

As I pass the sunroom, I see Khunying pacing the silk Persian carpet while talking on her phone. She sees me and lifts her hand, signaling for me to come in and sit down.

I do as I'm told, and take a seat on one of the couches. I feel exhausted from the day's craziness and wonder how much more I can take of this. But Khunying smiles at me as I sit. Strangely. So I'm guessing this isn't to crap me out? Maybe she wants to talk about everything that happened here this evening.

"Jemma," she says, finally hanging up her phone and sitting down on her Marie Antoinette armchair. "How are you doing? Are you OK after all that?"

"Yes, I'm alright, thank you, Khunying," I say weakly, feeling suddenly really tired.

"And the girls? They got to bed alright?" I wonder why Khunying didn't come check on them herself after the ordeal, but guess she has been too busy trying to get a lawsuit together or something.

"Yes, they are OK too. They were quite upset, but they calmed down. I had to read them extra books," I add, wanting her to know how upset they were in case she didn't notice.

"Now, about the police," she says, completely missing my pointed comment, her tone businesslike, "or more specifically, about your statement."

Great. So I didn't get away with it after all. I brace myself for the monster – here it comes. Psycho bitch is about to unleash herself because I didn't lie to the police. I look down at my hands, not wanting to meet her eyes as I'm sure they are about to flare over and I can't take much more today.

"You didn't want to have him arrested?"

"I'm sorry?" I ask, looking up in confusion. Her face isn't one of rage, or icy indifference, or even cold disapproval. Nothing I'm used to from her. She looks at me, head cocked to one side.

"Well, I was about to have him arrested, but your statement put an end to that."

"Oh," I say, searching for some kind of hint as to whether I'm in trouble or not. She really doesn't seem angry at all – just talking. Like a conversation. Like between two normal people. It's bizarre! "Oh. Well, I just told them what I saw, Khunying."

"Do you realise he is an abusive man and father and probably does much worse than just shout and scream when he's drunk?"

"Um, I don't know him, and –uh – this was the first time – uh . . ."

"Yes, I suppose you don't know any of the history. I am good friends with his wife. She is an ex-Miss South Africa runner-up, do you know? Terrible story, her falling for him, or rather his money I should say."

That's a laugh. She's one to talk!

"So, sadly, later in life, she started losing her looks thanks to his abusive nature, and now he's turning into a violent drunk on top of all the years of emotional abuse! I've tried to get her to leave him for ages, but she just won't, for the girl. Today was my opportunity to have him arrested and show her how dangerous he is. But all he'll get now is a charge for drunken behavior or disturbing the peace or something."

I listen to Khunying, feeling a deep sadness for Taylor. The poor little girl, caught up in such a horrible family situation. I wonder if I should have just agreed with Khunying's story after all. Khunying watches me for a while, and I feel as though I should say something.

"I'm sorry. About your friend, and for Taylor. But, you see, I didn't want to lie to the police."

"Some people are worth lying for, Jemma."

"You mean him?"

"No. I mean Taylor."

I take this in. She may be hard on the outside, she may be irrational and act bat-crazy from time to time, and let's face it, she's downright bitchy most of the time, but right now I see her in a different light. She wanted to help Taylor. In her own way, even if it wasn't exactly the right way. And I messed it all up. I'm confused. I don't know what's right or wrong any more.

"I'm sorry," I say again, feeling terrible.

"Oh, cheer up!" Khunying says, laughing at my solemn expression and clapping her hands together. "I forgive you. It's not my daughters after all!

What can you do? Now. Let's talk about school. Tomorrow is Friday, which means you don't have any after school activities with the girls, do you?"

I'm confused, surprised and astonished all at once. She is asking about the girls' school schedule! She never shows any interest in their daily routines with me. It's as if sparkly Khunying from the Sun City trip is back again, revived from her torturous slumber by this horrible incident today. Maybe she is bi-polar.

"Uh, well, yes. We usually come straight home . . ."

"Well, then, I will come with you to fetch them, and we will all go for a lovely lunch afterwards."

Did she just say that? Khunying? My employer Khunying. I'm floored!

"Oh! Wow. That will be wonderful!" I say, knowing it will be wonderful for Tasanee, not so wonderful for Lola, or me for that matter. "The girls will be so pleased!"

"Let's keep it a surprise, then, shall we?" she says through a radiant smile. Even her voice has changed and gone light and wispy. I feel like the whole planet has just done a flip and everything is topsy-turvy. Back on the roller-coaster we go.

What a day. I honestly can't take much more of this.

As I leave the room and head up to bed, Khunying stops me at the door. "Jemma?" She has got up and come over to where I am standing. She puts a hand on my arm. "I'm happy you are here. For the girls."

I can tell she means it. A genuine moment. Rare. I spend the whole night lying awake with my thoughts. She is human too; one with strengths and flaws and hurts just like anyone else. I want to understand her. I can feel myself starting to feel sorry for her. I think she might be the most deeply unhappy person I've ever met, except for Taylor's family maybe.

For the first time, my heart really goes out to her.

Chapter 25

· · · · · · · · · ·

I turn Peaches' non-power-steering wheel and park at the flat. Wow, this car sucks. Every time I have to drive it these days, it feels like such an effort. It's like navigating a brick, compared to driving the Porsche. I really must look into getting a new car. Maybe take a loan or something. I haven't actually saved anything yet – my salary seems to just slip away every month – but I'm sure I will start saving soon. Things went so well at the lunch with Khunying, maybe I'll start being paid overtime? She was surprisingly pleasant, engaging and asked me all about myself. I mentioned I wanted to buy a new car, and she commented 'Oh yes, you would do us all a favour if you got that wreck off the road!' and tinkled with laughter, so I took it as encouragement rather than an insult. If she started paying what I am truly owed, I could pay the loan back then. And she was right - I really need a new car. I mean, who drives under these conditions?

Pulling into my space, I see Troy's car is parked in our visitors bay. That's funny. I didn't know we were seeing her tonight? Unlocking the door, I drag my suitcase into the flat behind me, kicking my shoes off at the door. "Jason?" I call into the darkened flat. "You will not believe what happened!"

I flip the lights on in the kitchen and grab a water bottle out the fridge. Maybe they've gone down to the complex's communal pool. Sometimes Jason likes to go for a dip after work . . . I step onto something cold. Eew!

I look down, ready to squirm if it's a wayward slug from the veld or something, yuk, but . . . there are wet foot prints on the floor. And what I just stood on is a wet bathing suit . . . No! Is that what I think it is? A bright purple Brazilian-cut bikini top! And swimming trunks.

Troy! And Jason?

Before I can gather myself from the sudden reeling in my head, Jason comes running out of his room and slams the door shut behind him. His hair is all ruffled and his face is blood red.

"Jason?" I'm dumbstruck.

"Jemma! You're home."

"It's Friday night."

"But you're . . . uh . . . early"

"She let me go early . . ."

"She let you? Wow. First time . . . er . . ."

"Ya, you won't believe . . . wait . . . what's going on?" I almost forget myself, desperate to tell my brother all about the past twenty-four hours, but then snap back to the dripping purple thing at hand. I narrow my eyes, point a finger at him and lower my voice to a hiss. "Is Troy in there with you?" I hear a thud from his bedroom, and a quiet swear word muttered in the unmistakable throaty female voice. Jason's eyes widen and he stands awkwardly, spreading out a bit like a guilty-looking balloon fish, trying to hide the passageway to his bedroom behind him.

"Oh, well, um, no? No. Why would you think . . ."

"I saw her car downstairs."

"Oh."

"And this?" I say, flagging the purple bikini.

"Oh, oh – that. OK. Well, she was just – uh – just helping me – um – pick out some new outfits for work," he laughs nervously. "You know, with you being gone and no one to tell me if this shirt is horrendous with that tie . . ." His eyes are darting back and forth between his guilty conscience and me. He flinches every time another bump and swear word emanates from his bedroom.

"Oh really, then explain why it's on the living-room floor? While helping you organise your wardrobe? Because?" My tone is a hushed quartet of accusation, horror, sarcasm and disbelief.

"Oh, we had a dip in the pool, you know. And. Ha. And well you wouldn't believe it! She got changed, of course, and was about to hang her wet top on the windowsill to dry out when . . . uh . . . well, you see . . ." His eyes are ricocheting all over the place. He is useless at lying.

"Oh really, Jason? Exhibit A, in all its purple glory, and the offending wet tracks. The wet tracks leading to your bedroom door! I can't believe it! You're cheating! With Troy!" This week just doesn't get better. If a drunk in a suit is not attacking me at work, if it's not Khunying pulling a complete one-eighty, throwing me way off again, it's my brother, my faithful best-guy-in-the-world brother cheating on his long-term girlfriend! With my friend!

"I'm not!"

"Jason, what about Tracy?" I say, forgetting to whisper and not hiding the judgment from my voice at all. I stare hard at him and wait for his answer. He flames up and puffs out a tiny bit more, but seems to get a slow leak. His face clears, and suddenly he looks incredibly guilty. But there's something more. Hurt?

"Tracy," he says gruffly, looking down. "The thing is, Tracy and I kinda broke up."

"You what? When? How? What happened?"

Jason pushes his hands through his hair, looking tired, and walks past me to sit down on the couch. "Actually, about six weeks ago already. She met someone in London. She has been with this guy for like three months already. Behind my back. Three months and six weeks now, I guess," he adds bitterly.

"What? Why didn't you tell me?" I drop the bikini top back to the floor and sit down next to him. This is awful. My brother – my twin – my best friend in the whole world kept something like that from me. He must have been going through such a hard time; he must be so sad and hurt! Another sound from Jason's bedroom door grates my sisterly pity. Hurt, I guess, but not too hurt to seek comfort in Troy's clutches. Why would he tell her and not me? Is it because of the Ryan thing? Maybe he hasn't forgiven me. But why should that matter?

I'm so confused, I don't even know where to begin. I'm angry, but I also feel I've let him down. I feel awful! And the fact I can hear Troy scurrying around in the bedroom just makes it worse. I knew she had her sights set on him! All that Cherry Monster . . .

"I tried to tell you, Jemma. But you couldn't talk."

"What?" Oh man, how could I have not seen this. How could I have been so selfish?

"You never seemed to be able to talk. You had so much going on. You know, that woman and all." He keeps his head turned away from me and is staring out of the dusky window at our nightlight illuminating the tiny porch outside.

"And you and Troy–"

"Just sort of happened. I mean, we obviously have chemistry and there's been this flirtation for ages," he looks sheepishly at me. "Maybe that's why I was so upset when you accused me of – things – because maybe there was some truth to it. But I would never have cheated on Tracy, you know that." I do. I know my brother. Still, I cant help but have a sinking feeling Troy might use him up and spit him out too. Suddenly I realize all the similarities between her and Tracy. What if the cycle is repeated? What if Jason falls for another man-eater who has her fun with him but bores and tosses him aside? I try to focus on what Jason is saying. "But after it was definitely over with Tracy, I mean, I told Troy. I would have told you, but, well, you know. So then I guess it just happened." Jason is playing with a coaster, flipping it over and over in his hands like he's practicing the coin-finger-flip-trick-thingy with it. I know him, when he plays with something like that, he is trying desperately not to deal with the issue at hand.

"You should have told me anyway," I say, feeling a mixture of guilt at being such a crappy sister and heartache for what my poor brother must be going through. "I would have helped you, you know, even just to talk about it. The least I could have done is get you horribly drunk on bad cheap booze. Even if I seemed too busy, I would have made the time."

He laughs and shakes his head slowly. "I know. But also… telling you would have made it real. I didn't want it to be real – I wasn't ready to admit it was real. I guess that was stupid – I mean, it is real. It is very, very real . . . and now . . ." Jason pauses and looks down at the bikini top. A fresh grin spreads across his face. "Now I guess this is real too."

Right.

"But it's OK," he continues, smiling shyly at me. "Don't worry. I'm doing OK. Good riddance, I say."

"Ya. And it's probably a good thing you found out about the cheating now instead of wasting more time with her."

"Exactly. Tracy the Tramp," he nudges me, looking to lighten the mood.

"Trashy Tracy the Tramp!" I say emphatically. I nudge Jason back and giggle. He laughs, and puts down the coaster.

"But just promise me one thing, Jemma. Please give the idea of Troy and me a chance. For me. Because I really need this."

I sigh. "OK Jason, I'll try. But only for you."

Later in the evening, a fully-dressed Troy and Jason are sitting together on the couch, and we're all trying a little too hard to act like nothing's weird.

But I can't help sending Troy a death stare or two. That's my brother! And I'm concerned he is fragile at the moment, and Troy might. . . Jason seems to notice my demeanor and tries to distract me with my favourite subject.

"So Jemma, what's new with Mrs. Totally Lost the Plot?"

"Oh, well–" I hesitate. Now I'm not sure if I should tell Jason all about yesterday. Somehow it feels less 'big' in the light of his collapsed long-term relationship and subsequent new-found flame. But he's looking at me expectantly, waiting for me to dish. "I feel bad only ever talking about my stuff," I try.

"Are you kidding me?" laughs Troy" We live for the latest episodes in the days of your crazy upside-down so-not-normal au pair life! It's what keeps us going, babe!"

We? Us? Already? I'm trying really hard to be OK with this, but this is Troy. Seductress Troy. She goes through men like a teenage boy goes through Kleenex, and now she's draped all over my brother. My heart-broken, vulnerable brother. I can feel myself glaring at her again, but I did promise Jason I'd give him and Troy a chance, so I calm myself and tell them all about the crazy drunk man, When I get to the bit about Khunying expecting me to lie to the police, Troy laughs out loud.

"Wow, she really is insane!"

"Actually..." I move on to tell them how much Khunying seems to have changed. The way she is speaking to me differently, and the lunch. Even talking about her boyfriend in Italy, and giving me style tips. Not that I think I needed more tips, but I guess the queen of Vogue would know.

Jason has been looking more and more concerned as I tell him all this. His brow deepens in a frown and eventually I can't take it anymore.

"What! What's wrong now?" I throw my hands up.

"It's called Stockholm Syndrome."

"What?"

"You know – she's got you captive there, you feel trapped, and then you go through this traumatic experience together, so now you're bonded or something. It's not real."

"No man, I know what Stockholm Syndrome is! But this isn't it. I mean, she gave me that champagne at Sun City, and was nice to me before. And didn't you listen? She came to school with me today. Out of her own free will. Then took us all to lunch. To lunch! And she was so nice! OK, not nice like normal people nice, but, well, nice for her. I mean, you should have seen her! She was so–"

"Nice. OK, I get it. Very descriptive, Jem. I'm convinced." Jason rolls his eyes and Troy giggles.

"I'm just saying," I say irritably, "that this could be the turning point in our working relationship. The point where we start to get along."

"And I'm just saying, I wouldn't hold my breath if I were you," says Troy.

They've been together for like a second and already she's speaking for him?

I stand up and stretch my legs. No point in going on about this. Jason just doesn't understand. And Troy. Well, she's just in it all for her own gain, obviously. I wonder if she ever was my friend at all. I've had enough for one week and could do with a long relaxing bubble bath. I turn to walk out of the room, "I'm gonna have a soak."

"OK, but don't you want to call Frederick about doing something tonight first? He was quite upset by the dinner plans falling through . . ." starts Jason.

"No thanks." I call from the bathroom, already opening up the taps. "Not really in the mood to do anything tonight."

Jason walks in behind me, looking surprised. "But. Well, he was saying he couldn't get hold of you yesterday, for obvious reasons, I know now. Still, he wanted to see you."

I sigh deeply. "I'll chat to him later, promise. Just not tonight. I'm really tired. I want to relax and go to bed early."

"Alright then, old lady."

"Haha," I say scornfully. "Well, what about you? What have you two got planned?" Troy, close behind, looks at Jason, a devilish glint in her eye. He returns her wicked smile with a wink.

"Out!" I order and bang the door shut. Do I really have to deal with this now?

Chapter 26

· · · · · · · · ·

With Kobus gone, things are different at The Palace. I feel as though I've been floundering, trying to find my feet again with the new situation, almost like starting at a new job all over again. Sitting in one of my new, daily meetings with Khunying where she gets me to help her deal with some things Kobus used to take care of, she hands me a laptop.

"You can't be expected to book me flights if you don't have one," she explains. "Kobus didn't need to take it with him, so it's yours." I open it up and I swear I smell cigarette smoke, but the computer is slick and light and I love it.

"Thank you, Khunying!"

"Before you go, those are for you too," she gestures to a bag at the door. "Some more of my old clothes – probably all too small for you but some things may fit."

My heart skips a beat. It started with a shirt she didn't want any more, and I happened to walk past as she was telling Ramie to toss it. She caught sight of me, looked me up and down, and changed her orders, and told Ramie to give it to me, who then handed it over begrudgingly. I suppose

· · · · · · · ·

Ramie would have kept it for herself if Khunying hadn't seen me, but that's hardly my fault.

"Oh, and that Chanel top I just got in Italy – stupid maids not reading the care instructions properly and a seam unraveled! I should deduct it from their salaries. But may as well not go to waste – it's your colour so you can have it."

"Oh, thank you, Khunying!" I can't help but gush. I know the top, and I was instantly in love. For a simple V-neck three-quarter-sleeve beige top, it was exquisite I never expected to actually own anything Coco!

"Now that you are the new Kobus, you should look like one." Does this mean I'm the new PA? Nothing has been said about job descriptions. I only help Khunying in the mornings while the girls are at school, and then I'm back to being the nanny. Nothing has been amended in my contract and certainly nothing has changed in my bank account. Still, this must be a step up. I take the clothes gratefully and feel a wave of pride. "Shouldn't you be fetching the girls now?" she says pointedly.

On the drive I call Frederick and put him on speaker.

"Dahling skattebol. Where have you been? What's new in la la land?" he says, but his voice is strained. It's probably just distorted because of the car noise.

"Oh nothing. I'm just the proud new owner of Le Coco Chanel, that's all." I put on a fake French accent.

"Hm?"

I kind of expected more from him. Maybe he doesn't quite get it. "It's this new trend with Khunying. Every time something doesn't fit right or look right or seem right in the wrong light, she sends it my way. And amazingly, we are both the same size with the same size shoe too! Which is just the lucky fairy-star-dust at work, if you ask me."

"Definitely. Nothing pink, I suppose,"

"Does Burberry come in pink?"

"BURBERRY!?"

That's more like it.

"Good gaga child, you will be the best dressed pet in the play park!"

"Hah! I'm hardly the pet. She called me the new Kobus,"

"Is that like a Devil Wears Prada thing?"

"I don't know, but I get a lot of cool new stuff so I don't mind."

"So many changes! First JaRoy, now you. . ."

"Who?"

"You know. The hot new couple? Jason and Troy – JaRoy."

"Ugh. I don't like talking about them. Not just yet, ok? I still need to come to terms with the whole thing. Let's rather talk about something else."

"OK. You could tell me what it's like without Kobus being there? Or I could tell you about my new project. . ."

I wonder how Kobus is doing, away from the madness. I wonder if he managed to quit smoking. I wonder if he is working with Alak, but I don't hear from him. But change is good. Maybe it's the change of temperature in the air that has calmed me down, or maybe it's the change of temperature at The Palace that has warmed me up – either way I suddenly realize I don't really feel the need to find solace from my working situation in Kobus, my friends, or Alak anymore. Not that there ever was much of that, I suppose.

"Jemma? You still there?"

"Sorry, my mind was elsewhere. Ya, It's different without Kobus, but I think it's better in a way? Not because he's gone, but because of the shift in Khunying. It's quite nice to be on such civil terms with her."

"Civil? With Mrs Totally Lost the Plot?"

"Oh come on, it's different now."

"Oh? So she's taken down the black bags off the staircase then?"

"Well… Not exactly, no. But anyhow, listen, I just got to the school. Speak to you soon!"

Time proves me right. Khunying has changed, despite what Frederick says about black-bagged stairwells. Over the next few weeks, besides the meetings and clothes, we have moments – not quite warm, but definite human moments. She greets me every time she sees me, sometimes coldly, but sometimes she has these bouts of pleasantness where she talks a bit about the girls rather than just giving more orders. Even when the orders do come, they don't seem quite so robust any more, but rather as strong suggestive requests. Not that I have a choice but to obey. Still, it's nice to be asked. And her new found 'fondness' makes it easier for me to avoid Jason and Troy. The more I think about it after catching them that night, the more upset I've become. I just can't get my head around them being an item behind my back, and I start to spend less and less time with them. I even offer to stay at The Palace a couple of weekends, to take the girls to various birthday parties, but really it's to stay away from home. Frederick tries to swing me round and be all pro "Ja-Roy", but it just makes me more annoyed he is so easily swayed to be on their side. So I avoid him too.

All this avoidance is working for me on a professional level. The extra time with Khunying and the girls is slowly but surely soothing all my old nervousness around The Palace. Even Lola is more relaxed and happy around her mother.

Today I'm wearing an ensemble gathered over the weeks: le Coco Top, some long brown flat Stella McCartney boots, and a flowy sand-coloured D&G boho-skirt, all given to me by Khunying. When she sees me in her runway-hand-me-downs, she usually laughs and says something like "Who would have thought my throw-aways could re-create an entire new human being!" I never know whether that's an insult or a compliment, but I don't really mind. I get the clothes after all.

"Who wants to know what today's surprise is?" I ask the girls leadingly as we all climb into the car after school. They both bounce up and down full of excitement.

"Oooh me me me!" they shout in unison.

"We are going ice-skating!"

The girls stop bouncing. Neither of them speaks.

"I said . . . we are going . . . ice-skating!" I repeat, wondering if they heard me. They look at each other, and then back at me, their foreheads knit in frowns.

"What's wrong? Don't you want to go ice-skating?" I ask, perplexed. When I was a kid it was my favourite thing to do.

"We can't skate," says Tas, sounding disappointed. "Can't we go for ice-cream or something instead?"

"No, you cannot go for ice-cream instead. If you can't skate, I can teach you. Don't you want to learn?"

"We've never been," says Lola.

"You've never been ice-skating. Seriously?"

They both shake their heads. I can't believe it. These two have been everywhere and done everything. Except for the conventional childhood things it seems. They rode an elephant in Thailand, a camel in Egypt, and I wouldn't be surprised if they had ridden an extinct saber-toothed tiger in the Siberian Tundra . . . but they've never been to the ice rink at Northgate?

"Oh, you poor deprived children." I say, in disbelief. And Khunying said I was the one who was sheltered. Hah! "Well, it's your lucky day because your mother already gave me permission to take you. Ooooh, you are in for such a treat!" I say, egging them on. "Ice-skating is so much fun."

"Really?" asks Tas, her eyes widening and a grin starting to spread over her face.

"Hello Kitty says," I say, smiling back at her in the rear-view mirror.

. . . .

* * *

At suppertime I take the girls down to the dining room for dinner. I notice there are four places laid this time instead of three. The girls run to their places and sit down, but I hover a little, not entirely sure where I'm meant to sit again. Suddenly Khunying sweeps in, smelling of diamonds and evening perfume, and places herself in the chair at the head of the table. I follow suit and sit at the empty place setting, next to Lola.

"So, did you have fun?" Khunying addresses the girls. They tell her all about the skating excitedly till they have run out of things to say, and then tell her everything again. I keep quiet most of the time, feeling somewhat awkward with the new dining arrangement and not wanting to do anything I shouldn't.

"I have an announcement," says Khunying after the girls have calmed down and turned their focus to eating their supper. "Giorgio was so disappointed not to see you earlier this year, that he has offered me something very exciting! We are all going to Italy for the term break to stay with him."

Both girls jump up and cheer eagerly.

"Don't squeal like that," says Khunying crossly. "You sound like pigs being slaughtered. Lola. Sit down and eat your food. Anyway. As I was saying. We are all going to Italy, so Jemma, I will need you to book all the tickets, and arrange with Giorgio for the payment."

"OK, yes, I will do that for you," I say, wondering how long they will be going for and if I would have to go home. I don't really want to stay at the flat. Maybe I could take a trip somewhere too. I probably can't afford to go and see Mom and Dad in Cape Town, but I could probably go and visit my friend in Ballito or something. "Just give me the dates."

"I'll send all details to you tomorrow." Khunying says. "Do you have a valid passport?"

"Me?" I say.

"I don't see anyone else here who I would ask."

"Oh."

"Well? Do you?"

"Oh, do you mean, are you, am I going with you?"

"Of course you are coming with us. Honestly, Jemma, sometimes I wonder about you. Who on earth would look after the girls while I spend time with Giorgio?"

I'm going to Italy? I'm going to Italy! Oh wow. This is so fabulous. Italy!

"Jemma!"

"Sorry, Khunying," I say, jumping at her angry voice. "No, I don't have a passport, but I will sort it all out first thing in the morning."

"Good. I thought you had gone deaf there for a moment," she scowls at me impatiently. But I don't care. I'm over the moon. I beam back at her, smiling all round the table.

I'm going to Italy!

✳ ✳ ✳

"No freaking way! You lucky, lucky little . . ." Jason is ogling on the other end of the phone line. I couldn't wait for dinner to be done and got the girls into bed in record time tonight so I could call him with the news. "Well, I guess the job does have its perks, doesn't it?"

"Oh hell yeah." I'm so excited. I've never been overseas before and have a hugely romanticised idea of Italy in my head. "Hello, Milan! I'm sure we'll go there. Hello shopping. I'm sure we'll do loads of that. Even though I probably won't have enough money to buy myself much . . . although I'm sure I could borrow from you and pay you back, right? I'm sure I'm still going to love seeing it all. And I'm sure Khunying will shop up a storm!"

"Are you sure you're sure? How sure are you really?" he teases.

"As sure as the freckles on Giselle's nose!" I shout, giddily.

The excitement accumulates the more I work on getting my passport, and all our visas, flights and hotel bookings sorted out. It's a logistical nightmare following Khunying's orders, but I do it all with determination. I had to postpone another trip she was meant to take to accommodate the Italian holiday, and even though she was the one who told me to do it, I got the distinct impression she blamed me for her not being able to go. And I heard her shouting on the phone about money and maintenance again. I don't know what is happening on the divorce settlement front, but Khunying fires a few more of the house staff, leaving only Jim, Suda, Ramie and myself behind. A gardening service takes over the grounds that come only twice a week now, and there is no longer a laundry shoe-elf. Ramie has taken to doing most of the laundry, but seems to forget my things quite often. I don't really want to cause a stir with her – after all, she is the only one who knows about me snooping – so I just quietly do my own things. I usually go out to the laundry room at night, after the girls are in bed, when I have enough dirty clothes to do, and sit there reading one of the books Khunying has passed down to me, waiting for my things to dry.

It's freezing tonight, but my laundry has piled up a bit, so I carry it down, wearing extra layers to keep warm in the outside room. The usually heated marble floors have gone cold. I wonder if it's just the weather, or if someone turned the under-floor heating off? While separating my whites from my colours, I decide to phone Frederick. I still haven't got around to telling him about the Italian trip – I spoke to Jason on the phone for so long the other night it sort of slipped my mind.

"Hello?" he answers. I'm rather surprised; he usually answers my calls with something cute and playful.

"Darling." I drawl. "How are you?"

"Hi, Jemma," he says, not playing along. "What's up?"

He never treats me this way. I wonder what's going on?

"Um, is everything OK?" I ask, wondering if something happened at work. Or maybe he spoke to his uncle today. That usually puts him in a pout.

"Fine. How about you?"

That's strange. It's as if he just doesn't want to talk to me? I'm not used to this unfriendly Frederick. OK, I guess he's been more distant lately. Or maybe I have been. But I've just been so busy . . .

"Oh. Uh. Fine here too. I just, you know, thought I'd call to catch up."

Silence.

"It's been a while since I called you," I say, laughing nervously and trying to keep the conversation flowing. "I've missed you."

"It's been a month, Jemma."

"Wow. Really? That long, huh? I guess I have, uh, kind of been busy. You know?"

"Oh I know. Ja-Roy keep me informed."

Silence. Again.

This is hard. I know I haven't seen much of him lately, but I honestly thought he was busy too.

"Guess what," I say, trying to ignore the iciness.

"What," he says dryly.

"I'm going to Italy!"

Silence.

"Italy," I continue. "Like overseas. First time! Khunying is taking me with her to look after the girls on holiday. Italy. Isn't that exciting?"

"OK, if you say so. Well done."

Sheesh.

I pick up the detergent and start to fill the dispenser distractedly in the machine. There is a pool of water in the drum that hasn't drained out yet – it must have been left there from the last load Ramie did earlier today. Maybe the settings were wrong or something. I double check the dial, put in my whites and turn the machine on.

"Frederick," I say, breaking the awkwardness between us. "I'm really sorry. It has been crazy and I don't know how a whole month went by. How did your flower show go? Didn't you have that?"

"Yes, that was three weeks ago. It went well. I got quite a few new clients."

"Oh, well that's good."

Silence again. What – am I going to have to grovel to get more information?

"So, I'm doing my own laundry, can you believe it," I say, snorting ironically.

"I do my own laundry all the time," says Frederick, an edge to his voice. OK, that was moderately bitchy. Didn't expect that from him.

"Uh, ya, but – well – I'm at The Palace."

Silence.

"Er . . . and the shoe elf got let go. You know, the one who cleans our shoes and used to do the laundry. She got let go. Actually it's been crazy here and there has been so much going on!" I start babbling, trying to make up for the lack of conversation. "Lots of changes to staff and you won't believe what's happening . . ." I realise I'm rambling, but it's so uncomfortable talking to Frederick like this. Maybe if I just act as if nothing's wrong he'll ease up. He loves clothes, especially designers, and Calvin Klein is his favourite so I keep going. "Oh, and you won't believe it, but she gave me a genuine Calvin Klein jacket last week! I mean, can you believe it? I would totally give it to you if I thought it would fit, but it's this cut-off military thing in cream. Stunning, though! I mean, of course you can try it and if you like it it's yours," Frederick doesn't jump to the conversation just yet, but I hope the CK jacket got a bit of a rise from him at least. Maybe if he understood I've been under a lot more pressure than before, he wouldn't be mad at me for being scarce.

"But anyhow, so there's been a lot more work around here, since her personal assistant quit. Remember? Anyhow, so I've been doing some of his work while the girls are at school, and of course still looking after them all afternoon and – well, now I guess I'm doing laundry too!" I laugh, trying to sound lighthearted and friendly.

"Well, if you are busy I guess I should go," he says simply.

"Oh."

Wow, he must be more upset than I realised. It can't be me. He must just be having a bad day or something. I mean, Calvin Klein didn't work? "Oh, well, no I mean,"

"Like you said, you're crazy busy."

That was as hard and cold as a slap in the face! "OK," I say, giving up. If he's not going to try, why should I? I mean, I phoned him – isn't that something? And now he isn't even trying to make conversation. Well, I don't need that in my life right now.

"Enjoy Italy."

"Oh, that's only in like two months' time, I'm sure I'll see you before . . ." But he has already hung up.

I stare at my phone. What just happened? Was it a fight? Is he just being pissy? Suddenly a horrible rumble comes from the washing machine making me jump. Foam starts spurting out from under the lid, and the awful rumble gets louder. I quickly open the top and try to press the "cancel" button. Thankfully the rumbling stops, but only because a terrible grating sound drowns it out . . . What have I done? I didn't do anything wrong? I used the machine exactly as I have for the past few weeks, nothing different at all! I frantically dive over the machine and pull the plug out from the socket in the wall. There's a flash behind the emerging plug, then everything goes quiet.

I look at my wet, soapy clothes inside the machine. It looks like way too much water went in for some reason, and nothing is draining out. It's too late to call Ramie to help me, not that she would even if I did, so I just take out all my things, dripping and cold, and squeeze them out in the hand basin. I use one of the empty soap dispensers to scoop out the water from the machine. I guess I will have to take my laundry home this weekend to do at the flat in our ancient twin tub. Ugh, how annoying! I bang the door closed behind me as I leave, feeling all the injustices of the world weighing down on my shoulders. I so don't need this!

Chapter 27

. . . .

"Hey now, hey now, my daddy's back!" Lola is dancing around in her cute goofy way, singing her version of the hit song from the sixties, "My Boyfriend's Back". Sometimes I wonder how this girl knows about these things, but then again, she seems to have a photographic memory for music.

"Lola!" I scold, trying to get her to stand still so I can pull a bright white dress over her head. "Stop dancing for just a second! I need to get you ready for your daddy and I can't if you don't stop dancing."

Alak has a big business conference over the weekend, and is flying in and out for it. He only had tonight available, which is also the night of the girls' art exhibition at the school. Without Kobus to act as buffer I had the lovely task of telling Khunying that Alak wanted to see the girls. She was less than charmed, and I could tell she was about to forbid it, when for some strange reason she looked at me, lifted her chin as if sizing me up, then said: "He can see them, with you, of course. Make arrangements. It's up to you to make sure they are safe." I know of course she was referring to the 'kidnapping' warning she had given me earlier, but now we are sort of friendlier, she seems to trust me to not get them stolen.

. . . .

We decide to do an early dinner and then all go through to the school hall together. I haven't actually heard back from Khunying yet whether she is going or not, so I decide to take the chance and confirm plans with Alak. He is their father and has just as much right to be there as she does. More so, in my books!

"I'm so glad Daddy's back," says Tasanee, admiring her red dress in the mirror. "You two look like the Rose sisters." I smile at her reflection.

"The who?" she says, turning away from the mirror and sidling up to Lola, both girls looking up at me expectantly. Their earnest faces show they are eager for me to tell them one of my tweaked-but-old-fashioned stories. It's amazing, even with iPads and SpongeBob SquarePants, they still want me to tell them all the old fairy tales I grew up with. I glance at my cellphone and see we still have a bit of time, so I put down the hairbrush, go over to the sofa in the bay window, and sit down. Immediately both girls bound over and jump up to sit next to me, one on either side, nestling into the throw cushions.

"Well, the Rose sisters were very sweet girls," I start the story, "and very beautiful. Just like you two! Their names were Snow white, and Rose Red . . ."

When Alak arrives, he is dressed in a beautiful crisp white shirt and midnight-blue jeans. "Don't you two look lovely!" he says as the girls emerge from the house and climb into his Bentley.

"I'm Snow white, and Tas is Rose Red," explains Lola, a huge smile on her face. "They were princesses! But nobody knew. It was a secret."

Alak looks at me questioningly and I shrug my shoulders. "Story hour," I explain, and he nods congenially.

"In that case, let's take the secret princesses out for something special tonight."

We decide to go to Illovo for conveyer-belt sushi at a trendy new restaurant. Sitting wrapped round one corner, Tas and Lola in the middle, and Alak and I on opposite ends, we eat our sushi while chatting. Every now and again I look over at Alak and wonder if he would ever move back to South Africa. It would be so much nicer if we could do this kind of thing more often. Sure, things have been better with Khunying, but in all honesty, I would rather work for Alak, like Kobus now does. In his house. With the girls. Me, Alak and the girls. We make quite a troop. If they can't have a normal family, isn't this so much better? Healthier? Sitting here with two adults who clearly get along and who both love them. Not cooped up in that big, hollow shell of a home with a mostly absent mother who has flipped her lid, a black bag spiral staircase and a father they hardly ever see. I know we would never be romantic – but I wonder if we could end up being one of those strange platonic couples. Friends, despite our age and social status differences.

I realise I am staring at Alak when he turns and catches my eye. I quickly turn away, averting my thoughts back to the girlish banter at the table about who is better, Hello Kitty or Princess Elsa. But my mind keeps on wandering. Maybe I could talk to him about my thoughts? I wonder if Alak has ever thought of using more of his joint custody. Keeping the girls for half the time – and I could go with them. I decide things are friendly enough between us for me to ask him these more private questions some-time soon.

By the time we arrive at the school, I'm so warmed by Alak's com-pany and lost in my own mutinous thoughts of leaving Khunying behind, I almost forget to change the girls into their school uniforms. After a quick trip to the bathrooms, we are all ready for the evening's events.

The girls skip along next to us, filled with bubbly excitement at being on their school grounds in the evening. There is something magical about being in a place so familiar at nighttime. In the dark, the buildings look mystical, and the lights give the windows a warm glow that is every bit as inviting as it is exciting. We follow the signs, lit candles in sandbags, and all the other arriving families towards the exhibition entrance. We get welcomed as we enter the hall by smiling teachers and bustling groups. A young lady in a black and white waiter's outfit hands a glass of champagne to me, and Alak accepts a glass too. There are so many waiters in this place it may as well be a high society event, not a primary school art show! The hall looks wonderful too, filled with colourful displays of art and little winding footpaths labeled "Grade Tours". I feel a tad underdressed next to the rest of the mothers, their hair up and their Louis Vuitton heels clicking on the old original wooden floors. I may be wearing le Coco top and hand-me-down nude heels, but I'm in jeans.

Alak leans sideways, conspicuously close to my ear and whispers: "I think maybe the jeans weren't exactly the right idea?" signaling to his own usual casual attire.

"Oh no, you're fine," I whisper back. "I'm the one caught out and about without my pearls! I feel like we just stumbled in on an episode of Revenge!"

"Is that what Revenge is all about?" he asks.

"Not really. I was just saying," I'm about to start explaining the greater plot of the popular TV series when I see a twinkle in his eye as he grins at me. I stop abruptly and feel a blush rise. Is he ripping me off for watching? I mean, I know I'm like twenty years younger than him, but still. It's not as though I follow series all that closely – in fact that one is pretty much done, isn't it?

"You do like to take things seriously, don't you?" he teases as I frown slightly.

I smile awkwardly, and take a big sip of champagne to hide my embarrassment. But I suddenly feel indignant. I don't take things too seriously. Why would he think that? And why is he teasing me about comparing these people to a Hollywood made cast? Do I still look as if I don't fit here, as if I don't belong? I would think that in my new wardrobe I blend in a whole lot better with these kinds of people. I've noticed it at the birthday parities – more and more often now the other mothers compliment me on my cardigan, or skirt, or handbag (all of which were Khunying's of course). But it makes me feel good. I suppose saying something stupid like "I'm in an episode of Revenge" is the only thing that still shows the difference, and separates me from these people. And from Alak.

I shrug, feigning casualness, and change the subject. "The girls are quite the little socialites, don't you think?"

Tasanee has already found her Gucci-Grade-Oners and is eagerly pulling them along, chattering amongst all their artwork. She bounds over to us and gives me a pencil she made, bright feathers bursting from the back where the eraser should be. I notice all the other mothers carrying hand-crafted designs from their girls too, and take mine, giving her a big hug, thanking her. I feel honoured! She rushes back to her friends, and Alak and I follow, forgetting our secret conversation about how out of place we feel. As we come around a big display of what can only be described as a waterfall of rainbow-coloured knitting wool and old mops, I walk almost smack bang into the back of Khunying.

"Oh! Oh, I'm so sorry!" I say, completely taken aback and in shock. I totally forgot she might be here! "I didn't realise . . ."

She turns slowly, a look on her face that quiets me instantly.

"Nicole," Alak says, giving his ex-wife a small kiss on the cheek.

"Alak," she says, returning his greeting with cold callousness. "I see you are having fun with," she pauses, looking me up and down, "the help."

Ouch!

Her eyes scan my outfit, each and every piece being something she threw out over the past month, and suddenly I feel like the soft expensive material is filled with itching powder. It burns on my skin as I watch her face, knowing here, next to her husband, dressed in her clothes, none of this seems as normal or innocent as it all did before. Her jet-blue eyes linger on the bright, feathered pencil in my hands, and then finally reach my face, seething through to the back of my skull. I feel like Harry, facing Voldemort, caught red handed trying to steal his ex-husband with nothing but a pink feather duster for protection. So to speak, of course.

I'm not trying to steal anybody's anything here.

A woman jumps forward, breaking the spell. "Oh, Lord KhunChain! So lovely to see you again! I met you last year at the end-of-year function, remember?" Tasanee's teacher stretches her hand out towards Alak. He takes it and smiles politely.

"Yes, of course. Loraine. Lovely to see you. I hear you are doing a wonderful job with my Tas. She is enjoying her classes very much."

"And she is a pleasure to teach," smiles Mrs Arend, patting Tasanee on the shoulder warmly. "In fact, I was just telling Jemma here only yesterday how lovely it is to have such a well-spoken–"

"Lorraine was just showing me some of Tasanee's pieces," interjects Khunying, addressing Alak while stepping forward and blocking my view of the teacher.

Crap. I've definitely moved back onto the dark side of the moon.

"Uh," says Lorraine, momentarily deterred. "Yes, here we have a lovely one Tasanee made earlier this year. Our theme was 'Save the Planet', and as you can see she had quite a clever interpretation of the Greenpeace movement." We all look at a painting of a globe with arms and legs sitting crying with what looks like a gash on its knee. There is a little girl next to the hurt "earth" with long brown hair, putting a Band-Aid on the knee.

"I'm helping saving the planet," says Tasanee loudly, grinning round at the group. "And look," she adds, proudly, "this one has me and my mommy." We all shift focus to the next painting, entitled "My Role Model". Khunying is portrayed as a tall woman in a light suit, carrying a briefcase, while Tasanee is standing next to her in a matching suit and carrying a matching briefcase, only smaller. The real-life Tasanee is standing at her mother's side, glowing up at her expectantly.

"It's lovely," says Khunying simply. "Though you really could have done a better job with my hair. You made me look like one of those awful reality stars! I find the TV switched to all those trashy channels often, now we have the au pair living in the house," she adds in a stage whisper to Lorraine. I know she meant for me to hear – and Alak. I feel my cheeks redden and avoid eye contact with any of the adults. I look over at Tasanee, who is still looking up at her mother, but her face has fallen ever so slightly.

"Oh, sorry, Mommy" she says, in a small voice. "I didn't mean to mess up your hair."

"Here's my favourite one!" says Lorraine brightly, trying to move on. "This one is called 'Home Time.'"

We all stare at a large drawing on the wall amongst the others. Most look as though they must be family portraits, with three or four figures in each. Two adults, one or two children and some pets. But Tasanee's has a group of six people. I recognise the characters instantly. There is Suda, Alak, myself, Lola, Tasanee and Khunying, all in a neat little row. The grey creature next to Khunying must be Bruno the dog.

"Very nice drawings!" says Alak, smiling down at Tasanee. "You have all our heights perfect! And look at that, you even drew Bruno. Well done!"

Tasanee smiles weakly, but I see her watching her mother. Khunying doesn't make any more comment, and stares stonily at the drawing. Eventually she looks down at Lola and takes her youngest daughter by the hand.

"Come," she says sharply. "Let's see yours now, Lola."

We all follow Khunying, who is marching across the hall to the kindergarten class section, dragging poor Lola along. Mrs. Arend makes her apologies along the way and rushes off to another group of people. Smart woman. I would also love to make an escape right about now.

When we reach the section where Lola's drawings are up, I stare in horrified disbelief. For a moment, everything goes silent, and I can feel the air draining from the room. An underwater quality seems to pulsate in my eardrums.

There, under the title "Best Friends", Lola has drawn a picture of herself, Tasanee, and me.

Very definitely me.

Under the title "Holiday Fun", there is a picture of Lola, Alak, and me. Once again, definitely me.

And no Khunying.

I chance a glance at Khunying, but see she is glaring at a third picture, her mouth set in a line. I follow her eyes, fearing what the last depiction will be of. The title is "My Family" and there, with Lola's undeniable crayonmanship, is a picture of Tasanee holding hands with Lola, and on either side of them, Alak and me.

Not Khunying.

Me.

Before anyone says anything, Khunying turns and walks out of the hall. I stand there, the awkward silence grating away at my forehead like a wave pulling a big broken piece of shrapnel along the shoreline, then suddenly remember Lola. No one has said anything about her drawings yet!

"Oh, Lola!" I say, feigning enthusiasm. "What beautiful drawings! And that one has got such lovely colours! You are a real artist!" I pull her closer and give her a squeeze. "Both of you, I'm very proud of you both!" I say, nodding over at Tasanee too, who's face has taken on an ashen shade.

"So am I!" says Alak, coming to from the unexpected awkwardness and picking Lola up to sit on his hip. "I think our budding little artists need a reward, don't you? Maybe ice-cream boats with five different kinds of toppings?"

Lola smiles and nods her head eagerly as Tasanee silently watches the empty gap in the crowd where her mother has left the room. I can feel the awkwardness prickling at the back of my head like a bad omen. I look over at Alak – his forehead has sort of hardened, causing him to look closed off, protected. He catches my eye and smiles, but somehow doesn't soften.

"Well, what are we waiting for, then? Let's blow this popsicle stand!" he says, trying to sound as though nothing just happened. I fake a small laugh, and take Tas by the hand.

"Ooh, that sounds good! Come on, then, who's keen for some yummy pudding with your daddy?" I look up, hoping to ease all lingering tension and find a companion in Alak.

But he has already started walking out of the room, following the scalpel track his former wife so neatly cut through the crowd.

Why do I feel as if I have a hangover? I only had that one glass of champagne, but my head is pounding as though I had drunk the whole bottle! I go over it in my head again. The rest of last night went badly. Alak changed. He was no longer as chummy and attentive as before. We all got through our ice cream in a stunted sort of way, smiling and laughing forcedly at things that weren't funny. Finally, Alak dropped us back at The Palace in silence. There was no sign of Khunying, which I thanked my lucky fairy-star-dust for. Honestly, it was just a few kids' drawings! But still, it was bad. Really bad.

Lying in the four-poster princess bed I stare up at the silky covering above my head. OK, Jemma. This isn't so bad. Let's be adults about this. So a child who spends a lot of her waking hours with her nanny drew a few pictures with her in it, rather than her mostly absent mother. It's bound to happen, isn't it? It only happened because she is so young and isn't controlled by the socially accepted way of these situations yet. Tasanee didn't draw her mom out of her pictures. It's just a matter of Lola having to accept a few things. Well, that's the way I hope Khunying will see it. Unfortunately, I can't rid this sinking feeling she will see it quite differently. I guess I should just get up and face the music.

I go over to the girls' bedrooms, only to find nothing but tousled bed linen on their empty beds. That's strange. They never wake up before me. Maybe Suda or Ramie got them up this morning. I head down to the kitchen to see if they have started breakfast. As I pad barefoot towards the end of the ice-cold passageway, I hear voices. Tasanee's voice is booming from the dining room, and I hear Khunying. They are gossiping and laughing like old friends.

"And Mommy, her hair wasn't even done up. Just a ponytail," Tas's husky voice comes wafting over with the smell of bacon and scrambled eggs. She is talking louder than usual, with a tone I've only heard her use when she is trying to boss Lola or pretend she is older than she really is. I don't like it at all.

"Well she is just a teacher, darling," Khunying says, and then stops briefly. Probably sipping her coffee from her china teacup. Sure enough, a second later I hear the clink of her cup resting back in its pretentious saucer. "Teachers are no better than maids. Or au pairs." I notice Tas's laugh sounds strained. As if she is sucking up big time to her mother, and laughing at anything the woman would say, whether she likes what she's saying or not.

I decide not to interfere just yet, and turn to tiptoe back to my room.

"Oh. You're still here." The Voice catches my retreating figure round the throat and pulls me back. I turn slowly to see Khunying in her silk gown, standing in the dining-room doorway, a hollow, frosty stare locked on me.

"Khunying! Good – er – morning. I didn't want to disturb you – and the – er–"

"Why are you here? It's Saturday."

"Oh. Um. Well, I did mention it to you earlier this week. That is, we discussed it and you said, well, you suggested that, um, the birthday party today, er . . ."

"Honestly, can you never formulate a full sentence before opening that vastly brainless and under-glossed mouth of yours. I don't need you today. I will see you on Monday. Meet me in the study for a performance review right after you drop the girls at school."

She says the words "performance review" like a judge issuing a death sentence. I stare at her, feeling the blood draining from my face. I whisper "Yes, Khunying", turn, and flee to pack my things.

Chapter 28

* * * * * * * * * *

"**S**he's not going to fire you?"

"Of course she isn't, she's taking me to Italy. She said performance review, not disciplinary hearing!" I'm pacing back and forth in our cramped kitchen at the flat.

"Jemma, would you please sit down. Honestly, I've never seen you this worked up. Relax!"

"Yea, babe. Relax," adds Troy. "Even if she does fire you, who cares? You can get a promoter job again."

I turn and face my brother, Troy wrapped around him like a 1920s fox-fur, all lovey-dovey and googly-eyed. Who does she think she is? Not only do I need this job, I want it. Promoter? What? Does she think I'm going to go back to selling shots in clubs? Like I'm not worth more than that? I'm the governess to a high-society family, practically royalty! My company car is a Porsche! I am a close, personal friend with a Lord now, and I'm practically the only guardian of his girls who are practically princesses. What has she succeeded with recently? Besides get into my brother's pants that is!

"For your information," I breathe, smoothing down the True Religion jeans Khunying tossed my way when she got a small tear in one of the knees, "I'm not going to be fired." I don't really believe it myself, but I try

* * * * * * * *

to convince them regardless. "I'm going to Italy with them, and the ticket is already paid for, booked in my name. I just don't want there to be any unpleasantness. That is all. I'm not going to be fired. I'm very important in that household." I feel my chest rise and fall, burning with anger and self-doubt.

As if fueled by my indignation and hell bent on challenging it, Troy throws me a sarcastic side-glance. "Oh, come on. You're a babysitter. She could take anyone else with her." Jason is actually nodding in agreement. Since when is he on her side and not mine?

I want to grab their thick-as-thieves heads and smack them together. "Actually, Ja-Roy," I spit, "I'm being prepped for a really important role there, not only au pairing. Look at me. Do you think she would give me all this if she saw me as just a babysitter?" I gesture down at my figure, starting at the studded D&G button-down shirt, sweeping past the Gucci belt and ending with the nude Jimmy Choos. "She's molding me for more."

"She's molding you alright," says Troy, half under her breath, "'cause you sure aren't the Jem I used to know. You've been body-snatched."

"Excuse me?" I shout, sticking my hands on my hips. "You listen to me, you fair-weather, brother-stealing hussy!"

"Woah! OK, that's enough," Jason vaults up, almost dropping Troy to the floor as he does. "Sorry baby," he adds, offering her a look I recognise as something he reserved only for Tracy in the past. It makes my blood boil and I can feel my fingernails piercing into the palms of my clenched fists. Jason looks back at me, a fire burning in his eyes. "You will not speak to my girlfriend like that." Troy flickers a look of delight up at Jason that ignites me even more. I throw my hands in the air. "She is just being a total . . . a total . . ."

"A what, Jem?" Troy eggs me on, a smirk on her face. "Say it. What am I?"

I feel it boiling, bubbling, rising up inside me. Everything coming to a head. Every last little bit of everything.

"A CALOUS BITCH!"

The room is silent. Echoes of the explosion rattle in my head. All I can hear is the heavy breathing coming from my own swollen throat. Jason is staring at me, mouth open. He closes it after a moment, and straightens his shoulders. I can see he has also made fists and is holding them tightly down next to his body, breathing dangerously. Troy, also staring at me, but with a look of triumph, uncurls herself from the couch and puts a hand on Jason's arm.

"I'll let you two chat, baby," she purrs in his ear, infuriatingly calm. She leans up for a peck before turning, walking past me and out of the door, leaving a trail of perfume lingering behind.

"Nice one," Jason finally says in a low, rumbling voice. "Calling your best friend a bitch. Getting all high and mighty thanks to a few pieces of overpriced material on your back. Treating me like a piece of dirt under you new, designer six-inch-heeled shoes. Or is it under your highly self-wor-shiping barefoot feet? I can't tell."

"It all depends whether I'm indoors or outdoors," I growl back.

"Wake up, Jemma! This will not be your last and only job. That's all Troy is trying to say. You will not be with them forever. This is not a career! The girls will grow up, leave school. Even if you stayed until then, what do you think you would do then? You have so much more to do with your life. You have so much potential. Do you really think you will be happy being her lackey? PA at best? You are worth more than that. You let that . . . that . . . insane woman dress you up like her own personal Barbie doll right down to the snotty attitude! Don't tell me you really believe this is the life for you?"

"I will be whatever I want to be," I say, feeling a wave of tears suddenly threaten the backs of my eyes.

"You want to be? You? No, Jemma. It's her. You are becoming what she wants you to be. I've watched you slowly but surely lose yourself in that place. First Ryan, and now Troy. Not to mention Frederick."

My skull burns. "What? What the hell have I done wrong to Frederick? He just turned on me! Not me on him," I insist, wiping at my face to try keep the anger-induced tears at bay.

"No, it was you. I watched it happen. You started to freeze him out. Don't ask me why, but to leave a friend, a close friend, stranded with no contact, no phone calls, not even so much as a flipping like on Facebook for so long is as bad as a slap in the face. You were his only friend here in Joburg, Jem, you know that. And he loved you. You guys were inseparable! You nurtured him, gave him all the sweetness you are capable of, then you turned all your attention to those girls and just dropped him. Replaced him. Don't think he didn't see it coming. And he noticed all the nastiness building up in you, believe me. So no wonder he didn't feel the need to chase after you, hunt back a friend he wasn't even sure would be the person he used to know any more."

"So I'm his keeper now? He can't make any other friends?" I hear the words coming out of me, and feel the bite, but choke on them. I feel so terrible, knowing my brother is hitting the nail on the head. I did neglect Frederick. Even though he didn't need a mother or a keeper, he did need a friend, and I was that friend. Then I just dropped him when I had other things to do.

"And what about Mom?" he continues, driving the wound deeper. "When last did you call Mom?"

"What? I call her all the time! I spoke to her just the other day!"

"Oh really? When. What about?"

"I – I – Oh, I can't remember exactly! Sheesh, man, would you get off my back! Mom and I are just fine!"

"You didn't speak to her the other day, you haven't spoken to her in weeks! And I know this because she called me crying about it, and I had to calm her down and let her know you are busy and will come round eventually. What kind of a daughter are you?"

I feel myself crumbling. I know all Jason is saying is true, but I don't want to back down. If I don't fight now, I will lose control of everything. It will mean all my hard work with the girls wasn't for the greater good. All my hard work with Khunying. Everything I've done for the past six months, in fact. A failure as an au pair and a failure as a person. I just want to cry and collapse into a bundle of nothing. So I grit my teeth and storm out instead. I bang down the passage, stomping as hard as I can in stilettoes to my bedroom, fuming all the way.

"Fine! If that's what you think of me, I will just move out! I'll find somewhere else to stay where no one tells me what to do. I won't stay here to be abused by you and your little, little, your, urgh!"

I pull down my biggest travel suitcase and slam it open on the bed. Jason comes in and stands in the doorway, watching as I pull clothes, shoes and scarves out of my cupboard, tossing them in a flurry of furious colour.

"OK, listen, let's just sit down and talk about this. Let's not get ahead of ourselves." He has softened his voice to try to calm me. I ignore him, staring at the mountain of things I've thrown into my suitcase. I'll never get the thing shut with all that junk! I start sorting through it, tossing clothes angrily back in the cupboard to make space.

"Come on, Jemma."

"No! There's nothing left to talk about. You have made your point very clear."

"I'm just trying–"

"You are just trying to run my life for me. Well guess what, it's my life, not yours. And this is my new life. This is me. Deal with it!"

Jason watches me, pausing before he replies, taking a deep breath in and letting it out again.

"Jem. This isn't your life. This is someone else's life. And the sooner you realise that and leave, the better."

"Don't tell me what is or is not my life. I am the one in it! And I'm there for the girls – I can't just walk out on them."

"No, it used to be for the girls, but you are so far beyond that now. There is so much more going on. Just look at your suitcase," he walks over to the bed, gesturing at the contents.

"What's your point?" I say through gritted teeth.

"This!" he says, holding up a pair of beige CK capris. "And this," he picks up a white Jenny Button blouse, "and this and this and this. No colour! Not a stitch of your old clothing. Nothing resembling the old Jemma at all! Nothing pink!"

Watching him going through the things I ended up packing, I suddenly see it. Almost as if a parting in the haze has just hit me in the chest with a boring beige mallet. He's right. I haven't packed a single thing I used to own, only the new, beige and white and neutral designer clothing Khunying tossed my way. I stare at the suitcase, feeling my eyes sting from the harsh reality at hand. Then, as quickly as the fog has lifted, it closes down again. No. I will not be told what to do. I will not have this taken from me by everyone who is against me. I will not give up!

I slam my suitcase shut, lock it and pull it off the bed. Grabbing a few other trinkets, I shove my way past Jason and out of the front door.

Driving blindly, I finally let the tears flow. I drive just far enough to be sure Jason won't see me, and then stop Peaches on the side of the road to have a fat blubber. I cry, scream, hit the steering wheel . . . It feels as though the whole world is against me and I don't understand why. I don't understand all this anger inside me, all this emotion. I don't know what I'm doing anymore. Where I am? Who I am?

And where the hell am I supposed to go now? After being turned on by so many of my friends? My own family? Where will I go? Eventually, all cried and kicked and spluttered out, I sit back in Peaches, wipe my nose and turn the ignition back on. My petrol light is on now too. I think I have some cash left in my purse, so drive slowly to the first petrol station

I can find. My head is so fuzzy I don't realise I've driven right past two Engens and a BP before I finally stop at the Caltex at the beginning of Rivonia Drive, probably driving on fumes. When I open my purse to see how much money I have, moths may as well fly out. There isn't anything in there other than receipts, till slips and ATM printouts. I stare, eyes glazed, at the pathetic contents of my pathetic wallet. And feel utterly pathetic.

"Madam?" asks the petrol attendant, standing expectantly at my car window. I turn and look at him, but he is all blurry. I'm crying again, blubbering like an idiot. I don't even have any money to buy petrol to drive – to drive – nowhere! I have nowhere to go and no way to get there! My whole life is useless.

Apologising wetly, I decide to try one last thing and get out of my car, go inside the Fresh Stop, and head towards the back of the store where the ATM machines are to try to see if I can draw even fifty rand out of my most likely fleeced account. I make my way past the racks of Simba chips, jelly tots and braai brickets.

"Jemma?"

Oh no, the last thing I want right now is to be seen, and this is probably the last person I want to be seen by.

"Jemma! It's my lucky day! How lovely to bump into . . ."

It's Alak. I turn my mascara-smeared face towards him and try to smile. It must look more like a grimace because his friendly expression transforms instantly into deep concern.

"Jemma! Dear, what's wrong? What's happened?" he rushes forward and puts a reassuring hand on my shoulder. I look up at his lovely face, his eyes dark and gentle, and find myself sobbing. My whole body starts to shake again as I try desperately to say something to make sense of my being here like this, but fail dismally.

I've never been rescued by a fireman, carried out of danger's way by a hero in a big jacket and heavy boots, but this must be what it feels like.

Alak says things to me, words that don't really register in my brain, but rather feel like a soothing blanket, wrapped around my shoulders, as he leads me out the convenience store and puts me into the passenger seat of his Bentley. I manage to focus slightly and arrange his words in my head as best I can. Something about "coffee" and "someone will come and fetch your car", "don't worry, I'll arrange a tank of petrol".

"Knock knock? Anyone alive in there?"

I open my eyes, squinting against the dimly lit room. A stream of early morning freshness shines right on my face through the open crack in the door where a figure stands. Oh no. What did I do? Where did I go? Did I–

Then suddenly I remember everything from the night before.

"Morning, Alak," I croak, pushing myself up against the cushions and clearing my throat, feeling wretched.

Alak creaks the door a little wider, shining light onto the side table. "I wasn't sure what you like to drink in the morning, so I had the housekeeper bring up coffee, chai tea and some of that red bush stuff you South Africans all seem to like." His tone is gentle.

"Oh, that's – thanks. Thanks so much," I say, smiling weakly at him behind blurry eyes. I can smell the coffee now and look over to see the tea tray on my side table, laden with cups, steaming cup-sized pots and some French Danishes on a side plate. Boy, is this the royal treatment! Literally.

"So, she's just cooking up some breakfast," he continues, "I always do a full fry up on Sundays. Would you care to join me?"

"Oh," I say, pushing the hair out of my face and trying to look as awake as possible. "Oh, yes, thanks. I'll come down. I'll just, uh . . ."

Alak laughs. "O.K," he says, "Good then. You take your time, no rush. See you downstairs when you're ready?"

"Thanks."

He closes the door behind him, and I look around the room. I didn't really have a chance to look at it last night. The guestroom in Alak's Morningside house is as full of the creature comforts as The Palace is. Possibly even more so. I feel the sheets with my hands, spreading them over and smoothing the wrinkles down. It's so soft and luxurious, but I don't feel happy at all. I feel like the living dead.

In the morning light everything's clearer again. My head is swollen and stuffy from all the tears and rage that stormed in there last night, but it's like a dreaded calm after a tornado. Just as the dust settles, before the survivors come out from their hiding places to see just how much damage has been inflicted. I look into my open suitcase, taking out some fresh clothes to wear. Beige clothes. I hold them in my hands, staring. I remember my brother's words. He was so right. I am lost. Lost in a neutral haze with nothing pink left. No beautiful sunsets. Just confusion and a sense of loss of something I never even had to begin with. I stare at the suitcase, feeling an unmanageable guilt building up inside me, topped with sadness and finished off with a spritz of what the hell was I thinking.

Temper tantrums are never attractive. Looking in the mirror at the dark circles under my eyes just deepens the blow. Not even my newly sculpted eyebrows-ala-Khunying's beautician can hide the ugliness of last night's emotional outburst.

At breakfast, Alak treats me tentatively. We make some idle chit chat, but mostly sit in silence, the noises of scraping toast, clinking coffee cups and silverware slicing gently across greasy eggs keeping us company.

"So," he finally says, taking a sip of orange juice. "Did you sleep well?"

"Oh, yes, thank you. I mean, Egyptian cotton sheets! Who wouldn't?" I try to smile convincingly.

Alak throws his head back and laughs heartily. I feel some of the weight on my shoulders lift immediately. "Ah, Jemma," he says, still laughing. "That is why I like you. You say whatever comes into your head. As if everything is the best thing in the world – as if it's the first time you have ever experienced such things!"

I smile at him, but focus my attention on cutting a piece of bacon, not feeling quite up to my usual cheer yet.

"Jemma." Alak suddenly sounds serious. I look up at him, and see his smile has changed. He has a look in his eyes I haven't seen before. Something sad. Vexed. "I can see me bringing you here last night may look, or may have come across in an inappropriate way, and I'm sorry for that. I just wanted you to be ok, and it seemed you had no where to go." He pauses, but I feel I should be quiet and wait for him to carry on. "Having said that, I'm glad you're here, because I think we need to talk about the other night at the school art exhibition."

Crap. Like I need this right now. Talk about kicking a dog when it's down!

"Mm," I mumble half-heartedly through a mouthful of bacon.

"Well. I just… You know it wasn't you, right? None of it was your fault."

"Oh," I say, thankful this is how he's starting out. "Thanks, but. Well, thanks."

"But . . ."

Great. Of course there's a 'but'. There's always a 'but'.

"But the thing is, Jemma. We are friends, right? You and I?"

I look at him, confused. "Uh, yes. I guess. Friends."

"Yes. Exactly. Friends, and you work for me." He pats my hand, a natural action for him, but then, as if catching himself, quickly moves his hand away again. Oh no. Does he think . . . ? Could he possibly . . .? Oh crap. Crap crapity crap.

"I am a simple man, and I like to keep things simple. I follow my heart – sometimes blindly. I like that we get along and enjoy our encounters. It makes it really easy when I want to see my girls and things are – well – you know."

I shift uneasily in my chair. I'm fairly sure I know why he is saying all this. I nod my head, dreading the rest of the 'talk' and he carries on.

"The thing is, well, I like things the way they are. You are great with the girls and I hope you will be staying around for a lot longer. I just wonder if I haven't maybe been a bit too familiar with you. I realise I may have done things, may have given you conflicting signals. The perfume. And bringing you here – that could definitely have given you the wrong idea. I hope we understand each other. As friends, that is? Just friends."

Yep. There it is. He thinks I want to jump him.

This is so embarrassing. I can feel my cheeks start to burn. I mean, honestly, what does he think, that I expect him to fall all over me, a girl twenty years younger than he, give up whatever life he has now and run off into the sunset with me, Tas and Lola in tow? That's just crazy. OK, so I did have some weird thoughts about spending more time with them as a family, but I only thought . . . not like . . . it wasn't as if I thought . . . Oh, I don't even know what I thought.

"Of course," I say, forcing a smile, and fake-punch him awkwardly on the shoulder. The moment is tangibly strange. "Friends," I echo, hoping he forgets the arm punching and let the whole thing go.

"I just want to make sure there's no confusion – I realise you had nowhere to go last night, so bringing you here was just to. . . I know it might have seemed...I just want you to understand where we stand?"

Please, please can the earth swallow me whole?

"Absolutely. And thank you. I appreciate it, really I do."

He smiles at me, then stretches out and takes a deep breath. "It's OK, you know. To have bad days. I have them too. I don't like not seeing my girls. I do feel like I miss out on a lot with them. But I have to keep on. My work is just too demanding. It is what it is."

I look at Alak, and suddenly see him in a whole new light. I see an old tired man. One who has spent most of his life chasing a dream that didn't exactly have space in it for children. Or a wife, I'm guessing. For the first time, I see little flaws. Tiny cracks in the rose-tinted glass. He is wearing spectacles again this morning instead of contacts. They are a bit too big, like the bottle stoppers they used to wear in the seventies, aging him slightly. His hair is less of a 'sprinkled-with-ash' colour in this light, and more 'growing-out grey'. The creases on his forehead now speak of many, many hours slaving away at his work, and his skin looks sallow and pitted.

Looking past him to the table in the corner of the open-plan dining-living area, I see a study desk, littered with papers and envelopes. His laptop is on and I realise he must have been up early working this morning. Maybe I've judged the whole situation too hastily. Maybe Khunying is just a work-widow who eventually had had enough. Maybe Alak isn't the wonderful father he could have been. Maybe he sacrificed the wrong things.

I think about my own parents and how involved they always were in my life. Still are. I think about how wonderful they are and how loved and cherished they have always made me feel. All they ever want is for me to be happy and fulfilled in life. I realise I've been pushing them aside, not wanting to talk about my life with them because I was afraid they would call me on my mistakes. I suppose I did cut my mom off because I didn't want to have to tell her how bad things were getting, how much I was changing. How deep the black hole had become.

I decide it's time for me to take a step back, a step out, and a look at myself in this situation from a different perspective. I'm too close for all the trees, or something like that . . .

After breakfast, I say my thank yous and goodbyes to Alak, and head Peaches back home. Amazing how he got someone to bring her here, just as he promised he would. I practice my apology all the way, talking out loud to try hear it before I have to face saying it to someone. But when I get home, no one is there. I look around and see Jason has packed a bag too. His toothbrush is gone, and so is his work briefcase and car. He must have gone to Troy. I try calling his cell phone, but he doesn't pick up. After calling him four more times, I try Troy's number instead, but it rings twice, then goes to a busy signal. So she obviously rejected the call. After trying her landline, I decide to leave a message.

"Hi Jason. And Troy," I say, my voice shaking, "I'm really sorry about yesterday. I didn't mean what I said. I'm just under so much pressure, and, well, I don't really know how to handle things right now. I know you're probably both still mad at me, but, well, I'm sorry. There. That's all I can say really. I'm sorry. Please, please call me. Thanks. OK. Bye."

I sit staring blankly at the walls. I stare at nothing for what seems like ages, not moving, just holding my phone in my lap and staring. The silence in the flat seeps into my ears and taunts me. I feel a wrenching in my chest and a fresh wave of emotion tumbles out.

Frederick. I need to call Frederick.

He doesn't answer either and his phone goes to voicemail. "Hello, dis Frederick se phone. Los asseblief 'n boodskap en ek sal terug bel. Dankie." When did he change his voice mail? It's so serious all of a sudden. I'm almost thrown; it's not often I hear him speaking Afrikaans. He sounds so different. So serious! So not gay.

And now here he has a new voicemail and I don't even know my own friend's voice. I really have been gone for too long!

The phone beeps its signal for me to leave a message, and I feel a lump rise in my throat.

"Hi, Frederick. It's Jemma. Obviously. OK, I know I've been a really bad person, and body-snatched, and mostly a terrible, terrible friend. And I'm sorry about that. I really am. It's all my fault – I'm so so sorry. Please call back? I need you right now." Tears start to well up in my eyes and I feel them pool into huge drops, spilling over onto my cheeks. "I'm such a mess. I don't know who I am or where I'm going. And I had a horrible fight with Jason and with Troy." My voice is quivering horribly and I splutter snot-tily though my words, black streaky mascara-tears soaking down my face, "because of the Cherry Monster and I don't really care if they are a couple but I just ended up feeling left out and ganged up on and … and, and Alak thinks I'm trying to get him, like… like that, and Khunying hates me and, and you are talking Afrikaans and, and, the girls, and I can't, I can't and… and, and I swore at Troy, oh, everything is so awful!" I'm sobbing now, like a child. "And I just really need a frieeennndddd!" After a few more sobs, I finally hang up the phone, wet with misery.

That was utterly useless. Silence cocoons me in self-pity.

Settling further into the couch, I pull a duvet round me and press play on the DVD remote. The tune of "Moon River" starts, a yellow cab drives up the familiar deserted movie-scene streets outside Tiffany's, and I clutch the crystal wine glass filled with milk close to my chest, sniffing and sobbing as Audrey Hepburn bites into her sugared pretzel bun.

Chapter 29

. . . .

"Is it just me, or are you the saddest Little Miss Daisy ever to have drunk 'n dialed?"

I open my eyes; they're thick and sticky from smudged make-up. It's dark, except for an eerie blue glow coming from the TV screen. Frederick is sitting over me, leaning to one side and stroking my hair.

"She awakes!" he says, straightening up.

The DVD is long finished, but I don't actually remember watching much of it. I must have fallen asleep. I look around and see it's pitch black outside the windows. "What time is it?" I ask, rubbing at my swollen eyes.

"Nearly nine oh cock, my darling chicken. You must have passed out here."

"9? Wow . . ."

"What did you have in that glass anyhow?" he asks, reaching over and sniffing my empty crystal glass. "That was quite a dronk-verdriet. You must have Pink Flamingo'd yourself."

"Just milk," I confess.

"Whoa, so all that blubbering on my voicemail – classic by the way, I'll never delete it – all that really was a self-pitying cry for help, and not just a

. . . .

317

result of too much alcohol?" I frown at him, but see a glint in his eye. He's teasing me and it feels so good to be back on this end of the loving Frederick again. I try to smile, managing a small twitch in the right direction.

Frederick slips an arm around me and gives me a squeeze. He presses play on the remote and we start to watch together. We don't speak at all, but I lay my head on his shoulder comfortably. Eventually I take the remote from him and push pause. Without looking him in the eye, I say "I'm so sorry" in a very small and pathetic voice.

"Shhh, bokkie" he says. "My maag skeer when I see you like this."

I start to cry, feeling the weight of his words. "Why do you put up with me?" I ask.

"Because, my dear, you are innocent, delightful and charmingly adorable."

"No, I'm not. I called Troy the 'B' word." I end in a whisper, barely mouthing the words.

He laughs out loud, shushes me again and tut-tuts, patting away at my hands as though trying to make me put something down. I turn my empty palms facing up obediently. He takes my hands in his. "You can be mean, you can lose yourself. But to me, you are Audrey Hepburn in Breakfast at Tiffany's, only dressed all in pink."

I look down at my clothes. I'm wearing a now-crushed plain T-shirt and the beige capris.

"Well, not right now obviously," he adds quickly, looking at my clothes and pulling up his nose. "Disaster! But we can fix that. Come on dah-ling. Up with you. It's time to fix this mess, go back to before The Palace. It's time to get into that awfully lonely wardrobe of yours, refresh, revise and recreate your look! Starting with something pink!"

"Frederick," I say, holding him back. "I need to do this. The job, I mean. I need to figure it out for myself. I need to stay. I don't know for how long, but I need to find my own way out."

. . . .

He smiles at me and gives my shoulder a squeeze. "I know. I'm just going to make sure you are properly accessorised for the task."

Arriving back at The Palace I look up at the property. It sends a chill down my spine. The house looms out from the darkness making those Greek statues look downright Gargoyle-esque. I climb out and walk across the crunching pebbles. Hard clinks scatter under my steps, like thousands of tiny bones cracking in a moonlit graveyard. As I pass the fountain, I glance down at the Koi, bobbing and swishing in the water with annoyingly bright tails. Obnoxiously bright. Like the colour of hell fire.

After dropping the girls at school, I walk up to the staff entrance and pause, taking a deep breath. Time for my performance review – time to face the music. I close my eyes and try giving myself a pep talk. Just remember, you can't judge anyone till you have walked a mile in their shoes. OK, bad example considering how many of her shoes she gave to me and I've been walking in those shoes for a while now . . . Not the point.

I'm back to me. I look down, slipping out of my purple clogs and placing them neatly at the door, thankful for something familiar right now. It won't be so bad. Just let her have her say, let her get it all off her chest and then she will feel better and it'll all go back to normal. Like with those written warnings. Her bark is worse than her bite.

There are some muffled voices coming from the piano room. I creep forward, Khunying is in there talking with Ramie, and then Suda comes out and looks straight at me. For a while she is silent, her face worn and heavy. She looks burdened. I wonder if she has also been having a performance review.

"Come," she says eventually, "you come now." She walks back into the room.

Once standing in front of Khunying, I feel all the panic return. She looks livid - about ready to roast me on a spit and feed me to Bruno! I'm so glad I didn't eat anything today – I might have just thrown up I'm so nervous.

"You have a lot of explaining to do." Her opening words bite through me and I feel my blood rush in fear. "Is it true you used the washing machine for your own personal use and broke it?"

What? I thought this was about . . . I look over to Ramie who is standing to one side, arms folded, a smug look on her face.

"Er, I did use it, Khunying, but only because my things weren't being done and I–"

"And you felt it would be OK to use my machine, my water, my detergent to do your brother's laundry too?"

"What? No. No, I didn't. Only my clothes worn here at work."

Khunying narrows her eyes. "Don't lie to me. Ramie has seen men's clothing. Jogging pants and sweat shirts."

"Oh," I say, bewildered. "Oh, yes, well, I do wear some of my brother's old things when it's really cold, to sleep in. Honestly."

"Honestly? Hah! You are about to tell me you haven't had men visit you on this property?"

"What? What men?"

"At Lola's party. You had strange men visit you. And you invited one of them to stay afterwards!"

"Oh, Khunying, that was my brother! I just wanted to show him around. I'm so sorry I didn't ask. I'm so, so–"

Khunying holds up a hand to silence me, surveys me for a minute, then continues. "Things have been going missing in the house. Ramie tells me that food is gone, and even some money. Have you got anything to do with this?"

I don't even know what to say.

"Khunying, I haven't taken anything you didn't give me. I swear, I haven't stolen anything–"

"Then why is it that Ramie found this in your bedroom?" She reaches beside her and holds up – no, could that be – the tiara! I stare at it bewildered.

"I… I have never, I don't know why, I, it couldn't have been in my room!"

"It was," puts in Ramie, stepping forward and addressing the room like an audience. "In between all the lovely clothes Khunying gives to her. She repays such kindness with theft and betrayal."

Khunying waves at Ramie to keep quiet. "Are you telling me you never took this? I saw you looking at it when I wore it to the ball! I suspected something when I saw your face, but decided you were just coveting it – I had no idea you would go so far as to steal it!" Her accusation grips me with fear. Crap! Now what do I say. Of course my face was guilty as sin that day at Sun City, but admitting that would be admitting to snooping in her room and finding the . . . oh dear . . . oh, oh no.

"I, I didn't touch – I promise I never took–" I stutter, not believing this horrible situation. Looking past Khunying, I see Ramie glaring at me. A grin spreads across her face. She did it! She planted it! She is trying to get me into trouble!

"It wasn't me, Khunying. I didn't take it. It was put there by someone else."

Khunying laughs a horrible, disbelieving laugh. "Oh really? And who would possibly do that? Who would go to all the trouble? No, Jemma, things have never gone missing in this household before you arrived. Now the fridge isn't even safe!"

I suddenly remember all the times I saw Jim coming out of the freezer, laden with boxes. All the times I saw Ramie whispering in corners with him, and taking bags to the maids' quarters. I look at Ramie and flare. She knows I know! "Khunying, I've never taken food. Perhaps someone else, someone with easy access to the freezer."

"Are you accusing my staff?" Khunying's voice is raised, getting more and more robust with every syllable. Ramie lets out a snigger from her corner. Khunying, not missing a thing, snaps round like a snake. Ramie jumps and presses her lips shut tight. Khunying looks at Ramie for a second, and I think she is about to see through the lies. But then, as if choosing to ignore the truth, she turns back to me, staring hard with her piercing blue eyes. I watch her eye me up and down, like a lioness sizing me up.

"You're not eating them yourself, if you are stealing them," she says, almost as a side note to herself. I hold my breath, hoping.

"I swear to you, Khunying. It wasn't me. Ramie and Jim . . ."

"Jim doesn't work here any more."

"Oh, I didn't know. But before, when he did–"

"Don't speak."

Crap, that was the wrong move. Her nostrils flare and she stands up, patches of red starting to appear at her neck. The last time I saw her getting like this was when she threw the cream at me. Anything could happen now! But instead of hurling random objects, she turns to Ramie. "Did you put this tiara in her room? You were the one who found it, after all. How would you know where it was hidden?" Ramie's eyes bulge at the accusation. Clearly she didn't see this turn of events coming.

"Well? Did you?"

Ramie's eyes are getting bigger and bigger. Haha. Her nasty plan is backfiring!

"No, Khunying, of course not! I did not! She is the one who is lying. She even snuck into your room and looked in your TV cabinet when she first started here! I found her wearing the tiara!"

The world goes fuzzy.

Khunying rounds on me, dangerously crazy-eyed. I gulp guiltily and feel myself whiten.

"You – did – what?"

"Khunying," I plead in a horrified whisper, "I only did it once and I'm so sorry. But I swear I never took anything of yours."

"So that is true? And the other is not? And the washing machine thing is true, and letting strangers into my house is true, and the rest is not? How am I to believe you?" Khunying shakes her head, and her perfect hair starts to look a little less perfect. The expression on her face is terrible.

"I'm not here for any reason other than to do my job. To look after the girls. That is all I care about."

Khunying pauses for a second and I think there might be a chance she is calming down. I take the gap and keep going. "Honestly. I know it was wrong of me to look in your room. I made a mistake. Please, you have to believe me. Ever since that day I've been doing all I can to be the very best au pair for the girls, for you and the girls." My voice is trembling violently. "I am here for you and all I want to do is help you. I never meant to screw up, I'm so sorry it happened. The rest of what Ramie is saying isn't true. I promise. I would never try to take anything from you."

At this, she narrows her eyes at me again, and I see the red rising in her throat, working its way up her face. "You would never take anything from me? What about my husband," she hisses, coming closer.

"What? No!"

"Did you or did you not spend the night with him this weekend?"

HOLY CRAP.

How on earth could she possibly know? She never speaks to him, never gives him the time of day. Who on earth could have told her? "Oh, Khunying, it's not like that!"

"Did you or did you not spend the night with my husband," she repeats, shouting louder and louder and coming closer.

. . . .

Her Chanel perfume mixed with Evian breath claw at the back of my throat. "I, no, I, I . . ."

"Did – you – or – did – you – not – spend – the – night – with – my – husband!" she demands, spitting the words inches away from my face in an aromatic assault. My whole body begins to tremble.

"No! Well, I did stay there. But in the guest bedroom!"

"How stupid do you think I am? I know about the gifts. I know about the

money he has been giving you on the side. I know about the sunglasses, the perfume."

How the hell? I start to panic. How on earth does she know about it all!

"And you want to preach to me about making mistakes? About never wanting to do me wrong? About only caring for my girls! When the whole time you have been snooping around my personal things! Fooling my husband! Working your agenda. I'll sue you! Taking my private property! I'll sue! You think I fell for your game? Your agenda was to replace me all along! Don't think I didn't see you two, parading at the art show? It was disgraceful. And you standing there dressed from head to toe in my clothes – trying to be me – trying to replace me! Do you think he will love you? You and your cheap haircut and your bad style and your common upbringing? He is a lord! You will never be good enough. You will never be me. You will never have him and you will never steal my daughters from me!"

I start to cry, unable to control it any more. "No, Khunying! No! I promise, Alak and I are just friends! You can ask him! Nothing is going on there! I don't want to steal anything. I'm not trying to take over. I don't want to be you! I don't! I don't!"

Khunying is beyond reason as she shakes her fists in my face. She looks out of control, as though she is having some sort of fit. I'm so afraid she is about to hit me, or worse. She suddenly throws her hands in the air, and lets out a blood-curdling scream of exasperation.

"AAAAAAAAAARRRGGGHHHH!"

The room falls silent. All is dead quiet except for the sounds of my sobbing. Khunying breathes heavily. We stand there for what seems like an eternity. Finally, I notice the slightest movement. Her shoulders fall an inch, and her eyes droop. I hold my breath, trying not to make a sound, but splutter out a few more tears involuntarily. Ramie is inching away, making a break for the door with barely noticeable moves. Suda is standing behind us; I can feel her at the doorway. After what feels like a lifetime in hell, Suda comes forward.

She walks over to Khunying, and takes her arm gently, leading her back to sit down on the couch. Khunying obeys, suddenly as meek as a lamb. She puts her head in her hands. Then Suda turns to me, and quietly ushers me out the room. I move in a trance-like state, unable to feel my legs. The shock is so severe I can barely breathe. Suda helps me to the stairs and says quietly: "Just a fight. No problem. Let be. You take you things and go home now. I call you later."

"I'm not going with her to Italy," I whisper bitterly through tears. "She can sue me for that too."

"Now just go. It will be fine. You see."

I nod solemnly, and slowly head up to my room to fetch my things. One foot in front of the other. Step by step. Like a robot, going through pre-programmed motions. Once in my room my head suddenly reels. I feel faint, completely out of breath. I sit down on the bed and put my head down between my legs, breathing fast. I take huge gulps but don't feel like I'm getting any air into my lungs. I must be having a panic attack. I can't breathe! I need to get out of here! I can leave my things – it's mostly her clothes after all, and now I see them as tainted. Designer clothing that came at a price. I can't take any more of this emotional trauma. I feel completely brutalized! I hate to think of leaving the girls but I can't work in a house where some are plotting against me for no apparent reason, and others, well, others have just gone downright barking mad! I can't breathe – I can't breathe! I realise now I feel as though I haven't been able to breathe for the whole time I've been working here. Black stars leave blind spots in my vision, but I get to my feet. I just need to get out.

I walk faster and faster, heading towards the stairwell, desperate to get out of the house. The air starts to leave my lungs again and I take huge gulps, rushing forward. Ramie is at the base of the stairs; I see her as I look down but everything is blurring again and I start to question if she really is there or if it's just an apparition glaring up at me. But I don't care any more. I need to get out. I start down the stairs, barely feeling the slippery surface under my feet. One foot in front of the other, go go go! Keep on! The black bags shift dangerously under my feet, but I'm nearly there. Ramie picks up Khunying's watch lying on the table at the base of the stairs and slowly, deliberately shoves it in her bra. She is staring right at me, daring me to challenge her, to stop her.

Forget that! Forget the staff entrance, forget the shoes – just go! I have to get out. Go go go! I feel my feet slide on the treacherous surface. I feel my iron grip on the hard banister slipping. I feel my arm jerk into my shoulder socket and a loud pop seems to come from it. My head reels and black stars smear across my eyes. . .

And suddenly I feel nothing. For a second, I'm in the air, completely weightless. Then everything goes black.

Chapter 30

Cold.

Legs. Cold.

Freezing.

I blink my eyes open. They feel sluggish. I'm not sure where I am or how I got here. I'm cold.

"Jemma!" Jason almost jumps on top of me. I'm in a bed in a strange room and he is pawing at my head wildly. "You're awake! She's awake!" he shouts over his shoulder. "Oh man, I was so worried! Oh, I'm so glad you're awake! How do you feel? Do you feel anything? Are you sore? Can I get you anything? Do you need anything? How many fingers am I holding up?"

I stare at my brother holding two fingers up like a peace sign and start to giggle. I'm not entirely sure what's going on, but I've never seen him so frazzled and all over the place. It's really funny! Mr Together is practically coming apart at the seams.

"Dude," Troy's face appears above me too, a mixture of worry and relief on her face. "He's finally lost it." She smiles at me, putting a warm hand on my arm.

It's so nice and warm!

"I'm cold," I say, hoping she will be able to magically spread the warmth all over me.

"A blanket! Another blanket!" shouts Jason, jumping out of my vision again. "Told you she needed another blanket! She sleeps under a freaking duvet and all kinds of layers even in the summer! A blanket! Quick!" I hear him rummaging around the room, open and close a door, and seconds later I feel something heavy being laid over me. Aah, better. I smile and close my eyes.

"No! Jemma! Jemma! Don't go back again! Stay away from the light!"

Sheesh! I open my eyes and stare at Jason irritably. He is leaning right into my face, slapping me on the cheek.

"Stop that you moron!" I say, trying to pull my head away.

It won't move.

What the hell? Why can't I move? "I can't move!" I say in alarm. Things start to come back to me. The fight, the stairs – I must have fallen! I must have cracked my spine and now I'm paralysed and I am lying in hospital and I'm . . .

"Haibo! Give her some space," says an unfamiliar voice. "Hello, Miss Richardson. You've given your brother here quite a fright. How do you feel?" I see a wide face and triple chin above me coming out of a nurse's outfit.

"I can't move my neck," I whisper feebly. "Am I paralysed?"

She clicks her tongue loudly. "Of course not! You're wearing a brace so you don't move. Silly thing. What have you been telling her?" She slaps Jason away, turns back to me and starts to look at a bunch of tubes and buttons and a chart and all sorts of scary stuff around my head.

"Not paralysed?" I say, lifting a hand to my neck and feeling the brace. I realise my hands, arms, legs . . . pretty much everything else can move. But I'm still trying to figure out what is going on.

"No," she says distractedly while doing all her nursey things. "No, no, you just knocked your head, dislocated your shoulder, have a small crack in your thoracic spine, a broken hip and your neck needs a few more x-rays, but you were very lucky. Nothing permanent or too serious, and probably no surgery needed. Just a few stiches, and you'll wear that neck and back brace for a while. We will need to monitor the swelling for now. Bed rest, then physiotherapy, and you'll be back to normal. The doctor will be in shortly to check up on you."

It's a lot to take in. "So I broke my neck?"

"We need more x-rays, and the physician has to take a look – but a most likely a cervical fracture, yes. How's the pain?" Jason's head keeps popping in and out of my vision. "Hamba," the nurse commands him, irritably.

"Uh," I say, trying to focus on individual parts of my body to see if I feel any pain or not. "No, I think I'm OK."

"That's good. Now you should probably get some more rest. The body heals itself more while you sleep. And you," she adds to Jason, "you should take a walk and calm down before I give you something to calm you down." It sounds more like a threat than an offer.

"I'll take him," I hear Troy say from the end of the bed.

Then someone else speaks. "And I'll stay with her." My heart stops. I can't see the person who spoke the words, but I know that voice. The Voice. I widen my eyes at Jason, but before he can say anything, Khunying's face appears above me.

"You go and get a cup of coffee or something, Jason. I'll stay here with her till the doctor comes," she smiles at my brother, putting a hand on his shoulder. He smiles back! He's been poisoned! Manipulated! No, Jason! No! Don't leave me with her! I want to scream but just lie there and stare at the terrible scene above me in horrified silence.

And then I am alone in the room with her.

She looks down at me and puts a hand on my arm. I flinch. "Are you OK?" she says, suddenly looking worried. "Shall I call the nurse back?" Her eyes look so tired. They are blood shot, but her face is the thing I'm staring at. She looks different. Scared. Worried. And somehow softer. She looks at me, her eyes milky pools of gentle blue, waiting for my answer.

"Um," I say, finding my voice. "Um, no, I'm OK. But. Um. Well. What are you . . . doing here?"

She looks taken aback, and then laughs. A soft, tinkly sort of laugh that kind of reminds me of a Christmas tree. What the hell is going on? Has the world gone mad?

"Oh, Jemma, you are funny. I came with you in the ambulance! Don't you remember? I held your hand and you kept saying sorry to me," she laughs again, this time louder. "Sorry! As if you needed to apologise for falling!"

"I... I don't remember . . ." Held my hand? On what planet?

"Yes, the doctor did say you might have some trouble remembering the events around the accident. Well, let me help. Let's see. We got you into the ambulance, I went with you, as I said. You told me your brother's name, I called him from your cell in the ambulance. Lovely man, by the way. We got here, they took you off for tests and treatments and, well, here we are." She smiles at me radiantly. "You were asleep for quite a long time, but that's pretty much it."

I don't know what to say. Everything is too confusing. After that horrible scene! She looked just about ready to kill me the last I remember, why would she be nice to me now? As if reading my thoughts, Khunying softens her voice. "Jemma. I know what really happened now. Ramie was trying to get you fired. We are downsizing, you see. I'm going to be putting the house on the market soon. I won't need so much staff. She knew I was about to let another one go, and I suppose she decided it wasn't going to be her. Suda suspected it. She explained it all to me and told me you couldn't have done any of those things, and then Ramie confessed. Of course, now, I absolutely will fire her."

She reaches down and strokes some hair that has strayed onto my face out of the way. It all feels so wrong. So twilight zone. Her eyes focus briefly on my hairline. "This is awful. Remind me to send you to my stylist when you get out – we have to do something about your colour." It's my natural colour; of course she wouldn't like it. But I relax slightly at her interrupted niceness. It feels a bit more like her. "Don't worry about the girls," she continues, "I had one of the other moms take them home after school for the afternoon. I'll bring them to visit you later this evening. I just wanted to make sure you were going to be O.K. first."

"Oh, uh, thanks, I guess," I'm unsure of what I'm meant to say.

"And I called Alak before he got on his flight. He's going to be here soon to see you. He is very concerned about his new friend."

So she doesn't think I'm trying to steal her ex-husband after all? Wow! Maybe it took a bash on the head and near-death experience, but I think things might be looking up.

Khunying sighs and speaks again.

"I'm sorry, Jemma. I should have taken down those black bags ages ago. And I'm sorry about the meeting too. I get a little crazy when I'm angry – sort of lose control . . ."

No kidding.

"I always feel bad afterwards, when I see how... well, how far I've gone. Like when the fog rises and the dust settles. It's as if I'm suddenly in the aftermath of an earthquake; everything is calm and I can see all the damage I've done. You know?"

I stare at her, disbelievingly. Is she really saying this to me? It's exactly the way I felt! After my temper tantrum with Jason and Troy. I can't believe she actually has the same feelings as I do.

"Ya, I guess," I reply, not quite believing it. This is absolute madness.

· · · · · · · ·

"You gave us all a fright! I think you shocked me more than I have ever been shocked before – worse than my own accident even."

I look at her beautiful face, one of the first genuine smiles I think I've ever seen on it, and wonder if the shock brought on this change or if she's just being nice for the time being. A million thoughts fly through my brain. I still think I should quit. Even if this change sticks. But I don't know how I will manage leaving. I think about the girls again and feel a pain in my chest. Who is going to look after them? What if Khunying fires Suda too? They will have no one.

"Did someone call a doctor?" Frederick interrupts my thoughts, appearing above me with a nurse's hat on and what looks like a bright pink stethoscope around his neck. "Good Gaga, child! You're paralysed?"

A broken neck is no joke, but I must have had some strong lucky fairy-star-dust raining down on me that day because I came off with only a minor compression fracture to the C4 area. Soon enough I am ready to go home – with all my spoils. Whenever Frederick came, he brought me oodles of delicious home-baked goodies, and he managed to find me a pink neck brace, though he said he'd never reveal his sources. The doctors gave their approval, but I have to wear it for 2 whole months! Alak brought the biggest bouquet of flowers I've ever seen and a teddy holding a balloon saying, "Get well soon". The bouquet was done by Joburg's hottest new talent, he explained proudly, someone named Frédéric. My parents flew in from Cape Town and were there by the evening of the accident, Mom fussing over me like there was no tomorrow. Tas and Lola made me glittery cards and picked Nicole-Annelle roses from the garden for me each time they visited. Suda came and actually joked, saying: "You start with bang on head, you end with bang on head." She smiled so broadly it almost cracked her stern face! Even Ryan came to see me. He brought me a bottle of Omega oil capsules as a gift – something about helping fight inflammation, and went on about crossfit as possible rehabilitation when I'm better, offering to coach me. I still don't really know why he would forgive me, but it was so sweet of him to come, and I was glad to be able to apologise, and re-invite him into our group as a friend. Troy, on the other hand, brought me a whole bunch of thick, page-turning (she assured me) fashion magazines, pointing out that vibrant colour was the new black, and a bottle of vanilla-flavoured vodka. "For when you're off the meds," she explained, "though if you really want to have a good time maybe you should drink it with the meds – and you can send some my way too." I got showered with gifts and flowers and chocolates and phone calls and text messages till my nurse accused me of milking it for all I was worth. But she was nice, in her own special grumpy way, and I hugged her goodbye. I'm almost sad to leave.

"Ouch," I say, cringing in the back seat while Jason drives over a bump in the road taking me home from the hospital.

"Sorry!" he says, looking at me in the rearview mirror. "Almost home. I'll try take it a bit slower."

Once in the flat, I am so happy to be home. It feels like home for the first time in months! Troy and Jason have both forgiven me, mostly out of pity, I'm guessing. Still, I won't turn my nose up at the sympathy vote. I stare out the window at my beloved veld where a cathartic scene greets me; low lying black clouds but with a break in the sky where a vibrant stream of sunlight highlights the cosmos, shimmering wildly in their natural setting. I breathe in deeply and can smell the electric earthy promise of a Joburg thunderstorm. I allow all the events of the past few months leave me.

"Jason," I ask after he and Mom have helped settle me onto the couch with all kinds of cushions and bedding to prop me up to optimal comfort. "Please stick around when Khunying comes?"

I know she has been unbelievably good to me since the accident, visiting me twice a day, and buying me all kinds of fabulous gifts, but I'm still nervous to be alone with her.

"Sure. Have you thought about what you are going to say?"

Khunying is due to visit me in a week to discuss my job situation. I haven't told Jason what I've been quietly thinking yet.

"I'll tell you what she's going to say," says Mom, fluffing a bright pink stuffed heart and sticking it behind my head. "She's going to let that woman know exactly how much of this was her fault and she's going to . . ."

"Mom," warns Jason.

"Sorry," she says, taking a breath and stepping back. Jason has had to do a lot of damage control with our mother, promising we weren't hiding all kinds of atrocities from her and she should just let me work this thing out for myself. And he has forbidden her to use the phrase "I told you so".

"I'm not sure," I say to my twin, after our mother leaves the room. I pick up a water bottle from the table set up next to me laden with every possible food and beverage item I could want, magazines, remotes and even an aromatherapy candle filled with glitter Frederick bought me for "sparkly healing". I take a sip and continue: "It's not like I can go to Italy now – she'll need someone else."

"And what about after Italy?" he queries, probing cautiously.

I am completely torn, not knowing whether it would be better to think about myself and quit and do the thing I've been going over and over in my head while lying in hospital, or staying for the sake of the girls. I pick up Vogue, paging through it without actually looking at it.

"She has been really nice to me, hasn't she?"

"I know. You split open your head and she's the one who ends up with the lobotomy! Go figure."

I laugh, but it hurts my neck, so I stop. "Troy says it's 'cause she's scared I'm going to sue her," I grin.

"Troy might not be half-wrong," he smiles back. "Not just a pretty face, that one. She's very shrewd." His face goes gooey again, the way it does whenever he speaks about Troy these days. He's clearly fallen harder than I thought he had for her, and I'm glad to see him so happy. I laugh again, quickly holding my hand up to the back of my head to try stop the pain. "But that's not you, Jem."

Suing was only something we joked about before. When Troy said it now, though, there was a moment when I wondered. Jason is right, however; I wouldn't do that. Besides, Khunying paid all my hospital bills, after checking me into a private ward in the Morningside clinic, one of the nicest medical centres in Jo'burg. She handpicked the doctor – one who is famous for his research in spinal injuries, and she insisted on all kinds of expensive tests to be done on me. She has already paid her dues as far as I'm concerned. I smile and nod just as Mom peeks her head out from my bedroom door.

"Jem dear, your phone is purring in my handbag – should I bring it to you?"

I look over at Jason, suddenly feeling misty. "You changed it back to a purr?" I ask.

"Not me," he shrugs.

Loud rustling and the sound of shopping bags fills the room.

"Darlings!" announces Frederick, standing in the doorway, his arms laden to the brim with Woolies packets full of groceries. "Prepare for a culinary voyage!"

Chapter 31

⋅ ⋅ ⋅ ⋅ ⋅ ⋅ ⋅ ⋅ ⋅ ⋅

Now here's a scene I never imagined: Khunying sitting in my intimate flat on my rescue-couch, sipping instant coffee from my chipped mug. The one with the ridiculous fat fairies all over it, that is so old it leaves shimmery bits of paint flecks on your hands after using it. I smile to myself, finding way too much delight in this little fact.

Jason is in the other room, as I had requested, listening at the door. Just knowing he is there makes me feel more capable of having the conversation.

"Now we both know you won't be able to join us in Italy anymore," she says, taking another sip of cheap coffee, leaving a few glittery specks on her pristinely done mouth. "But I think we need to decide what is going to happen when we get back."

"I know," I say slowly, taking a deep breath. "Khunying, I, I... you have been so kind to me and I really appreciate all you have done, but I," I gulp. This is harder than I thought it was going to be. "I . . ."

Khunying reaches forward and puts a hand on my arm. "If I may interject," she says in her posh voice. "Jemma, I think I should go first. You have been wonderful. So I think it's time I make you an offer.

⋅ ⋅ ⋅ ⋅ ⋅ ⋅ ⋅

"As I mentioned to you, we are moving out soon. Probably in about six months or so, maybe longer depending on how long it takes to sell the house."

A fifty million rand estate . . . I think it might take a bit longer than six months.

"I am opening a new wing of the business Alak and I used to run, and I'm going to need a help - personal assistant of sorts. Both at home and at the office. The pay is triple what you were getting as my au pair, and of course you will still get weekends off. But it's a sketchy time for me and I'm taking quite a few chances – I need someone I can trust. And you are exactly the kind of person I want. I know we have had our differences, but I've watched you grow and change, and am very pleased with the work you did for me after Kobus left. You are becoming a very capable young lady. It's even apparent in your wardrobe! Uh, your work attire, that is." her eyes sweep over my current outfit: pink toe socks, cosmic swirly purple leggings and a slouchy gym top stolen from Jason.

"I'm sure you will be out the brace and healed enough before we move, and I'd love it if you came back to us when you are ready. So, what do you say?"

I can't believe it. I was all ready to quit so I could go out and find myself, professionally, so to speak. I had all these ideas about starting a party-planning business or joining an events agency, something that would involve creating wonderful things. Or maybe a job of a completely different kind. Sales. Marketing. I don't know. I just know I need to do something new. It was going to be the first adult step of my life. But it was going to be really scary. It was going to be a shot in the dark. It was going to be my time to venture into a grown-up world where I could carve out a grown-up career. It was going to pay more than babysitting! But I had no idea where I was going to start or how I was going to get there. Now here it is being offered to me on a platter. It's almost too good to be true.

A voice niggling at me in the back of my head makes my stitches prick. 'Just because it's right in front of you doesn't mean you should take it.' That has got to be Jason's thoughts finding their way into my brain. I consider everything Khunying has just said. She says I'll have weekends off, but I know her. That will never happen. She says it will be different, but somehow I don't believe her. Even if it is, she wants me to be different. She wants the beige wearing Jemma I became at The Palace, not the person I really am or want to be.

"I tell you what," says Khunying, obviously sensing my inner conflict. "You take a little time. Don't answer me now, tell me when I get back from Italy." She puts down the coffee mug and gets up. I watch her smooth down her crisp white shift dress, my eyes stuck to the dull shimmer left in streaks behind from the mug debris on her fingers. She picks up her handbag that possibly costs more than a year's worth of our rent, and starts to head towards the door.

"Wait," I hear myself say. Khunying stops and turns to face me. This is it. The moment where my life is about to change forever.

Epilogue

⚬ ⚬ ⚬ ⚬ ⚬ ⚬ ⚬ ⚬ ⚬

W alking through Sandton City, I round the corner looking for Frederick. His business has truly taken off, and after his third magazine feature, the massive corporates began hiring him for shows. No more small time anything for our Frédéric. I've come with him to help get things for a big gig he has at the convention centre, but I can't keep up with him. Even though it is a new year, I completely all my physiotherapy and I feel like a new person, I've struggled since the accident that ended my time at The Palace. I'm just about to give up and take my cellphone out to call him when I see something emerging from the crowd that demands my attention.

Khunying is walking with the girls, hand in hand on either side of her. Lola spots me first, lets go of her mother's hand and runs straight for me with Tasanee hot on her heels. I crouch down to welcome her with a huge hug.

"Oh, I've missed you!" I say, hugging them both. I haven't seen them since they got back from Italy. Khunying wasn't exactly thrilled I turned her job offer down, and decided it would be better to make a clean break while they all transitioned – her with the new house and business, and them with the new au pair. She asked me not to call or contact the girls while they got used to their new nanny to make it easier for them. It was

⚬ ⚬ ⚬ ⚬ ⚬ ⚬ ⚬ ⚬

hard not to see them, but Khunying had been clear she didn't want the girls to be more traumatised. They were both in floods of tears when we said our final goodbyes, but it was Lola who had been inconsolable. It broke my heart not to be able to see her again, but Khunying is their mother and I had to respect her wishes. And to tell the truth, I needed to stay away too. I had to break the bond, to move on with my own life. But I never stopped thinking about them.

When Khunying reaches us I stand up again. "Hello, Khunying," I say awkwardly, feeling at a loss as to what the protocol is now. Do I shake her hand? Do I wave? If this was the army and she was the sergeant major general, I'd get away with saluting her every time we bumped into each other for the rest of our lives. But this isn't that simple. My arms hang awkwardly by my sides, tingling with confusion. Khunying greets me with a big smile, reaches forward, and air kisses me on each cheek.

It's too weird.

"You look thinner without the brace," she says in typical Khunying style. "Aren't optical illusions marvelous."

Lola tugs on my shirt and I look back down at her. "Look, look, Jemma!" she squeals in delight. "I got my ears pierced!"

"We both did," says Tasanee self-importantly, "and I didn't scream. Lola cried."

Lola shoots Tasanee a glare. I laugh, missing them even more. "Oh, you both look so beautiful!"

"Yes, well," says Khunying. "They wouldn't let us pierce with any real jewelry – no diamonds or pearls or even an insignificant, harmless little tanzanite – so I guess we will be forced to live with these barbaric scraps of metal till the holes heal." My earlobes itch – I'm wearing the exact same 'barbaric' earrings the girls have in – stainless steel studs set with coloured glass like fake diamonds. Tasanee has chosen blue, but I see, with a wave of sentimentality, that Lola went for pink. Just like mine.

"So," continues Khunying, stroking Tasanee's hair. "I hear you are now planning children's parties?"

How on earth does she do that? She hasn't seen me in half a year, and she still knows everything?

"Er, yes . . . I'm studying through Unisa, but doing parties to make some money." I wonder if she will be upset I used the contacts I made while working as her au pair, with all the other mothers from Tas and Lola's school to get it started.

"Well, as you know," Khunying says, reaching out for her other daughter to stroke her hair too. "Our little Lola has a birthday coming up – and she has been begging me to do something special this year." Lola leans against her mother's thigh and smiles up at me, missing two new teeth on the bottom. "She's quite into this Disney character at the moment from that movie – you know the one – Snowy or Winter or something–"

"Frozen," I correct without thinking, then catch my mouth. "Oh, sorry, I didn't mean to interrupt, Khunying."

She laughs. A light breezy laugh that could light up a room.

"That's the one. I'm still new to all these things, but the girls are teaching me, aren't you?" Tas and Lola beam up at their mom and nod emphatically. The new dynamic between them is wonderful! I wonder what changed?

"Do you think you could arrange a theme party for us then, Jemma? And find Lola a blonde wig? She'll be the only Queen there, of course. The belle of the ball! She is the birthday girl, after all."

"Of course. What a wonderful idea."

"It was Mommy's idea," says Lola, smiling admiringly at her mother.

"Oh, I can't take all the credit," says Khunying. "Someone once told me about an amazing Seasponge T-shirt party and I just worked from there."

"SpongeBob SquarePants!" The girls giggle loudly.

"It's lovely to see you all having such a nice time together," I say, not able to help myself. Khunying meets my eye as I say the words. "I'm so glad you are enjoying your girls."

"I'm trying this new thing," she says meaningfully. "It's called being happy in the moment you find yourself in. And I found myself here, a mother, to these two wonderfully perfect creatures. And I couldn't think of anywhere else I would rather be."

"I think it's wonderful, Khunying."

"Oh please, call me Nicole."

I lost touch with them eventually. I saw them a few times after doing Lola's birthday party, Khunying always greeting me happily and encouraging my visits. After a while, I saw them less and less as my party-planning business took off, and the girls' busy little lives kept them from being able to see me. I did go to Lola's first piano recital, and the second, third and fourth. I also cheered Tasanee on, alongside Khunying, or rather Nicole as she kept trying to get me to call her (unsuccessfully), in the swimming tournament when she qualified for the under-tens national gala. Eventually I didn't see them anymore.

But the last time I went to The Palace, I did notice three new photos in frames scattered across Khunying's beloved sunroom. One of her and Lola, sitting on the floor, littered with brightly coloured make-up and both grinning at the camera through thickly painted stage make-overs. Another was of the three of them, Khunying, Tasanee and Lola, all sitting on a beach mat, under a big white umbrella. The last and biggest was a recent one of the two girls standing together, Khunying's beauty shining unmistakably through Lola's childish face, and Tasanee lit up with a huge, confident smile. They were all dressed in pink.

Whenever I think about them, about my time there, it seems that The Palace changed me both for the bad and then for the good. Seems I changed The Palace too. . . after all, everyone needs a little something pink in their lives.